Reson

Approaching the Dark Age Series, Vol. I

M.C.Chivers

This paperback edition is published by Dream-State Drive Publications.

This book is a work of fiction. Any references to historical events, real people, or real places are used fictitiously. Other names, characters, places, and events are products of the author's imagination, and any resemblance to actual events or places or person, living or dead, is entirely coincidental.

Copyright © 2009 by M.C.Chivers

First Dream-State Drive Publications paperback edition, 2014

Resonance, Vol. I, the Approaching the Dark Age Series logo, illustrations, and book cover illustrations are all associated marks, names, characters, and images from the Approaching the Dark Age Series universe, and are © 2009 by M.C.Chivers and Dream-State Drive Publications to each of their own respective copyright, partnership, and ownerships.

Printed and distributed in the United Kingdom, France, and the United States of America by Lulu Enterprises, Inc., and Lulu Press, Inc., 3101 Hillsborough Street, Raleigh, N.C. 27607, USA, including all other associated distribution centres worldwide.

All rights reserved. No part of this publication may be reproduced, stored in a retrieval system, or transmitted in any form or by any means, electronic, mechanical, photocopying, recorded, or otherwise, without the prior permission of the publisher.

ISBN13: 978-1-291-65892-7

About M.C.Chivers

Matthew is a keen computer-gamer and board game enthusiast. He has been writing since 2005, although he had never published his first novel, Resonance, until 2011.

He has struggled with Dyslexia since birth, and he continues to overcome this disability on a day-to-day basis.

At the age of 3 years, Matthew was also diagnosed, by a Child Specialist in 1988, as mildly retarded and showing signs of Aphasia. However, having lived his life well, despite this diagnosis, he has enjoyed life since finishing his primary and secondary school years, and then went on to enjoy college immensely.

After college, Matthew soon found that, after many years of having the difficulty to learn his own native English language, he could finally write down his imagination (at least to a Dyslexic's standard). He spends his time continuing to write his books, whilst attending his fatherly duties foremost, and helps other Dyslexic authors attain their dreams at releasing their own stories through Dream-State Drive Publications.

You can follow Matthew via Twitter, **@MatthewCChivers**

Via his blog, **http://approachingdarkage.blogspot.co.uk/**

Or via his Facebook,
https://www.facebook.com/ApproachingtheDarkAgeSeries

Chapters

Chapter One	1
Chapter Two	21
Chapter Three	44
Chapter Four	67
Chapter Five	82
Chapter Six	112
Chapter Seven	139
Chapter Eight	169
Chapter Nine	191
Chapter Ten	224
Chapter Eleven	249
Chapter Twelve	272
Chapter Thirteen	291
Chapter Fourteen	314
Chapter Fifteen	334
Chapter Sixteen	367
Chapter Seventeen	391
Chapter Eighteen	409
Chapter Nineteen	434

Chapter One

The Tribal's Encounter

On the outskirts of a ruined city, in the distant future, lives a small group of human survivors known as Tribals. Peaceful and spiritual in nature, these nomadic peoples try to survive against the unstable elements or other dangers that linger in the Dark Age lands. They scavenge anything they can to sustain their existence, hunting in parties for whatever game may be available during this bleak period.

On a night like any other, many of them lay asleep in their camp, situated next to an ancient temple on a high hill, which overlooked the sprawling city nearby. Most slept in tents stitched from animal skins, while some slept beneath the stars and moonlight in this cold, unforgiving season.

Amongst the slumbering tribe, one was awake, gazing towards the descending moon and the ascending sun that crept over the horizon. Stars that littered the heavens were slowly conquered by a blood-red morning.

Maledream watched the dawn of a new day as he leaned on a marble banister in the crumbling temple. He could never sleep well. Most nights he would awaken from troubling nightmares that had plagued him for as long as his memory served.

When the sun came out, it afforded him some small comfort. He recalled his foster-father and spiritual leader of the tribe, Larkham, always saying to him, *"your memory will return to you when you're ready, and at the right moment."*

Maledream recalled waking up in the old man's arms as a boy in the war-torn city. The smell of smoke, shouting, screaming, and blood staining his hands haunted him like an echo from the past. That was the night Larkham had saved him.

Since then, he was never one to care with his cheeky remarks or attitude towards the other members of the tribe. On the other hand, he was introvert most of the time, and kept only to himself. Not one for much conversation, he was always a listener, and attended Larkham's storytelling sessions, which were given every few days during the mornings.

The speeches were intended to inspire the tribe through oral traditions, handed down to him by his ancestors. Even Larkham didn't know if these tales were true lore or fiction. Nevertheless, he handed down the knowledge anyway, in the hope that it would someday be of use amongst the people who followed him, if only to serve to entertain.

Rubbing his sore blue eyes, he sighed, and scraped back his long, dirty, knotted hair. The faint breeze caressed his cheekbones as he watched his fellow Tribals gradually awaken in the camp, to chat, cook, and feed their empty stomachs with whatever nutrition they had available. He could only sigh and shake his head at the scraps being prepared.

Maledream then noticed some commotion below. Larkham was gathering the children of the tribe for another one of his stories about the past, and how blighted the human race was, but of a much nicer tone than he himself would describe.

'Who am I kidding,' he thought. *'They're just as damaged as the rest of us and just don't show it. They already know we're damned.'*

Hearing the scrabble of children running up through the illuminated temple, Maledream watched Larkham steadily hobble up the stoned stairway with the horrid beasts in tow. They were making enough of a racket to wake the ancients. He watched them approach with his back casually leaning against the marble banister.

'Almost storytelling time, Children,' the old man spoke with a joyous tone.

His dirty white robes easily caught the sunlight as he strode on the balcony, only to see his foster son with his arms crossed and wearing his long, dark coat.

'Ah, I see Maledream wants to join us,' Larkham said, a grin escaping his dark beard.

'Don't count on it, old man, you know what I think about your stories. I'm just up here appreciating the dawn of a new day...' Maledream sighed.

'Oh, as always, my Son, as always... but, as always, an amazing coincidence that you're only up here when I'm speaking of old, silly traditions, eh Boy?'

Still stood with his arms crossed, Maledream turned away from the Tribal leader, muttering, 'just get on with it.'

Continuing to smile, Larkham turned towards the massing children, and uttered, 'hush now, little terrors! I will tell you my stories of old, and if you don't settle down, then I'll make this boring story last as twice as long!'

Maledream grinned. *'He brings it on himself,'* he thought.

Settling down, the children sat cross-legged in a semicircle around the old man, whom stood in the middle of the open balcony. Larkham closed his eyes with a frown to tell them his grim tale.

'Our desolate world is all that's left now, for Mother Earth was stripped of her natural wealth and beauty by the greedy, jealous tyrants of humanity, starving for her precious liquids and metals.

All across the globe, the oceans swamped the lands without pity, drowning many a creature. Black clouds filled the empty skies, turning all to darkness so that not even the sun could cast its glow. Lightning and thunder erupted from the heavens, sowing fear, and dread before our ancestors' eyes for what was to come.

Horrendous creatures, known only as Behemoths, rose from the depths of mother earth's vast oceans, and sank our ancestors' silver ships with no remorse.

Neither man nor woman had ever seen such creatures that should only belong to myth and legend, and the waters allowed their safe passage into the cities closest to the shores, where they readily devoured our ancestors whom tried hiding inside their grey-stone towers.

However, they weren't the only monstrosities to strike at us, for terrible serpents of old invaded our lands. Bearing horns and metallic scales, they waged a bloody war upon us, with fang and claw, killing and feasting on the weak and strong.

Mighty quakes then erupted, engulfing many of our ancestors in flames and molten metal. Our mighty buildings plummeted to the ground, shaken from their strong foundations...'

'That's a pleasant story, Larkham, but, to tell the children all of that at their age is, well, it's just a load of crap. If you ask me, we did this to ourselves, not some cocked-up version of a fantasy story. I wonder what their parents would say.'

The old man turned to face the sarcastic Maledream, eyes firmly locked with the young man. His weathered face looked far from amused.

'I would clip your ears, Boy, but at least you didn't disturb my storytelling... until the end, for once,' Larkham grumbled.

'Yeah, well, I get bored with the same stories repeated every so often, which is, you know, all the time,' Maledream groaned.

'Well, until you're old enough, and far more mature than these children, you're not going to hear another story,' Larkham stated with a raised eyebrow.

Some youngsters covered their mouths to hide their chuckles. Maledream seemed caught for words as he continued to glare at the old leader.

'Now, Children, please leave me and my son alone for a moment. Go outside and play,' Larkham cheerfully uttered.

Once the little terrors had scrabbled down the temple steps, Maledream rasped, 'your stories are nothing but old fools' tales, old man. The only dangers around this place are murderers, rapists, and beggars, and that's a known fact, by the way.'

'Well, I'm glad you've gained the manners not to say such things in front of the children, Maledream. These youngsters don't need to fear the world we all do today, only to be cautious of it from my tales of old,' the spiritual leader said with concern.

'Yes, old man,' Maledream sighed, turning his back to him.

'By the way, Son, I've been meaning to catch up with you. I want to know where you went the other day. You've found a few things, haven't you?' Larkham quizzed.

'None of your business, I've been in the city,' Maledream growled.

'Well, Boy, I've heard from here and there that you've brought something into the camp. I'm just curious as to what it could be.'

'Look, it's nothing dangerous, so nothing to talk about,' Maledream muttered, turning to stare his foster-father directly in the eyes again.

'I don't mind you venturing from the camp, but you know I'm against dangerous weapons,' Larkham returned, still keeping his tone civil.

'These weapons of destruction only exist in your old tales, old man. If you must know, I went off scavenging in the battlefield outside the city, and I didn't come across anything slightly interesting.'

'Please don't return to that place, Maledream. It's dangerous, I've warned you about it before.'

'Look, I went to that forsaken place and saw nothing but rusted metal and bones littering the landscape. I've no idea why you fear that barren wasteland more than this city, it's safer in my opinion,' Maledream barked without fear or consequence.

'It's your own skin at the end of the day. I should be thankful you don't drag anyone else into your stupidity,' Larkham uttered after a brief silence. 'Just remember who found and nursed you back to health.'

'Oh no, not this again, enough of the guilt-trip crap before you really piss me off,' Maledream spat.

Larkham grinned at him, almost as if he had won the conversation.

'Just remember that, Boy. If you don't have anything else to share, then...' before Larkham could finish, he watched the young man rudely brush past him, his eyes cast down at the cracked marble tiles.

'Don't care. I'm off to forage for more food, and then maybe find something else that isn't the slightest bit useful or interesting, you nosey old bastard,' he snarled, adjusting his large weapon underneath his long coat.

He did his best to keep it hidden from Larkham's prying eyes. It was a nice find, and although the old man could do nothing to stop him from possessing it, he knew it would create more hassle than what it was worth.

Larkham traced him striding down the steps of the temple, and then raised his voice on the verge of echoing.

'It's a sword, isn't it...?'

Maledream almost hesitated, but carried on in his stride and ignored his foster-father the best he could.

The Tribal leader sighed as he watched the young man leave the temple. Shaking his head, Larkham returned his gaze to the rising sun.

'That boy needs to spread his wings.'

* * *

Maledream travelled from the camp, staring briefly at the Tribal families getting on with their daily lives. It wasn't a life worth living most of the time. The fear of uncertainty was always a factor faced every day, such as when was the next meal.

If the stale scraps didn't kill them or make them spew their bile, then the sodden water would if it didn't rain, in order to be collected in skins or sheets. Truth be told, he was fed up living like this. This was all he knew. Trying to survive in a land filled with woes and fearful stories. Sighing once more and shaking his head, he continued down the slope of the hill towards the inner suburbs of the city. Eventually, he entered the city streets with a casual stride.

'*Nothing will change,*' he depressingly thought, kicking stones across the broken road as the sun gradually rose above the ruined skyscrapers to cast a full morning.

'That old idiot believes we'll all be fine if we keep following him, but I don't see anything changing. Spirits, psychics, and to top it all off, he keeps recounting crap that probably didn't happen,' he growled, kicking more stones in anger.

Maledream quickened his pace through the near-empty streets, save for the scant beggar or traveller trying to scrounge a living. He sub-consciously double-checked he had everything he needed for insurance in these streets.

He wore his usual patched-up leather armour, and had a couple of rusty daggers tucked inside his concealed pockets, along with the cumbersome two-handed sword that Larkham had referred, which was strapped tightly to his back in its shoddy scabbard.

Suddenly, a woman's cry echoed down the street. He stopped what he was doing and listened intently, but could hear nothing else. Moments passed as he stared down different streets. He wondered if he was hearing things. It wasn't uncommon for a scream to be quickly muffled.

'*Another murder or rape, I guess.*'

The Tribal shook his head, staring at the dirt beneath his boots. He looked up again in surprise. The scream resounded and the ground suddenly quaked beneath his feet. His sixth sense triggered. He glared to the east towards a ruined building overgrown with vines. A section of its wall crumbled into an adjacent river with fierce, resounding thuds of stone.

Maledream, at first, walked slowly out of curiosity towards the rumbling building as mortar dust took to the air. He heard the woman shrieking and screaming repeatedly. His eyes traced some beggars running from the scene.

'What's wrong?' Maledream shouted.

Ignoring his question, the strangers daren't look back as if their lives were in peril.

'Always the bloody same,' he angrily groaned.

Not a soul helped another and the screaming was unbearable to his ears. He had to investigate. Rushing to the half-collapsed building, he stopped at the blocked entrance.

'It's coming from in here, I wonder if someone's trapped under it?'

Maledream started to climb the crumbling walls to achieve some height. A building collapsing in the city was a common event. The decaying structures stretched generations in age.

The screams suddenly stopped. A chill raced down his spine, his eyes widened as he secured his footing to stay quiet.

'Something doesn't feel right.'

Looking to his right, Maledream noticed a small window he could squeeze through, so he went for it. Screaming ensued.

'Not liking this one bit,' he muttered.

Crouching and emerging through the window, he found himself on a small balcony inside. He saw the entirety of the building was covered in slimy, pungent vegetation, which smothered every vertical surface that survived the collapse.

Slowly, Maledream peeked above the balcony's ivy-covered marble banister, and gawked at an abysmal creature. Scales of every colour matched its vicious fangs, and horns ran along its forehead and down its spine. In place of fingernails, this monstrous alien sported claws on its club-like fists. It was tall, probably at around nine-feet by Maledream's guess. It was trying to reach for the screaming woman, hidden somewhere underneath the fresh rubble and dust.

He further surveyed the area below and saw six disembowelled human corpses nearby. They wore remnants of garments and armour, the likes of which he had never seen in the city before. Were they travellers? Rich traders?

Regardless, the creature had made short work of them as their bloody entrails smeared the cracked stone slabs.

His vision rolled back to the beast. It used its brute strength to move the huge stones. As thoughts burned though the Tribal's mind, the creature paused with a groan, almost as if it had heard something. Maledream trembled in the brief silence. He daren't move or think as a bead of sweat rolled down his creased forehead.

Once again, the young woman screamed in terror, and so the reptilian-looking beast returned its attention to the last pile of rubble that stood between it and its prey.

'*Larszarish Zandrishth,*' Maledream heard in a strange, echoing voice.

It almost sounded like it came from the bipedal giant, yet the beast hadn't opened its snout. It was almost through to the stranger, and its thick horns on its spine erected as if it couldn't wait to devour the woman.

Instinct took over and, before he knew it, Maledream's adrenaline was pumping through his veins as he slid down the nearby marble banister. Landing awkwardly, the Tribal reached for the hilt of the blade, clasped it firmly, withdrew the large, cumbersome weapon, and stared directly at the monstrous creature with a terrified expression.

The beast snapped its head around to glare at him with its large, abyssal eyes. Whipping its large tail threateningly, it struck the ground with a heavy smack, sending grey dust pluming into the rays of the sun that pierced the broken ceiling.

'Help!' the woman screeched.

Maledream felt a tightening in his chest, a stiffening sensation in his arms and legs as he held his weapon ready. All the symptoms he knew of as fear. He tried reassuring her, but his words came out weak.

'Don't worry...'

The beast launched itself at the would-be warrior, roaring something that sounded like a cackle. Maledream locked eyes with the reptile, and its cold stare penetrated his soul. The Tribal seemed lost in its hypnotic glare and, before he knew it, the monstrous creature was already upon him. With a mighty roundhouse-uppercut, it struck him directly in the chest with a clenched fist, and sent him flying a great distance through the air.

Maledream landed harshly in a nearby pool of water with a loud thud. He coughed erratically. Spitting blood from his mouth in agony, he tightened his grip on the sword and clutched his chest with his spare hand as sharp, shooting pains served to wind him.

The creature lifted its head high and roared. Its powerful vocal chords shook the ground and echoed inside the building like a bell tower. Its eyes glowed red with unearthly energy as it gathered a fevered rage.

'How the fuck do I stand a chance against that?' he thought, scraping his sword across the shallow water as he struggled to stand upright.

Breathing heavily, Maledream strengthened his resolve, trying desperately to bolster his courage.

'I'll give you a fight,' he shouted and coughed at the top of his lungs, as if to accept this roaring creature's challenge.

He charged with the blade, ready to swing it upwards in an arc. The beast closed in on him with foot-pounding thuds. The Tribal swung, sword and talons clashed, echoing loudly in the building.

'I have to keep moving,' he thought, darting in and out of the beast's powerful swings that could disembowel him with one swipe.

Gaining the upper hand, with agility alone, was much harder to do in practice. The Tribal ducked and weaved the best he could whilst scraping his heavy sword around, but his strength quickly subsided. Breath was harder to catch with every swing from the agony racking his ribs. The sword weighed a ton for someone unused to heavy labouring in some slave pit. Despite this, several strikes of his blade caught the creature.

Maledream almost felt as if a little progress was made. He dodged another deadly slash. However, his weapon seemed useless against its scaly hide as it merely rang metallic hymns.

Finally, the monstrous reptile caught him with another sharp blow to the ribs. Wide-eyed, Maledream was lifted to the air by the sheer force of the punch, and was sent flying through the nearby marble banister with a crunch. His skeleton heaved, easily fracturing on contact with the old stones.

As he came to rest amidst the grey, swirling dust, the bloodied Tribal knew he should try to get up. Adrenaline wasn't enough. He was losing consciousness from the pain surging through his broken body. His pupils dilated, and the world beaming into his retinas turned many shades darker. Just as Maledream's strength began to fade, he saw an image of Larkham's caring face in his delirious state.

'Sorry, old man, you won't be seeing me again. Sorry for being a bastard all the time,' he regretted.

Maledream saw his hallucination change into the beast's face as it stumbled over the rubble to reach him. All hope was lost. He closed his eyes and took one, last, agonizing breath.

'Sorry stranger.'

'Elin'shana dookilla shuen allina canshanna doom!'

A soothing voice appeared from somewhere. His ears twitched slightly out of his control. Then, waves of light, as bright as the sun, washed over him. The pain racking his ribcage faded. His eyes fluttered and flicked open. Miraculously, his fractures had healed in an instant.

'What the... hell just happened?'

With no time to spare, Maledream jumped to his feet and, with renewed vigour, leapt over the remaining banister to get away from the closing mountain of muscle. Missing him narrowly with a swipe of its talons as he jumped, the beast was unable to stop its own momentum and, with a deafening roar, crashed into the marble-tiled wall with an earth-quaking crunch.

Landing on his feet, he glanced and saw the girl was out of her hiding place, with her right hand pointed at him, and carrying what looked like a wooden staff in her left. Her dusty, green, and purple robes were also unfamiliar to him.

'What the hell are you doing? Run for it,' Maledream shouted, trying to catch his breath, the words barely escaping his throat.

The red-haired young woman had a worn, pale expression etched on her face. She had a look in her green eyes that was somehow different. However, her pale expression suddenly twitched to one of horror. In that split second, Maledream span on his heels, and narrowly dodged a blow to his face.

He was also now aware, in that moment, that his sword had changed, too. It now emitted a faint, silvery glow. He had no time to check it in finer detail as the beast swung its massive talons at his throat once more.

Something was different. His reactions quickened. The creature's swipe appeared slower than normal, and his palms that gripped the hilt felt strange. Warm yet also cold, it calmed him in some strange way. The Tribal dodged the second attack by rolling. Then, swinging his blade with a counter-strike, he struck the creature in its kneecap with a crack.

Bellowing with rage, the beast spun on its heels and uppercut him with great force, sending Maledream sprawling across the cracked slabs for many yards. The sword smashed, scraped, and sparked against the ancient marble tiles as he bounced and rolled. He refused to let go of it. His survival depended on it. Once he came to a halt, he coughed hard and caught his breath. The punch had almost smashed his ribcage for a second time round.

'Elin'shana dookilla shuen allina canshanna doom!'

Again, the voice appeared, this time behind him as he quickly regained his senses. It was the young woman. The pain that racked him from the punch just disappeared. This time, the sword clearly reacted to her voice. Multicoloured light shimmered on the blade's broad surface, rolling across its alloy like waves on a shore.

'What's going on?' he thought, eyes tracing the hypnotic colours racing up his weapon.

The monstrous reptile glared with a blank expression, barely able to stand on its legs as blood pumped from its crippling knee wound.

The Tribal wasted no time and got back on his feet. Panting heavily, he arched his weapon below the waist and, with all the strength he had left, sprinted forwards and held his breath. The stranger's mantra seemed to build up his momentum and, in turn, increased the weapon's sleeping power.

'Elin'shana dookilla shuen allina canshanna doom!'

Swinging his sword in an upward arc, Maledream roared, thrusting it into the scaly abdomen of the bipedal reptile. Helped by the momentum of the voice behind him, sparks flew. It felt like the blade would hesitate to dent the creature as its energy whined with a high pitch for that one, deciding moment.

An explosion, echoing like thunder, signalled the final blow, and a blinding flash of light filled the ancient library. Landing on his knees from the momentum in which he threw himself, the Tribal stared at the large sword in his hands as he came to a halt on his knees.

The hilt remained cool, yet the blade hissed at the surrounding air. Its energy seemed spent as the shimmering light faded. He saw the beast toppled, split in two halves. Slumping on his ass, he caught his breath and closed his eyes as the last of the adrenaline pumped its way around his veins. Maledream took only a moment to rest.

On opening his eyes, he stared at the large, bulbous, horned head of the beast, noticing then that its eyes were staring straight into his. Approaching it, he raised the sword with both hands and, lowering it harshly several times, severed its skull from its neck just to be sure of the kill. Maledream picked up the heavy head by one of its horns, refusing to stare into its dark pupils.

'No one's going to believe this… except the old man.'

He glanced in the direction of the young, strangely dressed woman, and saw that she now lay unconscious upon the rubble.

First, Maledream wrapped the horned head with a ragged cloak from one of the freshly slaughtered men. The horns constantly dug into his back as he fastened it. Next, he strode to the stranger, picked her up, and slung her over his shoulder with a heave. Steadily, he climbed and made his way out of ruined library. Wiping sweat from his forehead, he tried to understand what had just happened.

'Who are you… and what the hell was that?'

Chapter Two

Nightmare

Evening arrived as the sun set over the horizon. The Tribals prepared for another cold night by lighting campfires. As the eve progressed, rumours, imaginations, and emotions erupted as the Tribals gathered around the fires in their circles, discussing both Maledream, the red-haired stranger, and the severed head, which Maledream supposedly carried with him.

High above them in the temple, perched in darkness, was Maledream. Occasionally, the ascending smoke from the fires of the camp would waft into his nostrils. He looked on, lost in thought. The only way for him to believe what happened was to show the others.

It was a strange feeling for him. Something he certainly did not expect to come across in the early hours of the morning, on what seemed like another dull day. He cast his mind back to the fight, a battle that was utterly hopeless, and definitely should not have turned out like the way it did.

Averting and adjusting his eyes to the shadows, he stared at the serpent's head that he had unwrapped a while ago. It was like an atrocious nightmare, for not just Maledream, but for the other Tribals, too.

He thought about the young, red-haired woman he rescued. He wondered why he leapt into the fray to save her, instead of fleeing from something so terrifying. However, there was something about her. She reminded him of someone, and it haunted him. The young woman's strange ability to heal his wounds, which were certain to kill him, only made him think even deeper.

Strange words triggered off the blade's secret power, which he would not have known existed if it was not for her strange singing. Such power, such magic, was the stuff of fantasy that lurked within Larkham's mystical tales.

Guns were superior weapons, far more effective at close quarters or range than a weapon such as a sword. So why was it made in the first place? He decided he would ask the young woman how to achieve such effects, the likes of which he had never seen or known. Perhaps it was even something he could learn, which fired-up his imagination even further.

Larkham had been with the stranger ever since he brought her back to the camp. He was certain that the old man could help her somehow, just as he has always done with the sick or injured with his healing ways.

'People need someone to look up to in these dark times. I'm not the one they're looking for, but I may as well pose,' Maledream muttered with a passing sigh, staring into the abyssal eyes of the serpent's head as if he were speaking to it.

He figured it wouldn't hurt the camp to explain the tale of fighting this creature, whilst showing off the sword and head, of course. After all, the Tribals had settled down by the fires, and he could already hear the echoes of disbelieving gasps and laughter. He got up from his perch and grabbed the head by one of its thick horns.

Adjusting the sword in his shabby scabbard, Maledream made his way down the temple steps and into the camp. The events of the fight fed him a sense of purpose, a sense of pride, and, for once, it made him feel strangely optimistic.

* * *

Larkham sat with his eyes closed in the gloom, meditating, as the girl fidgeted in her sleep. Words escaped her lips from time to time, until she finally stirred.

'Stranger, help,' she muttered, flicking her eyes open in a dreary panic and bolting upright.

She took a while to check her surroundings. With a passing sigh, she gripped the rugged bedding in relief. It looked as if she was inside a tent crafted out of old clothes and well-preserved animal skins. A foul, damp smell assaulted her nostrils, but otherwise, it seemed a comfortable place to be.

A small handmade candle was present on the floor. Its flame flickered and waved from the invading cold draft. The flap of the tent was slightly open. She saw that night had fallen. Out of the darkness, in one corner of the large tent, came a voice replying to her mutter.

'That stranger is a troublesome young man in our small camp, young lady.'

'Who are you?' she screeched, eyes peering towards the darkness, hands clutching the blanket to her chest.

'You're safe here, have no worries,' the old man heartily laughed.

'Pervert! Reveal yourself!'

Slowly, out of the shadowy corner of the tent, Larkham appeared in full view of the pale light.

'I didn't mean to offend you, young lady. We have all been worried about you. You've been out cold since Maledream found you in the city, rescuing you from a beast of old, or so he says,' he replied, his hand reaching out to clasp hers gently.

Her eyes cast themselves nervously at the gesture, and then peered into his eyes to try to sift a motive.

'Yes, he did, I am very grateful. I've been on a long journey from the south with my companions.'

'I see. Well, young lady, you have a lot to explain to me from the sounds of it. Please, tell me your name, dear child of spirit.'

'Angelite Rose,' she replied with a nervous smile.

'What a beautiful name. I am Larkham, the leader of this band of Tribals. Please tell me, Angelite... what happened in the city, exactly?'

Angelite felt apprehensive at answering. She had only just awoken, albeit speaking to this nice but complete stranger. Her last memory was that of the young man with the strange two-handed blade. She peered into Larkham's eyes, wondering if he had a hidden aim. However, her intuition put her at ease.

'I travelled to this part of the world for knowledge hidden in books or other such historical artefacts. We found a ruined library, which I'm guessing must be nearby?'

'Yes, we're on the outskirts of the city in which you were travelling. Maledream left this morning to forage for food, and that is how he found and rescued you. Whom do you mean by "*we*"? Were you travelling with others?'

'Yes, I was with several others. We travelled across the ocean, far from the west. It's been a long journey of around several weeks, probably close to a month since we left my home, Meridia.'

Angelite was to continue, but the old man coughed abruptly. She paused in her speech as Larkham tapped his chest lightly with a clenched fist, before responding in astonishment.

'Meridia, you say?'

'Yes?' she returned, raising an eyebrow curiously.

'So, the spirits' whispers are right about this city, after all,' he uttered, staring down at the ground with his arms crossed, his hand serving to stroke his dark beard.

'Spirits have told you of it?' she pursued.

'Yes, my dear, I am a man who is blessed with the gift of hearing the spirits. I lead my Tribals the best I can through divining what they have to say,' he said, his grin brief.

'I see, there are a few in Meridia that have that gift, too, wise man,' she replied, shuffling upright with hands tightly clasping the old blankets, her eyes widening with positive body language.

'It's a hard gift to use but, from the travels and through the cycles of years, it has become easier. It is in my dreams that they speak to me the most, showing me visions of a glistening city. A salvation waiting for the people I care for.

It is a pleasant dream. I simply find it unbelievable that someone from my visions is actually here, in my camp of all places. Yet, from the look of your finely sewn robes, I can't question it, for the answer is staring right at me,' Larkham said, his voice almost trembling.

'It is very real, Larkham. I am a priestess in a guild. A guild called the Order of Spirit. It was my idea to travel to a part the ancient world for, you see, I'm a descendent from this city,' she said with enthusiasm.

'So, you are here as part of your Order to investigate the Dark Age lands?'

'Yes, this is the first time I've set foot from the safety of Meridia's walls. We landed in our ship to the far south. Our aim was to collect anything of interest as we headed north, and then to rendezvous with a Meridian port after our long travel. I wish I hadn't now, though... my friends that accompanied me were killed by the beast,' she said, her voice beginning to quake.

Tears glistened then swelled in her eyes. The old man got up and shifted towards her, sitting on the edge of the bed to cuddle her for comfort. Timeless moments passed as her tears ran into Larkham's sodden sleeves.

'It's okay,' he said, gently cradling her from side to side for a short time as she sobbed.

'I've known nothing like it. Why did I leave?' she murmured.

Half of the candle melted as she let out her pain. Larkham continued to hold her tightly as she hyperventilated.

'Sorry,' Angelite sniffed.

'That's quite alright, Sweetheart. I must confess, losing a loved one or a friend is never easy. It's commonplace in these dark lands. By nature, beasts, or even by other human beings,' he sighed.

'Thank you, wise man. Sorry, I should gather myself. Thank you for taking care of me. I used so much of my energy when I saved that brave man from some nasty wounds. I could have done the same for my friends, but that Anunaki decimated half of the library before I had any time to react. The screaming was horrific,' she sniffed, trying to hold in the tears as she hugged the old man even tighter.

'The suffering my friends went through as I struggled underneath the rocks, stuck in total darkness, unable to help. All I could do was scream...' Angelite paused to catch her breath, using a hand to wipe away the tears off her cheeks. 'I thought I was going to join them. There were only a couple of stones left for the creature to move. That's when I spotted a young man at the top of the library's balcony. I watched him slide down the banister with such grace, telling me not to worry,' she sniffed, pausing again to catch her breath.

Larkham smiled at her tale. To think, his foster son acted with such zeal and bravery against an ancient menace from his legends.

'Her voice must have struck a chord in him, perhaps sparking something deep inside his soul,' Larkham thought.

'I wouldn't have expected Maledream to jump straight into the fray like that. He often plays it safe and never seems to care, but now, I think we both know differently,' the old man smiled and nodded.

'He had no fear! I managed to escape the rocks and was able to work my healing on him. However, I thought I felt another presence inside the building.'

'What was this presence?' Larkham interrupted.

'It felt like it was an old soul. You may not believe it, but it felt like it came from his sword. It was resonating to my speech and the energy that I was focusing into him.'

'I knew Maledream was keeping a secret from me. Funny how a sword popped into my mind when I asked him about it this morning,' he said, raising his eyebrows over the thought.

'He used it well, almost as if he knew how to strike with it, but, at the same time, I saw how dumbstruck he was at what he was holding. As I was saying, this weapon glowed, many runes and glyphs shimmered on its surface, and before I knew it, I fell unconscious as a bright, blasting wave of energy rippled from it. And now I'm here in your tent,' she finished, glancing at the nearby candle.

'Sounds like quite a tale, young lady...' Larkham replied, his shifty eyes hiding the desire to repeat this story to those in his camp.

After all, this was new material.

'Where is this young man now? You said his name is Maledream?'

'Yes, yes it is. We'll find him, just so long as you're sure you've had enough rest to get out of this bed,' Larkham grinned, slowly retreating off the thick rugs and animal furs to pick up his walking stick.

'Yes, let's find him,' she smiled.

* * *

Elsewhere in the camp, Maledream recounted his story to a large group of Tribals that had just returned from a foraging run. They were eager to hear of his bloated yet entertaining story after a long trip.

'So, Maledream, what's this going around the camp that you've slain one of those ancient creatures from Larkham's tales?' asked one of them, a familiar tone of disbelief filling the air with laughs or jokes.

Many knew what he was like. Some had branded him a coward in the past.

'See for yourself,' Maledream replied, tossing the wrapped head to the dirt.

Roll by roll, the head unravelled itself until it ended up at the feet of the middle-aged, straggly-haired Tribal who asked the question. The circle gawked or gasped as they glared at the horned skull in disbelief.

'Get that cursed thing away from me!' the man shrieked, jumping back with a stumble, almost tripping up and over on some wire and tent pegs in the process.

Other Tribals shared the same view as they, too, moved away from its presence in quick fashion, yet, at the same time, unable to take their eyes off it in amazement.

'I took it down with this,' Maledream continued, drawing his heavy blade from its shoddy scabbard and planting the tip of it in the earth.

'How in the name of the Great Spirit did you do it?' one asked, each of them comparing the size of the sword to Maledream's average height.

Many were guessing the size of the creature by the sheer volume of the head alone. He stood there for a moment, not answering any questions, only returning a cheeky smirk. It wasn't every day that a creature from an old man's legend came to fruition.

In fact, it was the first.

'I defeated it, but it was a narrow victory...' Maledream said, the commotion quieting down as he spoke.

It wasn't like him to say anything, especially without being rude. However, this time, Maledream somehow seemed different, sincere, so they listened at great length to this young man's encounter.

'... If it wasn't for her strange magic, I wouldn't be alive now,' Maledream finished.

'So, why isn't your sword glowing now, then? For all we know, you could've found this head lying around, knocked the poor girl out, and then changed one of Larkham's tales to make yourself out to be some kind of mythical hero,' one of the gathered laughed.

Disbelief in the malnourished man, and his ability to kill anything, set in. Some were not inclined to believe his fanciful tale, despite the horned head. Maledream decided not to argue, he had no energy to prove it.

'Give him a break,' another said, the camp siding with or against his account.

'Either way, I don't care what any of you believe,' Maledream muttered.

'What a surprise,' another echoed from the crowd.

'Right, well, now that I've shown you the head, you can keep it for all I care,' Maledream chuckled without bother.

The small crowd quietened down as they watched the young man stick his cumbersome weapon back into its scabbard. Walking away from the light of the fire, Maledream made his way back to the ruined temple.

The Tribals chatted quietly, where as some moved their tents and other sleeping apparatus away from the hewn head. Regardless of whether they believed Maledream or not, they stayed well away from such a cursed skull.

* * *

Maledream's feet ached, along with his arms and back. On the bright side, he had proven something to himself. The experience opened his mind to what Larkham had been saying all this time in his legends.

'Perhaps all he says is true,' he sighed.

The Tribal turned his attention to the night sky. His eyes casually browsed the twinkling constellations. The wind was calm tonight, and the moon appeared brighter than normal as sparse, silver clouds drifted gently across the dark-blue aura of the galaxy.

'I still can't believe what happened this morning. Who is she? What is she doing here? It went by so quickly, I didn't have enough time to take it all in.'

Several hours had passed, and the Tribals below had settled down for the night. Maledream knew something about him had changed, deep down. He also believed he was there by sheer luck and nothing more.

'Elin'shana dookilla shuen Allina Canshanna Doom.'

That voice of hers shook his very soul. Breathing in the autumn air, Maledream outstretched his arms and legs before releasing a sigh. He continued to stare at the stars as he leaned on the balcony's broken banister. Something was up, and he knew he would have little peace of mind until he had some answers.

'Thought you'd be up here, my Son,' a familiar voice echoed from behind.

Startled, Maledream turned and saw that Larkham had arrived, and with the attractive young woman.

'Thought I'd never see you again, old bugger. So, what's the news?'

'We've a lot to discuss, but I'll let Angelite begin. You can never keep your eyes open for more than two moments if I speak,' Larkham jested.

'True,' Maledream grinned.

Maledream seemed lost as his eyes settled on the gorgeous redhead and her voluptuous curves, even behind all of her thick travelling robes. He recalled her beauty when he saw her in the morning. He snapped himself out of it and caught his words.

'Uh, it's nice to meet you... Angelite, was it?'

'Yes, nice to meet you, too, young warrior,' she returned with a sweet and gentle tone, accompanied by a cute grin.

'Warrior? I think you have the wrong man. I was just in the right place at the right time,' he weakly smirked.

'Is that so? I'll try to explain why I'm here, and what happened during the fight with that beast,' she said.

'Okay then, I'm guessing you'll explain a lot of the questions I've been asking myself. I always thought they were just something the old man conjured up.'

'Yes, they've been a threat to us since the turn of the Dark Age, which, my sources say, is over a hundred and fifty years ago. Apparently, they were thought of as myth to our ancestors, too, before the Dark Age occurred.'

'Just as I have told you many times in my stories of old,' added Larkham, his voice ushering a deep concern.

Maledream put the information in his mind for the first time. He tried to remember Larkham's long, boring tales.

'I can't say they don't exist.'

'I'll continue,' said Angelite. 'Since the arrival of the Dark Age, which decimated our world, we've had a very special gift unlocked within us. We still don't know how this happened exactly, but it happened.'

'You're beginning to lose me, what happened?' Maledream interrupted.

Angelite lifted up her right hand and pointed it towards the stars. In the other, she carried her staff. Etched on its surface were many symbols, crystals, and strange runes. At the top of her staff was the largest of all the crystals, which contained in its smooth, transparent surface, faint letterings that pulsated with a gentle rhythm.

'I know you might not understand right at this second, but that comes in time. Now, witness the gift of Resonance and that of the stars,' she said, striding to the circular clearing on the balcony.

Still holding her right hand skywards, she turned around. Then, slowly lowering her spare palm to grip the staff of power with both hands, the shaft's symbols began to illuminate, as if she controlled them.

'Innanania triatus, sooulish contempas inan hispostitius,' she chanted.

Her green eyes began to glow a gentle violet in hue. Maledream could hardly believe his own eyes. He tried his hardest to doubt what he was watching. Both he and Larkham remained silent, in awe of her craft and beauty.

Once her melody gained momentum, the floor illuminated a bright radius around her feet with a golden aura, like a template, mimicking the runes on her staff, while her long, red-hair defied gravity.

'Illafimia Denetus Shantanna Quialataluis Natu-aouri.'

The balcony glowed, almost as if many sources of moonlight brightened the circle, radiating outwards and touching all corners of the temple.

'What you are seeing is the energy within us, the magic of science, sound, and spirit. This is the power of Resonance. I can teach you how to find your energy,

Maledream. I can take you back to my home. A home we all call Meridia. Will you come with me?'

'Yes, he will go with you. It's far too dangerous in these parts for a young lady to travel by herself,' Larkham stated, his tone firm.

'I can make up my own mind, old man,' Maledream muttered.

'It'll be a full month's journey, and Larkham insisted that you would. Meridia is a safe haven, a place free of disease, famine, and danger. You will love it, I promise... my Tribal warrior,' she finished with a sweet and addictive smirk.

Maledream couldn't help but to grin at her. Her voice was in sharp contrast to the power behind her spiritual energy. Green and golden auras arched out like birds stretching their wings, unfolding in shape and fading away like a flame to the wind. A moment later, the native vines, ivy, and moss that clung to the eroded, stony walls grew in an instant.

Angelite finished her show-and-tell, and her hair was caught by gravity once more. In a quick rush, the energy stored in the symbols on the staff dispersed to the ether, whilst sweet smells of lavender filled the air, captivating both Maledream and Larkham's senses. As her spell faded, so too did the glow, leaving the threesome with just the moon for a light source.

'Anything else you would like to know?' she pursued.

Maledream could hardly decide where to begin.

'Were you responsible for what you did to my sword? How did you heal my wounds? What were you doing in that building in the first place?' he rushed.

'Hold on, one question at a time! I'll begin with the sword. In Meridia, we have weapons with runes and crystals crafted in them, so I am guessing you must have something similar. Where did you find it?' she probed.

'I found it in the ancient battlefield, it lies just outside the city towards the north,' he confessed.

'Against my words of advice, it was only this morning that I warned you about that place, again,' Larkham interrupted.

'Oh well, I'm still here, aren't I? What else could I use to bargain for fresh food inside the city? All the gangs' trade weapons for supplies,' Maledream sighed.

'That's not the point,' the old leader grunted.

'Ugh. Please, Angelite, continue for both of us,' Maledream said, turning to the priestess.

Angelite smiled at the quarrelling pair.

'To answer your other questions, we travelled from the south in search of objects of interest such as books or scrolls.'

'"*We?*" I'm guessing you're referring those people I saw inside the building?' Maledream pursued, before realising what he said as he stared into her saddened eyes.

'He had to ask, the poor lady is close to breaking again,' Larkham frowned.

'Yes, they were friends travelling with me. We ventured northwards until we reached this city in the early morning. We finally found what we were looking for. Then it all happened,' Angelite answered, bravely containing her feelings.

'It's okay, I know,' Maledream said, watching Larkham walk over to place a hand on her shoulder for comfort.

'So, yes, we were going to keep travelling north, to a port where we were to rendezvous,' she added.

'I see. And that creature?' he wondered, not knowing if the question would upset her further.

'They're called the Anunaki. It was the first time we saw one in the flesh, so to speak. We have records of their existence, but most of our journey was uneventful. We never dreamed of coming across any,' she answered.

'Indeed, young lady, these parts of the land are rife with danger,' replied Larkham.

'You're telling me, old man. I'm still having trouble believing what happened this morning, let alone believing what I saw. I'm just glad you're safe,' Maledream said, his eyes focused on her sweet face.

'I'm so grateful, thank you. There will be more time to explain everything in more detail when we set off,' she replied, finding the courage to let out a small smile behind a small yawn.

Maledream brewed over the dangers in his mind. The petite priestess didn't seem the type that could handle a fight, or even make it travelling such perilous continents. At least he was born and raised in the Dark Age lands.

'When are we leaving, exactly?' he asked.

'At dawn, we'll have to traverse through the battlefield to reach our destination to the north. Any who, I guess we could save this for the morning, I'm pretty tired,' she said.

'She's lying, she's still upset. What really pisses me off is the fact the old man roasted me seconds ago about the battlefield and now we've got to go through it?' Maledream thought, glaring at Larkham's cheeky expression, before rolling his vision back to the priestess.

'I guess this makes me your personal warrior?' Maledream jested, hoping his words would perhaps lift her spirits.

Her reply was a simple grin and a nod. Larkham looked on, also nodding his head side-to-side with a smile.

'I wish I could come with you both, but it seems fate would keep me here with the tribe. Both of you be careful,' said Larkham.

Moving to face Maledream, the old man placed his hands on the Tribal's shoulders. 'I sense that something big is awakening inside you, Maledream, but I give you this warning that you must heed, so please listen carefully to my words. Do not succumb to the temptation that does not belong in your heart, for it will threaten this young woman and everything you would strive for with your choice of freewill. Listen to your heart. If it were not for the heart, we would not have survived this long, as humans, or a tribe. The incident this morning proves that you have grown into a proper man. You've always been restless, my Son, so go out into the world and find your true path in life, find your meaning, find your purpose.'

Maledream smirked at the old man's serious face. He didn't have it in him to make fun of what he had to say this time. This was getting too serious for his dry sense of humour. Gently, he removed the old man's weathered hands from his shoulders.

'Well, for a while now, I've wanted to leave, so, in a way, this'll give me a good reason to,' he replied, averting his gaze from the old man to the priestess.

'It's as if this has been your calling all along,' said Larkham.

'I don't know about that, but I'll go with the flow.'

'All things happen in life happen for a reason, Maledream. I don't for a moment believe in coincidence,' said the Tribal leader.

'You could be right, but I think I'll wait a little longer till I have a final judgement on that one,' replied Maledream.

'In time you'll see. I for one believe in it, this fate, a synchronisation of spirit,' said Angelite.

'We'll see what our trip brings. I want to get out of this place, feels like I should be moving in some way,' Maledream smirked.

Larkham bid one final farewell to the pair, and retired for the night in the camp below. Angelite turned and strode on the balcony and peered at the blue abyss that contained the twinkling constellations. Maledream joined her out of curiosity. For a lengthy time they gazed at the stars in silence, save for the cold wind that softly brushed them as it whistled through the broken temple.

'She's beautiful,' he thought.

'Beautiful night, don't you think? I love the stars, they're so different in this part of the world,' she said.

'Uh, yeah, I quite often stare at them, too. I just wish the city provided something more pleasing to look at. The people in the streets are best avoided when we get going,' he sighed.

'I know. Meridia is nothing like the Dark Age lands. I would love to chat more, but we'll have to save it for the morning, if that's okay?' she said, unable to contain another yawn.

'Not a problem, I'll walk you to your tent,' he nodded, kindly showing her the way.

Chapter Three

Deeper Understanding

After showing Angelite back to her tent, Maledream returned to his own, and rested the heavy blade on the ground. He was unable to take his eyes off the weapon. He couldn't see any visible markings. It looked dull, almost rusty in tone, just as he had originally found it.

'How did she make it work? I felt something, more than physical, more spiritual, sort of like when she showed us what it was in the temple.'

An idea struck him. Leaning on his knees, he held the blade in both hands and began meditating with it out of curiosity, in the ways that Larkham had tried teaching him in the past. Drawing deep breaths, Maledream began to picture a vast ocean in his mind, sitting on a cliff's edge near a beach.

He filled the empty space with sea gulls flying high in the heavens, whilst imagining the waves, below, rhythmically crash against the shore as storm clouds formed. He could almost feel the drizzle on his face.

* * *

Taking a sudden twist, Maledream suddenly found himself in his own imagination. Standing up within his vision, he wondered why he was no longer in his tent, but within this inner world. This worried him. He could not open his physical eyes, for now he was living in this place, seeing through them, breathing in the ocean air, and feeling real rain.

'Where am I? Am I actually experiencing this?'

The clouds grew darker. Lightning erupted in the distance, followed by a swift crack of thunder rolling its fury across the sky. Soon after, the drizzle turned into a rainstorm. A sound he was not familiar with boomed and echoed through the airwaves. He rose to his feet and wandered up the grassy perch.

What he saw next utterly shocked him. Climbing over the muddy ridge, he saw thousands of human soldiers, and thundering war machines, march with purpose across the entire landscape. The tracked tanks lit up the sky with thunderous flares as they fired their salvos.

His eyes followed their neon tracers through the sky like shooting stars, only to find them greeting monstrous, towering creatures. It was sickening to watch these large, translucent insects roam across the horizon like looming spectres. Slamming into the creatures, the powerful shells exploded against their gelatinous hides.

Maledream watched in horror as the enraged monsters strode forward on their long, insect-like legs, towards the men and women on the battlefield. Shaking the ground violently with their strides, they easily scooped up handfuls of soldiers with their tentacles, and tore them asunder in showers of red gore.

Falling to his knees, he experienced an epiphany. These creatures, easily the size of skyscrapers, lurked within Larkham's legends. Behemoths.

'This isn't happening, this is my imagination. It has to be.'

Looking behind, he saw something just as terrifying. Turning out in their thousands from the sea, and much like the one he fought, were more of the Anunaki creatures.

Turning around, he noticed the battlefield was quickly emptying of the human soldiers whom fled in terror from the thundering Behemoths. They smashed the tank columns aside like children's' toys, putting to rest the mighty cannons.

Seeing what was about to happen to the troops, Maledream rushed towards them, waving his arms around maniacally in the vain hope that they would see him.

However, when he spoke, no words left his vocal chords. As if they were spectral, they passed through him with no hindrance, only to leave him with their cold, emotional horror. He felt the soldiers' loss of hope and dark despair. With every spectre rushing through him, he staggered back, recoiling from the terror, trying to keep his footing in the middle of the bloody chaos.

Lightning fast, the Anunaki beasts pounced upon the broken soldiers, eviscerating them once they reached the shore. The men and women hopelessly fired their weapons into the horde, and with little effect. The swift tide of the fierce creatures swallowed the soldiers in a sea of horns and scales.

The sky flashed before his eyes with a deafening boom. The downpour was harder, the clouds darker. Maledream averted his glare to witness the arrival of a stout leader of humanity. This man seemed unbothered by the death that surrounded him as he strode forwards in thick, alloy-hardened plating. He was a human war machine on two legs, shouting orders at the men and women under his command with a stern, bellowing voice. He looked bigger, stronger, compared to an ordinary human.

Standing at almost nine feet, he was as large as the monstrous Anunaki, and easily towered over the regular soldiers. Then it caught the Tribal's vision. Sticking out in this man's right hand was the blade that Maledream now possessed. Gawping, he watched as the armour-plated man charged straight into the mass of scales and blood. Bursting with ionic power, the blade hacked away at the Anunaki from left to right. The stranger easily tore through the beasts without mercy.

However, whilst Maledream could only hold the heavy blade in both hands, this large man held it in one solid fist. He continued to watch the man tear into the mass of horns and scales. With the blade bathed in ethereal energies, its keen, blood-soaked edge hewn any foe that dared get within its deadly, sweeping cleaves. Those that got close could not tear into his armour long enough to kill him, or drag him down off his feet as he swung and kicked.

Maledream then noticed that, on the back of the large human's hood, were some symbols that shimmered and glowed. The soldiers, however, roared their last, defiant stand – trapped, with no hope, between both the gigantic Behemoths and merciless Anunaki.

Overwhelmed, Maledream couldn't awaken from this nightmare. Another strike of lightning and thunder roared across the battlefield. Maledream could only watch as the brave warrior, whom wore the plated armour, was slowly swallowed by the horde of claws and scales. Striking him off his heavy feet, the blade flew high into the air, before embedding itself with a squelch in the blood-soaked mud nearby.

It was in that moment that Maledream furrowed his brow. He thought he had just heard a word on the wind pass from the man's lips.

However, his attention returned to the tens of thousands of soldiers who had been decimated. Any survivors were feasted upon, their ribcages cracked open like eggs in bloody fashion with fang and talon to reveal their still-beating hearts, twisting intestines, and hyperventilating lungs.

Maledream, for the first time in his vision, managed to let out a deafening roar of sheer terror to outmatch the guttural cries of the feast.

Silence fell across the battlefield. His scream seemed to garner the attention of all the beasts for miles around. In silence, their horned craniums turned, and their crimson eyes coldly glared at him. Ecstasy widened their snouts.

Without a second thought, Maledream sprinted towards the sword, in the vain hope that he could awaken from this nightmare. It was so close. Slowly and surely, Maledream fought with all his heart to keep going, stepping through the slaughtered human phantoms that lay beneath his feet. All around, the evil presence he felt grew stronger. The Anunaki closed in, sprinting far faster than he could.

As he got closer to the blade, roars of thunder synchronised with his every step. Disfigured souls grabbed at his ankles, groaning at him to save them. With the Anunaki only mere strides behind, he closed his eyes and leapt with arms outstretched.

'Please grab it...'

The black sky now rhymed with his heart and, with each beat, a boom of thunder echoed across the field of battle. Feeling the grip of the handle in his palms, he tightened his fists as the icy wind and rain battered him. He opened his eyes.

Tearing the blade from the crimson-soaked earth, Maledream held the weapon aloft and roared.

'Wake up!'

* * *

'No!' he deliriously bellowed, heavily panting in cold sweat, eyes dilated.

Glancing at the blade, Maledream promptly chucked it aside, before crawling from his tent to wretch his bile. It had freaked him out to such an extent that he was tempted to pass out, but something inside him made him refuse.

'No,' he muttered in repeat for several minutes, feverishly swaying his head.

For the rest of the night he could not sleep, no matter how hard he tried, even after hiding the blade under the fur rugs and out of his sight.

* * *

Glaring at the morning sun from the balcony of the ruined temple, Maledream went over his frightening vision before setting off with Angelite. The Tribal looked very pale, and a serious expression was engraved on his face.

He thought back to the ancient battlefield. This was a place he had frequented lately, but only ever near the beach or the outskirts when he had been out scavenging. Going through his inventory, he knew that a long journey would mean travelling as lightly as possible.

'So much for getting a good night's sleep,' he thought, letting out a powerful yawn. *'That bloody woman ready yet? It'll be the afternoon by the time we get anywhere.'*

Maledream's knee gave way as he felt something blunt whack the back of his leg. He jumped around in fright, only to see Angelite with an attractive cheeky grin etched on her face. He guessed that was a good enough reason to forgive her.

'Give it up, it's far too early for games,' he moaned.

'You seem jumpy and serious today. I thought I'd get your attention. I've been stood behind you for a while now, and you didn't even notice!' she said, pointing her finger at him, and so closely, that he had to cross his eyes.

'Why, was I meant to?' he jested and grinned.

'The cheek!' she said, whacking her staff on his ankle.

Maledream let out a yelp and comically rubbed his leg up and down. She threatened to hit him again, but he accepted defeat and held his palms out in defence.

'Good, she seems much happier,' he thought.

'Silly man, you'll get more of where that came from if you're just as disrespectful!' she laughed, leaving Maledream to shake his head and smirk.

'Why are you in a good mood then? Did the old man get it up after all these years?' he laughed.

'That was uncalled for!' she protested, raising her staff once more to see the Tribal flinch away.

'Just thought I'd get even, I don't like getting hit, especially in the mornings,' he joked, holding his palms out once more.

'Anyway...' she replied, gently placing her index finger on his lower lip. 'Let's get going.'

Maledream gave her a firm nod and, slinging his sword to his side, made one final check before they set off.

Larkham watched the two leave the safety of the camp from the balcony of the broken temple, before the children approached him for another round of stories to start their day. A concerned expression troubled his slightly wrinkled and weathered face.

'Look after each other, you two, and be careful.'

* * *

It was the start of their month-long journey back to Angelite's home, Meridia.

Chatting away, the pair walked steadily down the hill and into the city. They passed plants and other wildlife that had taken over the grey-brick walls. Birds of all varieties, nesting in the ruins, sang their songs as the sun appeared over the horizon. It was peaceful as the couple strode through the empty streets. Thanks to Maledream, they avoided the most dangerous and hazardous areas in this part of the ruined city. Along the way, Maledream told the priestess about his disturbing vision.

'I think that, whatever it was, you were definitely experiencing something from one of the many last battles. Perhaps your weapon was there, perhaps it's older than I thought,' said Angelite.

'Yeah, I think so, although it doesn't look anywhere as good as it did, but the power was released in the same way as it was during the fight with that Anunaki,' replied Maledream.

'I expect it just needs polishing, it looks rusty. After all, dreams are different from reality,' she said.

'I'll leave it how it is, besides, I prefer the old look, doesn't look so valuable. Anyway, how does all this magic work?'

'I wondered how long it would be until you asked. I guess I should start from the beginning. All magic that you know or heard of, including the world around us, is formed from a single source of power, known as Resonance. It's everywhere you look, from you and me, to even the stars in the heavens,' she chirpily replied.

'The stars?' he queried.

'The stars also have to come from somewhere, too. In the heavens at night, in this great spiral of life, emanates a sound, a Resonance so strong that it creates all the stars and more. Do you get the idea? It's like a living heartbeat for all things...'

Maledream stared blankly into the distance, the conversation made him think deeply. He refocused his attention as Angelite leaned forward in her stride and clicked her fingers in front of his eyes.

'Sorry, please carry on, I'm listening. So, uh, how does this energy work, exactly? From what I've seen so far, it's like it comes out of nowhere,' he said.

Angelite stopped Maledream gently by holding his shoulder. She looked around for an example.

'You see that small puddle of water just by your feet?' she said.

'Yeah, what about it?' he muttered, his brow stooping in confusion.

'This free energy, Resonance, has been named scientifically as particles or, in more basic terms, atoms. Atoms are the hollow carriers of free energy. Everything you see or touch is created from these atoms. So many in fact that it's countless,' she replied, glancing at him.

'Okay, just trying to get my head around your words. So, if these atoms are hollow, how do we even exist to begin with?'

'Let me finish, I'm getting to that!' she smiled.

'All right, but this isn't my old man's legends, this stuff is deep. Anyway, carry on,' he said, grinning.

'These hollow atoms are locked with certain charges which orbit them. These are called electrons, protons, and neutrons. Each charge, or atom, has the potential of changing itself into something else. Atoms are energy, and energy can freely change its form. Simply put, these atoms can change their frequency, or energy field, and can be manipulated with the most basic energy of all... sound.'

'Sound? Let me get this right, so these atoms or energies can be manipulated by sound?'

'Yes. There are some sounds you cannot hear, and there are, unbelievably, many sounds that manipulate the known world, and, in fact, the universe. However, most are invisible to our ears.'

'So, uh, what's all this got to do with a puddle?' he smirked.

Angelite knelt and picked up a pebble. Standing back up, she raised her arm above the shallow pool and then let it drop with a splash.

'Ripples?'

'Imagine that the puddle is a round, hollow atom. Now, imagine that those ripples are waves of sound inside that atom,' she said.

'Oh, I see, that's actually quite clever and simple,' he remarked, thinking he had finally grabbed the basic gist of what the priestess had taught him.

'What these protons, neutrons, and electrons do is lock that sound frequency into certain energies or forms. The rim of the puddle, you could imagine, is that barrier, locking in place that one puddle or frequency of energy. Energy only changes form, it's never destroyed, so, therefore, this one puddle could change its frequency to look like, or represent, some different form of Resonance,' she added.

'That bit sounds a bit more complicated. Sorry, it'll probably take me longer to better understand it, but I think I see what you're talking about now,' he said with a cheeky grin.

'I'm glad you do,' she said, excitedly clasping her hands together.

Maledream continued to stare at the puddle as he went over the lesson, until Angelite tugged his shoulder to move on.

'Continuing from what I've just taught you, Resonance connects all kinds of life together, such as spirits, which we can't see normally with our eyes, unless we encourage the Resonance inside of us. We are connected, heart and soul, to everything that exists, even if a person doesn't know it! There is so much more to learn and understand, though. I don't hold all the answers.'

Angelite paused for a quick breath, and, while holding Maledream's hands in a caring fashion, asked him, 'you sure you're okay? You look so tired.'

'Yeah, I'm fine, thanks, don't worry about me, I'm just thinking about what you're saying. So then, what's the connection with your singing, and the runes that glow on your staff, or on my sword? Does that have something to do with this Resonance, because words are sound?' he wondered.

She found it hard to answer his question as she glanced at the young man's rough stubble and blue eyes. Realising what she was doing, she let go of the Tribal's hands in an embarrassing fashion, before proceeding to rush her words.

'Uh, yes, yes it does. My staff is a tool that helps me focus these energies, and the runes serve to enhance certain Resonance spells. The crystals on my staff act in a similar way, but it all depends on what you use and what combinations work best. Because everything in existence is a resonating frequency, we can tune our words, objects, and spirit into these resonating sounds. Some tunes work well, while some do not at all. It depends on the structure of your notes.'

Maledream raised another confused eyebrow, replying, 'you're starting to lose me again. Tune into Resonance? Do you mean what you did last night with the different colours and your singing?'

'Okay, for example...' she said as they continued walking, 'a flame has certain energy or magic, known as Resonance. If you wanted to conjure a flame, then all you need to do is tune into that certain fire frequency to use the energy that the flame shares. However, it takes a lot of mental focus to achieve this, and you need to strike a balance with your words, thoughts, or a combination of the two. I can't actually conjure any flames without a source of it nearby. The strain is too much until I improve.'

'Well, if it wasn't for you yesterday, I wouldn't have stood a chance, so I think you're doing just fine at the moment,' Maledream grinned.

'Thank you, I tried my best, but as I said, I'm still improving, it just takes a lot of practice. Some members in the Order of Spirit can attain creating fire with just their voice alone, but it is very rare for a person to accomplish the desired effects without some sort of instrument to work with, such as my staff, crystals, or runes for example, which can be used to amplify the Resonance you wish to harness. That's why I use crystals. I believe they hold the key for me, personally. Runes serve to enhance the energy of the person's mind, body, and spirit, to help further tune the desired Resonance that you want.'

'I think I'm beginning to understand, it's still confusing, but I think I'm getting the point of how it all works. We should be at the bridge soon, it takes forever to cross,' he replied.

The pair continued onwards through the deserted city streets. The sun was fast approaching above their heads, and bad weather loomed on the horizon.

'I hope it doesn't rain. I'm not in the mood for those dark clouds,' he let slip with an irritated tone.

'Yeah, it would be a shame. I'm having a nice time on this walk, similar to when I was travelling here. I do feel a lot safer with you beside me,' she said.

Angelite glanced at Maledream as he strode with his hands in his coat pockets, staring at the ground in thought, with a grin stretched from ear to ear. He looked up and their eyes met.

'You know what? I can't remember smiling so much,' he uttered.

'Me neither,' she nodded, casually linking arms with him.

They came to the bridge and began their long trek to the other side of the city across the large, winding river below them. The bridge looked crippled in places where the weather had taken its toll over the years. Rust blanketed the ancient iron. It stood to serve as a testament of what humanity had achieved in ancient days in terms of engineering. Birds that nested in-between the girders flew high above, enjoying the last of the light before the dark clouds drew near. The river that led out to the ocean glimmered with a red hue as the sun turned a shade of crimson. They gazed at the tranquillity as they traversed silently, enjoying the view that surrounded them.

Maledream broke the silence, 'can I ask you something? Why did you and your friends leave the safety of your home? It's so dangerous here, was there any real reason?'

'I wanted to learn more about the Dark Age lands, I guess you could say I was bored. I have heard of many stories from the refugees that stumbled on our city, and they would tell us of where they came and how dangerous it was. You could say this fired up our imaginations. It gave some of us wanderlust. I wanted leave and search for a place that held knowledge, which could be of great use to Meridia, such as books, scrolls, anything that may prove valuable. I promised the Order that I would find useful artefacts and bring them back for study. It was my decision alone in the end. My sense of adventure got the better of me and I convinced some friends to come along. Until I came here, I have always lived behind the protective walls of Meridia. I wanted to experience what it was like on the outside,' she sighed, drawing a quick breath before continuing.

'Unfortunately, we weren't the only ones in that library. The Anunaki attacked from the nearby river, killing my friends as it did so. Before I could use my abilities to try to save them, as I did with you, the creature brought half the place down during its attack. I was just alive by inches under the stones and, by then, it was too late to save them.'

Tears crawled down her cheeks. Angelite fought them back by wiping them on her sleeve. 'It was horrific... they were my closest friends...' she sniffed.

Maledream didn't know what to say. He almost felt unemotional about her companions' deaths. It was a regular occurrence most days, in or outside the Tribal camp.

'Well, they may not have known the danger involved, but they did their best to save you. They died, but now they will wander the spirit realm, at least, that's how the old man puts it, a better place than here.'

'You're right, may their spirits know peace. I can't help it, but... it's not something I should accept,' she said, wiping the tears from her cheeks.

A quiet moment fell on the duo. Maledream struggled to pluck up the courage to speak, still not knowing what to say.

'What else can you tell me about where you're from? You've mentioned this Order of Spirit?' he asked, hoping it would take her mind off the past.

She eventually held in her tears once they continued pacing.

'Yes, that's right. I'm a priestess in the Order of Spirit. We mainly practice Resonance and aid in any way we can for the greater good of Meridia. We specialise in teaching others how to use Resonance,' she sweetly replied.

A brief smile appeared on her face, she gained some small comfort in remembering her cause and homeland, of the greater good she wished to achieve for her people.

'Certainly sounds like a good group you've got going,' prompted the Tribal.

'Yep, we work well together, and we link with other guilds, but you'll find out more when we reach my home,' she said.

'What's this city you keep speaking of? Is it a wall, a temple, or a tent?' he jested.

Angelite found the courage to smile at his silly jibe.

'No, it's not a cardboard box, cheeky man. It's a beautiful city! It's filled with people, happiness, and Resonance. I can't wait to get back. I can show you all the sights. You won't believe your eyes... Hey, I'm just wondering, have you lived here your whole life?'

Maledream was quiet for a moment on hearing this question. He was raised by Larkham since he was a child, and he only had dim memories of an old friend that had probably been killed since that time. He replied, changing the conversation again.

'What about the rest of my people? You say this city of yours is safe, yet all my people are back there at the camp?'

His eyebrows creased, a subtle hint of pessimism settled in.

'Calm down, silly man, I've already arranged a plan with Larkham. I have a way we can get them to Meridia in total safety, without having to risk everyone's lives. As there's just two of us, we should be safer going this way as we're less noticeable,' she smiled.

He nodded in agreement. If the entire tribe travelled through the city and beyond, they would draw too much attention from outward forces.

'Anyway, we're almost on the other side now,' Maledream uttered, as if he couldn't wait to get off the windy death trap that they traversed, no matter how beautiful the view might be.

Striding down the last segment of the bridge, the two sat down for a moment to rest.

'You know what, you've taught me a lot, and the day isn't over yet. Resonance, it's never fascinated me until now. Maybe I needed to find a more interesting teacher than my boring old man,' he jested.

'I think you would make an excellent student,' she grinned.

'Probably. In the meantime, why don't we find ourselves something to eat? We've got a long way to go through the last parts of the city,' Maledream said, staring deeply into her eyes as he spoke.

Striking him hard and fast, his head thumped in pain. Falling with a fever, the Tribal collapsed on his knees whilst holding his scalp.

'What's wrong?' she panicked.

'It's nothing, just a slight headache,' he muttered.

Kneeling down next to him, she put her arms around him to hug him tightly.

'It's going to be alright, okay?'

The Tribal nodded in pain.

'Right, I know what the problem is. Let me cook something up, I bet it's hunger that's doing it. This will cheer you up and add a little protein to you,' she said, whipping out a mechanical stove and emptying her bag of rations and supplies.

'They have things like that all over the place in Meridia?' he remarked, staring at her fingers as they activated a red, crystalline orb beneath the stove.

'You mean this? It's just a simple travelling cooker. We have many things that make our lives easier in Meridia. You could say we have many luxuries. I don't envy the existence of your tribe. Once we reach Meridia, I'll make it my top priority to get your father and your tribe back in one piece, I promise.'

'You make Meridia sound like one of Larkham's spiritual realms that he keeps on and on about,' he chuckled.

'Well, I wouldn't go that far, but, once you get there, you'll probably feel cheated. You'll probably not grow so tired of it in some ways, like I did before I left. You'll have more respect,' she uttered.

'I see, I guess now that you're sitting on my side of the ocean, you look back and think how lucky you are, gives you a sort of new respect for your home, doesn't it?' he pursued, staring into her eyes as the food began to heat on her stove.

'No other way of saying it, but yes, you're right,' she nodded.

'I wouldn't worry. You've been through a lot travelling through these lands. When we get back to your home, you'll be saving many, many lives,' he assured.

Maledream's words warmed her heart.

'You're right, that's our mission really, isn't it?' she said, smiling at him with hope-filled eyes.

Soon enough, the smell of food wafted through the breeze as the pair ate their meals. After they finished, Angelite offered him some healing. Placing her hands upon his shoulders, his head began to clear. He winced in pain a moment later, and felt her hands and fingers pressing into his back muscles.

'Better?'

'A lot better, thanks. What was that you did? I almost fell asleep. My joints feel a hell of a lot better,' he exhaled.

'Just a bit of something called message. And with some healing Resonance, of course,' she grinned.

'It works. I may have to make it a hobby,' he jested, turning his gaze to the clouds on the horizon. 'Anyway, we should get going before it gets too dark. We've been sitting here for too long,' Maledream finished, moving his shoulders and arms around in circular motions, almost in disbelief.

'You're right, let's get going,' Angelite nodded.

Chapter Four

The Packs

The sun continued to descend as if it retreated from the dark, brooding clouds. Angelite remarked about the sunset, that it was a beautiful sight to finish off a pleasant day's journey. Maledream wished he shared the same philosophy.

A storm front was massing, and it could be felt on the light, warm breeze. Many lights flickered into being throughout the ruined cityscape like glowing fireflies, showing then that the grey walls catered life. Uneasy and restless, the nightlife was about to begin after sunset, and get far more interesting.

'We have two options,' Maledream whispered, 'we can either find somewhere very safe to sleep, or the second option is to keep moving. I recommend not stopping around here for long, and go with the second.'

'What makes you so uneasy and scared?' she worried.

'Trust me, bad things come out at night, and it's usually of the human kind, not the monstrous kind.'

'We're both exhausted, though,' she yawned.

'I know, but trust me on this. We don't want to be here. I'd rather keep going,' he persisted.

'You're starting to scare me,' she said, subconsciously tightening her grip on her oaken staff.

Reaching out and holding her hand, Maledream looked at her with a firm stare.

'We'll be fine, trust me,' he reassured.

With a nod, they continued through the darkest part of the ruins.

'Be light on your feet, don't let go, and we'll be alright,' he whispered.

The nightlife was certainly out. Shouting echoed through the gloomy streets. Shadows of people darted across the walls from the faint illumination of fires that were set alight in rusty bins.

'Why so much shouting?' Angelite whispered.

'Usually gangs fighting each other because they've got no other purpose. Preying on the weak, mugging, raping, disembowelling, you name it. It's all here. Utter chaos. These gangs are called Packs,' he said, trying to keep his voice low, watching his every step on the rubble as he led the way.

'You make it sound like they're a bunch of ravenous Anunaki,' she stammered.

'That's what these Packs are, nothing but dangerous assholes. You're safe with me, don't worry, just keep moving,' he said, squeezing her hand.

Louder echoes resounded of the lawlessness that existed. Engines of various archaic machines roared with high-pitched revs, providing a chorus of noise as the Packs began their nightly raiding at high speeds on makeshift bikes or other wheeled contraptions, performing hit and run attacks on each other's territory. Some Packs drove trucks mounted with an array of weaponry to slay their opponents for mere table scraps.

'I've never seen anything like this before, I can't believe my eyes,' she whispered, watching one such war truck speed passed the ruins in which they hid.

'Yeah, this is a real desperate struggle to a lot of people,' he sighed.

'What's that other noise?' Angelite wondered.

'Shit,' he panicked, tugging her backwards.

They retreated into the depths of the building, and took refuge behind some marble pillars. Crouching, they peered around the column to see what it was. One of the Pack gangs had showed up twenty yards away on the broken road. Sitting on their bikes, they idly chatted and yelled at the tops of their lungs after revving their whining engines.

'Great, this will slow us down,' Maledream thought.

'Is everything alright?' she whispered.

'Yeah, I'm not crushing you am I?' he whispered back.

'Couldn't be better, I guess,' she joked.

'Good, quiet,' he smirked, scanning the Pack's movements as he listened closely to their words.

This particular gang was the Ruthless Pack. It suited their nature, and of course, the paint markings on the bikes gave it away in the faint light of their flaming torches. Maledream would have no chance but to fight if they were discovered, given this gang's reputation as one of the most feared in the city.

Clad in rustic metal plates, thick furs, and leather armour, these powerful men were far from diplomatic. If it was one thing he knew about Packs, regardless of clan, is that once they had found somewhere to settle, they would most likely get off their bikes and scavenge for anything that was useful.

Deciding it was the logical choice of action, Maledream reached slowly for his sword. Balancing the large cumbersome weapon, he removed it from the scabbard. At the last second, his strength failed him and, with a gasp, his arm gave way to the weight of the blade in his awkward position. The blade's tip struck the ground with an echoing clang. It was the worst possible moment. Just as he dropped it, the Packers switched off their bikes and stopped bellowing.

'*Shit.*'

He saw the Pack get off their bikes, wielding weapons such as clubs, chains, knives, and broken bottles. They surely heard him. They stared towards the duo's general direction in the darkened, ruined building. Rising slowly, he pulled Angelite off the floor, and quietly hid her behind another marble pillar in the darkness.

'No matter what happens, just stay here and stay hidden, don't come out, even if I'm in trouble,' he whispered.

Angelite was going to protest, but he put his index finger on her lips to prevent her. He pulled his hood over his head. He didn't want any witnesses to see his face if, of course, they managed to escape. Preparing himself, Maledream stood ready to strike. Adrenaline coursed into his veins. Angelite watched, her eyes glistening with fear. She gripped her oaken staff, and drew her own hood over her head.

'Who's there?' shouted one of the burly men.

'I heard it, boss, right big clang it was. Sounded valuable if you ask me!' uttered another.

'I know what you heard, runt. Come out and face us like a man, you little girl! We won't hurt you too much. We'll just smash your knee caps, is all...'

A loud roar of laughter from the person that said those words ensued. The Pack followed in their leader's laugh, and then stopped when he did. This unusual act showed great fear and an odd respect for their boss.

Angelite whispered her words of Resonance, praying to come to no harm. Maledream stood motionless with his arms aloft, holding his heavy blade. He was ready.

'Something tells me you're hiding behind these shadows and pillars like a coward,' the Pack leader snorted.

The Pack slithered into the darkness, and steadily surrounded the couple's position, searching for them, making as much unnerving noise as possible by banging their weapons and roaring at the tops of their lungs. There was no way to escape. One of them was nearby, gradually stepping closer and closer.

Maledream risked one more whisper, 'whatever happens, Angelite, stay h...'

As the nearby Packer arrived around the corner, creating a racket with his iron pipe by striking the columns, he, without realising it, struck Maledream on the head. The Tribal responded angrily with a sweep of his sword. The Packer stood no chance from the lashing shadow. His head was separated from his neck in an instant.

In panic and grace, the Tribal stepped back into the darkness. Surprisingly, the other Packers didn't notice the noise. Again, another Packer strode closer, stopping just out of range for a safe hit. This one carried a torch.

'Leo's dead, boss, his head's rolling on the floor!'

A roar filled the ruined building.

'Find the bastard responsible,' yelled the Pack leader.

In less than a breath, more torches were set to flame, flooding the building with wavering illumination, and leaving few shadows in which to hide.

'No more games, time to die, asshole. No one gets away with killing just one of us,' snorted the leader.

'I need to get them away from her.'

With a leap around the pillar, Maledream took down the nearest Packer with a mortal cleave across his victim's spinal column with a vicious crunch. This man was no Anunaki. He was fragile flesh and bone, and his two-handed sword split his target in twain. In doing so, however, Maledream revealed himself to six more of the gang.

'Get him!'

Maledream lowered his large weapon for another swipe. The attack was fast and swift as they charged into him. The Tribal was in a flurry of defence against all odds. He knew he couldn't keep it up for more than a minute before his arms gave way to the weight of the sword.

Parrying a blow, he dived through the mass of bodies and, spinning around, clumsily swiped his blade at one unfortunate's ankles, cleaving his feet from his legs in one swoop. The man roared in pain, shock, and horror as he hit the ground with a thud, blood spurting from his stumps.

Maledream raised his cumbersome weapon once again, and brought it down firmly across the ribcage of another as fast as he could swing. Bloody flecks pelted his face with an accompanying squeal of pain. Two down, four to go.

Twirling to his left, then right, he clumsily dodged and fenced off a barrage of attacks. Before he could dart away, however, his hands felt the stinging sensation of a thick, iron chain. With a powerful tug, Maledream's balance was lost. Dragged off his feet, he went flying, head first, into an adjacent marble pillar.

* * *

Closing his eyes on impact, the Tribal opened his eyes and saw something he did not expect. He seemed to be in another one of his visions. Maledream saw himself with his back to the sea, staring blankly at the commander that once owned the blade. The giant of a man stood before him, his facial features clouded by the shadow of his hood.

The adrenaline that he once felt coursing through his veins had vanished, as if he were never in the ruins fighting. Confused at what he saw and felt, a loud, echoing voice invaded his thoughts.

'Retrinumun.'

The blade's hilt hummed to the word, before a sudden flash of light took his sight.

*　*　*

Opening his eyes, the Tribal's head cracked and bounced off the hard stone. Concussed, but with every ounce of strength, he pushed himself from the pillar, swinging his hand and sword loose of the chain in distraught panic, and cut through the links in a shower of sparks.

'I'm not going down,' Maledream roared defiantly, his voice filled with renewed vigour.

Exploding into life, the sword cracked the air with an echoing power. Its energy rolled across the dark, rusty-looking alloy. Raising the blade above his head, he brought it down upon a Packer with a satisfying blow, cleaving the attacker's skull in half. However, it did not stop there. The blade sliced through the rest of the man's torso just as easily in a vertical line, and only stopping once it struck the earth.

The Pack continued their relentless assault with renewed bloodlust. It was as if killing them just made them stronger. Maledream found it difficult to wield the weapon, or even understand its power, whilst concentrating on the fight at hand.

Spiked-iron chains, broken bottles, and knives tried to gut him as he dodged and parried. Going around in circles, Maledream flung himself from pillar to pillar, leading them away from the priestess and, in turn, chased by the Packers' weapons that rang out mere inches behind him.

'Get that adrenaline running, Pack, makes the meat taste better!' their leader bellowed with laughter.

Suddenly, Maledream's boots slipped on a smooth, marble slab and, before he knew it, fell and cracked his chin on the stone. The silhouettes of the Pack's shadows on the nearby walls showed the assailants jumping in for the kill. They piled on top, overpowering him by sheer weight of numbers as they pinned him.

'We're going to enjoy gutting you like a fucking pig,' one hissed.

Maledream's eyes widened. He was about to die. He thought of her above all else.

'No,' he roared, his voice echoing louder than the entire ruckus inside the ruins.

With a push, he rolled onto his back and brought the weapon to bear on the closest of them.

'Retrinumun.'

In an instant, the sword activated and, as bright as the sun, crackled into life. In an explosion of bright energy, the remaining Packers viciously flew into the walls and pillars with a booming thud. It left nothing but entrails, half-disintegrated torsos, and blood smeared on walls and pillars.

'Looks like it's my turn now, fucker,' the Pack leader roared.

As he approached, Maledream saw he was far taller and muscular than the others he had just defeated. The Tribal tried to stand to meet this new threat. However, his knees buckled and he fell to the floor. Blood gushed from many horrendous stab wounds inflicted by the Pack that had jumped him.

Maledream began to lose consciousness, and his body stiffened to the fear. In shock, he tried breathing desperately for air, but blood filled his lungs, and all he could do was helplessly gargle. He glanced at the blade, only to see its surface growing dull.

'Not so hard now, are you. A damn chicken could take me out compared to your runty ass,' the Pack leader scoffed.

Maledream's pupils dilated, he struggled to calm his heartbeat that sprayed his life on the cold stone.

'Angel... ite...'

'There aren't any angels where you'll be going, shit head. You're going straight to hell!'

'No he isn't,' Angelite shrieked.

Halting in his tread, the boss of the Pack turned to face this unexpected woman.

'What's this? What's a little slut going to do, huh...?' he snorted, glaring at Angelite's petite form.

However, falling silent for a moment, he winced when he took notice of her attire, and that of the fallen Packer's torch that she held.

'Well shoot my ball sack. You're a fucking Witch,' he growled.

Angelite said nothing. Instead, she raised her free hand. Focusing on the embers, her eyes reflected the white, orangey glow of the fiery stick. Twirling her fingers around the naked flame, the primal energy flowed and danced with every passing action of her index finger. Her voice echoed, and her eyes shined with a violet hue.

'You're not killing him, and I'm not a slut or a witch!'

Taken aback by Angelite's shriek, and by her way to manipulate fire, the Pack leader broke a sweat.

'You're gonna' die, bitch, but not before I fucking have you,' he bellowed, charging towards her in his frenzy with two large clubs in his hands.

The priestess let the swelled energies spill from her hand. Her Resonance easily manipulated the hot energy. Within seconds, the flame grew in immense size and super-combusted to the free air as she screamed. With no time to react, the helpless large man was engulfed in a cacophonous sea of white-hot flame. The inferno shed his skin and muscle from his bones in an instant, and his bellowing war cry disappeared as the rush and roar of the intense spell swept over him.

Overly roasted flesh filled the priestess's nostrils. Her legs quaked from adrenaline. Dropping the torch, she dashed to the Tribal.

'This... this can't happen again,' she cried.

Uttering some quiet words, she clasped her hands together and knelt beside Maledream. Resting the Tribal the best she could on her knees, her hands took to green and golden glows that grew in intensity the more she focused. Fate lines on her palms illuminated with a dull, white glow. She feared she was too late.

* * *

An hour had passed. The pair lay still in the dark. Maledream breathed quietly and occasionally snored. Each time he did, Angelite panicked and held her hand on his mouth.

'Wake up, wake up for spirit's sake,' she said, nudging him.

Eventually, her efforts paid off. His eyes fluttered. He dozily glanced at her.

'You almost died,' she whispered, staring at him with a violet glow in her eyes.

Maledream attempted to get up with a passing moan, but fell on his knees trying to do so.

'Your wounds are sealed, but I can't replace the loss of blood. Your strength will gradually return, but you need rest,' she whispered.

'We don't have time. We have to move,' he groaned, forcing himself to his feet by using his blade and Angelite's help to steady his balance.

More chaos echoed down the streets. They were in no position to fight. They had to run.

'To their bikes,' he spluttered.

Quickly, they searched the Packers for keys and then rushed outside of the shadowy building.

'Do you know how to work one of these?' she asked.

'Kind of, I haven't ridden one for years. You'll be okay, just get on,' he ordered.

She nervously hopped on the back seat whilst Maledream sat on the front. The rusty suspension creaked and heaved, as if the bold, rubber tires were not bad enough. Inserting the keys with a twist, he put his foot down on the clutch, starting the bike and revving it hard.

'Tighten your arms around my waist,' he uttered over the noise of the whiny engine.

The pair sped through the gloomy streets on their rickety ride. The Tribal avoided the rubble and potholes the best he could. They darted through Pack territories that threatened them, dodging firebombs, rocks, and gunshots that aimed for them precariously.

'Faster, faster, faster,' the priestess shouted, even though she was terrified and clung to him for dear life.

'I'm going as fast as this piece of shit can go, hold on,' Maledream bellowed.

He screeched the bike's brakes, sending the archaic ride skidding around a darker street corner.

'Shit.'

They glared at a brick wall barring their path. A shot rang out from the building above, puncturing the rear wheel tire with a double bang. The pair jumped off in desperation and, backed against the tight corner, Maledream withdrew his weapon and pushed the priestess behind him.

An overpowering searchlight beamed into life, blinding the pair as a voice shouted at them from one of the apartments above. 'Is that who I think it is?'

Chapter Five

The Unexpected

A familiar voice from long ago echoed to the duo. Maledream tried to match the man to someone he knew, deep down, but was too busy struggling to stay on his feet from the loss of blood. The voice called out again.

'It's Neveah. Get your asses in here.'

'Neveah... no, it can't be,' Maledream thought.

After Neveah spoke, the powerful searchlight, located high above, dimmed in power. No longer blinded, a thick iron door opened before them, an entrance into the multi-storey building. The pair hesitated for a moment but, as the bellowing of more Packs echoed their war mantra in the streets, they decided they had no choice.

With a nod to the priestess, the twosome quickly stumbled towards it. They stepped through the doorway and into complete darkness. With a mighty slam, the pair was locked inside, and once it closed, a red light above the door flickered to life.

Two Packers stood on each side of the iron frames, armed with pole-arms strapped to their backs. They wore scraps of leather for protection, forming similar coats to Maledream, with the exception that chain mail or plates of iron armour protected vital areas. Both sported strange hairstyles, similar to other cuts adopted by Packs.

'Up here,' yelled the man from upstairs.

'Go on then, Neveah won't wait all night,' one of the guards muttered.

'Why don't you help me carry him up? He's too weak to move by himself!' Angelite burst at them.

Glancing at each other, then at Angelite, and then back at each other, they grunted with a firm nod, and then took Maledream off Angelite's hands and helped him up the flight of stairs.

'Quite a lady with a back bone,' the guard said cheerfully, bearing a small grin.

'Don't get many women like that anymore, that's for sure,' the other jested.

'Uh, thank you, I think,' she replied with a raised eyebrow.

'No problem,' the guards grunted.

The pair was led up to the first flight of stairs and, once a little way down the corridor, ushered into a room filled with burning candles. It was a shambles. Old electrical equipment and other unused objects were scattered about the room.

In the centre of it was a table, stockpiled with rusty-ranged weapons and crude ammunition. One wall was home to a rack, sporting knives, swords, and other weapons for close quarter's combat in a similarly poor condition. Some had never even been wiped clean from the blood of their victims.

Maledream could guess whom Neveah was by seeing him sat on a broken, torn couch with some others, smoking a pipe full of tobacco. Tobacco was a treat for the leader of the Pack, and handing it out freely was an honoured privilege. It was very hard to procure.

Neveah wore an eye-patch, which covered a gruesome battle-scarred eye that stretched halfway up and down his face. The Pack leader also sported a thin goatee, and his head was shaved right down to the scalp. Neveah wasn't only the tallest in the room, he was also the largest in bulk. His naked torso showed off his impressive wide frame that sported large, compact muscles.

Stood by the broken window, like a shadowy spectre, was the man with the large gun that blew out the bike's back tire. He kept watch of the perimeter that the Pack had set in the street below.

By the side of him was a large, stationary searchlight, the same one that was used to blind them. The power for it came from a humming machine down the hallway, a few doors away, with power leads running to it. Diesel fumes wafted into the room, meaning that a portable generator was responsible for the electricity.

Sitting the couple down, the guards returned to man their posts. Neveah glanced at the priestess. She seemed agitated and uncomfortable with all the rough-looking men, bar one woman, staring at her.

'Can I offer you buggers something to eat or drink? Water? Meat? Bread? Thin air?' Neveah jested.

Maledream's memories of his younger years rushed back into his mind at an alarming rate. He could hardly believe it. Ignoring his homely patronage, the Tribal blurted, 'what happened to you?'

'Aye, we'll move on to the history lesson after we've discussed drink and food, you two look more than worn out,' replied Neveah.

'Worn out isn't the word for it. Water would be good,' muttered Maledream.

'Yes, me too, thank you,' Angelite uttered, her voice edgy.

With the raise of his hand and a snap of the fingers, the surrounding gang members handed them flasks of water.

'Drink up, it's the cleanest source we have,' Neveah announced, watching Maledream take a long swig.

'Thirsty?' Neveah chuckled.

Angelite sipped hers slowly. She couldn't shake her uneasy feelings.

'Is this your woman?' Neveah asked, almost causing Maledream to choke on the water.

'No, nothing like that, bit of a long story,' the Tribal coughed.

'Fair enough. Does this lass have a name?'

'Angelite,' she spoke up.

'Angelite? Nice to meet you,' Neveah grinned and nodded, before turning to face the Tribal.

'Do you remember when we were attacked all those years ago, mate?'

Looking dumbstruck, Maledream paused before answering. 'Kind of, but I lost some of my memory. I can barely remember what my parents looked like. Larkham and his Tribals adopted me out on the outskirts of the city. By fluke, I still remember a fair bit of you from our teenage moments, but that's all, really. I assumed you were buggered by the Packs, or worse.'

Neveah exploded into loud, boisterous laughter at the last comment. It forced a smile on Angelite's lips.

'It seems to me your dry humour has kept you alive. So, you're one of those Tribals now? I can't tell you how good it is to see you, mate, it must be fate, or some spiritual shit like that. I lost all hope, and no, I wasn't buggered. I'll tell you what happened,' Neveah uttered, shaking his hand.

The big man paused to inhale a large dose of tobacco from his pipe, exhaling as he continued. 'We were part of wandering group of refugees. You, me, and our families were on our way to the north. We were trying to find a sanctuary that was rumoured to exist. We travelled for years, avoiding many troubles, that is, until we crossed this city, then we were separated during a battle. Until now, I thought I was the only survivor. Since then, this is where I've remained.'

Maledream nodded in turn. He recalled his bloodstained palms.

'I'll take your word for it, I guess. Anyway, you've built yourself quite an empire here with this Pack of yours,' replied the Tribal.

'Aye, it ain't bad. I've gone through much struggle,' Neveah proceeded, taking in another full lung of smoke as he continued. 'To reach where I am now, I had to go through much hardship, much bruising, not to mention lose the sight of my right eye.'

He lifted his eye-patch to reveal a dark hole in his skull. The pair felt slightly queasy staring at the gory sight.

Lowering it with a smile, he said, 'I'll introduce you to the Pack. This guy is Crazy John. When he gets going in combat, you'll see why he gets the *"Crazy"* tag,' he laughed.

Crazy John glared at Angelite, madly grinning as he polished many knives set upon his lap. She felt uncomfortable looking into those maniacal eyes of his. They seemed to match his sinister look. His dark hair reached his shoulders, and his black leather armour lay beside him. The pair stared with harsh frowns at his naked torso.

'Why's your chest caved in?' Maledream wondered with a sly grin.

'You don't want to know,' Crazy John chuckled.

'Okay, who's next? Ah yeah, here's a brute called Pixie. Don't ask about that name or how he came by it. All I can tell you is that he loves his hand-to-hand combat, almost as much as he loves his trusty rifle,' said Neveah.

'My pleasure, you two, you will be safe with us,' Pixie uttered, his tone light and polite.

The man sported an unshaved face and a thick goatee. His large appearance almost matched Neveah, except there was no muscle or great height to him, just girth.

'You sure don't sound like a brute,' Maledream jested, bringing a smile to all the faces in the room.

'Well met, appearances are deceiving. I was once a refugee, too,' Pixie answered respectfully, stroking his goatee and large sideburns as he slyly winked.

Neveah continued going around the room.

'Hmm, who else, ah yeah, Boris here, only female in the Pack, but she's considerably crazier than Crazy John when she gets going and...'

'If you value your balls, Neveah, you'll finish off your words with something wise...' Boris interrupted.

Her hair was long and dark, a contrast to Angelite's dazzling orange. Her tightly hugging leather showed off her curvaceous, womanly form all too well. A couple of handguns dangled freely in holsters from her belt, and her exposed stomach sported tattoos of various designs. Unlike the other Packers, her ears were littered with silvery piercings.

'See what I mean? Don't mess with her, she and Crazy John are madly in love, of course, and fight harder because of it. Shame we can't all fall in love and fight harder, eh? Right then, last one here is Reckless. I would say the most sinister of the Pack. Isn't that right, mate?' Neveah said, his one eye glaring at him.

Reckless said nothing as he sat clutching his large gun. He glared at Angelite with his cold, brown eyes. She almost felt compelled to look away. The man looked rigid, twitchy, as if the wrong word could provoke him. His gaunt, straight facial features only highlighted this persona.

'All in all, it's a very tightly-knit Pack. There are others, but they're elsewhere in the building or outside scavenging because it's their turn tonight. Who you see in this room, right now, are the Packers who I've known and fought with, side-by-side, for many years, with the exception of Reckless. Others come and go. The two guards who let you in downstairs are new. Still don't know what to think of them, though...' Neveah said, glancing at Reckless as he did so, and vice-versa, both with inquisitive stares.

'They're fine, boss,' Reckless returned, his tone husky.

'We'll see. I want no backstabbing, mate.'

'As I said boss, all is well,' Reckless assured.

'Aye, it better be.'

Neveah had to make sure he maintained his position with authority. He could never be seen as weak. It would take many years for any new member to gain his trust. Assassinations were rampant in the city, power switched hands viciously on a regular basis.

'So, anything else you want to know?' Neveah uttered, turning to face the Tribal and priestess.

For a moment, the pair glanced at each member of the Pack in turn.

'Do you like this life, Neveah? Does the rest of your Pack like it here?' Angelite wondered.

'Hell no but, even if we had a choice, where would we go? The lands are filled with worse things than us humans,' he sighed.

The Pack leader got up and strolled towards another dark, broken window. Peering out of it with his hands clasped behind his back, his one eye glared at the ruined skyscrapers.

'If you want a way out of this way of life, then there is one option you can take. Join Maledream and me. We're travelling back to my home. Maybe it was the same destination you were meant to reach all those years ago?'

Neveah paused in his reply. He took full notice of her travelling attire as he turned to face her again. Her robes were of the finest silks that he had ever laid eye on, if greatly stained and dusty.

'You mean this sanctuary we've all heard rumour of?' he queried.

'Yes, my home, it's called Meridia.'

'This sanctuary you speak of is called Meridia? What proof do you have that it exists, this Meridia? Do you really believe it could be a safe haven for us?' Neveah wondered, suspicion tipped on his tongue.

'We've all heard the rumours, they're a load of bollocks,' Boris interrupted, also unconvinced with the others in the room whom grunted their pessimism.

'Well, I'm going to find out, you lot can stay here and keep killing each other if that sounds any better,' Maledream uttered in her defence.

'Aye, that so?' Neveah grunted.

'Yeah, look at what she's wearing, for instance. Have you ever seen silks as fine as this?' replied Maledream.

'They do look odd. What other proof do you have? You can't expect us to risk our lives with you two. Give us some hard proof and we might consider it,' Crazy John added with arms crossed.

'Just watch, I'll show you my proof,' Angelite nervously smiled, bravely standing.

Maledream settled down to watch with an arm crossed behind his head. Neveah passed him the pipe of tobacco as the Packers erupted in conversation.

'We could do with a little more light in here,' she said.

Withdrawing her oaken, rune-chiselled staff, she held it aloft and pointed the crystal tip toward the centre of the room.

'You may want to move yourselves away from the candles,' she added.

In no time at all, the Pack retreated to the walls of the room, dragging with them their broken couches. Angelite asked for quiet so she could concentrate. The runes began to glow upwards from the base of her staff, until gradually reaching the crystal that sat at the top.

'*Flamash, Flamash, Flamash, Gionistisa Triatus,*' sang the priestess.

The candles in the room flickered briefly.

'Flamash, Flamash, Flamash, Gionistisa Triatus. Fire light the beacon, fire be my light, fire be my guardian,' she continued in song, enthralling all that looked upon her as she worked her spell.

Each word strengthened the intensity of the flames.

'Fire, be my sun, fire by my creation, fire give breath to the ether. Flamash, Flamash, Flamash Gionistisa Triatus.'

Energy from the runes hummed with static. Her staff glowed with an intense, amber aura, whilst the crystals beamed fantastic arrays of multiple hues that radiated deep inner-glows. The candles placed all around the room led a gradual river of hot, swirling gold from the naked flames, slithering through the air at unimaginable angles, until they orbited the crystal atop her staff. Rings of fire danced and licked the air, lighting the room as bright as day. Hair floated on end, and loose clothing tugged towards the fiery vortex, as if a gravitational force existed within the hot, swirling rings.

'Like a droplet of water to the ocean, like a candle lit flame to the sun. Flamash, Flamash, Flamash.'

Finalising her spell, the rings of fire exploded into a nova of ether, disappearing from the room, and equally shocking her audience as they cowered with fear. With her Resonance complete, hair and clothes took to the natural pull of the earth once more.

'Convinced?' she grinned.

'Aye, fuck me,' Neveah gawked.

'That was strange Witchcraft,' the others said with frightful glares directed at the young woman.

'She's a cursed Witch?' Crazy John spoke up.

'With power like that, that's one woman I wouldn't mess with,' Boris jested with a wide, beaming smile.

'I think that might be all the proof we need...' Neveah added with a stammer.

'If she was truly a Witch, she would have incinerated us right here, right now. This is the first time I've seen someone using such Witchcraft by singing it, like it was a fine craft,' replied Pixie.

'I agree, people with chaotic powers can't control them like she just did,' added Boris.

'I've seen and killed many of her kind, but she's different,' said Crazy John.

'So have I, this one's different alright,' Boris concurred.

'Not to mention, she doesn't have any skin mutations or the likes, her clothes are of the finest quality, and her Witch-staff is quite alien, yet intriguing,' said Pixie.

'Pardon me for asking, but, what do you mean by *Witch?*' Angelite wondered.

The name sounded derogatory in how they used the term. The Pack fell silent for a moment, almost reluctant to answer.

'Aye, Witch's in this city can do weird shit, similar to what you just did. They're chaotic, distrustful, and have strange, destructive powers that have been known to wipe out entire Packs in one go. We stay away from them the best we can. They can make the skin rot just by looking at you. We don't know too much about them, but as Crazy John and Boris just mentioned, they've had a couple of encounters with them in the past,' Neveah answered.

'Yeah, mean sons' of bitches,' Crazy John nodded.

'She definitely isn't one, her skin's in better condition than mine,' Boris said, focusing on Angelite's alabaster complexion.

'As you can see, we're quite fearful of such power. We have no way to fight it, as such. If this was any other Pack, they would've killed you by now,' said Pixie.

'I see,' Angelite nodded, keenly remembering the Packers she and Maledream had encountered earlier.

Reckless remained speechless, unsure of what to say as he eyed up the red-haired woman with distaste.

'The thing is... I'm not the only one in my home that practices Resonance. There are many of us that do, and we've existed in peace for over a hundred and fifty years, and we have only ever used our arts for defence, learning, and healing,' said the priestess.

'Aye, as Pixie said, you could've melted us or burned our place down. Now, I ain't saying we'll ever trust your strange Witchcraft, but you're not insane either. Long ago, me and Maledream travelled with our families to reach such a place, till we ended up here, that is,' Neveah said, staring at his group with his one eye.

'So, what do we do then, great leader?' Boris smirked.

'Well, okay, we'll take the hint that you come from this strange sanctuary of yours. Who here will join me with Maledream and Angelite? She's living proof that this Meridia exists, for that I'm certain,' said Neveah.

The pack muttered and nodded, reaching various opinions. Soon after, they made up their minds, and some rose to their feet.

'I'll come along for the ride,' Pixie stated.

'Me too, anything is better than this shit hole, right? As long as there's killing to be had on the way,' said Crazy John, glaring at everyone with his mad grin.

'I will, but we need to remember that this Witchcraft is dangerous,' replied Reckless, lowering the high atmosphere.

'And why so, runt?' replied Neveah in turn, his one eye staring coldly at the new recruit.

'I'm beginning to think you've lost all your minds, she's dangerous,' Reckless added sombrely.

'I'm sure little Angelite is more than able to help us with her Witchcraft, and that's part of the reason why I'm prepared to risk the journey. She doesn't look it, but you can just feel the silent power from her, somehow,' replied Neveah.

'Even so, I don't trust Witches, and neither should any of you. How do you know she won't turn on us once we leave the safety of our base? She could melt our skin with her ability to control fire! Burn us alive in an instant!' Reckless barked in rising fear.

'That's enough out of you,' Neveah shouted, slamming his fist on the table.

He feared his words would kill his Pack's enthusiasm. Neveah wanted a way out of the city, but needed a good reason to leave the safety of their territory to make such a break. Now that Angelite and Maledream was here, he could see a possible way out, finally.

Neveah carried on, staring at each member as he growled, 'I won't hear any more shit about her. I'm well aware of the stories of Witches or beasts that exist in this shit hole. I don't see this sweet girl doing anything like that. So shut your mouth, before I smash it in with my fist.'

Reckless seemed fearful of the Pack leader, resentment clouded his eyes in the gloom. Neveah spat on the dusty floor as he turned to each member of the group, examining them in turn, making sure he hadn't lost any respect. None argued against him, although Crazy John decided to antagonize Reckless with a snide smirk.

'Then it's settled, you two won't travel alone. If we meet trouble, then we'll all fight by your side,' Neveah uttered with confidence.

Angelite seemed hurt by Reckless's comment, but tried to show no weakness as she sat back down next to Maledream.

'Isn't this fantastic?' the priestess uttered to the Tribal, only to discover him lightly snoring.

'I'm surprised the commotion didn't wake him,' Pixie quietly uttered.

'He's lost so much blood, I hope he's okay,' Angelite thought, stroking his face. 'At least he's getting some rest, I guess,' she smiled.

'Aye, must have been one hell of a day. You'll have to tell me all about it at some point. We'll leave in the morning after gathering our supplies and weapons. You're also in luck, we have a transport covered and guarded downstairs. It'll greatly speed up our journey,' Neveah said, his mind going over the tasks that needed doing before they left.

'I can't thank you enough for your help,' the priestess graciously returned.

'That's no problem, Sweet,' Neveah nodded.

'I do have something to add, though,' she said, hesitatingly. 'We have to travel north, through the ancient battlefield.'

At hearing this, Neveah and the other Packers glanced at her. A swift silence fell.

'You know what exists there, if, of course, we're unlucky enough to cross them,' Pixie replied, his tone disturbed.

'I'm not sure what you mean?' Angelite wondered, raising her eyebrow.

'I'll tell you about it tomorrow. We should be fine, though, it's just superstition. After all, we live our everyday lives fighting in this city, so what does it matter if we cross this fabled battlefield and shit hits the fan? Anyway, if that's all, then everyone get some sleep. We'll get up nice and early,' Neveah finished.

Nodding or muttering in agreement, the Pack got up and left the room to leave Angelite and Maledream alone to sleep in peace.

* * *

Angelite perched herself by the window and, peering out of the broken glass, focused on the blackened sky. Her thoughts wandered back to Meridia. The ever-menacing clouds continued to shower the broken city. A cold, light wind entered the room while the drizzle spattered on her tired face. Although she felt drained from her use of Resonance, she was unable to sleep. She found the rain refreshing on her skin.

On her lap, she held journals and other books she took from the ruined library. She opened one, trying to decipher the text, which appeared to be written by a poorly adept hand. Others were clearly printed by technology from a forgotten time. She spent a couple of hours restlessly reading the notes in the gloom. Occasionally, she glanced away from the books to see Maledream snoring away on the couch.

Letting out a powerful yawn, Angelite quietly stepped off the window's ledge, and closed the books with a subtle clap. With a stumble, she did her best to tiptoe across the dark room to reach the couch. Stopping, she thought she heard something. She tried adjusting her eyes to the darkness. Suddenly, shadows of people, once merged with the walls, dashed for her in silence.

Before she could scream in fright, someone grabbed her from behind and covered her mouth with a filthy hand. Panicking, she tried calling out, only to muffle a pathetic whelp as a foul-smelling rag was shoved in her mouth. Her eyes were quickly blindfolded, and her wrists and ankles also bound in rough, skin-cutting rope. Several assailants worked together. She felt their hands reaching in between her robes and garments to tightly squeeze and grope her.

'The more you struggle, the more pain you're gonna feel, Witch. Move, and we'll slice your throat,' said the croaky whisper.

'You're ours for the taking,' another gleefully whispered.

She struggled as much as she could, but it was no use. The priestess was quietly carried out of the room and into the hallway. Quickly, the assailants jogged a long distance down the pitch-black halls, and then entered another room.

Thrown to the floor, Angelite landed face first with a thud. She tried in vain to undo the rope that kept her hands and feet bound. A foot landed in her stomach, winding her easily with the blow.

'We think you weird types aren't good for business,' the voice muttered in her ear as she felt a long, wet tongue run down her exposed neck.

Another kick pounded her abdomen. She struggled to breathe through her nose.

'In fact, we think the world's a better place without Witch-whores,' spat another man.

The strangers kicked and beat her relentlessly. Her senses turned dizzying when a blunt object cracked against her skull.

'Your staff feel good, bitch? This Meridia doesn't exist, you filthy slut,' another spat.

Tears streamed through the blind covering her eyes.

'Your kind deserves to be sliced up, but not before we screw your warm body first,' the voice said, tongue licking away her tears.

'Could keep her alive for several rounds, all we have to do is keep that mouth of hers shut so she can't curse us,' another laughed.

Without warning, the priestess was picked up and thrown against a nearby wall. Muffling in pain, her legs were repeatedly struck by her own staff.

'They're going to kill me,' she cried in thought.

After twenty strikes, she was thrown back on the floor, only for the men to rip off her robes, leggings, and undergarments. They swarmed all over, groping her exposed flesh, and viciously tugging her waist-long hair as if she were a fine catch. She could barely struggle. Claustrophobia and terror gripped her tense nerves.

'Not like this.'

She felt their strong, iron-like grips desperately trying to prise her legs apart. She fought against them with all her remaining strength.

'Come on, asshole, stick it in already, we all want a turn,' one spoke in agitation.

'I'm trying, but the bitch keeps squirming. Hold her down, for fuck's sake.'

Suddenly, a voice echoed from outside the room.

'Out here, assholes.'

The would-be rapists halted in what they were doing.

'What? Who's that, who's there?' one of them uttered in panic, signalling for everyone to stay quiet as they didn't recognise the voice.

'You two check it out,' one ordered.

Angelite caught her breath. She continued tightening her legs, just in case they tried again. She couldn't help but focus on the cold draft entering the room. It was calming, something to keep her mind off the situation.

Kicking the priestess again, one of them applied pressure on her neck, uttering in her ear, 'stupid whore, you're going to die after we've all had our turn fucking you. You aren't casting any of your spells on us, Witch.'

Angelite violently coughed through the rag, trying desperately in vain to breathe through her bloodied nose as thick, cold fingers firmly wrapped themselves around her throat. Outside the gloomy room, struggling of some kind erupted from the black hallway.

'I'll stay with the whore. You two go and see what's going on,' a voice ordered.

'Save us some, we want our fair share of that beaten Witch.'

'Don't worry…' replied the man holding his hand over her throat, 'plenty of warm holes to fill.'

The cold, sharp sensation of a blade then pressed on her throat. So hard was the pressure, she could feel slithers of her warm blood trickle down her neck.

Once the other men had left the room, more struggling resounded outside. Metal against metal echoed with the cries of the two men, signalling their swift defeat in the dark hallway. Angelite prayed it was someone coming to help her.

'Maledream's asleep, who could it be?'

The stranger stayed motionless for a moment, trying to hear anything in the gloom.

'If you want a job done, do it yourself,' the voice bitterly rasped.

Thankfully, the man released his hand and knife. Angelite breathed the best she could through her bruised nose. Lying on her back, the tear-soaked blindfold was now loose, covering her nostrils, and allowing her eyes to adjust to the dark room. The sound of a weapon unlatching from a strap caught her attention. The rigid figure held a menacing pole-arm, sporting many sharp, serrated edges.

'No, it can't be Neveah,' she thought.

'Show yourself, assassin,' the man spat.

Maledream stepped around the corner, pulling back his hood, and brandishing his sword. The Tribal spotted the priestess on the floor in the darkness. It was difficult in the gloom, but, from what the Tribal saw, she was covered in bruises, blood and, assuming the worst had already happened, raped and murdered. He turned his head. He couldn't bring himself to stare.

'I'm too late.'

His hands squeezed the hilt, fury ignited in his eyes.

'Reckless, I'm going to fucking kill you,' Maledream roared.

His blade awoke to the anger. Illuminating the runes in a hue of crimson, it hissed at the air as if it was a roaring fire. The blood of its recent victims visibly coursed down its broad surface.

'We'll see, looks like you're no stranger to Witchcraft either,' Reckless bellowed.

Maledream charged into the fray, his sweeping blade clashed with the Packers pole-arm. The light given off by the sword bathed the room in red, and the two combatants silhouettes danced to the glow. Toying with him, the Packer used his lighter weapon and fast reflexes to hit Maledream in the head with the butt of the shaft. Staggering, the Tribal swung around, thrusting the blade towards the Packer's face.

Too slow. Reckless parried Maledream's blow aside, and threatened Maledream's head with a quick sweep that the Tribal narrowly ducked. Another clang echoed as the two squared off with their two-handed weapons. Anger grew and festered inside Maledream's spirit, thoughts raced through his mind of what they had done to her, and this fuelled him.

Reckless struck Maledream again in a quick swipe across the chest. The deadly pole-arm was narrowly deflected, absorbed by his leather armour and thick coat. Releasing a quick kick, he hit the Packer square in the crotch, following it swiftly with an elbow to his face.

'*No mistakes,*' Maledream thought, backing off to inhale some quick air.

He was tiring quickly. The scuffles in the hallway, where he had dispatched Reckless's accomplices, didn't help. He brought his sword to bear in an arc for another cleave, but he wasn't fast enough to plant a killing blow on the Packer, whom merely rolled and darted to the side, leaving the blade to ring against the brick walls.

Reckless swung his weapon around with ability, keeping the Tribal busy. Maledream parried one blow after another until he had the chance he was waiting for. He plunged his weapon towards Reckless's pole-arm, trying to disarm him after locking them.

Reckless saw what was coming and, with a snap-kick, caught the Tribal with a trip. Falling forward and losing the lock of weapons, Maledream's blade lodged itself in the wall of the room with a thwack. Concrete dust covered the pair.

'Shit.'

The pole-arm's blade narrowly wedged itself beside his right ear. Staring at the menacing edge for just a second, Maledream reached for the two rusty daggers concealed in his coat. Spinning on his feet, he lunged at the lanky man who, twirling his weapon, faintly deflected each of Maledream's quicker strikes.

Then, changing tactic, he thrust one rusty dagger towards Reckless's chest. Blocking it as expected, the Tribal suddenly jumped on the pole-arm's shaft, forcing the serrated blade into the flooring. Now off-guard, Maledream catapulted over and firmly stabbed one knife into Reckless's back. Landing on his feet, Maledream spun on his heels and sliced his remaining rusty blade across the exposed tendons behind the kneecaps.

Reckless roared in guttural agony, and clumsily, span with the intent to decapitate the Tribal. Grabbing the pole-arm by the shaft after dodging the sweeping blow, the Tribal used all his strength to twirl the flimsy maniac in a circle. He then released, but not before the Packer landed a solid fist in his face. Maledream stumbled to his two-handed sword.

Reckless couldn't keep his balance, fell backwards, and landed on his ass. The Tribal gripped his weapon once more, trying to free it. Reckless taunted him, blood filling his punctured lung.

'Not fast enough. To be honest, that bitch of yours was crap, I've had better…' he spluttered, coughing blood all over his chin.

Believing the lies, Maledream roared in anger and ripped the blade from the concrete with gritted teeth. He turned and charged towards the Packer, bringing his sword up and down with unbelievably fast, vicious blows. Sparks showered the two combatants each time the Tribal struck the pole-arm with resounding clangs. Then, spinning around on his feet, Maledream swung the massive sword as if it were a club.

Screaming his hatred, he ploughed the crimson-glowing blade into Reckless. Powerful energies leapt up from the sword in an instant. Blocking the blow, Reckless's pole-arm shattered under the intensity of the enchanted weapon.

With that, a huge force drove him from the floor, to the air and, with a burst of crimson light, hurled him through the wall of the apartment room. In a fantastic display of dust and mortar accompanying the deafening crack of power, Reckless twirled like a crippled sparrow to the world outside, where the force of gravity gripped him. He screamed his last defiance at losing the fight, before a finalising crunch echoed through the dark, stormy streets.

Silence fell as Maledream wandered up to the hole in the side of the building. He glared at the shattered cadaver splattered on the concrete, its blood mixing with the rain that fell from the abyssal sky. He watched as a few scavengers scurried out from the darkest shadows in the street, tearing off clothes, armour, and even fighting over the corpse for a source of food.

Falling on his knees and screaming at the sky, Maledream chucked his sword to the floor and clenched his hands. Gritting his teeth, he couldn't force himself to stare at Angelite's beaten body. His head span as the unwelcoming drizzle settled on his depressed form.

'Humph! Humph!'

Snap turning in disbelief, he stared into her living eyes.

'Angelite,' he shouted, dashing to her side and skidding on his kneecaps.

Unbinding the rag around her mouth, he took off his thick coat to cover and keep her warm.

'Thank you,' she whimpered in his ear.

Clutching and cuddling her hard, he sighed with relief, his anger quickly subsiding.

'I'm sorry I fell asleep...' he stammered.

'Silly man, it's okay, all I've suffered is a little bruising, I'll be... fine...' she muttered, falling unconscious and slumping in his caring arms.

Rubbing his cold, bloodshot eyes, he picked her up in both arms and rested her on a nearby couch. Taking a seat next to her, he used some clean cloth to wipe her blood off her face.

'What the hell was that noise? Why is some of my Pack dead, just what the hell's going on?' Neveah announced as he entered the room with a bright lamp.

Several more of his gang walked in to see what the fuss was. Getting off the couch and stepping forwards, Maledream gave him a cold, silent stare. Neveah only took a moment to assess the room and situation. He noticed Angelite's robes and undergarments, torn and bloodied, resting on the floor. Like Maledream before him, he assumed the worst.

'Take a wild guess,' Maledream growled.

Stunned for words, Neveah stared at him blankly.

'She needs dry clothing. I'm sure you have more than looted weapons in this place. Hurry!' the Tribal ordered.

Neveah nodded and, with a raise of his hand and click of his fingers, the loyal Pack left the room to get some dry, clean clothing.

'I'm sorry, mate,' Neveah said depressingly, glancing at Angelite's unconscious form.

He rested a reassuring hand on Maledream's shoulder. It was the only compensation he could grant.

'It was Reckless. He's on the pavement outside.'

'Aye, then we'll let the bastard rot, he was a piece of shit anyway,' Neveah nodded, wandering to the hole in the wall.

Peering down, he saw a river of blood leading away into the shadows of an adjacent apartment building. It was obvious the beggars had dragged away their spoils.

'What the hell did this?' Neveah thought, brow creasing, his hand briefly feeling the rough circumference of the gaping hole.

Chapter Six

Ancient Battlefield

In her dream, Angelite strode through a dark, foreboding forest. Upon walking to the edge of the lush woodland, she saw Larkham standing before her.

'Do not succumb to the temptation that doesn't belong in your heart, for it'll threaten this young woman and everything you would strive for with your choice of freewill,' he said, before evaporating in a thick cloud of noxious darkness that slithered its way into her lungs.

***

Startled, she awoke to the smell of burning fossil fumes assaulting her nose, and heard the dull, loud drone of an engine. She felt incredibly fatigued, and she found herself lying down on a lengthy seat, and covered with a thick, fur blanket.

Angelite saw Maledream and Neveah were also there, sat on some seats in the mid-section of the mechanical transport in which they rode. The priestess closed her eyes, but listened to the men's conversation as she continued resting.

'Many Packs hate and fear such people, such as the Tribals or Witches. Many Packers are superstitious. I try to find members who aren't rapists and killers, but unfortunately, I can't see what their hearts are truly like until something like last night happens,' said Neveah.

'Why are there so many assholes around? If I had my way, I would wipe the lot of them off the face of the planet,' Maledream cursed.

'Mate, I know where you're coming from, but people can't help where they're born and raised, even us. You're starting to sound like someone who'd believe those stupid myths about the planet turning on us,' Neveah chuckled.

'Perhaps the planet was right, if the legends are true. It's people who turned our world into a shithole. And now look at it, nothing but ruins and death wherever you go,' Maledream rasped, glancing at Neveah before looking back at the desolate landscape through the window shutters.

The sprawling cityscape appeared smaller the further they travelled. It was odd seeing the city this way. They always lived in it or just on the outskirts. The group traversed in a large vehicle capable of carrying around fifty passengers, which sported two decks in total. The upper deck was exposed to the harsh elements, whilst the lower deck served as a lukewarm cabin.

Occasionally, strong diesel fumes from the rickety engine would waft through the passenger's lower deck. It was enough to bring on a queasy headache. Adding to their discomfort was the state of the seating, which was torn and buckled throughout the transport. It resulted in the most uncomfortable, bumpiest journey on one's ass. However, the Tribal was thankful. They could have travelled on foot in the vicious downpour that pelted their ride.

'What did you call this thing again? What are we riding in?' asked Maledream.

'We call this beauty the Battle Hammer!' Neveah proudly boasted.

'Battle Hammer? What kind of name is that?' Maledream laughed.

'Trust me, when you see this beauty fire up to full power, you'll understand why. Even the upper-deck is sported with weapons, so there's no problem when it comes to firepower,' Neveah grinned.

'I'll have a look later. I'm quite content with sitting here for the time being. I'm not in the mood to get damp,' Maledream sighed.

'Aye,' Neveah nodded.

* * *

Several hours passed as they snaked up old, broken roads. Angelite awoke once more after drifting off. Maledream and Neveah remained seated, staring out of the half-drawn shutter windows in silence as the rain continued. The priestess moved in great pain, her stomach made it hard work. She was still in rough shape.

'I hurt,' she moaned.

The two men turned to greet her with smiles.

'Up at last, I'm glad to see,' Neveah uttered as Maledream picked up her robes that lay beside him.

'Had them cleaned and stitched to the best of our ability,' said the Tribal.

Angelite drearily looked beneath the blankets at what she was wearing. Nothing. Blushing, she was struck for words.

'No need to worry,' spoke the two at once.

'We didn't look. Boris changed you!' they chuckled, both trying to be comical to lift her spirits.

'You could've fooled me,' she smirked, realising their intention.

The sweet blush quickly vanished, however, as she returned, 'anyway, how far away are we from the battlefield?'

'Well, it shouldn't be too long now. We've been on the road for a while, so we've got to be close,' said Maledream.

'That's when we're going full throttle through that place,' Neveah added.

'Why? It's not dangerous, I went there when the weather was fine a while ago,' said Maledream.

'Not when the sun isn't shining, mate. Around there, they say the shadows themselves rise up and take the unwary. They don't like the light, that's the rumour in the city, at least.'

'What shadows? You sound like my daft old man with his warnings about the place,' the Tribal jested.

'They come from a place that the ancients used to call the *Heaven between Heavens*,' Angelite interrupted.

'Aye, well, whatever you call them, or wherever they're from, I couldn't care less, just as long as we make it through in one piece. The common theme going around, back in the city, is, that these shadows are fallen soldiers, or some such shit. Far worse rumours have sprung up from the Packs who've ventured there to salvage weaponry, and then again, most are too afraid, and most don't return,' Neveah muttered in monotone.

He looked grim as his one good eye peered out through the window towards the horizon. Struggling over the pain and holding her stomach, Angelite drew a breath and coughed from the wafting diesel fumes. Maledream was fixated on her, waiting to hear of any knowledge that she had on such things.

'These beings aren't entirely made of shadow. They are just solid enough to appear to be. They hail from a zone that nestles in-between the dimensions on many planes, as far as what I have learned back home. They apparently feed on our deepest fears, and live on such emotions to sustain themselves in our physical world. It's a sort of synthesis,' she said.

'So, Angelite, did the ancients call the shadow creatures home the *"Heaven between Heavens"*?' Neveah probed.

'Yes, from what we've learned of them. Written records contain accounts of these shadowy entities when the world was different, back in older days. They seem more solid now compared to today's sightings and old witness statements, and can now show themselves to possess or kill. Since the arrival of the Dark Age, the world's Ley lines have opened and spilled all over the planet, meaning nature took its course.'

A dark mood fell on Neveah. He struggled to comprehend Angelite's wisdom. To him, most of it was superstition, myth, tales from a fearful city.

'Larkham once mentioned a story about the earth's energy. Something about an axis change at the poles, or some crap like that. Is that what you mean?' Maledream quizzed.

'Yes, well, we suspect something like that could have happened to trigger the power of Resonance, but we're not certain. Do you remember what I taught you yesterday? Anyway, these beings can take on many forms, and are often beings that have never lived a life, so they seek to devour souls to sustain themselves in our world. They have an insatiable hunger for emotional energy, too, such as fear. They can even attack you in your dreams,' she replied.

'Sounds like a nasty bunch to me. One good thing going for us, at least, is that they hate any sort of light. Well, that's the rumour at least, and I hope, for our sakes, that it's bloody true,' Neveah frowned.

'Not if this weather persists,' Maledream sighed, watching the rain fall so heavily that it drowned out the noise of the engine.

It was getting chillier in the Battle Hammer's passenger cabin as an icy wind set in and stole the warmth.

'Not to worry, I've got ways to expel them if we encounter any. That is, if I can pull off the Resonance. I've not actually had an opportunity, let's say,' said the priestess, her words far from reassuring to the men.

'We'll worry about them if the time comes. Anyway, how are you feeling?' asked the Tribal.

'I'm getting there, I've been using my healing techniques to ease the pain, it's working, but it takes a little time to heal. A drink of water might help, if you have any?' she returned.

'Sure thing,' Neveah replied, chucking her a flask.

Catching and glugging its contents, the priestess proceeded to get up slowly, whilst clutching the blanket around her. She shuffled her way to the Tribal's seat, sat next to him, and then hugged him tightly.

'Thank you for last night, Maledream,' she said, kissing him on the cheek.

The gesture made him grin. He couldn't help but to turn his head away in embarrassment.

'Uh, no problem,' he stuttered.

Rising from his seat, Neveah laughed heartily at the sight with his bulging arms crossed.

'Let's go up deck and let her change. Besides, a little wind and rain will cool you down,' Neveah bellowed, patting his hand on Maledream's shoulder.

Springing off his seat, the Tribal smiled and nodded at her, before making his way up the iron staircase with Neveah in tow.

'Oh, by the way, Sweet...' Neveah uttered as he put his foot on the first step, 'sorry about last night. I'm truly and deeply sorry for what happened.'

'Yeah, uh, thank you. It's not your fault, so don't worry, I'm okay,' she replied, raising her palms up and waving them with a weak smile.

Nodding with a warm grin, he gave her the thumbs-up and left her to it.

***

Sporting many ranged weapons, the Battle Hammer was certainly crafted from many hours of hard labour. Inches of iron and steel plating from various other vehicles were wielded onto the large chassis, turning the ride into a mechanical beast. However, some parts rattled as if they were about to fall off. Overall, Maledream felt it was a comical vehicle. He just hoped it could protect them if they hit any trouble.

The Pack sat about on stools with sheets covering them from the rain, smoking pipes, and swapping general rude banter to pass the time. The Tribal was surprised that Neveah commanded so many people, his Pack numbered at around fifty from the rough head count. Among the Pack, he saw Crazy John, Pixie, and Boris huddled around each other, discussing the situation and taking shelter under one such sheet the best they could.

'Certainly a beast isn't she!' Neveah announced above the wind, rain, and the sound of the engine as he leaned on the thick, metal railings at the forefront of the vehicle next to Maledream.

'Yeah, not bad at all, quite a daemon,' the Tribal jested.

'Aye, this baby can take anything on, although, some of the Packs we left behind in the city have mechanical beasts twice the size of this one. I'm pleased you look impressed.'

Falling silent for a moment, the two stared at the gloomy horizon. The battlefield was almost in reach.

'You ever get that feeling, Maledream, where it feels like, where you are at the time, is meant to happen? Seeing you and Angelite should have shocked me, but somehow, it didn't. You ever get that, or know what I'm talking about?'

'Sort of. I just go with the flow because it's easier. Man, I'm starving...' Maledream groaned, his hand briefly gracing his stomach.

'We've got fresh fish stocked up in the deck below if you fancy a snack. Well, not entirely fresh, a lot of it smells like shit, but the offer's there if you're desperate,' Neveah laughed, slapping Maledream hard on the back.

The force almost sent him flying over the slippery railings.

'Thanks, but I think I'll pass. I don't want the shits,' Maledream smirked.

* * *

Lightning flashed and thunder boomed in the tearful clouds. Angelite donned her clean robes, taking note of the careful stitching at the seams where they were torn. With a sinking feeling, she looked out of the shutter window at the dark, looming sky that spat ions across the heavens. Putting any dark thoughts to the back of her mind, she gripped her staff, and then steadily made her way up the metal staircase, covering her head with her hood as the rain fell like an angry omen.

'What's going on?' she asked the two men.

'Glad you could join us, we're just admiring the view,' answered Maledream.

'Not far until we're at the battlefield. Once we've passed through it, Angelite, which course should we take next?' Neveah probed.

'Uh-huh, keep heading this way, don't change direction,' Angelite nodded, pointing northwards.

'Aye, no problem, I've heard some hills lie that way somewhere,' said Neveah.

Another crack of lightning and thunder illuminated the foreboding clouds. The storm was gathering strength, and the wind viciously whipped the Pack's rain sheets. Maledream saw the battlefield ahead. For a moment, when the lightning flashed before his eyes, he thought he saw something odd in the distance.

'Something's coming,' Angelite said, eyes widening.

Neveah joined Maledream in trying to see what lay ahead. Their frowns turned pale.

'Battle stations, Pack, fire up all the lights,' Neveah roared, raising a clenched fist to the air, signalling them all to take up arms.

All at once, the loyal Pack got up and armed their archaic rifles and pistols amidst their bellowing war cries.

'Neveah, the torches are damp, they won't light,' Pixie panicked.

'These things are hopeless, you can't even burn skin with them,' Crazy John added, trying in vain to keep his torch alive by keeping his palm millimetres above the tiny flame.

All fell silent, save for the wind, rain, and engine of the Battle Hammer. Their eyes focused at what was coming from the darkest recesses ahead. Shadowy forms unnaturally sprang and surged across the ground, approaching them from all angles once the vehicle ploughed through the edge of the battlefield, crushing bones, rusted metal, and stone on its monstrous tires and tracks.

Evidence of many failed expeditions lie scattered for all to see. They sped past many vehicles, similar to Neveah's own Battle Hammer, rusting away on the battlefield, alongside other countless war machines from an era long forgotten.

'It's the shadows. There isn't enough light to keep them away,' Maledream said, a tremor present in his voice.

'Aye, can our weapons kill these things, Angelite?' Neveah seethed.

'If they're solid enough, then probably, I'm not too sure. They'll have to be physical enough to get to us, just be on your guard,' she cautioned.

The shadows flickered in reality between the flashes of lightning, yet somehow, they kept up with the momentum of the Battle Hammer. Many shadows shot out of the ground, forming various shapes and sizes. Some were humanoid in appearance, whereas most formed snouts and sported four, six, or even eight legs.

Galloping with daemonic speed, the hellhound apparitions raced faster than the Battle Hammer, telepathically barking inside the minds of the living occupants like ravenous canines. Everyone glared at them in horror, staring into the dark creatures abyssal eyes.

'Don't fear them, they only grow stronger if they can feed off your dark feelings,' Angelite shrieked.

Gunfire erupted as the Pack finally lost their nerve. Hot lead pelted the oncoming phantoms. Closing in from all directions, the beasts easily fed on the humans' fear, causing their shadowy retinas to burst into misty balls of red-neon flames.

Clenching his weapon, Maledream got ready for any other surprises that might creep up, whilst Neveah drew out his pole-arm and roared at the mass approaching them.

Angelite gripped her staff, trying to quell the festering horror growing within.

As she began chanting her words of Resonance, Pixie fired blindly at the oncoming horde with his assault rifle. The powerful rounds tore into the daemonic ranks, easily passing through the shadows with no hindrance. They merely quickened in speed. Crazy John and Boris delved into their leather armours and whipped out many concealed knives, and prepared themselves for the inevitable like the others.

Lightning flashed once more in the harsh, beating rain and, for a split second, the shadows disappeared in the light, yet were even closer when the gloom returned.

Maledream could feel something was wrong. His body shivered with a sudden sensation of pins and needles. Spinning around, he saw a shadow leap high in the air, with all four paw-like appendages ready to strike Angelite down. With only seconds to react, he raised his blade in one hand and, pushing Angelite down with the other, struck the hellhound in-between its fiery eyes with a wide swing.

Cutting the beast in two, it disintegrated to the rushing air in a plume of silvery ash. Passing through it as if it were nothing, Maledream buried his sword in the iron railing, sending sparks flying.

'Oi! Watch what you fucking hit, mate,' Neveah cussed.

Many other beasts had the same idea, having already latched on to the flanks of the large transport. Clambering up the metallic monster with click-clacking scrabbles, screeching their horror, they sought to sustain their existence with emotional fuel. The Pack gave up shooting them, and instead withdrew their trademark pole-arms to slice at the creatures with length of limb.

'Do something, Angelite, quickly,' Maledream said, helping her back on her feet.

'If you can stop them getting to me, then I might have time to think,' she muttered.

Many of the phantoms suddenly leapt over the decking from both flanks, trying to lop off heads as they did so. Some succeeded knocking the unwary Packer off their beloved ride. The abyssal hounds devoured the men as they fell. Their rich source of spirit and flesh, it seemed, was readily absorbed. The beasts barked with ecstasy. Terror filled the Pack, they screamed for their lives as they battled fruitlessly with their weapons.

However, the battle took an unexpected, horrifying twist when the hellhounds pounced many to the decking. Consuming their spirits in an instant, the living shells of the humans turned possessed. The whites of their eyes turned dark, and the hounds' vision glimmered through their retinas like a red fire seeping to the wind. Bringing their weapons to bear, their old comrades sowed havoc among the living.

These were easy targets for Pixie. He had no reservations for the frothing maniacs who were once his friends. He could do nothing but cross his heart with one hand, before blowing away their chattering skulls with his assault rifle.

Crazy John and Boris cut through their former comrades them with ease, without fear or consequence. Once their vessel was broken, the shadowy entities spilled from every orifice with the intent to possess once more.

Neveah's Pack slowly dwindled. If he didn't quell their fear, they were doomed. Neveah spun round, cutting through four of the beasts that tried toppling him all at once with great cleaves. Graceful blows and solid arms insured that he could defend and counter-attack with quick reflexes, lopping them in halves in a whirlwind of hits. His one eye glimmered with an iron will.

'Don't fear these beasts, they're nothing, fight you mongrels!' he roared at the top of his lungs, his words and actions inspiring his Pack.

'Fight, Fight, Fight,' he bellowed and, swinging his weapon again with greater strength, buried another shadow into the metal grating with a fierce clang.

Gradually overcoming their fear of the red-eyed beasts, the Pack were now standing more of a chance as their fearless leader showed even greater feats. Roaring with vengeance for the dead, they fought with a renewed vigour and boosted morale. Crazy John and Boris sliced at the shadows that threatened their unity. Almost like a dance of death with blades, they performed a great deal of agile attacks with quick accuracy.

As the battle raged, Maledream rolled his vision to the priestess.

'Something big is coming,' she uttered, turning to face him.

Out in the distance, he saw a large mass of shadows gathering, before emerging from the earth, snaking to the air like vines. They reached the storm clouds, before spreading underneath them like sickly veins. Watching with widened eyes, the shadowy tendrils spiralled towards the earth, circulating like tornadoes, and growing larger with every second.

Maledream's vision turned dizzying. Suddenly struck off his feet, his blade was thrown from his hands and into the grating with a clang. Flying over the side, his foot was caught by the iron railings of the Battle Hammer. Banging his head on the open shutter on the driver's side window, he peered in. The driver was now nothing more but a cadaver, the accelerator trapped by its bony foot. A nearby shriek twitched his ears. Twisting his head, he saw a hellhound leap for him.

*　*　*

Angelite focused her energy. Her eyes beamed a violet glow as three hellhounds jumped for her. Raising her staff and stepping one foot forward, she raised her hand towards the creatures. With eyelids tightly shut, she called forth her inner-flame.

'*Illumani' Penetrana Sheol Dagadan.*'

Shrieking for the kill, the hounds were almost upon her, their forms distorting from the energy flux. Resonance snaked its way up Angelite's arm and into her palm, illuminating her fate-lines as she released her spell. It took the form of a golden, resonating barrier, rippling like a puddle as her magic bore life. The beasts made contact against the high-pitched, rippling shield with booming thuds, serving to shackle their writhing, twisted forms.

Their crimson eyes blazed in terror, they screeched in pain against the golden light that held them suspended. Spinning with her robes and cloak in full flow, her staff gripped, the priestess swung the crystal tip in the centre of the rippling light.

'Be gone from this plane.'

Hissing defiantly, one beast exploded in a rushing cloud of silvery dust, its embers racing through the decking. Spinning on her feet again, she swung the staff at the second entity, roaring her defiant attack once more. Vast energies from the crystal exploded into life, shattering the hellhound with the same result. Then, twirling her staff, Angelite finished and swung the rod of power against the last creature's abdomen.

The crystal tip burst into a plethora of multicoloured light, fully releasing the swelled power. No longer binding the creatures, the rippling, golden light dissipated to the strong, whistling winds. With a violet glare, Angelite paid close attention to the huge shadow storm ahead. She took a forward stance, holding her staff skyward.

* * *

Maledream stared into the beast's eyes. It closed in for him as he struggled to loosen his trapped foot. A roar boomed from above, signalling Neveah's entrance as he swung his long weapon into the shadow below with precision, severing the creature in two, and narrowly missing Maledream's head. He broke into a cold sweat, and his heart raced.

'Grab hold,' Neveah yelled, Maledream doing as ordered with a solid grip.

The Pack leader's powerful, bulging arms swung him up in the air, allowing Maledream's foot to loosen as he did so.

'Be more careful next time, will you?' Neveah smirked.

Landing on the deck with a clang, and gripping his large blade, the two nodded, before turning to see Angelite take on three of the shadow beasts. Gawking, the two watched the clouds of silvery ether rush through the gangway as she completed her combo.

'Everyone, protect Angelite,' Maledream yelled.

'You heard the man,' Neveah bellowed.

What was left of the dwindling Pack gathered round the priestess the best they could, fighting back-to-back against the seemingly infinite horde. Onwards the Battle Hammer charged, gaining speed from the stuck accelerator in the cockpit. Maledream stood side-by-side with Neveah at the front, cutting down any shadow that dared interrupt Angelite's concentration, and then...

* * *

As the Tribal drew his sword up above his head to drive another shadow hound away with a swipe, a flash of light took his visions, and he found himself somewhere else within his mind again. Surrounded by nothing but green grass and a bright blue sky, he heard Larkham's voice echo words of wisdom.

'Use the power of the elements. Use the energy of the sky. Use the energy of the beating drums.'

On hearing these words, Maledream watched a dark cloud unnaturally form above, booming with thunder that shook the earth beneath his feet. Lightning spat from the heavens, striking his sword with a frightening clang. Humming in his fists, the sword spoke as if it had a voice of its own, its glow softly pulsating to one word.

'Retrinumun.'

A chill ran its course down his spine. He heard this word before. Glowing, the sword hummed.

'Retribution, dispense it well.'

* * *

Cutting through the air with a descending stroke, he awoke from his vision. The sword crackled. Energetic Resonance danced down its surface, and, as he glared into the shadowy hound's hellish eyes, roared intuitively.

'Retrinumun.'

A resonating, booming power burst from the sword as it awoke. A beam of arcing, golden Resonance swept forth the battlefield, easily dissolving the beast in an instant, and tearing up the land in its wake. The blow was overkill. Rain evaporated in the near vicinity of the old, sizzling weapon.

'What the... what the fuck was that, mate?' Neveah stammered, unable to help but gawk in shock and awe at both Maledream and his blade.

'I don't know,' Maledream responded in similar shock.

'What the fuck? What the hell do you mean, you don't know?' Neveah said, returning his glare to the distance.

The Tribal joined him in silence amidst the continuing rainstorm.

'Bloody vultures,' Neveah muttered, seeing hundreds more of the shadows galloping towards them.

Guided by intuition, Maledream moved to the forefront of the deck and placed his right foot on the railing, the wind threatening his balance. Lifting the two-handed blade above his head and, not knowing what to expect, lowered it once again.

'Retrinumun.'

In mid-swing, the runic weapon channelled its Resonance in a sweeping arc at the amassing creatures. Striking one, then three, then thirty, it split in the gathering mass like a chain reaction. The battlefield glowed instantaneously for miles around in a flash of light.

'That's sorted them...' Neveah muttered in a daze, still amazed at what his old friend possessed in his tight fists.

However, he spoke too soon. The large, tendril-like shadow storm was almost upon them as they continued speeding towards it. Maledream repeated the steps he had just performed, but the blade grew dull.

'Why isn't it working again?'

'Come on, mate, pull off that trick again, that piece of shit stands no chance,' Neveah jested.

'I don't know, I've tried, but it's not working now,' Maledream cussed.

A deafening roar echoed from the titanic, swirling pillar of darkness. The remaining shady entities suddenly disappeared, phasing out as fast as they had originally faded in. Looking down at the rushing earth over the railings, they saw them all converging towards the storm to join it.

'This will be difficult,' Angelite muttered.

Ideas coursed through her mind. She needed a way to overcome the abyssal storm. She knew their only hope was a very strong source of light. While the priestess was busy thinking, Maledream kneeled on one knee from exhaustion. Glancing at Neveah, he muttered.

'Is this it?'

'Looks that way,' he groaned, giving his eye patch a scratch.

Breaking the silence, Angelite stepped forward. 'Get back, what I'm about to do is dangerous. So give me some room, please.'

Doing as ordered, the pair stepped away from the front of the pointed deck and let her take the lead. The very ether around Angelite began to shift and distort once her energy flowed. Orbs of white light appeared and began frantically encircling her. She chanted, channelling the energies within.

'Illumani' Penetrana Sheol dagadan, Illumani' Penetrana Sheol dagadan. Elin'shana dookilla shuen Allina Canshanna Doon Mitsubargui shui.'

Raising her rod of power towards the cloud-ridden sky, the runes on the shaft spat excessive energy. The force of the Resonance was more than they could handle. Still, she carried on.

'Bring me sun, bring me light, bring me fire to burn this plight. Illumani' Penetrana Sheol dagadan, Illumani' Penetrana Sheol dagadan. Elin'shana dookilla shuen Allina Canshanna Doon Mitsubargui shui.'

Her eyes glowed with an unearthly violet. Using herself as another spell-focus, she forced more Resonance into the crystals and overloaded them. The runes spat raw, unstable energies to the icy wind. Cracks appeared on the large, crystalline tip that shined with a strong, orange light, growing in intensity, until it could no longer contain the power.

Exploding with a shattering crunch, the crystal fragmented into hundreds of shards, yet they did not fall to the force of gravity. Instead, the pieces flew around of what was left of the core of the large crystal. Surrounded by multicoloured energies inherent in each remnant, they dashed in clockwise and anti-clockwise motions. Appearing in existence were darting, silvery lights that surrounded the priestess with similar motions to the fragments.

'She's going to kill herself if she keeps this up, she can't control it,' Maledream yelled and, before he could stop her, Neveah held him back with an iron grip.

'Just stay back, mate, she said it was dangerous.'

'No, let go,' Maledream roared.

Wriggling free with adrenal strength, the Tribal pushed past his old friend. Then, the sound was, for a moment, drowned out as Angelite completed her final incantation. All of the glowing energies fluxed and flashed with white noise, whilst the silvery particles culminated at the fragmented core.

Wind flowing through her hair, rain pelting her face, Angelite twirled then swung the staff with iron-gripped hands towards the sky. The energies coursed through her being as she overloaded the runes, each bursting to flame in synchronised fashion as they travelled up the shaft until they reached the top. A cacophonous explosion resounded from the shards and core, the force easily throwing Maledream, Neveah, and the Pack bouncing down the gangway decking with resounding clunks and clangs.

The force of the release almost crushed the priestess's body. Groaning, the metal decking visibly warped and dented beneath her as if stomped by an invisible force. All eyes keened on a ball of silvery, golden Resonance that shot from the fractured, crystalline tip, roaring skywards like a fiery meteor and faster than the speed of sound. A familiar crack of a sonic boom echoed across the landscape and, at the same time, the floating crystalline shards shattered into grains finer than sand.

Hurtling into the clouds, the ethereal comet disappeared and, in their last fleeting seconds, the group feared for the worst. Still racing towards them were the menacing tendrils of shadow, seeking to snuff the life of the last living members on the mechanical beast.

'Look up,' shouted Neveah.

The clouds began to twist and swirl, opening a gap in the sky rapidly, and unnaturally, growing wider against the wind's direction. Then, as the heavens opened a little more, the group saw what looked like a bright star floating at its centre in complete silence.

Deafening screams then erupted from the swirling, abyssal column, forcing most of the group to cover their ears. But not Maledream. He ran towards the priestess. Blood dripped from his ears and nose as the screeching became unbearable, drowning out any of his thoughts.

Suddenly, the glimmering star of Resonance exploded like a supernova. Rippling against the atmosphere like a pebble to water, the shockwave cleared the sky for several miles with an instantaneous boom. The clouds dispersed, leaving a ring of blue in the heavens.

Rays of the sun raced across the ground, overtaking the group with speed. Any individual shadows that had not merged with the large column burst into clouds of silvery ash. Ending its screech, the shadow storm retreated from the sky and into the ground, leaving behind a violent, false wind that buffeted and dragged the mechanical ride.

Burning their skin was the welcome warmth of the sun. Sprinting down into the lower deck, Neveah shoved the ragged corpse of the driver to one side to slow down the transport. Maledream finally reached Angelite and shook her gently.

'Come on, wake up,' he said, eyes wide with worry.

Coming to a halt, Neveah ran back up the metallic steps and barged through the Pack. Putting his ear to her mouth and his hand on her chest, Maledream listened as all fell silent. A faint breath graced his ear.

'She's alive,' he sighed in relief.

Roaring in victory, the Pack celebrated their win over the hellish daemons.

Neveah laid his hand on the Tribal's shoulder. 'She'll be all right, mate, take her down to the lower deck for now.'

Maledream agreed, leaving the Pack above deck to count the remaining survivors and check the total damage.

Chapter Seven

Forsaken Wilderness

The Battle Hammer coughed and spluttered. Crazy John inspected and tended to the engine the best he could with the survivors. Black fumes plumed from the hot cracks littering the engine's surface, and the smell of oil lubricant assaulted their nostrils. Neveah watched, hoping that they could somehow repair his beloved beast.

It was bad news. The cam belt had snapped during the inspection, the radiator coolant was wasted, and the pistons were bent or cracked. The armour plating of the vehicle, as thick as it was, needed a lot of work. Many of the front tires were also punctured during the harsh ride, and were now nothing more than grounded-down discs.

Even if they had the materials needed to make the repairs, it would take several days of consistent hard labour to get the engine working again. A bigger problem presented itself when the Pack found that even the fuel tank caught a leak, putting an end to any idea of ever driving it again. The Pack was disheartened at the sight. They didn't look forward to travelling on foot into dangerous lands that lay undiscovered. Their only knowledge came from rumours.

'This isn't good, boss,' Boris said, throwing the last of the supplies from the upper deck to the ground below.

'Aye, our baby's shafted,' Neveah groaned, sighing with depression and shaking his head.

'Think I can safely say we aren't getting her going again,' Crazy John added, wiping his oily hands on a thick, putrid rag.

'On the bright side, we did get through in one piece,' Pixie replied as he polished his archaic rifle.

Neveah stared into the lush wilderness before them, trying to put any conceivable dangers to rest in the back of his mind for now. He could not show weakness or despair at losing their only ride on this long trip. His one good eye followed the plume of black smoke rising high into the sky. The surviving Pack took all the supplies they could carry with them as they prepared to head into the depths of the forest. Neveah could only give the order of pressing on regardless, hoping that his Pack wouldn't be deterred by stories of Witches haunting the green wilderness.

'Can't believe we made it with all those bloody shadows catching us off-guard out there,' said Crazy John.

'If it wasn't for Angelite, I don't think we could've made it at all,' added Boris's feminine voice.

'Our pack has dwindled severely, only thirteen of us left after the count,' said Pixie.

They glanced back at the battlefield. It was hard to believe they made it through at all from the amount of men who lost their lives. The thought of it twisted Neveah's stomach, only further adding to his growing concerns. He turned around to see Maledream staring at Angelite's unconscious form.

'She'll be alright, mate, don't let it get you down,' he said.

The Tribal looked on in silence with the rest of the group, gazing at the tranquil land before them.

'What do you think is in there?' Maledream muttered, nodding in the direction of forest.

'From what I've heard, I can't say, because I don't know for sure...' Neveah replied, his voice ushering concern.

'Maybe we'll find out? It'll most likely be nothing to worry about,' said Pixie.

'Aye, maybe, but I think its best we try to find another way,' said Neveah.

'It could add more days to the journey if we do, and Angelite said to keep heading this way. If we change direction, we could end up getting lost,' said Maledream.

'Damn... I wish she would wake up,' Neveah groaned, staring at her.

'She looks very weak, and her staff's in pieces. It's something we definitely can't fix on our own. I've never seen anything like it in the city,' replied Boris.

'Well, don't worry about it for now. Let's just carry on,' said Maledream.

Nodding, Neveah bellowed his order, 'pick up your shit, we're heading in.'

With no other choice, they advanced further into the strange woodland wilderness with quiet reservations. The Tribal strode behind the Pack with Angelite slung over his shoulder. The sun beamed through the green canopy of the autumn forest, all thanks to the priestess.

Casual banter took the Pack, they seemed happy to have swapped the grey walls of suburbia for this green expanse, despite the rumours. It seemed the Packs' superstitions were gradually easing the further they ventured in.

'So, Maledream, we going to talk about what happened to you and your disappearance all those years ago?' Neveah asked.

'Not really in the mood. Can't you leave it for some other time?' the Tribal moaned.

'I know you might not want to talk, mate, but you ain't helping yourself.'

'I don't really know. All I can remember is some stuff about our childhood, but I can only remember you, barely one else. I remember something like a very long journey. I remember shouting, screaming, and blood, then, after that, I was saved by Larkham,' Maledream sighed.

'Aye, but I can help you remember who you are. I may look like an ugly ogre, but I ain't all that bad,' he said, chuckling to lighten the mood whilst wiping the sweat from his brow.

'Pity there ain't a breeze, the trees soak it all up it seems,' Neveah huffed.

'Doesn't look like the rain has reached the ground in these parts either,' replied the Tribal, staring at the dry twigs, leaves, and earth beneath his stride.

'It's unnatural, but then again, nothing seems natural lately.'

'Right, well, get on with what you have to say then, Neveah, otherwise you'll just keep bugging me until we get back on the topic,' Maledream smirked.

'Aye, so be it. Right then, well, all those years ago, we came from the far south, and believe it or not, a place much worse than the city. The bastard-lizards overran our old home. We got away and travelled far from any water with our families and friends. We journeyed on foot for months, then years, avoiding danger at most turns until...' Neveah paused, 'I know what could jog your memory, mate. Eventually, we came across four robed travellers. They owned weapons that looked similar to the one you carry. I don't know if their swords could do what yours can, but the resemblance is uncanny.'

'What? Who were they? They had blades much like mine?' Maledream pursued, his brow raised at a harsh angle.

'Aye, as I said, similar to your own. They told us of this safe haven, and to reach it, we had to travel north, but they didn't agree to come with us. They talked a little to the Elders in the group and pointed us, in what we thought, was the right direction. They had some sort of weird symbols on the backs' of their hoods, too. What was also stranger was that you couldn't see their faces, it was like they were covered by the shadow of the hoods they wore. You remember anything?' Neveah finished, turning to eye the Tribal with a raised grin.

A cold sensation ran its course up his spine as Maledream thought about his vision.

'No,' he lied, secretly wondering if the hooded figure was perhaps linked to Neveah's memories.

'Maybe it'll come back to you, but, as I was saying, we set off on a difficult trek through dead grasslands, forests, and mountainous terrain. I'm surprised you can't remember anything, mate, it was quite a journey. Built up our legs like they were nothing but muscle. Seeing this forest reminds me of all that travelling, it's a welcoming site compared with everything else, since we ended up in the city, that is.'

Maledream wiped the sweat from his forehead and heaved the priestess on his other shoulder. His mind fruitlessly tried to recall these apparent memories. A subtle breeze greeted the group as they pushed deeper into the forest.

Neveah reminisced, 'those blades they had, though, were something else. You seemed quite drawn to them. You went on, and on about them until you drove us mad. It was something to talk about and we were all a little curious ourselves. These strangers even had trophy teeth and other mementoes hanging from chains on their necks from the beasts they slaughtered. Some of these chains were finely crafted, some of the finest metals you ever saw. Quite dark characters, but it was a misconception of who they were, if you get my meaning?'

Pausing shortly for breath, Neveah glanced at Maledream, 'got off the point slightly, but I was hoping you might have remembered something. You were obsessed about them.'

'I'm sure it'll all come back to me, eventually,' Maledream breathed heavily.

'So, what about this sword of yours, how the hell did you come across something just as weird as Angelite's Witchcraft? It's had some of the Pack asking some understandable questions, and I don't know what to tell them,' said Neveah.

'I have no idea what it is. I found it a while ago on the battlefield, except a bit closer to the coast, and during daylight,' muttered the Tribal.

'Shit, makes me want to go back and find something like that for myself!' Neveah jested.

'Yeah, it scares the crap out of me, but it's saved me a few times now. The first time I saw its power was when I first met Angelite the other day. Saved her from something called an Anunaki,' Maledream panted.

'Anunaki?' Neveah asked, his brow stooping curiously.

'Remember the bastard-lizards you mentioned? It was one of those things. It almost killed me. If it wasn't for Angelite saving my ass with her Resonance, I wouldn't be here now,' he recounted.

'Ah, so she saved you then, damn-well figures!' Neveah laughed.

'I prefer to call it team work...' Maledream smiled. 'Back to my original point, though. When she healed me, it seemed to awaken the blade and, well, most of it was a blur, but in a mere second I managed to cut the bastard in half.'

'Aye, quite a tale, mate. After all I've seen, I can believe you easily. To hear you speak of defeating one with that sword is hard to imagine, yet also believable. If I didn't see the power of it myself, I would've told you to fuck off,' Neveah mocked and grinned.

'It's one thing to hear of them in old stories, but it's another seeing them with your own eyes. It was about twice your height, too,' Maledream said, recalling the fight all too well.

'Twice my height? Shit, you're joking?' Neveah chuckled, shaking his head.

'Let's just hope we don't come across one. Its scales are thick, and they're crazy bastards. If it wasn't for this weapon, I would have been dinner.'

Neveah stared into his friend's eyes for a moment, easily gleaning the visible fear in them.

'Anyway, let's rest, it's been a long day, and we've walked a fair few miles,' said Maledream.

Neveah ordered the rest of the Pack to stop and rest on some fallen trees, ridden from core to bark with thick, slimy moss. Laying Angelite down in a comfortable position on the dry earth, the Tribal stroked her hair affectionately.

'It's a shame our Battle Hammer died on us. I'm severely grieved, Neveah, I put so much of my heart and soul into that piece of rusted crap!' Crazy John uttered, sparking some conversation amongst the Pack.

'Aye, it's a damn shame. We didn't have the fuel to make it all the way to this Meridia anyway. We knew we had to walk at some stage, but not this early on, that's for damn sure,' Neveah grunted, scratching his eye-patch and wiping his forehead.

'This forest gives me the shits. It's gotten a lot quieter, too,' Pixie said, gleaning the lush, green landscape anxiously, as was the rest of the Pack.

'Nothing we can do, except kill anything that has a problem with us being here. Anybody heard anything about this place?' asked Boris.

'Nope, apart from some rumours surrounding it, which we've all heard of in one crappy bar after another,' said Neveah.

'Plenty of lumber around if we want to burn something for the hell of it,' Crazy John added while sharpening his knives with a thick whetstone.

'Aye, don't touch anything. No telling what's watching us and what'll get pissed off if we do something like that,' the Pack leader muttered.

'Not much chance of that happening, we'll need heat later on,' Boris sighed.

Neveah eventually nodded, 'don't want to freeze at night, either. Let's have some munch, and then we'll continue. I don't like being sat down for too long. Could be any manner of beasts, shadows, or damn Witches in this place.'

Falling silent, everyone seemed paranoid that something was staring at them from the dense, wild overgrowth. The occasional twig snapping in the forest, or even a burst of whistling wind, alarmed some of the group on occasion. Thankfully, it was nothing but their fraught nerves.

'So, Neveah, what else happened? How were we split up, and from what?' the Tribal asked, referring to their separation in the city.

Drawing in a deep breath, Neveah continued to enlighten him the best he could whilst sharpening the blade on his pole-arm with a whetstone.

'Well, we blindly set foot in the city during the day but, as we travelled through it at night, all hell broke loose. We weren't ready for the intense fighting in the city,' he said, his one eye reflecting the shower of sparks from his weapon.

'You mean that's when we first met the Packs?' Maledream elaborated.

'Aye, anyway, to cut a long and bloody story short, we got separated during the battle. I was caught with my back against the wall, facing a few big guys. One of them went for me. Bastard tried gutting me with a single thrust. I can barely remember the fight, save the blood afterwards, but it was clear I swiped his own blade across his neck. There's more to it, though...'

Neveah stopped talking for a moment, his hands still as he glared at the surrounding forest, thinking he had heard something. Maledream turned his head but saw nothing. The Pack leader continued in a careless tone, his hand repeating its flow.

'Since then, I've taken charge of these guys. It's how Packs work, as I'm sure you know. Take out the biggest brute who leads them, and you become the leader. However, facing the loss of my family, friends, and not knowing the way to this safe haven, I decided to take refuge in that bloody city. For many, many seasons, I gave up on almost everything, except leading this Pack. I soon learnt their ways. It wasn't in my nature, at first, but I found myself caught up in their way of life with no choice. Over the years, I created a Pack I could rely on. I'm thankful for my physical strength, Maledream. At times, it may not have been enough, but I pride myself over my ways more than anything else in this blood-soaked, shithole of a world.'

Neveah paused to examine his blade's edge, checking whether he had sharpened it too much or too little. Adjusting his stroke, he continued with his story, 'I never did find out what happened to you. I presumed you were dead, just like everyone else in the attack. It's great to see that you made it. I shouldn't sound so surprised, though, you were always good at hiding. We shared many laughs, you were always a comedian.'

Sighing, the pair thought in silence for a moment.

'It's a hard one isn't it,' Maledream muttered, before staring up at the trees above to continue, 'I can't remember much, but I do have nightmares. Sometimes, I think it's my memory trying to tell me, but, to be honest, I go with what my old man told me once. *"Only look in front of you, never look back."* Even Angelite has helped me take my mind off the past. I want to look forward, not back, if you get what I mean. I don't think my past matters to me anymore. I just want to find a safe home, away from all this bullshit in these dark lands. I think it's time I started growing up properly and stopped being an annoying idiot like I usually am.'

'Aye, but it what makes you, you, Maledream. Remember, looking back allows you to reflect and change and it makes you a better person. Things happen from time to time, but it's all a learning experience for the spirit in all of us.'

'You're starting to sound like Larkham with all this wisdom. Ah, there is one thing I do remember, and that was you were chosen to be a spiritual leader when you were younger, or something like that.'

'Ah, see, your memory is coming back! Yeah, I was going to be chosen to be such a leader back in those days, but that was before we had to face the violence in the city. I've tried to reaching out with these teachings to a few of my Pack, but only my closest mates, mind. The ones you killed, back at the base, were rotten shits, but you get them occasionally,' Neveah grumbled.

'No arguments there,' Maledream concurred.

'Anyway, once everyone I knew was dead, I turned into a barrel of hatred for a short time. I was hurt from losing everyone I cared about, or even loved. I met one woman but, sadly, things didn't turn out the way I hoped.'

'Really? Who was she?' Maledream pursued.

'Aye, she was beautiful...' Neveah's eye seemed to water at the thought of whoever she was, before coarsely brushing it off. 'I'll tell you some other time, pisses me off just thinking about it. Anyway, I was a barrel of hate and then, after my woman, I became worse. I led the Pack on many brutal, pillaging sprees. Then, after a while, I began to grow tired and weary with this hate lingering in me, and since there was no one around for spiritual guidance, or some crap like that, I had to contemplate things all by myself for years,' Neveah said, pausing for a moment to see his Pack muttering in their own conversations.

He continued with a lighter tone. 'It was an endless cycle, Maledream. It's weird, but over the last couple of months, I've felt more tranquil in myself. Some of the others have felt this way, too. *"Something's different,"* we'd all say, as if the wind was changing. Sometimes, I wished things turned out differently, like we reached this so-called sanctuary in the first place. I always used to say to my Pack that, one day, we'd search for it. Back when you and I were younger, mate, our group leaders told us that everything in life was planned, as if it were all a great big spider's web, and that coincidence only existed to serve as ignorance for us humans. I thought, until yesterday, that it was all a complete load of old shit. And then you decided to reappear with your runty ass.'

Neveah reached for his pipe once he had finished sharpening his pole-arm. The crude, raw tobacco smelled nice on the breeze.

'And now, Maledream, I've got no doubts. Perhaps life is planned, even with our choices. Maybe there's some sort of strange stalemate or something, you know, sort of like a balance. I don't know, maybe, makes you think, though, doesn't it?' Neveah said, eyeing the Tribal whom had his chin resting on the knuckles of his hand.

'You're right, something strange is up. Don't know about you, but I think this place is bringing a lot of peace to us all,' Maledream smirked.

'Aye, you're right. It is,' Neveah nodded, lying on his back in silence to smoke.

Maledream shut his eyes for a moment to catch some rest, rather than eat. It had been a long day, but now he was enjoying the sunlight and relaxing as the breeze caressed his being. After they finished their meals and drink, the group began their journey through the forest once again.

They crossed over many brooks and streams whilst the sun set over the canopy's horizon, creating a gloomier, more mysterious atmosphere throughout the lush expanse. The light wind blowing through the leaves of the trees created eerie sounds, reigniting some of the Pack's fears. Weapons were at the ready for any sign of attack from anything hiding in the darkening wilderness.

'We're going to have to set up some sort of camp soon,' said Maledream.

'Yep, we've earned a... what the... you all see this?' Neveah stated.

The group had entered an ancient, open grove containing a large, giant oak tree. The leaves seemed to have a golden, autumn glow about them as the last of the dying sunrays penetrated the tree line. Maledream sensed a pleasant atmosphere in the small grove. It was eerily similar to what he had felt before, when the priestess showed him and Larkham her Resonance back at the Tribal camp.

It had the same feel of raw energy.

Neveah raised his fist to halt the group. Cautiously, the Pack surveyed the tranquil area with stern eyes and tightly gripped weapons. Moments passed as all senses focused on what they could see and hear. Neveah strode forwards with his weapon primed, examining the area in detail. Gradually, everyone else followed his lead.

What was more unusual about the large, oaken tree, apart from its size, was the base of the trunk, which split in three parts, each joining into a centralised point like a pyramid. Its bark had unusual swirls and symbols etched on it, too. Yet, on closer inspection, they hadn't been carved by any man made tool. It was as if they grew naturally with the oak.

'Well, don't know about you bastards, but this place looks fairly safe. Let's sit our asses here for the night!' a satisfied Neveah announced.

Nervously, the Pack began setting up their skinned tents with renewed vigour, just so they could have, at last, a quiet respite with no disturbance from other gangs. Maledream lowered the priestess on the soft grass before stretching his aching muscles high in the air with a sigh.

* * *

Night soon fell on the grove. The moon shone brightly through the leaves of the great, mysterious oak tree, lighting the camp with cosmic-blue hues. Embers crackled and flowed from the campfire the group had ignited from dead branches and dry, golden-crisp leaves, which served to the warm them in the chilling breeze that owned the wilderness.

Around the fire, the Pack chatted, albeit quietly. Some felt it difficult to relax in such an alien environment. Such was there paranoia that everyone took turns parading around the perimeter of the grove, just in case.

Gradually, as the moon reached the highest point in the dark, starlit sky, they began their well-deserved slumber in their shoddy tents.

Maledream couldn't sleep. Another headache troubled him. He tried walking it off by walking the perimeter of the grove, before settling next to Angelite in their tent.

'Why won't you wake up? It's been a while now...' he muttered.

Eventually, the campfire died with a hiss.

* * *

Awakening in dreary panic, Maledream felt a cold, wet sensation creep through his clothing in the dead of night. He focused his blurry vision on the circular clearing outside the tent. The oaken tree was seemingly, and at the same time unnaturally, growing a fine sheen of frost that rose up its bark. Unsure of what he was staring at, he crept closer to see the moonlight shining on this white blanket of frost that seemingly came from nowhere. A thick fog, which had also appeared, took the darkened forest's circumference around the open ground of the grove.

Around the circular area were stones, standing several feet in height. They began to glow with an eerie silence, with many runic symbols flickering gently on their ancient surfaces, and the vines that had once completely camouflaged them grew and floated in an anticlockwise direction around the clearing.

Strangely, Maledream felt no fear in what he was seeing or feeling, so didn't reach for his weapon. Instead, he continued watching in awe, glancing to see if anyone else was awake.

'You bring weapons of war, stranger. This is our forbidden forest and Sacred Grove that you're desecrating,' a sweet, soothing voice echoed in his mind.

'What... who are you?' he muttered, all the while spinning on his feet to find the source of the voice.

'We're the warders, the protectors, and the most sacred. You have trespassed. What good reason do you have for setting foot in the Sacred Circle?'

Spheres of ethereal light floated from the leaves of the great oak, suspended high above as if they were many droplets of snow yet to hit the ground.

Shaking from the cold, he replied, 'we came from the city, seeking a place called Meridia. This forest was in our path, we didn't mean to offend you, whoever you are?'

'I sense death surrounding you. Give us a reason why we shouldn't banish such vile creatures from our Sacred Circle?'

Clenching his hands, he barked back at the lights in frustration. 'Don't threaten us. We haven't done anything wrong to you or this forest...'

Suddenly, he remembered what Larkham had once told him what to say about freewill and spirits. 'We claim freewill,' he asserted.

'A wise claim indeed. I see you possess a weapon lost from ancient times, young Spirit. Very intriguing, if we do say so ourselves, but please, stem your anger in this peaceful sanctuary.'

'We haven't done anything wrong,' the Tribal argued.

The strange voice changed its tone and topic, *'you have brought along a very spiritual being with you. Angelite, isn't it?'*

Maledream gawked. He looked back into the tent to see many pulsating orbs hovering above the priestess.

'I think it's time we revealed ourselves.'

The bright-white orbs glowed intensely, and whining shrieks echoed through the Grove. It was loud enough to rouse the slumbering Pack.

'What the hell is that?' Neveah yelled, shooting out of his tent with only his tight loincloth and pole-arm to bear.

Similar responses came from the Pack, each rushing for their weapons. The shriek gradually faded in pitch, seemingly disappearing back into the dark, foreboding wilderness.

'Don't draw your weapons,' Maledream ordered, glancing at the Pack unlatching their pole-arms.

'What the hell is all this frost doing here? And what's with those lights?' Neveah muttered, wandering over and taking his place by the Tribal.

From the opposite side of the great oak in the pale light of the moon, several strangers entered the circle. Their tread froze the grass beneath their stride and, at the same time, caused the very wildlife around them to sprout thorny vines. They watched the first stranger approach them in full visibility of the camp.

She was a young woman with long, black, coarse hair, and wore a shimmering, full-length white robe, sewn from rich-looking silk. The stranger's attire seemed to imitate frozen spider webbing that one would see on a winter's day. The woman also wore a circlet on her forehead, carved from fine tree-bore. It was decorated with many crystals, each placed in holes that glowed a cosmic blue. These hummed with resonating energies that seemed to emanate their cold spell upon her brow.

Two similar women appeared, dressed in the same type of robe, but without the circlet. Instead, both held warped, wooden staves. Whispers erupted throughout the group. It appeared that the myths surrounding the forest were true. The Witches had struck the chords of their greatest fears.

'My, my, my, three beautiful, shrieking women, just my lucky night,' Neveah groaned.

The voluptuous Witches glanced at the big man's tight, compact muscles as he leant on his pole-arm, unafraid, and complete with spare hand resting on hip. They could clearly guess he wasn't amused by the high-pitched wakeup call whilst the frost settled on his bulging loincloth.

'How very rude. However, this is not the time to teach you manners. You wish to know who we are, and I shall tell you...' replied the lead Witch, a sinister smile racing across her lips.

'Forgive us for such a rude entrance at this moment of night, but you have not only disturbed our Sacred Grove, you have also desecrated it by burning the oak. The Spirits do not look kindly to those that disrespect this most natural spot of beauty. We are the Witches of this Sacred Grove, and we follow in the footsteps of many a generation who have protected this holy place.'

From around the grove, the eyes of night creatures caught the group's attention, glaring at them from all around the perimeter through the foggy haze. Their beady eyes glowed softly, shining hues of greens and reds in the pale moonlight.

'How do you know Angelite's name?' queried Maledream.

'There is much we know. We merely wish to help this unique soul, whom we also wish to heal,' replied the lead Witch.

'You've changed your tune all of a sudden. You threatened us, and now you wish to heal one of our companions. What are you planning?' Maledream pursued.

Gracefully striding up to the Tribal, the Witch put her cold finger on his lips, and paused to stare at him. The cold touch relaxed him instantly.

'We are Witches of the Spirit. It is our duty to protect this grove. There are many, many others, but you will not find them in this deep, forbidden wilderness. All groves are sacred places. They keep the world healthy and in full flow of sacred energies. We here, guard it, in hope of atoning for what our ancestors' atrocities wrought in the past. That sword you carry is not the only one. There are others.'

She paused, staring at Maledream's weapon as she circled him. Her stride stirred thoughts of apparitions by how she moved with elegance.

'We felt the very air thicken with an ancient taint this afternoon. We aided Angelite without her knowing, thus saving your lives on the battlefield. If it were not for us, then you would not have made it here. It's simply fate that you managed to stumble on our Sacred Grove,' she said.

'So, you're saying you're responsible for almost killing her?' Maledream angrily blurted.

'As I just said, you wouldn't have made it. We watched you fight the evil on that dead plane with childish courage. We helped you because we pitied you.'

'Pity? You almost killed her in the process. You can't justify that,' the Tribal bitterly retaliated.

The Pack watched silently with twitchy fingers.

'Aye, how did you witness us fighting? The battlefield is many leagues to the south,' Neveah probed.

'We have our ways, large man. It is the same way we found out Angelite's name,' replied the Witch.

Maledream and Neveah looked at each other and shrugged.

'Well, all this spying hasn't gotten you anywhere yet, and I'm still trying to comprehend your motives…' said Maledream.

'We'll discuss more soon. But for the moment, let's heal the priestess before her soul is too diminished to be saved,' ordered the lead Witch.

Silence fell as the group watched her push past with the other two Witches in tow. Racing underneath the priestess, the pulsating, ethereal orbs carried her out of the tent, humming brightly underneath and around her, and each leaving a trail of neon light in their flight.

Angelite swirled slowly through the air until she descended to lie underneath the great oak. The three spell casters sat down in a triangle around her. Laying their hands on her chest and overlapping one hand over the other, they did not speak. All the Pack could hear was the slight humming from the surrounding orbs as they weaved over and under the roots of the oak.

Many creatures appeared on the outskirts of the Sacred Grove, although they were not solid, as one would expect. There were cats, wolves, and crows, and their eyes glowed in the pale reflection of the eerie, blue light of the moon. They seemed to be drawn to the ritualistic ceremony by a ghastly instinct.

The foggy mist grew stronger around the perimeter, and seeped in from the darkness of the forest as more of the spirits gathered, only to add further to the chill and the highly-strung atmosphere.

'The spirits have gathered, and now it is up to nature in the realm of the spirit. These creatures of this ancient world will decide,' echoed the lead Witch.

Maledream was getting edgy, and although the frost was as cold as it was, a rolling droplet of sweat raced down his temple. A reassuring Neveah laid his hand on the Tribal's shoulder.

'It'll be okay, mate. Let them get on with it. I don't think we want to mess with them, no telling what curses they can inflict us with,' he whispered.

Howling, the wolves trotted into the Sacred Grove, their fur coats a pristine white, black, or grey. Remnants of tattered flesh, revealing bone, hung from some who had not fared so well in their former lives. Strong, rotten smells also accompanied these spectres.

The group was weary yet vigilant, tense with terror and superstition at what they were witnessing. Some gripped their weapons tightly, whereas others jumped in a shocked fashion as the ghastly animals passed through them, leaving them with a subzero chill.

The wolves sat around the Witches, seemingly communing with them in silence. They stayed a short while, howling in unison, before signalling their retreat to the outskirts of the Grove. Once more, they took their places in the darkness of the overgrowth, watching with their piercing vision.

The cats entered next, their cries echoing as they were piercing. Many in number and variation, some looked similar to the wolves, like rotting carcasses. They squealed as they sped into the inner circle, sitting before the Witches. Like the wolves, they too returned to the outskirts of the grove, their eyes beaming at the group as they scurried between their twitching legs with phantasmal speed.

The spirits of the crows did not move from their trees, and instead cawed from their perches. Their eyes glowed at them with dark, hazy blues.

Maledream eagerly waited for Angelite to recover. His impatience grew. Nothing seemed to be happening.

'How long now?' Maledream seethed, clasping his hands together in a vain attempt to keep them warm.

'Quit your worrying, it's not going to speed anything up,' Neveah nudged him, the look on his face etched with fear.

'So mote it be,' the Witches uttered to the spectral, pulsating orbs.

Energies manifested through their arms and hands, flooding Angelite's body with golden-green Resonance. Singing and wailing with hums and sighs, they worked their bizarre spell on the priestess. The group could only watch and stare with a sense of amazement.

Dissipating from their cold, gentle hands, the orbs ceased their flow of energies into the coven. The ritual ended as soon as they stopped chanting. The woodland spirits, such as the wolves, cats, and crows, sank back into the gloom of the forest and, when they did so, the fog gradually subsided from the Sacred Grove, giving back a little warmth to those that were shivering.

Gradually, the mysterious, pulsating orbs raised Angelite from the ground once more, before elegantly twisting her form through the air and into her tent, where they set her down in her original position. The lead Witch approached and peered at the Tribal.

'You wished to know how we receive our information, so I will tell you. You know of Larkham, young Spirit?' she asked.

'Of course,' Maledream nodded.

'He has once told you about communing with Spirits, such as us, but you would never listen to him. You still have much to learn, but then again, so do we all. Isn't that right?'

Confused by her riddles, he merely nodded. She enlightened him.

'In basic terms, young Spirit, we communicate with him, and many others, across our sick planet. It is through means of travelling through this existence, in spirit, that we can find out such information, or keep an eye on certain people. People like you and this priestess.'

'You've been watching over us for some time then. A request from Larkham?' Maledream probed.

'He did ask. Nicely, I may add. If it was not for him, you would have been doomed,' she laughed loudly, easily toying with the emotions of those who were petrified of them.

'However...' she continued, her tone foreboding, 'we don't possess the means to fix Angelite's staff, nor the crystals. For such things, you will have to continue travelling north to the mountain range. Seek a hermit called

N'Rutas. She dwells in a secret glade covered by a waterfall. Be aware, travellers, for she may have a task for you.'

'Aye, what will she ask of us, Witch?' Neveah butted in.

'How am I to know? I know her, and she doesn't give willingly without a favour, especially for the prized artefacts' that she hordes like a dragon in a den,' she replied with a sinister tone.

'So then, are we to find this waterfall to the north easily?' Neveah growled, his brow stooped in frustration.

'Of course not,' she laughed cruelly, adding with glee, 'have faith and follow your best judgements. It's not easily missed, if you can follow the correct clues.'

'Damn you and your riddles, Witch. But, I guess a thank you is in order, so on behalf of Maledream and the Pack, thanks for helping Angelite,' Neveah graciously uttered.

'You see, that's how you talk to your elders,' she replied with a glance and grin.

'Elders? They look as young as us,' Maledream frowned.

'You can stay until morning. May the spirits protect you and, dare I say, you have our blessings this one time. We must go. We have spent too long talking. You had better be gone before the sun hits its highest point in the heavens, for we don't like lodgers. And Maledream, give Larkham our warmest welcome when you should encounter him next.'

Turning their backs to the group and with her two followers in tow, the Witches faded into the darkness of the forbidden forest.

'Wait,' shouted Maledream, 'When will Angelite wake up?'

His voice echoed through the dark recesses of the woodland. There was no reply.

'Great,' he muttered.

Neveah rested his hand on the Tribal's shoulder. 'Relax, mate, I'm sure she'll wake up in the morning. Let's get some bloody sleep, this cold is starting to bite my fingers and toes off just by standing here, not to mention my balls have shrunk to the size of fucking peanuts.'

Chapter Eight

Journey for the Hermit

Maledream awoke to find Neveah yelling in the cold morning.

'Cowards!' he bellowed.

'Are we under attack?' Maledream responded in kind, trying to find his weapon in panic.

'The bastard-Pack left us!' Neveah growled like a rabid beast, repeatedly punching a nearby tree.

'What?' Maledream blurted, jumping to his feet and out of his tent. 'Where'd they go?'

'Fuck knows, but they swiped all our food. I'm going to personally cut off their bollocks!' Neveah spat, stamping his feet hard on the ground.

Scanning his surroundings in the early morning of the grove, Maledream noticed that the orbs were gone, although his senses told him otherwise. The ground was moist, no frost apparent, save on the great oak that had icy cobwebs dangling and shining from the warm rays of the sun that penetrated the forest's canopy.

'At least they didn't take our damn weapons, but their balls are still mine,' Neveah seethed.

Maledream was relieved to find his sword and other equipment still present.

'They haven't taken anything of mine either...' before he could finish his sentence, both Maledream and Neveah heard a sweet voice utter to them.

'What are you boys shouting about?'

Angelite was awake, sitting upright, and rubbing her eyes.

'Whoa!' The two men cheered.

'It's good to see you're awake at last,' Neveah said in an upbeat tone.

It seemed the pleasure of seeing her awake dulled his annoyance about the morning's surprise. Maledream rushed to her and gently grasped her hand.

'We thought we'd lost you, are you feeling all right?' he said, smiling at her.

'Yes, yes, really, I'm okay. I just feel a little fatigued and thirsty,' she nodded, her voice dry and coarse.

'I'm afraid we can't help you with your thirst at the moment. My Pack buggered off with all the supplies,'

Neveah groaned, his one good eye gleaning the camp to see which direction they may have taken.

'Let's not worry about that for the moment. Where are we? I feel a very strong Resonance about this place, it's comforting,' she said, green eyes staring intently at the great oak in the centre of the grove.

'We stumbled across it after we kept on travelling north and into this forest. We came across a bunch of these Witches, well, that's what they called themselves. We apparently trespassed on their Sacred Grove,' said Maledream.

'Yes, as was intended,' said the priestess with excitement.

'Come again?' Maledream frowned.

'It was arranged with Larkham before we left your Tribal camp. I should have told you, but I didn't count on falling unconscious,' she grinned.

'That explains a couple of things,' Maledream smirked, his voice filled with relief.

'Aye, you knew we'd be petrified, so I can see why you didn't tell us about them before, or we'd probably have avoided the place. I counted on you having a plan,' Neveah replied, scratching his eye-patch.

'Yep, I intended to lead us this way through the forest. Larkham had told me about some spirits living here, he assured me they were nice,' she said, her hands casually clenching the fine grass.

'Sounds like something he'd say. Just to let you know, your staff broke when you cast that spell, and the crystals you used also shattered. We've retrieved some of the remains in a bag for you. Something else you might like to hear, is that the Witches helped channel their energies through you,' said Maledream.

'Oh, I see, so that's what the influx was, and you say it's because of these powerful Witches? How did they know we were travelling across the battlefield?' she wondered.

'Aye, that's what we asked them,' Neveah sighed, his arms crossed and his eyebrow lowered in deep thought over the events during the night. 'They didn't explain much, and some of what they explained we could hardly understand, not least my Pack. Apparently, they have their ways with the spirit, it was all rather confusing, especially for Maledream,' Neveah sniggered.

'I'm not as dumb as I look. Just because you're hungry you don't need to take it out on me, you complete ass,' Maledream retaliated.

'Only joking, mate, calm down,' Neveah laughed.

'Anyway, these Witches said that we should seek someone out called N'Rutas as we continue north,' said the Tribal.

'Why's that? Who's N'Rutas?' she pursued.

'An old hag that hordes treasure, apparently,' replied Neveah.

'Yeah, she can help us fix your staff,' Maledream nodded.

'That would be great. I wouldn't like to travel the rest of the way to the port without a staff. Maybe she can repair my shattered one. I wonder who she is...'

'Yeah, this is why we should seek her out. I expect she may be like those Witches of Spirit that guard this place,' said Maledream.

'Interesting, so, did they say where we could find her?' she asked.

'Sort of, the Witches just said to keep heading north and we'll come across a waterfall, or some such crap,' Neveah grunted.

'Yeah, that'll apparently take us to her,' Maledream added.

The atmosphere was picking up as the sun took its place high in the sky. Although neither sight nor sound was present from the animals that should be living in such a vast forest, it felt more alive than it did when they had first entered. It was almost noon by the position of the sun.

'I think we'd better get going and find some water, I can hardly open my mouth,' the priestess uttered coarsely, sifting through the bag that contained what was left of her staff.

'Right, well, let's pack the tents up and go hunting for some fresh food and water,' said Maledream.

'Aye, let's get our shit together then,' Neveah grunted, ripping his shoddy tent down with one flex of his arm.

Once the trio had packed and double-checked everything, they got to their feet and continued north. Neveah stopped trying to track his mutinied Pack, and instead, focused on his growling stomach while cursing occasionally under his breath about the betrayal.

Maledream followed Neveah as he helped the fatigued priestess walk through the deep woods. The two men enlightened Angelite on how the Witches appeared, what was said, and how they had performed a ceremony to heal her. After travelling for several hours, the three companions came across a river. A fallen oak tree lay across the calm, sparkling waters, serving as a useful bridge.

'Fresh water at last,' Angelite praised.

'Looks mighty fine,' Neveah concurred, his steady eye gleaning the open surroundings of the riverbank across the other side, hawking for any potential threat or game.

The priestess sat down on the grassy bank whilst Maledream filled his empty flask. As he did so, he examined what lay on the riverbed.

'What are these?' he muttered, delving his hand into the water and disturbing the fine silt.

Drudging and drawing his hand out of the disturbed water, he opened his clenched fist to show many crystals in his palm.

'Take a look at these,' he said, holding them in front of Angelite's weary eyes.

She ignored them. Instead, she snatched his full flask from his other hand to drink it dry in seconds.

Wiping her lips, she uttered in excitement, 'oh yes!'

'What are they?' he asked, staring at the different colours.

'They're very unusual crystals. They look pure. I guess this place has many more secrets,' she said, examining each one and noting how perfect they were.

'This one is an emerald... and this one amethyst and, um, oh wow, a lot of them are different kinds of quartz crystals, very useful! If you boys can wait a little while longer, I'll have a quick swim and try to find a good sized one for a new staff,' she said, gently lowering the crystals on the grassy bank.

'You expect to go swimming in your robes?' quizzed Maledream.

'Of course not,' she said, disrobing before the two men.

'You can't do that!' he said, gawping, trying to avert his eyes with palms up.

'Watch me if you want, but, if you do, I won't forgive you for it! Besides, I need a wash, it's been way too long,' she finished.

'By the spirits,' Maledream muttered, slapping himself on the cheek.

Neveah didn't say a word, he just laughed at the pair with his bulging arms crossed, still glaring like a hawk towards the other side of the river.

'You two stay here, I'm going to find us some food over this tree-bridge,' uttered the Pack leader.

'Don't be too long, I don't know what she'll tear off next,' Maledream laughed.

'You cheeky pervert!' she gasped and grinned.

Stripped naked, she faced away from the two men as her red hair covered her buttocks. Both turned their heads away with grins as she peeked over her shoulder, uttering, 'don't be too long, Neveah. And Maledream, don't look!'

With raised arms, she dived into the river as smooth as a dolphin.

'Well, if that wasn't an invitation, I don't know what is...' the Tribal smirked.

Neveah laughed vigorously, before waving a quick goodbye as he crossed over the oaken bridge.

* * *

Reaching the other side of the riverbank in his casual stride, Neveah paused. His eye caught some odd footprints in the soft mud on the embankment. On closer inspection, he saw it was the trail from his Pack's treads.

'Just wait till I catch them,' he said, gritting his teeth.

His legs lurched forward in long strides as he bolted through the green maze, following the fresh tracks in a hypnotic fashion. Breathing heavily from the heat and lack of breeze, sweat easily dripped from his forehead.

Eventually, Neveah found himself in a clearing, only to be greeted by a horrific scene. Trees were battered and smeared in blood. It was clear a battle had taken place. He saw the remains of the supplies and weapons scattered about the clearing, but strangely, there was no sign of his Pack. Catching his breath and wiping the sweat with his spare hand, he caught a strange scent on the gentle breeze.

'Smells like… flowers.'

Keening his ears, he froze. Humming echoed from somewhere nearby, but he wasn't sure of the direction. The heavy foliage and forest numbed the noise.

'What the fuck is it?' he muttered.

Neveah's good eye saw that one of the nearby trees had a pole-arm buried in its thick, moss-ridden bark. Striding over the tracks, he examined the battered condition of the weapon. Ripping the pole's serrated blade out of the fresh sap, he carefully laid it to rest on the earth, trying to think what could've happened. The humming return, he looked around to check for danger, and then it stopped again.

'Could've sworn I felt a breeze just then. Where the hell are their corpses? Whatever killed them should have left them here, surely?'

He carried on examining the tracks, but all they could tell him was that a battle was fought, and that his Pack disappeared without a sign. He noticed that different bullet casings lay on the earth. From what he gleaned, the Pack was attacked from all directions. The thick wilderness masked any gunfire for miles around.

A disturbing sense of paranoia slowly seeped into Neveah's mind. He continued scanning the foliage, in what was, possibly, the deepest part of the forest. Strange scorch marks brushed the surrounding oaks in the vicinity. Neveah inspected them and saw that the wounds on the trees were recent. The scorches looked as if they were made by a fire of the sorts, strong enough to have set the trees alight.

'Maybe the Witches roasted them all?' Neveah wondered, remembering Reckless's concerns over Witches several nights ago.

His senses heightened as he struggled to come to terms with what he was seeing. He reassured himself that the Witches would not have attacked them. After all, they had offered safe passage last night once they were told to leave the Grove.

The scent of flowers caught his nostrils once more. Humming once again rang in his ears, but this time, growing many times louder. He glanced in all directions, but remained kneeling as he prepped his main pole-arm. He couldn't see it, but could hear and smell it. Neveah almost wished Maledream were there to back him up with that enchanted sword.

He was aware that the breeze was picking up all around, serving a stronger smell of pollen. He tensed his muscles, yet kept his legs loose for a quick reflex at any moment. Then he realised. The threat wasn't surrounding him. It was above him.

Catching the sound of the leaves and branches breaking above, he dived to his right and, in doing so, swiped his pole-arm in a wide arc at the falling foe. An ear-splitting crunch echoed as if he sliced through bone. Neveah rolled to his side once again as a harsh wind swept over him.

Jumping back on his feet with his weapon raised in a defensive stance, he saw what was stalking him. A chilling sensation raced down his spine. The creature flew wildly after the blow across its carapace, but it had only suffered a scrape. Refocusing its ocelli, it raised its abdomen and prepared to strike again with its many barbs. Its wings fluttered cyclonic winds in the vicinity with violent force, blowing leaves, branches, and loose dirt at him.

He gritted his teeth and struggled against it. Still, he held his ground like an iron wall. The giant insect dived at him, its mandibles dancing about its thick, bony skull. With all his strength, Neveah dived and thrust the point of his pole-arm's sharp, serrated blade into the giant insect's thorax, resulting in a satisfying crunch as he fractured and penetrated its surface.

Rolling to his feet, he delivered a killing blow in a deadly high arc, slicing through its thin, buzzing wings as it struck the trampled earth. Slicing off its great abdomen with quick, hard-crunching blows, he severed its thorax and head. Finally, to put the beast out of its misery, he brought the weapon to bear on its cranium, severing it from its thorax. Neveah stomped on it with his giant boot.

'Fucking bug, those Packers were mine. Question is what did you do with them all, huh?'

The scent of pollen wafted on the breeze. More humming echoed in the distance and closed in on his position. He looked up to see more of the large insects, many of whom looked bigger, and more menacing than the one he had just dismembered.

'Shit, ain't I glad I sharpened my weapon yesterday,' he smirked, steadying his stance.

Nudging another pole-arm off the floor with his boot, he gripped it with his offhand, staring at it briefly, before glaring upwards at the charging beasts from above.

* * *

Meanwhile, Maledream leaned on his back whilst Angelite continued diving for more crystals. Staring at the blue sky with his arms crossed behind his head, he relaxed. A person with red hair flashed in his memory. His eyes widened before he sharply sat upright.

'She reminds me of someone, maybe that's why my feelings are mixed?' he thought, trying to recall in more detail with what exactly he was remembering.

He then stared at the glittering, refracting water as the sun shone upon its surface. All he could remember was the long red-hair. Emotions stirred deeply in his heart. His thoughts were interrupted as the priestess emerged from the water, holding in her arms some crystalline chunks that barely covered her breasts.

'Put them away, woman!' he cried, averting his gaze in embarrassment.

Innocent, cheeky laughter was her only reply. Soon enough, Angelite had already clothed herself.

'You can look now,' she called, a flirtatious grin wrapped around her cheeks.

'About time. Neveah hasn't come back yet, so he must've found something interesting,' he replied.

'Aye, Aye!' she heartily mimicked, 'I feel better after the swim, my hair is all clean, my skin's clean, that water has worked its wonders with all those crystals underneath its surface! And...'

Maledream snappishly rose to his feet, distracted by something that appeared near them. Angelite's eyes traced the worrying Tribal's glare as she paused.

'What's that on the fallen tree?' she muttered to him.

'If I'm not mistaken, it looks like a wolf. There were some at the Witch's Grove last night, except they were ancient spirits,' he returned.

The wolf was stood on its four paws, and stared at them intently. It was large for such a creature, easily the length of Neveah, and almost the height of an average human. Its colour seemed unusual. Its fur was pure white and pristine, save for the silvery shimmer given to it by the sun.

'I thought wolves were extinct in the Dark Age lands?' she said.

'I thought so, too,' he nodded.

The wolf locked eyes with them, and then suddenly raised its snout to let out a long, terrifying howl. Maledream withdrew his sword, unsure of what to expect from such a large creature long-thought to be extinct. Then, finishing its howl, it turned tail and bolted in the direction of where Neveah went.

'Got your stuff?'

'Yep,' she nodded.

'Good, we've got some catching up to do. Neveah could be in trouble,' he said, gripping Angelite by the hand and dragging her with him.

The pair ran across the fallen tree to chase the wolf. Its howling continued, yet it kept pace with them through the overgrowth of nettles, brambles, and roots that threatened to trip them at any moment. Blinding them was the sun, beaming its strong rays through the scattered openings of the woodland canopy as they continued the chase. Then, the howling stopped. It was replaced by the near-deafening humming and strong winds that coursed through the forest.

Breaking through the overgrowth, the duo saw Neveah maniacally swinging around two pole-arms. Blood poured from scrapes across his torso and arms as he fought against the large, flying insects that dive-bombed him. The petrified priestess stood back and, hiding behind a nearby tree, hoped the massive insects wouldn't spot her. The Tribal, however, leapt into the fray.

'I'm coming,' he yelled, trying to be heard over the strong winds and rasping clacks.

Neveah swung his weapons against one of the many beasts, shearing its wings clean from its thorax and sending it crashing into one of the trees. Roaring as loud as he could, he continued his bloody rage against more of the attacking insects.

Maledream ran towards one of the flying creatures and, lifting his heavy sword up high, waited for the right moment to strike. Neveah battered another away, sending it plummeting into the ground. Clacking its mandibles threateningly, its antennas raced around its skull from the disorientating blow.

Just then, Maledream saw his chance to take it out. Jumping on the thrashing creature's abdomen, he swiped his blade in a low-to-high-arced fashion, striking the creature from behind. Passing through its body, thorax, and head, the sword cut right through the dense exoskeleton in a spray of ichor.

Landing on his boots, he carried on into the fray whilst Neveah skewered another one of the insects against a tree with one pole-arm, then slicing it, with exerted grunts, into three pieces with his other weapon.

Maledream saw he was weakening. His attention was drawn to another attack. He spun on his feet before diving to one side, avoiding a great, barbed stinger from an abdomen that pounded the earth. As it threatened to impale him for a second time, Maledream dived to his side and, with a side-swing of his blade, sliced through the creature's abdomen in a shower of sparks and gore.

It recoiled and fluttered like a confused moth struck by a hand. Neveah diligently brought his weapons to bear on the crippled pest. The humming was over. Nine of the giant wasp-like creatures lay dead, scattered around and severed in many pieces. Returning to its natural state, the strong, cyclonic winds returned to a barely noticeable breeze.

Maledream watched Neveah fall to his knees, before reeling backwards to lie on the earth, breathing heavily and covered in gashes. He noticed Angelite nervously entering the bloodied area. She tiptoed and squealed around the large creatures. The two men grinned as the antenna of one creature touched her foot, causing her to panic and jump with a screech.

'I think he needs some attention, Angelite. Could you work your healing hands on him?' Maledream prompted.

Nodding, and without saying a word, the priestess reached into her backpack to retrieve clean cloth's to wrap around Neveah's wounds. He lay on the floor, unable to move, and totally exhausted. She placed her hands on his chest, murmuring her Resonance to help with the healing process.

'These things are something, aren't they? I didn't realise they grew bigger than my fingernail,' Maledream said, examining one of their bony, yet furry, severed heads.

'I guess we learned something new, and deadly, about this place,' said Angelite.

Neveah just groaned and muttered for water as he slowed his breathing. The pair learned of the Pack's demise, and there was no sign of any food left in the scattered and torn supply bags. Maledream chucked his water flask to the big man.

'Drink up. I think we'd better leave here soon before more of these things show themselves,' said Maledream.

'Wise decision,' a stranger's voice entered their minds.

'Did you just hear that?' asked the priestess, the two men nodding their reply.

'Who are you? Show yourself, I bet it's you damned Witches messing with our bloody heads. I wouldn't put it past you,' Maledream uttered loudly, heaving his sword on his shoulder and looking in all directions of the forest.

A growl was heard nearby, silencing him with a chill. They listened to the telepathic voice speak again.

'Please be calm, I mean you no harm. I am here to help you.'

'Help us? All right, come out and show yourself, whoever you are?' Maledream said, relaxing his sword arm.

Motioning to the others to stay quiet and still, they waited. A fearsome wolf leapt from the overgrowth.

'Get back,' Maledream roared, ready to swing his weapon.

'I am the voice.'

Sitting itself down, the trio eyed the feral creature.

'You're that wolf from earlier, aren't you...?' Angelite stuttered.

'Yes, I am that wolf from earlier.'

They were, understandably, a bit surprised that the voice came from an animal. Maledream glanced behind him to see the frightened priestess hiding behind the Pack leader's bulky form. Neveah glared at the large animal as he got back up on his feet.

'It was me who warned you with my howls that your friend was in need of assistance. He could have fallen if you had not of reached him in time. Those Vasps can kill with their stings in a matter of minutes. It's good you weren't stung,' said the wolf.

'Vasps?' Maledream frowned, curiously striding closer with the other two in tow.

'Yes, they aren't merely insects, they're gross mutations.'

'How the hell can that mutt speak to us?' Neveah mocked.

'I'm a wolf, not a mutt,' it growled, his tone of voice not amused by the remark.

'This place gets weirder by the minute,' Neveah grunted.

'He looks so cute!' Angelite said, finding the courage to move closer to stroke the large wolf.

'You three must follow me if you would like to reach N'Rutas. We don't have time to waste. We must hurry before more return.'

'N'Rutas? All right, if you say so,' Maledream nodded.

'Wait, how the hell can we trust this mutt?' Neveah muttered.

'I'd rather follow him than wait for more of these awful Vasps to come back!' replied the priestess.

'Aye, guess you got me there,' Neveah sighed.

Maledream holstered his blade, 'let's get going then.'

'Bah, just when I was relaxing,' Neveah groaned, stretching his body and muscles in every place imaginable from the exhaustion.

'More running I suppose,' said Angelite.

'I guess we could just walk quickly,' Maledream smirked.

With one last check that they had everything, the three adventurers set off and followed the wolf northwards.

'I'll be taking you through a safer area. There are some places here that even the Witches can't claim because of evil taints,' spoke the wolf, his form elegantly trotting beside the priestess.

Darkness seemed to cover this part of the great, northern forest as they waded further in. The smell of pollen floated on the air, and the occasional hum of wings droned above the canopy.

'So, wolf, just to break the ice a little, do you have a name?' asked the Tribal.

'Indeed, my name is Silver.'

'Silver, quite a catchy name to match your fur,' Maledream jested.

'Yes, indeed it is...' Silver replied in monotone.

Legs and feet ached as the trio was led up and down steepened, brambly areas until they reached the edge of the darkened forest. The three, profusely sweating humans, followed Silver down the last of the steep slopes. The sound of rushing water echoed from around the bend of a rocky cliff face.

'Are we almost there?' asked the priestess, before shrieking and covering her mouth as another drone of wings resounded on the breeze.

'We won't be if you don't keep it down, woman,' Neveah cussed, watching his footing carefully, too, as they descended.

Silver leapt down effortlessly, bounding from one rocky ledge, to another, twisting and turning through the air easily, whilst the trio struggled to keep their grip. Maledream found the going very difficult as he constantly slipped in his shoddy boots.

'It's just around the corner. You'll know what to do and how to reach N'Rutas, as I'm sure the Witches instructed last night.'

The group finally reached the bottom of the slope, wiping the mud and leaves stuck to their footwear as they did so. The Tribal looked around, but he could not spot their new companion.

'Great, I think he's disappeared,' Maledream huffed, the other two staring about in confusion.

'You're right, where did he go?' Angelite quizzed.

'Aye, strange mutt,' Neveah muttered.

'Any idea on what he was, Angelite?' asked the Tribal.

'Not in the slightest. He's the first of his kind I've ever met, his unique thought-waves are something else, too,' she said.

'You're telling us. Anyway, forget about that mutt for now. We have to move and find this N'Rutas before more of those bastard-insects come back,' Neveah said, wiping his sweaty brow.

'I hear you on that one, let's get moving,' Maledream nodded.

Chapter Nine

Anunaki Council

Thousands of blood-red and black candles illuminated the triangular Council Chamber. A meeting was gathering. The race of the Anunaki, whom lived within great catacombs and deep underground cities, were high on the hot aroma of sulphur. Staring down at council from above were seats of power, obelisks of great Anunaki Kings and Queens of old in the likeness of gargoyle statues.

The chamber was gradually filling with the first political Sect of Anunaki, who wore blood-red robes and hoods that barely covered their large, bulbous craniums, and their scaly hide was of a greyish, scaly nature. They strode to their seats with purpose, like billowing spectres.

The second Sect of Anunaki that entered the triangular chamber bore robes of rich purple. Their scales were of a darker texture than that of their grey kin, dark brown in contrast. This signified the age of this breed, compared to their younger grey cousins. Their eyes were oval, large, and dark, and in which reflected the thousands of candlelights as if they possessed a hidden malice.

Sitting down and conversing amongst themselves, they awaited the arrival of the Black Sect. All in the chamber speculated as to why a council had been summoned. Rumours were plenty and scattered throughout the large, candlelit chamber with an echoing chorus of dispute.

Sure enough, during various arguments between the Red and Purple Sects, the Anunaki of the Black Sect entered from the opposite end of the chamber. The presence of these powerful figureheads was felt. Their ancient, scaly hides were of the darkest shades of reds, greens, and blues, far more exotic than that of their younger cousins.

Bearing gold rods of power with golden snakes intertwined up the shafts, and wearing robes of the darkest silks, they truly looked like creatures from an abyss. They bore on their foreheads a third eye that burned with hazy, orange auras. It took hundreds of years of service to the Royalty to obtain such a token of respect and power. Their original eyes were gouged out, their eyelids soldered shut and, unlike their Red and Purple Sect brethren, sported horns protruding from their bulbous skulls that measured over a metre in length.

Mass hysteria was building in the council chamber, rumours quickly circulated that Relic Weapons had been rediscovered. Wild accusations and conspiracies flew from one end of the chamber to the other.

'Before her Royal Highness enters, I would like to discuss the seriousness of this matter...' echoed the voice of Ganzath, leader of the Purple Sect, amidst the voices of the six hundred council members that quietened down.

'This weapon has great power, as we all know and, from the reports through the void, it is a Cattle who possesses it. We must discuss how to take back such a cursed weapon,' he hissed.

'Your words are weak, Ganzath,' shouted the red-robed leader, Tunzuulizh, causing most in the Council Chamber to listen amidst the continued outburst. 'Every single one of us here knows that we must attack, attack, attack, and take back what is rightfully ours. Forget this weapon for now, for all you know it is just an old story. Mythic weapons created by the cursed Creators in ancient days. Pathetic. It has no meaning to our magnificence in the here and now!'

Yet more squabbling between the factions ignited faster than an inferno, the halls barely kept the echoes to a minimum.

'What does the most revered Black Sect have to say? This information cannot be wrong. It is a lost Relic

Weapon! We must take it!' exclaimed Ganzath, hissing his forked tongue towards Tunzuulizh of the Red Sect.

'Enough!' echoed the thirty-three Black Sect in unison.

The fear from the two lower Sects was duly heard and felt. The entire chamber fell silent. One member of the Black Sect stepped forth into the centre of the grand council hall, slowly and elegantly striding with a bemused expression etched on his brow.

'Who is that, Lord Tunzuulizh?' a relatively new Sect member whispered.

'That's Quetolox, Initiate. Can you feel his power? It is strangulating, is it not? He is the oldest living Anunaki, and they say he is over a thousand years old,' Tunzuulizh quietly hissed, the Initiate nodding in turn with a scared rasp.

Quetolox, leader of the Black Sect, glanced in all directions with a slow, orange-glowing rhythm beating in his one eye. His ceremonial staff clunked on the marble floor with echoing thuds, and his one eye glittered like gold dust from the thousands of candle flames as he took residence in the centre of the great council hall.

Robes, drenched with silver and gold jewellery, draped from his tall, slender form from many ancient treasures of the surface world, which were also intertwined with exotic, colourful feathers of ancient birds that were centuries old and well-preserved. It almost seemed like he was of royal stock. He is the most trusted servant of the royal bloodlines, whom regularly sought his council. No one dared dispute his wisdom without careful, calculated thought. Scanning the room, he hissed his forked tongue and relished the feel of the heat against his ancient, multi-shaded hide.

'Before we speak of such matters in front of her Royal Highness, I command you all to watch what you say, as always. She doesn't like ill news,' he spoke aloud with a deep, echoing voice, his one eye glowing with a red haze for but a moment.

'We've captured some Cattle on the outskirts of the large woodland maze. That is a known fact. However, any rumours of a lost Relic Weapon have no backing, as of yet,' he added.

Some of his audience was confused by these words. Some were convinced that the rumours were true. However, it would be madness for anyone to question the Black Sect for fear of being unfavoured.

'We know what's good for all of you. For your security,' he hissed, licking his scaly lips. 'However, what we do know is that some Cattle still live fighting each other in ruined cities, or even in the wilderness. What we also know is that some Cattle are connecting with higher, dimensional energies. These are our main targets. We must not let them unlock their sleeping powers since the birth of our glorious Dark Age.'

Whispers were heard across the entire hall in controversy over the news.

Quetolox continued. 'Some of us here know about the secrets of blood. To even think that these Cattle can share our power is, well, quite unfathomable to say the least,' he sighed. 'However, it's true, the alliance we had once shared with their ancient ancestors. I don't like speaking of them, but it must be stated. These Creators, the highborn equivalent of the common Cattle we have today. Back in ancient times, our species mixed with their blood to create the Nephilim. Blood can be unlocked by any means given it the right symphony or note, lesser brethren. There are members of the mixed race on the surface, but they have chosen to ally with the Cattle, using their composition to stay hidden from us. They, as far as we know, are few in number and always have been, yet they, too, are our targets. They cannot be allowed to pass on dangerous knowledge to these Cattle, for it will have dire consequences for our security.'

He paused, bashing the butt of his staff into the marble flooring to intimidate his audience, to put an end to some whispers. Quetolox was known to all the Sects for repeating his history lessons in the chamber.

'Of course, this mixing of blood was a mistake and hasn't been allowed since the Dark Age. However, the damage was done, and I will tell you all that we of the thirty-three Black Sect will look after you, so there's nothing to worry about,' he hissed.

Quetolox's eye scanned the council room slowly. 'Now, for other matters to speak of. Ah, yes, as I mentioned before, we found some wandering Cattle in a fallen forest. They will be brought before us later, just before the great feast with the Queen. For now, they're being pleasantly tortured for information regarding these false rumours of any such weapons.'

Ganzath was angered at these words. 'I don't believe it!' he shouted, slamming his bony hands on the marble table. 'We have heard of reports that it was used on one of our most victorious battlefields, and that it split the dark clouds open.'

Quetolox gazed at Ganzath, leader of the Purple Sect. His scaly hide winced around his one eye in anger. 'As I understand the situation, this was not a Relic Weapon that could do such a thing. There was too much ionic activity to get a clear image from our Blood Adepts. However, we do have several images from the feedback before it was cut off by an unknown presence. This I shall share with you now, to put to an end any conspiracies, as I decrypt the information before all of you.'

Quetolox gestured his hand and, at once, ancient marble doors slammed open from the entrance of the chamber, revealing a flat monitoring screen that defied gravity. Levitating forth into the central hall, it was pushed by several small, grey Anunaki, dressed in white lab coats.

The screen was made of pure quartz crystal, while the edges were adorned with many smaller crystals, mainly amethysts, which were connected by a form of crystalline wires and conduits. It was heavily decorated with dangling gold and silver chains.

Placing the screen in the centre, near Quetolox, the Anunaki lab-coats pushed several switches. Instantly, the large screen floated high into the air above the leader of the Black Sect, so all in the hall could see.

'I will decipher the psychic images stored within the crystalline data-banks by our elite Blood Adepts,' Quetolox uttered, wetting his scaly lips with his forked tongue.

He rolled his large eye untoward the monitor. Crackling static broke the silence of the chamber as the screen activated. Ions hummed with fast, upbeat rhythms across its surface as Quetolox linked his mind to it.

'It's close, very close. Ah, yes. This is all we have, a short clip of these Cattle fighting mere creatures of the void, which I shall play for you now,' Quetolox hissed.

The whirring came to a stop, replaced by a sound like a flock of angry birds, mixed with interference like radio waves. A holographic image shot down out of the screen. The Sects watched a small part of the battle, whereby Angelite Rose fought off three of the shadows. The vision skipped. They saw her use her staff to open the heavens. The image quality was terrible, and it was hard to make odds and ends of what the council saw.

'Wait, there's something... else... Something I've missed?' Quetolox frowned.

The breaking news had many council members fiercely gripping their seats. Their eyes strained at the holographic images for any hidden meanings.

'The staff that breeder wields...'

The images flickered through, back and forth, rewind, play, rewind, play. Quetolox was certain he was missing something.

'There!' shouted Ganzath, causing Quetolox to pause on a certain frame in the image. 'It's blurry, but, as you can all see, it's a blade firing forth Resonance across the battlefield!'

Tunzuulizh raged with his own Red Sect's opinion.

'What excrement! Don't you know anything? It is ionic interference, you complete idiot. Your conspiracy theories do you no favours, Ganzath. You are imagining things. All you can see are energy bolts from the staff that the breeder wields. As Lord Quetolox has already stated, these are targets for extermination, nothing more.'

The hall was a mass riot of opinions from every Sect member. Tempers were heating.

'I'm more concerned about that female breeder. Whoever crafted that staff, whoever it was... there is a traitor in our ranks. Such knowledge could only be possessed by us, or possibly... a Nephilim,' Quetolox's voice boomed above them all.

Many Council members fell silent. Many wondered who it was among them that had betrayed them. Such was the growing paranoia in the chamber.

Quetolox continued to enlighten. 'Crystal minerals are a valued commodity, and are, of course, the most abundant resource that this planet has to offer. Crystals are the sacred substance that links the dimensions. This is why the Cattle can be especially potent adversaries when using such objects, such as channelling the ethereal energies. Thankfully, there are only a handful of Cattle that can channel such Resonance. However, she, that breeder... We must follow her steps, and see if she is related to any more Cattle that we do not know about on the surface. When we have our chance, we will annihilate them. That breeder will be sacrificed to our Royal Highness. Her blood will be drained to satisfy our thirst, and her supple, weak flesh will be served as a grand banquet,' Quetolox laughed, stamping his staff on the marble flooring, and enjoying his thought of the blood-soaked ritual.

The Council Chamber erupted with cackles or sinister grins. They, too, dreamed of the power and illumination of sacred knowledge that would be granted for the capture of such humans.

'So then, what is our first priority? Do we send our Blood Adepts to the last known location in the void in order to find them?' Ganzath forwarded to the council.

Tunzuulizh responded, 'we need an army! We need to assemble the once-great army of the Dragon Elite. That is, by far, our only way to achieve complete dominance and victory. Wasting time with spies in the void can be a long process. We don't have any more time to waste.'

Both the Red and Purple Sects started bickering amongst themselves once more. All suggested a solution. Quetolox continued to scan the data entries stored in the quartz crystal. He couldn't work out why, but he thought something was still missing.

'We don't have the power to summon such an army that size without the permission of new breeding initiatives. To produce such a hungry elite that you speak of, Tunzuulizh, would require vast resources, which are pushed as they are! In case you have forgotten, the vast and last army of the Dragon's Elite turned mad because of flaws in our DNA Engineering. They consumed far too much energy and, in turn, burned themselves out to the point of death. Others have ended up carrying plagues, or have just turned into mad, gibbering wrecks,' raged Ganzath.

'You know not what you speak of, fool...' Tunzuulizh argued, whilst Ganzath continued over him.

'You know they do not age due to the extensive stem cell activity in their brains and spinal columns. The ones that are left straddle the surface and are the last remnants of these soldiers, which are now hundreds of years old. While it is useful that they continue hunting the annoying Cattle, they now only serve themselves in madness or until they are killed. They are next to useless. To send another army of that size is impossible. We do not have the resources to support such a vast army, before or after victory. Until more research is done with the possibility of a renewable, biological fuel for such a new type of soldier, then your idea is idiocy.'

Tunzuulizh knew Ganzath spoke the truth, but decided to enlighten him.

'I do not doubt your *old information*, Ganzath. However, we have made many breakthroughs where we can program the DNA to draw in the infinite, dimensional energies by harnessing the potential of light-matter coexisting with Resonance that are, in turn, linked to the cells of every living organism. Once we have refined this technique, you can all expect an army that can never die of old age, or consume themselves in any other way. This is the renewable energy source that we can use to program our future generations, and it is almost a reality. Then we can start to colonise other worlds, thus increasing our expansion for her Royal Matriarch!' Tunzuulizh roared with the echoes of his Red Sect behind him.

'Anything the Red Sect has promised is a farce, much like your face, Tunzuulizh! This isn't the first time you've promised us something new,' Ganzath fiercely snarled.

'New ideas for plans and initiatives is what we're meant to come up with to better our kind. Unlike your Purple Sect, the Red Sect actually gets on with some work,' Tunzuulizh laughed.

'Work... Don't even make me spew my bile, or even laugh for that matter,' Ganzath spat.

'You have no guts, Ganzath. Since you have gained leadership of the Purple Sect, you have turned it into a sickly parasite. Your Sect has done nothing but turn down improvements in the aid of progress under your administration. As soon as conspiracies about mythical Relic Weapons spring-up, you're all over the subject, voicing your excrement...' Tunzuulizh paused.

'What are you trying to say?' Ganzath rasped.

'That you're traitorous scum!' Tunzuulizh spat.

The council exploded in an uproar. Ganzath quietened the chamber with what he uttered next.

'We must act, you are right. Nevertheless, going to war and taxing our precious resources cannot be the only option available to us. If we discovered a new Cattle civilisation, then yes, perhaps a new army is required. But they are so scattered and leaderless that they are almost pointless sparing the energy for...'

'Get on with it, I tire quickly of this,' Tunzuulizh interrupted, the Red Sect mocked and laughed.

'Tunzuulizh, what you're referring to is the great army that actually failed before we crushed the Cattle to near extinction. Let me remind you of our history on how we used the ocean insects under vast mind control programs to help squash any resistance, and how we judged the right moment to strike with all our resources. That is when we first used the half-breeds, the Nephilim, inside their governments to create infighting, instability, miscommunication, and misdirection, worldwide. All of that succeeded brilliantly compared to the Dragon's Elite once they were exhausted. After the great victory, we had no need for either the Nephilim or the neo-soldiers that you want to reignite,' he finished, feeling the lesson was a good reminder.

Quetolox shuddered as he delved deeper into the hologram. The ghostly visages of every action, and moment, were sifted through repeatedly. He was close to what he wanted and, at any moment, he would break the news to the rest of the Council. He chose to speak about the current matter at hand.

'Yes, using the Nephilim was a mistake. I am the oldest living Anunaki here and I saw it firsthand. The rebel Nephilim decided to join with the Cattle. They learned of our pure-strain plan, and chose to hide in fear of being purged. That is why we cannot risk such contamination again. It upset the royalty for hundreds of years. We are right in that we need to act. However, we must be patient. If we're wrong this time, then we'll have more than Resonance-wielding Cattle to worry about.'

Discussion was still high, along with the Council's appetite to learn more.

'What about hunting for any traitors? We cannot allow any newer technology to be made public as it could be leaked to the surface. We need to keep it all a secret if we're going to keep one hand above the Cattle and pull the strings first,' Ganzath uttered, raising his hand and pointing his scaly, pasty finger at all Anunaki in the chamber.

'We need to form a strategy. An offensive plan is what's needed. We all know this, just accept it,' Tunzuulizh urged with his war mantra.

Quetolox siphoned through the data at a faster rate, deciphering all barriers that had hidden abstract meanings as if he were one with the Crystalline-Pathways. The Anunaki lab-coats monitored the flow of information on smaller, hand-held quartz screen panels, which monitored Quetolox's mental levels. Their instruments crackled with a form of arcane power as they moved their fingers across similar images on the panels they held. They were more like ants then reptiles by the way they moved, interacting with the devices in synchronised fashion.

Now was the moment to break the news.

'I have intercepted a vision, right before the Resonance swept forth across the battlefield,' Quetolox hissed with agitation, 'I will relay the findings now...'

The hologram crackled to show what happened, and the thought waves of the recording were carried on the air through tinny speakers scattered throughout the chamber.

'... the power... elements, use... energy of the... use the... beating drums.'

All Sects racked their brains trying to understand what this could mean. Quetolox uttered with an echoing tone, 'I have narrowed it down to a Cattle who had this vision. Its name is Maledream. I will need the translating thought-formers to go over these words in the laboratory banks. I'm afraid I can't decipher all this babble myself,' he said, then suddenly, his eye glowed crimson.

'What's this? This can't be,' he roared.

His rage distorted the holographic image that was unfolding before his eye. Thousands of candles blew themselves out and reignited as Quetolox could hardly contain his demonic fury. Many in the hall froze in terror from any backlash, whilst the Black Sect members merely sat emotionless and still in their seats.

'May I ask what it is, my Lord?' Tunzuulizh quaked, unquestionable fear underlying his tone, his forked tongue rapidly hissing.

Quetolox's power could be seen. An abyssal aura briefly flickered around his being. This now worried some of the Black Sect, who shuffled uncomfortably in their seats.

'It can't be... It is a lost Relic Weapon, and after all this time,' he hissed.

Quetolox shuddered as the Anunaki lab-coats locked on the image and froze it, intensifying the holographic footage for all to see in the great council hall. Maledream could just be made out in the distorted image, using the deadly blade to great effect.

'I have seen it once before, but believed it missing. Now those Cattle have it. Nevertheless, everything will be okay, my Kin, we will capture that forgotten blade. Perhaps even present it as a gift to her Royal Highness,' said Quetolox.

Many whispers were abounding in all Sects. Ganzath stared across the hall with gleaming, reptilian eyes. He stood with an upright, arrogant posture, a smirk present on his face. Feeling defeated, Tunzuulizh withdrew to his seat for now to discuss yet more propaganda on how to undermine the Purple Sect.

Quetolox announced, 'so then, it is settled? We must do two things. Kill the Cattle and sacrifice the breeder. We cannot be hasty. There is no place they can easily hide. However, we cannot lose track of them. From the information gathered from the interrogations, we know where they were last travelling, so perhaps we should send out our Blood Adepts to find them. Once we do that, we can follow them and complete another aim, which is to discover if there are more Cattle who can wield the power of Resonance.'

Quetolox's anger subsided at his own well-thought, quick plan. He continued. 'We shouldn't worry about the blade. However, we have many more weapon variations in our vaults that can never again be touched. There is no known way to destroy these weapons but, rest assured, it is something we are always researching.'

Tunzuulizh rose out of his seat, his eyelids twitching with anger and resentment. 'What of these ancient Relic Weapons? There is no history of them, save for a few, pitiful scraps. What of the vision this Cattle experienced whilst using this potent weapon? We thought such things were stupid myths. Only now do you say they exist,' he shrugged.

'There is between twelve or thirteen such weapons to our knowledge. All look ordinary, save for a few. Within them, they posses their own life force. All are unique. Weapon smiths created them in darker days, Youngling.

And yes, I did not tell you before, as it is for your safety and security,' Quetolox hissed.

Many of the council members muttered amongst themselves about the new information. The Red Sect was still reeling from their crushing defeat in the chamber.

'Then, my Lord, please share it with us,' urged Ganzath.

'I shall. It was over twelve thousand years ago that the first mammalian civilisation sprung forth. Alliances were great and true between many races, not just the Creators or Nephilim, mind, but others, too, before we crushed them all in the name of our empire. Genetic engineering was at an all time high, and breeding programmes were well under way, showing us how we can manipulate Genesis Structures between unique races. It succeeded, and discoveries led to the creation of the Nephilim and more. They were the better days, when we, as a race, lived on the surface of this world. We were not forced underground by any great cataclysm. It was by the Creators, during the Great War, over twelve thousand years ago. There were problems with politics, sanctions on Genesis Data, and Dimensional Energy Data... you get the idea. In the end, our race was forced underground when the war ravaged the surface. It practically cost us all our technological advancements, and indeed, we have only relatively relearned of our past technologies and knowledge shortly before the turning of the recent Dark Age. The Cattle soon forgot us over the passing millennia, and that is when we used our knowledge to interbreed with the Cattle to infiltrate their research and governments a hundred and fifty years ago, much like we did over twelve thousand years ago...'

Quetolox paused as Tunzuulizh interrupted. 'Such great information, my Lord, it will indeed enlighten many here today who are not well versed in our sacred history.'

Many nodded in agreement. Quetolox continued in a calm tone.

'We teach the true knowledge, my Brethren. We must keep the faith and loyalty to the one true entity we serve, and that is her Royal Highness. I shall continue. Genesis was our secret weapon. When the time was right, we used the inferior Cattle against themselves, severing communications, and causing confusion. The time was right to send our armies out of the deep oceans and underground facilities to full effect. During this purge, Relic Weapons were utilised. Listen carefully. The Creators were great scientists and crafters, they researched many advances into Resonance and DNA and, ultimately, applied their skills to create these weapons,' he finished, stamping his golden rod on the marble floor to subdue the growing noise of the chamber.

He continued, 'they built them so that these intelligent weapons could harness the true powers of Resonance frequencies, turning the users whom wield such crafted weapons into, in all accounts, gods of destruction and creation.'

Clicking his fingers, Quetolox paused for breath whilst the Anunaki lab-coats brought over to him a chalice, poured with warm, human blood, carried on an exotic, feathered pillow. Grasping it steadily with a slight shake, his forked tongue feverishly emptied the contents. The feeling of the rich haemoglobin racing down his neck gave him a quick boost of euphoria. Many rasped their forked tongues at the sight.

'At the time, we had the dimensional technology that they needed. We wanted to trade some of this for most of their DNA advances. It was almost successful, until something went wrong. We do not have the ancient accounts to tell us what happened, exactly, but we were denied the technology that would have allowed us to forge these weapons for ourselves, before the ancient war occurred. Of course, we cannot use them due to a specific composition that we do not possess in our DNA. Only the corrupt nephilim and humans have any possibility of accessing their power because of this. Thankfully, those in the past who wielded such weapons of bane could never use them to their full, deadly potential, like the true Creator bloodlines once did. And so, when we had an outbreak or discovered such a weapon being handled by the lesser Cattle, we hunted them down.'

Tunzuulizh interrupted again, much to Quetolox's annoyance. 'My Lord, are you worried that, one day, a Cattle could harness such a Relic Weapon's limitless power?'

'Yes.'

The silence of the council broke into hysteria. Quetolox added with an echoing hiss, 'it is a possibility. I would not like to imagine the consequences of such devastation. We have all worked hard to cut down the population of the mere Cattle. Let us not allow them to rise again in vast numbers. If they were to discover how to use such weapons, unite, and assemble before us, then this would be an enormous problem. With such knowledge of Resonance and possession of Relic Weapons, they could wield vast powers incomprehensible. Knowledge is power.'

Moisture escaped Quetolox's scales, the holographic image shattered like glass and stardust once the energy feed stopped. Taking a deep breath, he stretched his fraught muscles from all the tension, before continuing to speak.

'We must not let this happen. The key to prevention is ensuring that there are no weapons to cause us problems. Another focus for our interest must be the female breeder that can wield such potent Resonance. We must discover how she could attain such knowledge, or artefacts, from the world above, with, or without assistance.'

Quetolox paused, his one eye glared around the chamber as if he were sifting through all the minds of the council members. 'Enough debate, Younglings.'

He raised his staff and, in one swoop, cracked his golden rod over a nearby Anunaki lab-coat in anger. The blow fractured its bulbous skull, killing it instantly. Its spongy grey matter spilled across the council floor. He stood on one of its large, black eyes, and continued with his plan of action.

'We'll send scouting parties to the surface immediately,' he hissed, snapping his fingers for another round of blood.

As he held out his chalice for it to be refilled by one of the Anunaki lab-coats, he continued.

'Our main objective will be to find and contain information of any such Anunaki technology or Nephilim whom still hide from us on the surface. We have many Blood Adepts at our disposal. As you all know, they are powerful in the arts of the void, and are extremely potent adversaries for these Cattle. After this assembly, the forces will be dispatched.'

Finishing with a hiss, Quetolox glanced at the remaining lab-coats. In turn, they started clearing the mess he had made. Satisfied with how the proceedings went, the

Red, Purple, and Black Sects quietly chatted about the findings.

Behind where the Black Sect was sitting, was a door like the one that the lab-coats had used to enter the room. This ancient entrance had noticeable differences in imagery. Exotic plumes of feathers, mostly blood-red in hue, were attached to its ornate, marble surface with many golden snakes adorning the door.

Many crystals were also embedded in its surface. These shimmered as the thousands of candles illuminated the great council hall. The precious stones mimicked star systems in the galaxy, each pulsating like a steady heartbeat.

Behind the door came the sound of a screech. The Queen of the Anunaki was approaching. The sound she made echoed into the council chamber with an impressive wail, almost as if she were some huge, terrifying beast of old arriving from the darkest recesses of the void.

'Quick, she's coming. Get rid of that quartz screen, get rid of it!' Quetolox ordered.

The lab-coats quickly turned off the machine and pushed it out of the hall. All fell silent as they waited for her Royal Highness to enter the triangular chamber to take her seat behind the Black Sect.

Quetolox sighed, hissing his forked tongue. *'Not long now, my Royal Highness, not long now,'* he thought, turning to stare at the royally sealed door that hummed and shook.

The exotic feathers waved from the vibrations of the quaking door. The many crystals began to glow in several colours, snaking upwards from the bottom of it, before gradually coiling up through the many crystals that represented the star constellations.

The door creaked open with a loud, bass hum and, at first, all that could be seen was the Queen's Royal Guard, who each towered over her petite form. Their muscles bulged beneath ceremonial, golden plating, etched heavily with thousands of intricate symbols, which were so small, that it was hard to distinguish an exact number.

These powerful guards looked similar to an Anunaki warrior. However, they were far more muscular and taller, and sported many horns protruding up their arms and through the gaps of the gold plates that they wore. This particular breed was rumoured to be as powerful and venerable, if not more so, than the Black Sect.

Some carried banners of royalty with many snakes and serpent gods of old, mimicking ancient battles on the fine, ceremonial velvet. They fluttered little as they advanced into the chamber with stoic and professional strides.

Fanning out behind the Black Sect, the Queen came into view. She was dressed in pure white robes. Her frail form moved as if she were a billowing phantom, swiftly taking her place behind the loyal Black Sect.

'Kneel,' Quetolox ordered, he himself kneeling down to face the Queen.

All followed his lead. Pulling back her hood, she revealed herself. Her skin was that of an albino, a trait only available in the Royal family. It is considered a godly trait among all Anunaki and, unlike the males, the young Queen sported a full length of dazzling, pure white hair that seemed to glimmer against the candles of the chamber.

Her scales were so fine that it was almost as smooth as human skin. Her facial features were elegant yet prominent, and her eyes were large and oval. If it were not for such little differences, then it would be easy to mistake the Queen, at distance, for a human breeder.

'Welcome, my Royal Highness,' Quetolox uttered with a fine tongue, and then peering up to ask her, 'how was your visit with our... allies?'

'It went well...' she said, her voice gentle.

The Queen glanced at those present in the chamber with her violet-glowing eyes. All who returned her hypnotic stare was greeted by a glow of swirling stars and galaxies pulsating deeply within them.

She continued with a hiss, 'although, many of our precious feeding grounds are almost out of stock. I hope you'll please me, Quetolox, by telling me that you have found a way to make up for the loss.'

'Yes, my Queen. We have a feast prepared and waiting for you and, upon your order, your bloodbath will be summoned forth. We have information of livestock on the surface that have found refuge somewhere in the mountains and forests. With your permission, we can start culling and breeding them for more resources,' Quetolox smirked.

'Of course, keep them in a cage. Now, I would like the feast to begin,' she replied.

He smiled, hiding his inner thoughts. 'Of course, my Queen, it is a pleasure,' he hissed.

Withdrawing from the centre of the council hall, Quetolox finally rested on his seat with the rest of his Sect.

'May the feast begin,' the Queen boomed, her voice commanding.

The doors from which Quetolox's lab-coats had retreated, once again slammed open, revealing humans stripped down to nothing but their bare skin. Regular Anunaki soldiers dragged them along by iron chains with sharp, curled spikes embedded into their ankles, wrists, and necks.

Leading the soldiers was an Anunaki called Lazzathrish the Torture Master, whom, day by day, took delight in capturing the Cattle, torturing them for information, or just inflicting pain and misery to fuel adrenaline into the meat. However, his appearance was not that of a soldier Anunaki. Instead of brandishing ornate gold or silver armour, he wore flayed human skins that were pierced on his natural horned hide. They were almost mummified on his scales, symbolising his deeply respected role.

Human blood stained the marble flooring. The few humans that struggled in their spiked chains pierced their arteries, thus spilling their life essence on the stone with gurgles or screams. The haemoglobin ran its course in-between the gaps of the cold marble, forming rich, intricate patterns and symbols that were now exposed to eyesight by red flowing streams. Screams from both male and female Cattle filled the hall in an echoing chorus of horror. It was a true nightmare for the human psyche to behold, to see hundreds more of these alien creatures in the chamber, jeering at them.

'Just look at these pathetic worms,' the Queen hissed with pleasure.

Her albino skin took on a shade of red from the blood forming in the centre of the chamber as it pooled.

'We, my dear Kin, are the rulers of this world, and if it was not for your loyalty and support, we could never have unfolded our agendas thus far,' she echoed.

Her eyes glowed, and the marble centre of the council hall collapsed in on itself with loud shunts to create a bath of congealing haemoglobin.

'Once again, I shall bathe in their blood, while the most sacred ancient ones watch over us all, so we may receive their mighty boons,' she wailed over the screams.

Pulling the last of the one hundred or so humans into the chamber by their chains, the soldiers began breaking or hacking a leg off each human to cripple them. After much bone fracturing, tearing of muscle, sinew, and flesh, more blood filled the bath.

The Queen strode past the Black Sect towards the inner-sanctum of the Council Hall, to take her place in her ritualistic ceremony.

Among the throng of victims was Pixie, one of Neveah's Packers. He was terrified, but refused to scream, even after his leg was fractured. His chains were rusty. He knew they couldn't restrain him. He hazarded a guess that the albino creature in the white robes was some sort of important person or guest.

'Just one chance at capping her. I'm going to die, so I might as well die trying.'

The large aliens that had dragged them by chains carried weapons that he was very familiar with.

'Pole-arms.'

The screams from his fellow humans was unnerving to him, but he tried to stay focused. With a broken leg, he would only have one attempt at killing the white one.

'May I bathe in the holy liquid in the presence of the Gods,' the Queen bellowed as her frail, voluptuous form strode towards the crimson pool.

Pixie felt his heart race. He finally let his burst of adrenaline flow from the anguish and fear that had filled the room.

Grabbing the chains that bound him, his muscled arms pumped and bulged. He strained for but a moment and broke the bonds that held him. Letting out a war cry amidst the mayhem, the naked Packer charged towards the nearest guard. Shoulder barging the large creature to the ground with force of weight and muscle, he ripped the pole-arm free from its back-scabbard. Swinging the weapon across the Anunaki's neck, he killed the giant reptile with one blow. His weary eyes glared straight into the pupils of the frightened Queen.

'Rot in hell, bastards,' he roared.

'One's escaped!' Ganzath shouted amongst the chorus that filled the chamber, urging the Queen to run.

'Stand together and fight!' Pixie yelled to his fellow prisoners.

Encouraged by Pixie's success, the humans fought back and dragged down the vast, large soldiers of the Anunaki to the ground in quick numbers. They ignored any wounds they had suffered. It was replaced with fury and vengeance. Guards rushed in from the great marble door, and many council members leapt off their seats and flooded towards the centre, to swamp the Cattle intent on killing their sacred matriarch.

'You're mine,' Pixie roared at the female albino.

With his muscles pumping adrenal strength, and his pores breaking sweat, he drew closer to his main target. With hands tightly gripping the pole-arm, he limped then leapt at the Queen.

'Enough!' Quetolox bellowed, his one eye burning with a crimson haze.

Suspended in mid-air, and mid-swing, Pixie was trapped by Quetolox's immense psychic power. He could only roll his bloodshot eyes.

'So close.'

Many of the soldiers began dismembering the Cattle, putting to rest any assassination attempt. The slaughter had begun, but it was unofficial, and the ceremony for the Queen was ruined.

The Anunaki Guards proceeded to eat the living flesh of the humans, biting into them as they screamed in either defiance or terror. Stomachs, hearts, and other organs were torn out of the living men and women. Those unlucky enough not to pass out from the pain witnessed their own living nightmare, as the ferocious beasts devoured them amid their echoing, gurgling screams.

The Queen was escorted from the slaughter, fear paramount that something else may threaten her life. Quetolox sighed as he glared at the naked Cattle that he held suspended with his power.

'What of this scum, my Lord, more torture? Shall I keep him alive with intravenous supplements so he can survive at his own displeasure?' Lazzathrish delightfully hissed.

'You can have all the fun you want with him. I have accessed the fool's mind, and now know all that I need,' replied Quetolox.

'As you wish, my Lord,' rasped Lazzathrish.

After surveying the gory, yet satisfying scene in the chaotic Council Chamber for but a moment, Quetolox's voice boomed to all present.

'Assemble the forces. We will act now or be damned for eternity! For the Queen!'

A cry of war sounded in the grand, bloody hall. Excitement rippled across all Sects at the opportunity to deal with the human threat.

'Thanks to you, Human, I now have the excuse I need,' Quetolox thought.

The leader of the Black Sect eyed Pixie inquisitively, before letting Lazzathrish take him back to the torture chamber.

Chapter Ten

Mysterious N'Rutas

'Well, here's the entrance,' Angelite said, standing before the one-hundred or so feet of falling water.

'I don't bloody see it, all I see is vapour,' replied Maledream.

'Aye, all they had for us to go on was *"follow your own judgement,"* or some such crap,' said Neveah.

'Come on, Boys, let's head around the sides so we don't get wet, and find a way in,' replied the priestess.

They began looking for an entrance enthusiastically and, after a while, their efforts slowed, and they wondered if this entrance existed.

'I'm stumped,' Neveah exclaimed, sitting down on a nearby damp rock to scratch his scalp, staring hopelessly at the bottom of the waterfall.

'It should be here somewhere,' said Angelite.

Nothing but weeds, roots, and ivy snaked up and in-between the cracks of the rocks as the group glared at the drenched, rocky wall.

'What signs did the Witches actually say to look for?' she turned and asked with both hands resting on her hips.

'Search us,' Neveah groaned.

'Well, that wolf seemed certain it was here,' said Maledream.

'For all we know, that wolf might be fetching the rest of his pack for a three course meal,' Neveah chuckled.

'If we can't find the clue physically, maybe we'll have to delve into the realms of the spirit?' Angelite wondered, before adding as her fingers twiddled her chin. 'It may be something that we can't see normally, so, if you two wait here a minute, I'll go and sit down somewhere more comfortable than these rocks and meditate for an answer.'

'If it's another option, then sure, just don't stray too far from us, okay? I'll keep watch along with Maledream,' replied Neveah.

The Tribal nodded at the priestess as she stared at him, her eyes changing to a shade of violet.

'How does she change her eyes?' Neveah quietly asked.

'No idea, maybe it'll be something she shares with us some time. I've only ever seen her do that when she's beginning to focus on her Resonance,' replied Maledream.

'Aye, possibly,' Neveah grunted.

They watched Angelite settle down on a dry, grassy area down river. They saw her removing the new crystals that she had acquired earlier from her bag. Holding each one up to the sun, she admired the pure, multicoloured crystal chunks that glistened and refracted the sun's rays within their cores. Then, holding one such crystal near her heart, she began to meditate.

Maledream leaned against a rock, taking off his thick, heavy coat, and other baggage, to rest more comfortably in the sweltering sun.

'Looks as if we just have to wait. Maybe that mutt will make his way back soon,' said Neveah.

'I'm sure we'll make some progress. I'm counting on Angelite to find a way,' Maledream sighed.

'Aye,' Neveah grunted, wiping the last of his sweat off his forehead with a dry rag.

'At least we can relax for a moment. This little adventure of ours is straining,' muttered the Tribal, crossing his arms behind his head, and looking blindly upwards towards the waterfall's source.

'To be honest, I need it, those bastard-bugs knackered me out. How'd they get so huge, you reckon?' Neveah wondered.

'Silver said they were a mutation or something. Don't ask me how, I'm not even sure what mutation means.

Larkham would probably know, but he isn't here, so, I can't ask.'

'Aye, at a guess, he probably meant they weren't normal, but altered in some way. I hope I never see them again. Those things were damned hard work. The deafening noise they made was unbearable to say the least, noisy shits.'

Neveah glanced over at Angelite, before nudging the Tribal to look as well.

'She's still at it,' said Maledream, smiling away at her.

'So, are you two actually a couple, then? I've not had the balls to ask this yet, but you both seem to be...'

Maledream quickly brushed in. 'No! Course not! You know the story. I only met her the other day.'

'Yeah, sure mate, whatever you say,' Neveah bellowed with laughter.

'No joking! We aren't... It's a long story, but yeah, we came across each other when I found her being attacked by one of those Anunaki. Anyway, I'm sure I've told you all of this?'

'Refresh my memory, we've got all day,' Neveah smirked.

'I won't go all the way back into it, but she does remind me of someone from long ago. It's not necessarily Angelite. It's just a very faint memory. I just can't remember, I wish I could,' Maledream sighed, scratching his rough stubble as he thought about it.

'Not sure who you mean, even if it is someone you are trying to think of when we travelled up north many years ago. I've forgotten most of them now, except for the ones close to me, of course. You were a kid that mixed with everyone back then. Feels like an age now,' Neveah sighed.

'It's been troubling me. That's why I think I'm so fond of her, even though we barely know each other, like, it's some sort of connection, which is really deep, I just can't put my fingers on it,' Maledream muttered.

'Right... deep connection and fingers... I'm afraid you won't know how deep she is until you stop using those fingers and use the real stuff!' Neveah said, barely holding back a laugh.

'Yes... no!' Maledream snapped, punching Neveah on the arm, 'full of innuendo today, aren't we.'

'Aye,' Neveah bellowed, 'perhaps it's something you need to work on, mate?'

'Seems so,' he smirked, turning to look at Neveah, 'I'll get there in the end, I suppose.'

'Aye, you sure will, keep working on your memory, it'll come back. Try not to worry about it too much. We've got a long journey ahead of us,' Neveah grinned.

'Agreed...' Maledream nodded, staring back up at the sky briefly, then back to the priestess. 'Just wish I knew more.'

Both men settled down in silence. Moments later, they were disturbed by a noise. Something was approaching. Gathering their weapons quickly, they rushed from the rocks, ready to take on any threat. A figure charged towards them over the rocky ridge.

'We're going to kill you!' screamed Crazy John.

Maledream and Neveah lost their balance at the surprise, falling backwards, and clumsily swinging their weapons away from each other as they both landed in a heap on the rocks.

'Damn you, crazy bastard!' Neveah shouted.

Maledream looked on in bafflement, and then led down on his back, groaning from the shock of hitting the hard stone. Boris appeared behind Crazy John with a smile on her face.

'You're both alive?' Neveah asked with a wide-eyed, gawping expression as he picked himself off the weathered rocks.

'Of course, although, from what we've seen back in the forest, it seems a big ruckus went down. I'm glad Pixie led the Pack in a different direction, rather them than us,' replied Boris in carefree fashion.

Neveah and Maledream just gazed at them in wonder.

'And to think, I fought extra hard to avenge you bastards, but looks like my Pack's still alive after all! What the hell happened? Why did you all bugger off this morning? Most the food and equipment was gone when we woke up. I thought you had all fucked off like a bunch of cowards,' Neveah said, his anger quickly subsiding.

'We carved arrows on tree bark to point which way we went. You should have seen them, but I guess you didn't?' Boris smirked.

'No, we didn't find any damn arrows. All I found was a bloodbath across a fucking river!' Neveah moaned.

'We left early to save some time in getting out the forest by scouting what was ahead because of the Witch's warning about leaving before noon. There was a forked path, so we split up from the main group. We didn't find much, except some old ruins. We heard gunfire from the direction Pixie led the rest of the Pack, but when we got there, we found nothing but hacked up wasps. We found some fresh tracks and followed them,' said Crazy John.

'Nice story on how you found us, but, no idea what happened to the equipment and rations, though?' asked Neveah.

'No idea, we let the rest of the Pack look after them because we were travelling light. You know our style, we don't do heavy,' answered Boris.

'Of course, what else can I expect from my best assassins? Pity we lost the provisions,' Neveah muttered.

'Yeah, I'm starving,' Maledream groaned, still lying down on the rocks.

'Aye, well, it's good to have you two back, the more company the better,' Neveah said, gripping the twosome joyfully on the shoulders with his large hands.

The group sat down, turning their stares towards the priestess.

'Wonder if she's making any progress?' Neveah asked.

'Probably, but she hasn't been the same with her powers since yesterday. She relied on her staff to do the things that she did,' answered Maledream.

'Sure saved our asses. She's some woman, even if she seems a bit weak in the arms. She's full of energy,' said Boris.

'Aye,' Neveah nodded.

* * *

Meanwhile, Angelite focused her breathing patterns and her inner energies as she connected to the Resonance of the cosmos. Moments passed as if all was becoming still and stagnant, time no longer having a bearing of age. Her mind gave way to the sensations of her body as she entered a clearing of light in the ether.

Her first vision was that of the stars and comets that raced through the void of space. Her second was that of the earth as if viewing it from high above. Everything she saw had a resonating glow, from the clouds, oceans, and mountains.

'Clearly, the Resonance of this crystal is helping. Spirits, show me a solution to my problem, please.'

A gentle voice suddenly invaded her mind.

'Kinanan Worshiphia Cunadun Valore Demanenor Kinesis.'

Then, before her third eye's sense, came an ocean from the horizon. It reached her at an impossible speed. The water swirled and changed form, morphing into the waterfall. She now saw the way to pass it.

* * *

'We've got to go, now!' Maledream bellowed, shaking her about, her eyes barely open after such a deep trance. 'The Vasps are coming, we can hear them.'

'Right, okay, give me a moment,' she returned, scrambling off the fine grass in panic.

She saw Crazy John and Boris nearby, but was short on time and merely greeted the pair with a nod.

'Everyone, follow my lead. I know what to do,' she said, eager to go before the Vasps returned.

'Right, we've got all our stuff. Do you know where the passage is?' Maledream asked, keeping his sword bound to his hands.

The humming steadily grew louder in the distance over the forest's canopy. Holding the crystal close to her heart, she chanted.

'Kinanan Worshiphia Cunadun Valore Demanenor Kinesis.'

Her words became more powerful as she continued. It felt like an age to the group as they watched the vast swarm approaching overhead. The stress of their auras could be felt, and Angelite struggled to channel even more energy from the crystal to help her.

'Spread this water, show me the path, show me the way and give us safety. Reveal yourself, hidden frame.'

With that, she stepped forward, the group watching her every move. By now, more than a hundred Vasps filled the sky, circling them in neat, hexagonal patterns. They had found their prey.

'They look pretty pissed off,' said Crazy John.

'Aye, shut the hell up. Don't know about you, but I don't plan to be the main course. I'll be damned if they're getting their pincers on my ass!' Neveah uttered.

Maledream turned to see Angelite's hair beginning to float on end, while some form of energies erupted around her feet.

Ripples formed on the river's surface with a dull, bass hum. Calmly moving the crystal away from her chest, she slowly knelt and placed it just on the skin of the water. A pale blue light shone from the crystal, rippling the river to such an extent that it disturbed the silt on the riverbed.

Shrieking, the priestess forced the Resonance through her being. The energies from the blue, pulsating crystal moved upstream at the speed of sound, creating a rift in the centre of the river like a vicious deluge until it reached the waterfall.

Winding up the wall of the rushing torrent, the Resonance reacted with it, illuminating many strange runes on the moss-covered rocks. The surrounding area trembled with power, like a small quake, parting the falling waters to reveal an entrance about halfway up its height.

'Climb and hurry,' an unknown telepathic voice uttered to the priestess.

Closing in, the noise emanating from the Vasps' wings was deafening.

'Climb!' Angelite shouted.

The group followed her through the parted river by jumping over the water's edge to reach the middle, where the silt was seemingly dry, as if no water had ever traversed the bottom of the bed.

'I'm going to break a leg trying to climb that thing with my boots,' Maledream groaned, barely able to make a sound from the humming.

As Angelite began scaling the slippery rocks, Neveah pushed the Tribal onwards with his first step, and then helped Crazy John and Boris. Following at the rear, and keeping his pole-arm ready, Neveah's bulging, spare arm helped to keep him going.

Angelite reached the mouth of the entrance, and peered into the unwelcoming darkness of the cave. She looked back down and saw Maledream in tow, followed by the others. As they progressed, the Vasps began their attack dives, and covered the once sunny area in shadow.

'By the spirits,' she gasped, horror etched on her brow.

Maledream looked down, feeling slightly nauseated from the ascension. He was slowing, and Boris and Crazy John climbed past him as he constantly slipped on the damp, uneven surfaces. Blood pumped furiously as everyone's adrenaline kicked in. Neveah caught up with the slow Tribal, trying to speed him up by pushing him faster.

'Hurry up, damn it! They're close, don't look down,' Neveah yelled.

Maledream groaned in agreement, gripping the wet and damp chunks of rock as hard as he could. Slipping and falling to his demise rested firmly in the back of his mind. The Tribal neared the top when a piercing sensation racked his ankle. Pain coursed through his nervous system in seconds, he struggled to breathe.

The Vasp latched on his torso and smothered him with its thick exoskeleton and, as it did so, tried pulling him off with its weight and furiously powerful wings. His fingers tightened on the rocks as he roared in agony. Neveah swung his weapon wide, knocking the giant beast away as he sliced through its cyclonic wings.

The large insect reeled in pain, screeching, and let go of the Tribal as it fell heavily towards the rocks. Crazy John reached down and pulled Maledream up and into the safety of the cave. He lay groaning, clutching his injury.

'Give Neveah some covering fire,' John shouted.

'Have some of this,' Boris screeched, madly grinning.

She whipped out her two large, silvery pistols, cocked them, and let loose with a hail of lead. Neveah had almost reached the entrance, followed by several Vasps out of the hundreds as the group gazed at the swarm. Crude shells pelted any droning beasts that threatened Neveah. Adrenaline pumped furiously through his bulky muscles. The bullets cut through the thick hides of the giant insects with ease, felling several of them with accurate aim. Launching up in one last go, Neveah made it to the entrance.

Clambering in, he furiously bellowed, 'fucking run!'

Neveah grabbed and dragged the Tribal with little effort as he continued clutching his ankle. Blood poured out of the cracks and holes in his footwear. Boris helped Angelite up to her feet and proceeded to pull her harshly. There was a roar at the mouth of the cave. The entrance shook and the ground trembled, sealing them in.

Silence fell in the short depths of the deep abyss once the group ventured further inside. Gradually, their ears recovered from the excessive ringing in their ears from the beasts deafening wings. They were now safe. The group lay in the dank darkness, catching their breath, and regaining some of their strength and wit.

'Looks like we made it,' Neveah said, his voice heavy and slow.

'Looks that way,' Maledream returned, wincing in throbbing pain.

'Aye... you're lucky you still have a foot, mate,' Neveah jested.

'Telling me... anyone got a light?' Maledream muttered.

'Not a problem, I've got an old one here, so long as it still works,' replied Boris.

Fumbling around, she delved into her leather pouches.

'Found it,' she said, repeatedly butting the small hand torch on the walls of the cave, until finally, the full beam switched on with a hard clunk.

'There we go. Is that alright for the rest of you?' she asked, shining the blinding torch at each of their faces as she grinned.

'Aye,' Neveah groaned, stretching his aching muscles, the light creating a ghastly silhouette of his shadow in the humid cave.

Crazy John sat silently with eyes closed, calmly breathing, and enjoying the moment of rest. Angelite stared into the darkness, trying to pierce the abyss with her vision. Turning to face the group, she felt it was her turn to speak.

'I think we should press on, N'Rutas's place must be close now.'

'Aye, let's go everyone.'

Neveah pulled Maledream up on his feet and helped carry him by the shoulder. Boris led the way with her torch.

'Looks like this cave hasn't seen much use in a long time,' said Crazy John as the group moved in single file through the tight cavern system.

'Looks it,' Neveah muttered.

'It's very peculiar,' said Angelite, her hands gently passing over either side of the cave's walls to feel every groove and damp surface.

Brightness grew at the end of the tunnel whilst cold, fresh air brushed the group's sweaty skin. As they waded deeper into the cave, it gradually widened, showing the real age of the underground network as stalagmites and stalactites grew larger until, eventually, Boris stopped on entering a huge cavern. Her light seemed to increase in strength as it refracted upon a field of glowing crystals of all shapes and sizes that jutted out of the walls, illuminating the entire cavern like a rainbow.

The group was in awe of what they saw before them. Angelite could hardly keep her excitement contained, clasping her hands together to her lips. Glowing auras of many colours took to the shadows as the group gradually inched forwards. As they moved, the flashlight continued to increase the crystals illumination of the subterranean labyrinth.

'It's beautiful, it's like these crystals have never been touched by light. They're making me feel more rejuvenated!' Angelite squealed.

'Aye, even I'm starting to feel like my old self again, being surrounded by these bright stones,' replied Neveah.

'Crystals, Neveah! Crystals! Not stones!' Angelite corrected him.

'Alright, woman, calm down,' Neveah heartily chuckled.

'It's a sight to behold, though,' Boris nodded.

'I think I preferred the woods,' Crazy John said with a patronising grin.

'Say that again and I'll boot your ass back outside,' Neveah muttered.

Water that escaped from the cracks in the rocky ceiling trickled down the stalagmites and filled various pools of pure mineral water. After wading deeper into the huge cavern, Angelite stopped the group to inspect Maledream's wound.

Neveah laid him on the ground as he winced in agony. Angelite took off his boot. Her nostrils twitched instantly at the unnatural stench. It was so bad that it even cancelled out the fresh air that flowed through the caves.

Neveah just grinned and bared it as he looked at the festering sting, which spewed nothing but pus. His veins had taken on a sickly, green tinge that slowly ran its course up his leg. Maledream could barely keep his eyes open. It seemed he was now unaware of his surroundings.

'I feel like I'm on fire,' he muttered, sweat dripping from his forehead.

'You need to rest, mate,' Neveah frowned.

'He needs more than rest,' Angelite thought, peering at the crystalline pools. 'Bring him this way and put him in the water. This'll help him, he's been poisoned,' she added with haste.

'Aye, come on, mate. Watch your step now,' Neveah uttered.

'I don't... feel too good...' Maledream gasped.

'Just hang in there, you'll be fine. I'm lowering you into the water now, all right?'

Neveah's strong arms helped Maledream into the pool of glowing water. The group watched in silence to see what Angelite could do. Withdrawing the crystal she had used for her spell to open the cave's entrance, she uttered her Resonance and used what little energy she had left to try to cure the poison in his bloodstream.

The Tribal took off his heavy coat and let it fall to one side. He also unlatched his shoddy scabbard and the blade fell loosely into the pool as his strength failed him and, as he did so, the symbols on the weapon's broad surface illuminated as it slipped into the water.

'That's odd,' Neveah grunted.

'It's like the sword's reacting with the crystals...' Angelite muttered, watching the crystals in the vicinity respond almost instantly to the blade. 'I think it must because it's linked or linking with them.'

Maledream slipped further into the pool.

'The water... it's warm...' he groaned.

The ancient blade let out a ringing noise as it was submerged, humming with power and life as it seemingly connected with its owner.

'I'm going to try healing him,' Angelite said, dunking her hands into the pool.

Golden and green energies began to glow and flow from the palms of her hands. Angelite's eyes widened and her pupils dilated.

'I'm not the only one healing him...' she murmured.

'How do you mean?' Neveah asked, raising his eyebrow.

'I can feel his sword is somehow healing him, perhaps because he is injured, but not because Maledream has control of it. It must be because the crystals are singing to the sword, and in turn, it's singing back, like they're a set of musical instruments communing with one another, like the crystals are hitting a certain sequence or notes to activate that power,' she said.

'You mean like back at the battlefield?' Neveah wondered, watching the runes on the sword glow almost in sync with the crystals in the cavern.

'Sort of, like it mimics the state of being of the person carrying it. It needs Resonance to activate, but it only does it on certain frequencies, it seems. I've seen it glow a dark crimson back at your old place, and, before that, he seemed to use it to devastating effect on an Anunaki,' she nodded.

'Aye, he mentioned something about a bastard-lizard,' Neveah concurred.

'Yep, he moved as fast as a lightning bolt when he struck it down. At the time, I was healing him from the vicious attacks, but it seemed my powers also awakened some of the swords potency.'

'Hmm,' Neveah grunted.

'I couldn't care less, it's still a powerful weapon either way, even if it does look ancient and deceiving,' said Crazy John.

* * *

The conversation around Maledream faded to faint echoes as he verged on losing consciousness.

'You wielded me once before, Maledream, and once before you unlocked me, and once again you can unlock me,' a female voice uttered. *'We are connected.'*

He felt a humming sensation in his palm, his hand still gripping the hilt of the blade. The sensation of weightlessness was overpowering. Colours dashed in soft, flowing lines. The song and chorus of the voice soothed his body and spirit. The burning sensation in his ankle faded. He opened his eyes to see green and golden energies racing in front of him, dancing on the surface of the water. The Tribal saw more symbols on the blade's surface. They seemed familiar in some way, like some distant memory.

* * *

'I feel... better,' he uttered strongly, eyes flicking open.

'Thank the spirits, you're all right,' Angelite smiled, her hands gliding to Maledream in the pool to hug him.

'Thanks,' he said, letting out a long-drawn sigh.

'Aye, by the looks of it, you're healed up,' Neveah said, patting him hard on the back.

'Let's get you out before you catch a cold next,' said the priestess with a grin.

Maledream put the sword back into its rough, shoddy scabbard. Piece by piece, he took off his clothes to dry them.

'Look at that, you skinny runt! Not a muscle on your scrawny body,' Neveah uttered with a cruel laugh.

Maledream was indeed a lot thinner than what his baggy clothes suggested. The Tribal merely stuck his middle finger up at the brute and smiled in retaliation. After a long rest, and once Maledream adequately dried his clothing and armour, the group got ready to move.

'We might as well press on then...' Crazy John uttered in monotone, before he was interrupted by peculiar, echoing laughter deeper inside the cavern system.

'What the hell was that?' asked Boris.

'Sounded like something is close to dying up there,' replied Maledream.

Neveah said no words and cracked his knuckles together.

'Me and John should investigate first,' Boris suggested.

'Not going to happen. We're safer in numbers. No telling what that was,' Neveah said, bracing his weapon.

Maledream finished donning his damp clothes and boots and, with a swift nod, Neveah began to lead the way down the passage. The cackling echoed continuously over short periods once they had made their way further into the brightly lit cavern.

Turning a corner, they stumbled upon an old woman. They knew they had found the source of the cackling. Her features were wrinkly and weathered, so much so that it was impossible to see any real detail as she stared at the group with a gentle smile. She was small in stature at a mere five foot. Her robes were brown and tatty, whilst her hood covered her unkempt, straggly white-hair.

'Are you N'Rutas?' Neveah asked, scratching his scalp.

'I am indeed N'Rutas, my Child...' the hag said, coughing.

'We were sent by the Witches in the forest,' the Tribal added.

'So it seems, young ones. Forgive me for all the hiding and secrets of this place, there's many things I hide from to stay safe,' N'Rutas said, her tone playful.

'Even though we risked death just by finding this little cave of yours?' Neveah grunted, eyeing the old crone with suspicion.

'It appears so, but my messenger has already given me all the details, so relax,' cackled the old hag, before turning her attention to the Tribal and priestess.

'You must be Angelite with that red-hair. And I know what you seek, young woman,' she said, limping closer towards her.

N'Rutas reached for Angelite's backpack and, plying it carefully free from her shoulder, stared into her eyes.

'The remains of your staff is one that I had crafted long ago, if you didn't already know?' she said, peering into the bag to see the dusty fragments of the oak and crystal.

'I didn't...' Angelite replied, her words barely escaping her gawping, confused expression.

The comment also stirred eyebrows in the group.

'What a strange woman,' Maledream thought.

Both he and Neveah looked at the others while shrugging.

'By any rate, this staff has served its purpose well. Anyway, Children, I shall tell you more once we have reached my hut and have fed your growing bodies. I can sense hunger festering in you. Follow me, and I shall stuff you all up!'

'You hear that everyone? Food!' Neveah bellowed childishly.

With a nod, the old hag led the group through the glowing, twisting, cavern system. While the others looked forward to fresh food, the priestess took her side by the mysterious N'Rutas.

'Did you know we were coming all along?' Angelite asked.

'But of course, Priestess, I have many ways like the Witches,' N'Rutas cackled, her body shifting back and forth as she did so.

'Then again, that shouldn't surprise us. You lot always seem to talk without opening your gobs. I don't understand it,' Crazy John muttered.

'You're quite lucky, my Children, not much longer until you reach Meridia. Anyway, where are my manners? I will tell you what this place is. Ahead of us used to be one of the largest volcanoes at the turn of the Dark Age. I took refuge here at the start of it, and turned this volcano around after it fell dormant. It's a basin paradise that I transformed and filled with rich fauna,' she said, cackling at her own expertise.

'That you transformed?' Angelite asked, almost in disbelief.

'You'll see, Child,' N'Rutas assured.

Slowly, the group followed this strange and eccentric old woman as she continued to speak. Angelite was constantly on the heels of N'Rutas, noting down anything important that was uttered. The group gradually approached the light at the end of the complex cavern system. After travelling through the refreshing, crystalline passages, they all had a renewed vigour about them.

Fresh mountain air brushed through the ranks as N'Rutas led them into her home, and, on exiting the lava duct, they entered the mountainous, volcanic glade. The group stopped in awe at the beauty of the place. Lush grasses, open fields, flowers, trees, and other such foliage stretched far towards the horizon.

Birds flew in the sparse, misty clouds that populated the ocean-blue sky. In the distance, they noticed that the sides of the circular basin reached further into the heavens, encapsulating the glade as if it were a barrier of rock. So large was the round glade that the sides of the volcano looked like far away mountains that ringed its circumference. Cairn stones, with runes pulsating on their surfaces, dotted the landscape and hummed with variations of colour, and chimed many faint sounds.

'I can't believe you've conserved some of the rarest animals, N'Rutas! Most of these species are thought to be extinct back in Meridia, how did you manage it?' Angelite exclaimed, seeing many varieties in the distance.

'Mind over matter, Priestess. If I were to tell you, I would be here all day. And you lot need feeding, so perhaps later,' N'Rutas smiled.

Chapter Eleven

Artefacts and Knowledge

The mysterious hag led the way through a slightly forested area towards the destination of her home. Reaching her hut, N'Rutas opened the oaken door with a subtle push, its iron hinges moaned against the old, wooden framework. Enriched herbs surrounded her home. Crushed crystalline fragments were strewn like fine sand at the stems, serving to enhance the growth of the plants like fertilizer.

'Please make yourselves at home. I'll whip you up something very soon. I hope you're all vegetarians?' N'Rutas wondered, scuffling inside and waving the others to follow.

'I fancy some meat, to be honest. Vegetables give me the shits,' Neveah grumbled.

'That's fucking disgusting,' Boris sneered.

'I agree, don't say such things, Neveah, you're being impolite,' Angelite added with a harsh frown.

'Aye, sorry,' Neveah chuckled and grinned, although, when he glanced at both men, he saw they agreed with silent smirks.

'I know what's good for you, young ones, this food is healthy enough to keep an army going for weeks,' N'Rutas replied with a firm tone.

'That will be fine, thank you kindly,' Angelite replied, smiling at the old hag.

'Now that's manners. Please sit down, make yourselves comfortable, and rest. Those crystals in the cave can dull your physical senses, somewhat, making you feel stronger in the short-term, when in fact you are as tired as sin! So rest, Children, I'll be back at dusk,' N'Rutas grinned.

The old hag left the group in the hut, shutting the door subtly. Most of them were happy to rest, but Angelite wandered around, keen to learn how N'Rutas lived. She saw mortars and pestles strewn all over one table in the corner, surrounded by ground crystals and herbs that littered the floorboards. Many variations of glass bottles were also present, filled to the brim with glowing liquids.

'Is it me, or does this place look bigger in here than it did from outside? It also looked shoddy,' said Boris.

'Aye, it does look shoddy, woman, but from the looks of it outside, and from what I've seen around this place, I wouldn't be surprised if this thing could withstand ten thunderstorms all at once,' Neveah laughed.

Crazy John peered outside the ancient glass windows, focusing on the deer and other meaty creatures that were grazing just a few metres away. He seemed unsure if he could wait for N'Rutas to come back with just vegetables and fruit.

'Don't any of you feel slightly cheated looking at this place?' asked Crazy John.

'Maybe slightly,' Boris nodded.

'I think we'll all feel more of that once we reach Meridia,' Maledream replied, sitting down on a rickety, wooden chair and resting his arms behind his head.

'I reckon so, and it'll sure beat killing back in the city,' said Neveah.

'That would be a shame,' replied Crazy John.

'Drag us down with your pessimism and there will be problems,' Maledream muttered, his eye flicking open to stare at the assassin.

'Calm it down before I hit both of you. I want no fighting, had enough of that shit back in the city. Keep your dark thoughts to yourself, John. Maledream, don't rise to him,' Neveah said, his tone firm.

An awkward moment of silence fell on the group as all eyes stared about the hut.

'This place has a strong aura about it. I suppose the pungent smell of herbs adds to its charm,' Angelite said, going off topic.

'Aye, it could do with a fire, but there doesn't seem to be anything we could use to burn, except the hut, but I think the old hag would add our fruit to her veg,' Neveah heartily chuckled.

Angelite stopped exploring N'Rutas's home. She remembered the old books she had retrieved from the library, so sat down at one of the oaken desks on the far side of the hut. From what she could decipher, there was a time human nations from all continents had been at peace before the Dark Age. She sighed as she studied the writing, immersing herself with the languages of old.

Taking a break, the priestess turned to stare at the resting party. Then, she glanced at Maledream's sword as it lay next to him. It was then that Angelite noticed that there were strange objects suspended in mid-air, just above the Tribal. The orbs resembled the planets of the solar system. Each one was crafted from various, colourful crystals, which hung from the poison ivy that crept through the gaps of the thatched ceiling. Squinting at the spheres, she recalled the names of each planet, while noting their formations.

'She's an intelligent woman,' she muttered, staring at the centre of the orbit of all the planets where the sun should be.

Instead, there was only a large, pure, quartz crystal latched in place by thin, taut string. Peering at N'Rutas's other wooden benches, Angelite spotted some very old maps. As she strode closer, she saw different star constellations on several of them, which noted positions on certain parts of the world. Very peculiar drawings of the earth's continents from other maps were of great interest to the priestess.

'The world's continents were tectonically changed. Could this be a map of the old world that I hoped to find in the library?' she asked herself.

She gazed at some new maps created by the mysterious hag, as if she had pieced together old ones to form what the world looks like now. Suddenly, the priestess felt a hand lightly grip her shoulder, startling her.

'Find my work interesting, dear?' N'Rutas grinned.

'Yes, yes... very,' Angelite sighed in relief.

N'Rutas shifted to her side, uttering, 'I have been alive for hundreds of years, dear.'

Angelite paused in her reply. An old woman who is hundreds of years old? Her eyebrows rose in curiosity.

'*It isn't possible, unless...*' she thought, replying, 'that couldn't mean... you're a Nephilim?'

N'Rutas peered into Angelite's eyes, and slyly morphed her pupils to that of a reptile's, before shifting them back to their human forms. The priestess almost shrieked, she clamped her mouth and bit her lower lip.

'Yes, you're a bright one. I can see why your mentors can't wait to see your full potential, Priestess. However, don't run before you can walk. You still have many decades left. I am what you would call a half-breed. Although, I prefer my old human form to that of my scaly hide. I find that I chaff in odd places,' N'Rutas cackled.

'So, you're an Anunaki, as well as Human?' Angelite pursued.

N'Rutas smiled warmly. 'Yes, although there are only a few of us remaining.'

'But, why couldn't I sense that in you, N'Rutas? I've encountered an Anunaki before, and it had a certain aura about it.'

'My dear, it's because I have the best of both worlds. Both shun me, of course. However, there is still prejudice lingering in many human souls, and so I stay here. I only visit Meridia when the need arises. The last time I travelled to your city, I dropped off that wooden staff for you, Child, because I knew we would meet today. That was... hmm... twenty-two years ago. Yes, yes it was, if I remember correctly.'

'It seems as if it was written in the stars,' Angelite said, as if it were a positive omen.

'It seems so, although I pictured you with short red-hair, not long. Perhaps it isn't the right moment yet. My abilities are fading, dear. I feel as if I am coming to the end of my life, which is why I need to tell you a few things about the path you must travel, but even then, I feel it's not yet time to discuss your journey further... end of my... tether...' N'Rutas muttered, frowning frustratingly.

Angelite held her hand, sensing that the old hag suffered from a form of dementia.

'It's okay, I'm sorry for asking,' replied the priestess, smiling warmly at her.

N'Rutas gripped hold of her hand. 'Its okay, my dear, things happen. Some bad, some good, you must learn to respect it. Besides, if we were all good and perfect, where would it get us? Meridia isn't perfect, as I'm sure you'd agree, but it is a step forward, that is certain, although I won't be around much longer to see it reach full fruition.'

'I guess you're right about Meridia. Just by being around you, though, I feel more connected with everything, even in your glade. I feel hope,' Angelite smiled, averting her vision to the maps and notes strewn across the tables of N'Rutas's workbench.

'Indeed, Child, hope is what we all need. We will talk again soon, but I must feed you and your companions. We must be ready. I feel something dark coming, so, its best I prepare your food, and then give you your new staff that I have been busy creating for many, many years. The day has finally come,' N'Rutas said, smiling.

Angelite's eyes widened. 'You crafted me a staff? That's too much, N'Rutas! I was only hoping to fix my old one,' she stammered.

'I know that you'll need it, and it isn't just any simple staff, my dear. I have placed some of my power and knowledge inside it, too. Of course, you will have to look after it. You can expend as much Resonance through it as you would like, and it will never shatter. It is a... well... let us call your new staff, Catalyst, shall we?'

'That's incredible, N'Rutas. I'm honoured!' Angelite raised her voice excitedly, almost stirring the group nearby.

N'Rutas beamed a crafty grin towards the young woman.

'I thought that would make you happy, dear. Now, I shall go prepare dinner, and tell you afterwards of where you will have to travel. First, a little more light is required, it's getting rather gloomy inside now the sun is disappearing.'

Angelite hugged N'Rutas, thanking her further for the gift that she would receive. N'Rutas then hobbled around the hut, lighting many handmade candles, which, thanks to their different coloured dyes, emitted odd and bizarre glows as they burned. She had prepared the meal by the time the rest of the group had awakened.

The party gorged themselves regardless of taste. They didn't argue over their stomachs. Gradually, as they finished, all of them joked and bantered. Spirits were high. Sadly, the group knew, deep down, that this respite would only last the night. They would be on the move again in the morning.

'That was some fine grub, N'Rutas. On behalf of everyone, thank you for your hospitality, otherwise we'd surely have died from hunger,' Neveah burped, wiping his mouth after drinking.

'You're more than welcome,' the old hag smiled. 'But now I must be serious with you, Children. I will have you escorted to a passage in the morning that will take you to the shore but, before the shore, you have obstacles ahead of you. As I am sure Angelite has already informed you, once you have reached the port, you will be greeted by the Watchman. They'll let you travel by boat across the ocean to reach your destination.'

She cackled lightly before gaining a little breath to continue. 'You'll have to continue north. However, you will need to travel across a wasteland, which is rife with a hidden danger lingering in the air. It is known as fallout, an unfortunate happening at the turn of the Dark Age. This radiation can make you ill for a few days or a lifetime, until gradually killing you. Angelite will look after you. Another danger I must warn you about is that there are still Anunaki warriors that inhabit that dead land. Be on your guard. You'll also be accompanied by Silver, the wolf you met in the forest.'

N'Rutas coughed, clearing her throat. 'Now, where was I? I shall explain a bit more about the radiation. In the olden days, before the Anunaki attack, there were weapons of wondrous power. They could turn any living being to ash and wipe out vast cities in one blast...'

The group drew closer around N'Rutas to hear her story. They eyed each other with raised eyebrows. Maledream recalled Larkhams' tall tales.

'These weapons were used against nations over trivial affairs, or, of course, to support manipulated agendas by governments desiring power. This led to escalating affairs. However, this was thousands of years in the making. The Mayan Prophets tried to warn of the approaching doom. They carried with them sacred crystals of wondrous power, which resembled human skulls. They were also the masters of the stars. They used to worship the Nephilim or Anunaki, and made sacrifices often to the Sky Gods. During this period, the Anunaki deceived them, and these skulls were gifts from those that hail from the heavens, those known as the Creators. They're also responsible for giving both humans and Anunaki conscious intelligence,' N'Rutas abruptly coughed.

'Old hag, I think you're confusing some of us. We know a little about fallout, but what the hell has skulls got to do with it? Who the hell are the Mayans? Neveah frowned.

'Yeah, I'm confused already,' Crazy John grumbled.

'In time you'll understand, Children, so keep listening,' N'Rutas returned with a beaming grin. 'The wise men, or Shamans, who knew of this manipulation, also possessed knowledge of the stars and how the world would come to be and come to pass. You'll learn more about the skulls when you reach Meridia.'

N'Rutas coughed again. Once she had cleared her throat with a gulp of water, she continued at length. 'The Maya knew what was coming. After all, they were the masters of knowing the constant. They had secret sects, which still exist to this day, hidden away. Mayan Shamans knew of the plight of what was to happen, so they decided, against the will of their masters, to disperse their people, to help the human race in the millennia to come. They evacuated their entire civilisation and disappeared overnight. This was because the shamans wanted to preserve the knowledge of the sacred skulls, for the better of humankind. They established other civilisations on the continents, leaving clues and artefacts. It did not take long before the Mayan forgot their deep ancestry, save for the few guardians. In keeping secrets, they were covering their own tracks, preserving their people and their secret knowledge that was handed down to each new generation. Therefore, young ones, there is a lot to learn and much I cannot teach you in one night.'

Drinking more water, she saw the bewilderment in the group's eyes. The priestess, it seemed, was the only one that could grasp N'Rutas's lecture. After all, Meridia had preserved much knowledge of the past.

'It's all valuable information, N'Rutas, thank you for sharing it with us. Can you tell us anything else?' Angelite uttered.

With a smile and a nod, the old hag continued. 'All I can say, Children, is when you have the vast amount of knowledge that I have collected for generations, you can easily derive a conclusion. Knowledge was protected in the form of artefacts or oral traditions. By fleeing, the Mayans ensured that their secrets were safe until they were needed.'

Neveah scratched his eye-patch, staring at everyone else who seemed to be deep in thought. He was a Pack leader, plain and simple. Fighting was his strong point, not knowledge, or learning. He couldn't care less about a civilisation that existed long ago, but still, he tried to listen.

'Before you go on your journey tomorrow, be sure to take the bags of food I have supplied you with, and the water also,' N'Rutas chuckled.

Maledream spoke up. 'It sounds very interesting, but surely, if these ancient people saw the future, or the constant, they should have stopped the trouble, shouldn't they?'

N'Rutas turned her gaze towards the Tribal, smiling intently at him. 'They believed that you couldn't stop the inevitable, and that you shouldn't even try, because it's impossible. Besides, many alternate states can happen in a constant, it is what makes reality so linear at times, and others, easy to manipulate. After all, free will is the universal law, for both forms of dualities, such as good and evil, for example. They possibly felt that the world needed to open its eyes, to see that humanity should appreciate itself and work towards a common goal. An evil threat would serve to unite the people. They knew this was what they had to do.'

Maledream wished that he had paid more attention to the old man and his stories.

N'Rutas took in deep breaths. Her age was showing. 'Now, I think it's time to give you your gift, Angelite. Then, Maledream, I must speak with you about that weapon of yours,' N'Rutas uttered.

She got out of her chair and hobbled from the centre of the room to the corner of her hut, where Angelite had found N'Rutas's maps and other materials. She lifted the wood on the table to reveal a long object, wrapped in leather and bound with strong, taut string. The wood creaked as if it were about to break as N'Rutas gently closed the desk, before hobbling back to the group.

'Use this in the radiated zone, Child, to protect you all. As I said to you earlier, Catalyst shall look after you very, very well,' she said, gently passing the wrapped staff to the priestess, who handled the package with great care.

'Go on. Open it, dear. You have made it this far, after all. Tell your mentors back home that you're ready for your next trial in your Spirit Order.'

'Thank you,' Angelite smiled, her excitement barely contained.

She gently untied the tight twine and unravelled the leather. The staff shone with glistening silver. Catalyst briefly hummed, almost as if it sang to the priestess. Symbols joined to runes very intricately, which, in turn, led up the shaft until reaching the top, where a bird sat and, like the rest of the rod, was also formed from the same metal.

'The statuette is called a swan, my Child. A beautiful creature, the name derives from an old language that means "song," or "sound." Human works of art used to show supernatural beings, called angels, bearing such swan-wings between their shoulders. They were considered, at least in art form, messengers for the old gods, the Creators. As the ancients once said, the first word was sound. They would be correct on that assumption, for all time,' N'Rutas said, her eyes and smile beaming like the sun towards Angelite's excited expression.

'Yes, it's beautiful! I don't know what to say, it's incredible,' she remarked, stroking the pristine staff with joy.

'It has the power of resurrection, Child. It also has many other powers at its disposal, but it is a power not to be used lightly. You could say that the staff is more powerful than I am and, if you're in a dire need, the staff can turn you into a force that few could reckon with. Bear in mind that such power will only last a short time, perhaps for three minutes at most. Once used, you will need to give it a length time to recharge. Anyway, you'll know when the time comes, Child. And now for...'

N'Rutas paused, averting her eyes towards Maledream for a moment, then to the sword next to him.

'That blade,' she said, stopping for a moment to take a sip of water.

'What about it?' Maledream quipped.

'I haven't gazed upon one such as this for a long time. Where did you find such a dangerous thing?'

'Dangerous? I found it over a week ago, kept it hidden from my foster... well, Larkham. Found it on that battlefield back from where I came from.'

'That weapon must have been left there after a fierce battle. Do you wish to know where it came from and who crafted it?' N'Rutas asked.

'I guess so. All I can say is that it has helped me occasionally, and has even showed me several things, which scared the hell out of me at first. I've wondered how using its power hasn't killed me, to be honest with you.'

The old hag shuffled closer to the young man to get a better look at the weapon.

'It works when you're in tune with it. You seem to share the same frequency it likes to work with. There are two ways you can use weapons or crystals like this. You work, either with them, or against them. Crystals are life forces,' she said, waving her hand just above the blade and shutting her eyes.

'It was crafted by the Creators. This weapon is slightly better in calibre than the staff. Incredible,' she added.

N'Rutas's wrinkly eyelids overlapped themselves as she delved deeper, and her eyes rolled back into their sockets. She gasped for a moment and shook her head, as if refusing to tell the group something about it.

'It's severely aged, and in need of a huge recharge. It has its own consciousness, very strong in fact. Yes, it's like the other Relics,' she said, opening her eyelids.

'Damn, now I wish I picked up one of those weapons, if you're saying there's more of them,' Neveah chuckled.

'These are dangerous weapons, and can be used by a skilled Nephilim or Human alike. They are designed so that no Anunaki can use them or their potential power. They are Master Creator Weapons and, if used properly, are potentially the strongest weapons ever made in creation.'

Neveah quietened down. The old hag seemed quite serious. N'Rutas sipped some more water and then shuffled back in her rickety chair. She sighed.

'All this standing up and running around! You lot are terrible,' she said, smiling to lighten the atmosphere. 'Those weapons were made for the planet, another gift, just like the sacred skulls. Thousands of millennia ago, eternal peace existed because no life was apparent, until an entity, called Conscious, grew. It is this consciousness that binds everything alike in song. This is what you would know as Resonance. The Relics were forged to represent a time when all the races agreed on peace and prosperity, under the watchful eyes of the Creators. It was then that knowledge was at a high pinnacle, everything seemed possible. However, it was not meant to be. I think it is what the Maya knew, having gifted knowledge for a second chance after the Dark Age's arrival. The crystal skulls and the weapons were gifts, perhaps a part of this second chance.'

Taking a quick breather, she sipped more water. 'Sadly, the weapon that you have with you, Maledream, was crafted more than thirteen thousand years ago, when the first major war on this planet erupted. The Creators, as they are known, made them with the subtle excuse of art, creation, and celebration. In addition, they forged them into superior weapons. Such Relics once destroyed the greatest human city on earth. To this day, they are either contained by the Anunaki, or lost. For you to find one, Maledream, and to even use some of its raw Resonance, shows that, even after many ages, they are still destructive.'

'So, what should I do with it, then?' Maledream muttered.

'I would say destroy it, but that is impossible, Child,' she replied with a slight husk. 'For you to find one suggests that some society had carried it with them for many ages, handing it down, until it found its resting place. As to the rest of your question, I would advise you not to overly use its power. It is not evil as such, but humans are easily corrupted. It is wise not to use it unless you know you can get away with it, especially when the Anunaki are around. If, of course, the only option you have is to fight, then you have to protect yourself.'

'I see,' he sighed, a worried look etched on his brow.

'You'll know what to do with it, Child, when the moment arises. If the Maya could have foreseen this moment, then it cannot be all bad. Another thing about your weapon is that it is crafted in the same way that I constructed Angelite's new staff, Catalyst, with exceptionally rare ore. The metal is also of the Creators' doing. Not much is left of it now. It is very potent, and cannot be smelted down with normal means. You have to bend it to your will. That is the secret of crafting such powerful, indestructible weapons with a dimensional alloy.'

Maledream looked at his sword again, fascinated by what he had just heard.

'What did you mean by charging the weapon? And how can I do it?' he asked.

'Meditation, or wait for it to wake up the more you use it,' she answered.

'I see. It would explain something to me, then...'

'Please, go on, Child.'

'Well, the night before me and Angelite left my tribe, I decided to meditate with it, something that Larkham always believed in. I thought I would try it, and then I had a vision I couldn't awaken from, and saw a huge battle take place. To cut a long story short, I had to run to this sword, which this man, with a strange symbol on the back of his hood, was carrying. It was knocked from his hands as he was swallowed by a horde of the Anunaki. This man was something else. Taller, and bigger than Neveah, and was wearing this powerful armour, too. There is one more thing. Occasionally, this weapon seems to mix its mind with me. It shows me strange visions, and I can hear it speak...'

The Pack eyed him and then glanced at the blade. Neveah couldn't help to butt in. 'Bigger than me? That takes a lot of beef to get as big as I am, I know that much,' he laughed, flexing his bulging arms while doing so.

'I think you've just injured his ego,' Boris jested.

'It's true,' Maledream said, smirking.

'Children, calm down,' N'Rutas ordered, 'I expect that man was a member of one of the secret societies that guarded the blade. I am not sure who that man could have been. Perhaps the symbol you saw would help. Jot it down here for me please, Maledream.'

Passing him an inkpot, parchment, and a wooden ink pen, they all watched as the Tribal sketched the round symbol on the floor.

'A bit rough, but that will do, I suppose,' N'Rutas cackled with a raised smile from her weathered wrinkles.

'Do you know what it is?' Maledream asked seriously.

'I think so. It has been a while since I have seen it. I'll need to think it over and talk to you about it again,' she uttered.

'I see,' Maledream muttered, now feeling slightly foolish for speaking of these visions.

He had been so sure that it was important, but if N'Rutas couldn't remember what it meant, or knew what it stood for, then what could it mean? He racked his brain while N'Rutas carried on speaking.

'It is difficult, Child, but don't let it get to you. You're still young,' she cackled.

Maledream looked even more troubled about the blade. His eyes were lost on its dark, rusty-looking surface.

'Now, all of you must get some rest. I especially need it. It has been fun talking and gifting you knowledge, but I am far too old to stay up this late. If you should wake up and find me gone, don't worry. I have many animals and trees to tend to. I have prepared water, bread, fruit, and freshly steamed vegetables for you all, contained in six packs. Maledream, you'll be carrying Silver's meat.'

'Hey, how is it that we've got to eat this green shit, and that wolf gets away with eating damn chicken?' Neveah grumbled.

The old hag laughed at him.

'He can't eat greens, you fool. Now stop whining, and be grateful that you have something to eat for your journey, before I clip your ear, or poke out your remaining eye...'

'She had you there,' said Boris, the rest of the party followed suit in poking holes at the big brute.

'I bid you all good night. Your food rations are just on the table behind you,' the hag finished.

The group bid the mysterious N'Rutas good night as she rose from her rickety chair and retreated upstairs.

'Well, that was an eventful evening, I guess,' said Crazy John with a heavy, bored sigh.

'Aye, it was. We're gonna sleep easy on these comfy rugs, makes a change,' Neveah muttered.

'Yep, think I'll stub out the candles, except two or three. This place has a nice glow to it. Any objections?' said Angelite.

'Whatever you wish, Sweet, I'm hitting the sack,' Neveah yawned, wrapping himself in the comfort of a woollen blanket on a nearby chair.

Crazy John and Boris slept next to each other, also wrapped in the thick blankets that N'Rutas had supplied them. Angelite went about the hut to extinguish the candles, bar a couple of them, before sitting down next to Maledream. Placing her new staff next to his sword, she casually stared at him as he gradually drifted off to sleep with his hands behind his head.

'Hasn't even taken off his boots, terrible man,' she muttered, smiling.

She took the liberty to remove his boots off the thick, white rugs, noticing then that he had already left dirty marks on them. With a grin, she rested her head on his chest and listened to his rhythmic heartbeat. Averting her stare, she noticed the Tribal had one eye open, returning the gaze at her with a smirk. Her heart raced. She had no will to turn away from his blue eye.

He broke the silence, whispering, 'you all right?'

She stared deeper, before realising that he wanted an answer.

'Yes,' she returned, her arms finding their way around his neck and chest as she cuddled up to him.

'Are you sure?'

'Couldn't be better,' she nodded, squeezing him tightly.

'Good,' he smirked, shutting his eye and letting out a quiet sigh.

'Sweet dreams,' she whispered.

Chapter Twelve

Into the Glass

The next day, and early in the morning, the sky was thick with red, silver-tinged clouds. Maledream stood outside the doorway of N'Rutas's home watching it happen. His ankle ached slightly from the day before. However, it was a niggling injury. Around him, he could hear a variety of birds chirping, which heightened in chorus as the day grew brighter.

A fresh breeze circulated throughout the glade. It was such a contrast to the bleak, ruined cityscape where he had lived for most of his memory. Watching the variety of animals gallop in the distance, he imagined the world having once been like this glade, before destruction had set in on the planet.

Over in the distance, trotting on all fours, and following the cobbled path appeared the familiar figure of Silver, the wolf. Smiling, Maledream waved at him. Angelite joined the Tribal and placed her hand on his shoulder.

'Up already?' he said, grinning.

'I wanted to enjoy the morning before we head off, it's a nice day, despite the clouds in the sky,' she chirpily replied.

'Doesn't look like it's going to shower today, at least we've that going for us. Can you see whose coming?' he asked.

'Ooh! It's Silver,' she said.

The pair casually walked a short distance to meet him.

'Miss me?' he uttered in mind.

'Of course, how are you this morning?' Angelite replied with a beaming grin.

'I'm fine, but we'd better be on the move. It shouldn't take long to reach your destination once we've passed the radiated plane,' he returned, his voice reassuring as it was deep and pleasant to listen to.

'Okay, let's get the others up and be on our way,' she said.

Soon enough, after much cursing from Neveah as Maledream kicked him awake, the group packed the rations that N'Rutas had prepared the night before. Everyone was in high spirits, each feeling their hard journey was nearly over.

Angelite stared at the remains of the melted candles, reflecting on what the day might bring. She felt her intuition was mixed and confused. Perhaps it was just her senses being clouded by the glade. She couldn't decide.

It took Crazy John and Boris a while to calm down once they discovered Silver could speak to them. They both assumed N'Rutas referred to a person during her lecture. After much reassuring from Neveah, Maledream, and Angelite, they let the topic drop.

'Aye, let's move out,' Neveah bellowed with his pole-arm resting on his right shoulder.

'Aye, aye, grand leader,' Boris humoured him.

Once the group began to stride at a steady pace with Silver in the lead, Neveah glanced at Angelite. 'Are you okay, Sweet? You've gone silent all of a sudden.'

'I... I'm fine. I just feel a little dizzy, in the spiritual sense, I guess,' she smiled.

'I've had that feeling, but just remember to keep yourself grounded, woman, and you'll do all right,' he said, grinning.

He put his hand on her shoulder to reassure.

'You're right. You do have some kind of spiritual leader in you,' she said.

Neveah laughed heartily at the comment.

'Some have said that in the past, even Maledream. Maybe when I can be assed, I'll try taking it up,' he said.

Maledream focused on the cobbled path. Staring up, he saw the clouds were still sparse. Their darkness was beginning to lighten as the sun rose into the deep-blue sky. The group was silent, save for the sound of their footsteps and noises made by animals in the grass and trees.

'There's so many animals here that I've never seen before,' said Boris.

'Aye,' Neveah grunted, his one eye also glancing at the creatures.

'That's why N'Rutas stays here and looks after them. A lot of them are from many parts of the world. This is a utopia for the animals, much like Meridia is for us. Very few species, except the birds, survived the arrival of the Dark Age. I'm amazed that N'Rutas has somehow managed to hold them up here,' replied Angelite.

'We're almost there,' Silver uttered.

Soon enough, after walking in the cool, morning breeze of N'Rutas's home, the party entered another lava duct that would lead them north outside of the volcanic glade. Angelite's new staff, Catalyst, glowed with a silver hue and, in turn, it illuminated the crystalline rocks littering the walls of the tunnel.

'The place which we'll be passing through is quite a sight. Those flying insects you fought yesterday were mutated by this radiation. It has forever changed them,' said Silver.

'You mean those Vasps?' replied Maledream.

'Yes. This place can either change you or kill you. To you humans, it would probably do the latter.'

'Which is why N'Rutas gave me this gift, to shield us,' replied the priestess.

'Correct.'

They made steady progress as they navigated their way around the lengthy passages, not speaking, but dwelling on the day still to come. The smell of purified water was welcoming in the glow of the caves. Silver continued leading them through spiralling passages and, occasionally, through large, glittering caverns.

Crystalline structures, the size of buildings, jutted outwards and glowed brilliantly each time they entered one of these large, spacious domes of rock. Purple, blue, red, and yellow hues painted the adventurers as Catalyst sang to the crystal-like towers with its silvery light.

'This is incredible,' Neveah announced.

'Yep, I'm going to come back and spend some time here in the future,' Angelite squealed.

'I have to admit, it's quite the spectacle,' Boris smirked, her fingers reaching out to feel the grooves of the rough, crystalline rocks.

'I never knew the earth contained such things. Sort of reminds me of Larkham's stories. He went on about the resources of the earth being abused by our ancestors. I wonder if he meant something like this?' Maledream pondered.

'More than likely. Caves such as these are rich, not only in crystals, mind, but other rare minerals, too,' said Angelite.

'It's pointless, there's no useful ore in this place, it's just filled with glowing rocks,' muttered Crazy John.

'N'Rutas regularly visits these surrounding passages to gather such crystals and minerals, she has many uses for them,' said Silver.

'Yeah, well, I don't see it,' Crazy John grumbled.

'I think a place such as this needs protecting. I doubt N'Rutas mines these passages, I expect she just picks up the loose bits that she needs,' replied Angelite.

'Aye, she can't move or speak without coughing half the bloody time,' Neveah jested.

'What do you think, Maledream?' asked Boris.

'Not sure, I'd have to agree with Angelite, I think,' he uttered with a grin.

'Biased bastard,' Crazy John sniped.

'Behave, John, or you'll get a slap,' Boris ordered, passing him a glare.

The Tribal raised an eyebrow at the assassin. Although, when the priestess clamped her hand on his arm, the swelling anger subsided at the comment. Averting his eyes from the massive crystals, he stared at her for a moment, noticing she had a deep, violet glow lurking beneath her shining green eyes.

'Aye, save your strength. We almost out yet?' Neveah groaned.

Without saying a word, Silver led the group out of the current cavern and around the corner of another duct. Greeting them with a punishing light, the group raised up their hands to cover their eyes from the bright sun as they exited the subterranean labyrinth. Not uttering a single word, the party gazed upon the bleak, sandy panorama.

They saw, in the distance, giant, transparent spikes, reaching high into the heavens, formed from curved or rigid glass. The glass spires were almost blinding from the sun. The structures acted like prisms. Multiple colours created glowing auras across the land. It seemed to give, what was left of the sand in the rocky wasteland, a heavenly look. The group marvelled at the sight of the different lights that fractured into all the colours of the spectrum. The complex, beautiful architecture was many miles in width and height.

'Ah, that would've taken your attention,' Silver said, before sitting on all fours to admire the view as he continued. *'Long ago, there were weapons that dealt massive destruction. It's unknown whether this particular sight was targeting the Anunaki or humans. This was once a desert. Humans, many years ago, created many potent weapons. They would burn like a thousand suns and, as*

you can guess, that is more than a summer's heat many times over. When sand gets too hot, it melts, and can turn to glass when it cools. This whole place used to be a desert, and now it's nothing more but a barren wasteland of irradiated glass spires that reach high into the sky.'

'Must have been some blast,' Boris said, amazed by the spectacle that seemed to stretch between eight to ten miles.

'Aye, if we had weapons back in the city like that, well, I'd rather not give it another thought,' Neveah nodded.

'I think the world's psycho enough as it is,' said Crazy John.

'This shouldn't surprise you. Our world was once a beautiful green and blue planet. This is one of the things that Meridia is trying to rectify, which is so many mistakes of the past,' Angelite said, leaning on her staff as a subtle tear rolled its course down her cheek.

Maledream said nothing, instead choosing to glare at the bright spectacle in awe as the sun painfully refracted the light into his eyes.

'If you look into your ration sacks, you'll find some useful goggles. I suggest that if you value your eyesight, you'll wear them now. Angelite, please begin using Catalyst to shield us from the heat and radiation. We don't want to bake. Oh, one more thing, make sure to avoid the bright sun spots, otherwise you'll burn in seconds. The *sun's rays are magnified many times over. You won't live if you stray far from Angelite's protection.'*

Nodding in turn, the adventurers reached into their bags to find another surprise from N'Rutas. Strapping the black onyx goggles on their heads, the complaints of discomfort sounded from the group. Maledream strapped a similar one on Silver's feral-shaped cranium at his order.

Growling, Silver's thoughts raced to the others. *'Stop complaining. I know it's very dark, but trust me, when we get down there, it'll look as bright as a normal day.'*

Neveah had one specially made with an eye-patch attached to it. A nice change, he cheerfully thought, as he tightened the thick leathery straps behind his scalp.

'Aye, stop bitching and head out. The faster we get through this, the better.'

'We made it this far, and I don't count on dying. Besides, this shit is getting weird, and you know how I hate weird shit,' Crazy John muttered.

'I don't lie, mate. Just do as I and the mutt say, and you'll make it out alive,' Neveah muttered back.

'I hope I've got your guarantee on that. I won't lose my only love,' said Crazy John.

'Look, mate, don't do this to me now, or your woman, just stay with it,' Neveah replied, gripping Crazy John's arm in an iron grip.

'What's up?' Maledream asked, wondering why they were both speaking in low tones.

'Nothing to worry about, let's move on,' Neveah returned with a nod.

Maledream raised an inquisitive eyebrow towards them. Crazy John ignored the Tribal and shifted his way back to Boris in silence.

Angelite uttered a few incantations and, in doing so, activated Catalyst's protection. A subtle blue aura irradiated from the rod of power, which coated each group member with faint, ethereal energy.

Everyone began to climb down the steep slope. At the bottom, the group navigated their way through the vast, hot spires of glass that inhabited the once-barren sands. The Tribal thought deeply about the place, his feet slipping from time to time on the slick surface as they further penetrated this bright hell.

The priestess expected to strain from the consistent use of Resonance, but her new gift, Catalyst, eased most of the stress caused by the flow of energies. It felt as if she was covered in a pocket of cool air, a sense of spiritual tuning accompanying the sensation. She felt that she could accomplish anything, although she did need to keep up her concentration.

However, something didn't feel right. Something seemed to be eating away at her soul, yet she couldn't put her finger on what was wrong. She brushed her fears to one side, and concentrated on following the others as they weaved around the hot spots that threatened to burn them to ashes. The glass spires towered over them like skyscrapers.

Occasionally, the priestess would pause in her stride for a brief moment. Whispers would work their way into her ears, their language garbled like an out-of-tune radio frequency. She tried to ignore it the best she could, but her ears flinched to each pulse of white noise.

'Wait,' Neveah said, halting everyone with a raised fist.

'What is it?' replied the Tribal.

'Look around and look up.'

All eyes slowly peered upwards. They saw blackened shapes of human skeletons surrounded them, preserved in the glass, which gave the glowing, gleaming hell a terrifying visage. The remains seemed to be in awkward positions, as if the deceased had flown through the air from some horrifying power, only to end up entombed when the glass hardened for all time.

Angelite stared at the skulls trapped in the glass with frightened eyes. The skulls, too, returned the stare from their transparent prison. Hundreds, perhaps even thousands of skeletons, were encased for miles around. The priestess couldn't take her eyes off their dark eye-sockets. The muttering noises increased in pitch.

'Help us.'

A chill graced her skin. Catalyst hummed in her palms. The voices filled her head, as if a thousand-strong crowd roared at her.

* * *

Tightly clutching her hair, the priestess squinted harshly against the invading thoughts. It was then that the whispers stopped. Opening her eyes and unlatching her hair, Angelite was now aware that something was different.

Her companions had disappeared in an instant. Instead, she found herself on the sandy plane that was now free from all the glass spires. Children brushed passed her, playing games, their laughter ghastly echoing on her senses. She stood still in complete shock as she watched hundreds of passing refugees traversing the sprawling dunes. Some travelled in light vehicles, whilst many others simply trekked along the soft sand that she felt beneath her feet. The whispers intensified.

'What are we being attacked by?' asked a nearby child to a parent. *'I don't know, princess, we just have to hurry.'*

Angelite watched the family stride by. Averting her vision to the heavens, she saw snaking smoke-trails racing back and forth in the stratosphere. Missiles screamed death from one end of the continent, to the other, through the blood-red dusk that settled on the clouds and arid expanse.

She refocused on the refugees taking cover on the dunes. Large flashes of light littered the distant horizon. Massive detonations followed and roared across the air. Screams grated and echoed on her senses, parents covered their children's ears, shielding them with their phantasmal forms. Gazing up once more, she watched one of the smoke trails side-wind in a confused manner.

'It's coming straight for us,' one refugee screamed.

Whispers continued to haunt her. She watched the missile descend in agonizing seconds as it screamed from the sky. Angelite stood still, watching, petrified from the terror that swelled inside her fluttering heart.

'It's okay, baby, always remember that we've always loved you. Nothing will ever take you away from us, nothing in this world will,' the parents cried in an echoing chorus, clutching the children they loved.

Hopeless hysteria ran its course among the tens of thousands of refugees. Angelite saw the powerful, white-hot explosion as tears streamed from her eyes. The ground rumbled as if a quake had struck and, for those several seconds, the bones of all the refugees shone through their apparitional clothing and skin as they bathed in dazzling radiation.

The heat surged through her in an instant. She felt every molecule in her being sear and blister from the heat-blast, before the blazing, molten sands swept through her body like a tsunami. The priestess screamed as the inferno engulfed and incinerated her with a deafening roar. Terror was etched on the refugees' skinless expressions for eternity. Trapped in the glass and forever staring at their demise, the parents were right to tell their children they would never be separated.

* * *

Everyone turned to see Angelite screeching. Confused looks etched themselves on their brows in panic. Maledream and Neveah were the first to her side, shouting at her to calm down as she injured their eardrums with hysteria.

'What the hell's wrong?' Maledream asked, trying to stare her directly in the eyes through the screaming.

'Sweet, what's up?' Neveah bellowed above the wails.

Angelite panted, babbled, and cried uncontrollably.

'Hold her down before she hurts herself,' Boris said, the two men nodding in turn.

They gripped her hands and feet, holding her down as she struggled and continued to mutter incoherently. Silver trotted to her, howling at her fiercely. So fierce, in fact, that it made the glass vibrate beneath the group's feet for a brief second. Angelite stopped and wrestled away from Maledream and Neveah. She kept her eyes shut, her hands covering her ears. Silver's voice cut through to her.

'It's me, Angelite. I can hear them too, but you must block them out. They are spirits forever trapped until they realise that they have to move on. They want our help, which we cannot offer them. Block them out.'

Angelite slowly opened her eyes, trying to keep back the tears that filled her goggles. She shook and nodded at him.

'Block it all out, all of it. Only listen to my voice, focus on me, Angelite.'

Long moments passed as the priestess sat upright, her breaths sporadic.

'Keep blocking them and don't let your guard down. It seems you're susceptible to hearing the spirits more than most.'

'Thank you,' she panted.

'You okay?' Maledream asked, watching Neveah pick her up slowly by her hand.

'Yes, thank you. Let's not mention this again. Let's carry on moving,' she stammered, trying the best she could to concentrate while wiping away the tears that crawled through the goggles.

Neveah shrugged and wondered what all the fuss was about, but decided it wise to ignore the commotion. It was the first time any of them had seen Angelite pull off such a worrying stunt. With hardly any words and reassuring pats on the back, they continued to traverse through the glass graveyard.

'I don't think we've much farther to go,' Angelite uttered, breaking the long silence that gripped them.

'Aye, certainly hope so,' Neveah nodded, grabbing a carrot out of his ration sack. 'You know…' Neveah continued, speaking with his mouth full, 'this reminds me of the time me and Maledream had when we were younger, when we walked through many odd places just to get to the city. My legs are starting to feel like rocks again. It's good exercise, I reckon.'

After wiping his mouth, he pulled a grim expression. 'Tastes like crap. We should be out of this place by the end of the night, shouldn't we?'

'Of course, as long as we don't slow down or come across any surprises. However, I do smell a tainted scent on the hot air, but I can't place where it's coming from.'

'I wish I was more use. I've had a clouded intuition ever since we passed through the cave,' said Angelite.

'I wouldn't worry. I expect your energies are at their most potent, and Catalyst will heighten your senses in many ways. I expect you still need to adjust to its energies,' replied Silver.

'I guess you're right. I haven't tuned myself to it, so I should expect some instability,' she replied in a daze, staring at him.

'Yes, I assure you, you'll be fine.'

Silver's words of reassurance made her melt. She weakly grinned. Her attention was then caught by the sunlight that split into rainbows from the prismatic glass.

'It's strange, our Chakra centres are the same colours, and in the same order,' she said.

'Sorry, what?' Maledream blurted, turning to look at her with a raised, sweaty eyebrow.

'Chakras are the energies flowing through your body. They all have different colours to represent your emotions. If you feel something deep inside of you when you get certain feelings, it could mean that your Heart Chakra is speaking inside of you. For example, the first colour in the Chakra system is violet, which is meant to represent infinite consciousness, or rather the spirit.'

Neveah butted in whilst scratching his scalp, 'I don't quite follow you. Are you saying we're just like rainbows? And is light the same thing?'

'Yes, sort of, to simplify things, I'll leave them at rainbows,' she cheekily quipped.

Seeing the priestess perk up lifted everyone's spirits. Angelite elaborated as Neveah laughed at the pun.

'I'll continue. It gets easier from here. The second colour is indigo, which is your Third Eye Chakra. It's situated in between your eyes. Psychic power, or other such spiritual potency, can be expressed through this energy centre. The third colour is of a sky blue, representing your vocal expression. It's more of the socialising energy point, as it exists in between your throat and shoulder blades.'

'Very, uh, educational, I guess,' Crazy John briefly interrupted.

'Now the fourth, which is the colour green, is your Heart Chakra, which stands for healing and your innermost feelings,' Angelite continued speaking enthusiastically about the subject. 'The fifth colour is yellow. It's situated in your stomach and stands for willpower and energy.'

The group listened intently as they stared at the prismatic spikes that fragmented the lights, for what seemed several miles in all directions. The inner-glass plane was now more like a multicoloured spiders-web.

'Number six is orange. It not only stands for your appetite, it also focuses its energy physically. It's in your, uh... how do I say it?'

'Spit it out, woman!' Neveah interrupted, nudging her with his elbow in gentle jest.

'Groin,' she muttered.

'What, you mean our balls?' Neveah laughed, his voice easily booming off the glass skyscrapers.

Others in the group were highly amused and joined in.

'No wonder I glow orange when I've had a good one!' he said, flexing both his of bulging, muscular arms in an upward fashion, before humping the thin air.

'What a gorilla!' Boris sighed in disgust.

'What? Best joke I've heard all day!' he continued to laugh sporadically.

'Yes, it does stand for sex, and, rather, how much energy you have,' Angelite finished, her innocent cheeks blushing a pale pink.

'Aye, good stuff, I was expecting Maledream to beat me at crunching the joke off first, but looks like he's too sweaty after last night,' Neveah mocked and bellowed.

The Pack leader jabbed the Tribal playfully with one arm whilst slapping a surprised Angelite on the ass with the other, before grabbing them both around their waists with a bear-like hug. Embarrassing them easily, Neveah relished every moment. Spirits were high once more. Angelite took the joke well and was glad he was around to lighten the mood.

'Orange aura, honestly,' she thought with a devilish grin.

She never did finish off the last Chakra now that Neveah and Maledream continued to joke about them for the rest of the afternoon.

'About time these humans lightened up,' Silver thought.

Chapter Thirteen

Dread Rising

An Anunaki Blood Adept traversed the glass planes. It wore blood-red robes lined with silver and carried with it a potent golden staff, adorned with many symbols that resembled those of the Anunaki Council Hall.

With its presence cloaked, it watched from afar, levitating just above the hot, shimmering surface. Its dark eyes, resembling those of a hawk, were transfixed on Angelite and her staff. Glaring at the other group members, it evaluated their potential threat. It was especially interested in Maledream's Relic Blade. Blinking rapidly at the sight of the powerful weapon, it closed its eyes and sent the information to the others nearby.

* * *

Gradually, the sun passed its highest point in the sky as the group carried on with relentless spirits. Before them rose two, mountainous areas on the edge of the glass plane, where a ridged-looking pass cut straight through the centre.

Crazy John muttered in his gravelly voice, 'looks like a canyon or something?'

'Aye, looks it,' Neveah replied, stretching his aching legs.

'I sense the Anunaki. We should quicken our pace,' Silver urged.

'Well, if there is any, I doubt we'll have to wait long to find out,' said Maledream.

'Look on the bright side, if they appear and we kill one, at least we'll have some fresh meat,' Crazy John jested, madly smiling at the prospect of cutting up such a lizard and baking it on the hot glass.

'For a start, that's just wrong...' replied Maledream.

'Of course it isn't, we can be on top of the food chain, too,' Crazy John sniggered.

'We've been travelling for a while, but we're not that far from safety now. I must ask you all to stay sharp until then.'

'Aye, everyone keep it down, no bickering. We can soon settle down and rest before anything else happens,' said Neveah.

With that, the group carried on in their stride. Gradually, they exited the hellish yet beautiful glass plane. Leaving the once-sandy expanse behind them, the group set foot on the hard, natural earth that led to the canyon directly ahead of them. Aside from the narrow escape from the glass spires, there was nothing but a cliff face, which seemed to encircle the desert.

'Some sight isn't it?' murmured Boris.

'Aye, looks like the only way is straight forward through this canyon. May as well take off these goggles now the sun's fading,' replied Neveah.

'I would advise keeping them on for now. The levels of light are still not safe enough. It seems like it is getting darker, but it is far from it. Until we reach the end of the canyon, keep the goggles on. Once we're in the shadows, you may then, of course, take them off,' uttered Silver.

'Fair enough,' Neveah nodded.

The group entered the mouth of the sunlit canyon. The air was dry, almost suffocating, and with no wind present, the group felt uncomfortably sweaty. Fortunately, Angelite continued using the protections of her staff, Catalyst.

Ancient bones of creatures and humans alike littered the ground in great numbers. Some were even carbonized into the walls for eternity at the mouth of the chasm. Their ashen shapes served as a powerful, yet sad ending, for the living that passed through this rocky corridor long ago.

Clothes were sparse, save for old shoes that crumpled and scrunched from the touch of the adventurers' boots.

'This place is terrible, not something I'd enjoy walking through more than once,' said Angelite, her voice filled with unease.

'I'm glad. This place isn't for the living, only the dead. Harsh as that sounds,' replied Maledream.

'Aye,' Neveah concurred, surveying the passing rocky crevices with his one eye.

Maledream paused in his stride and, for a moment, felt a chill. He rolled his vision back to the glass plane. For some reason, he felt unsettled, tense.

'Maledream...'

It wasn't Silver's telepathic tone. It was something else. It was almost familiar. Without any thought, he dropped his backpack in a shot and withdrew his heavy blade.

'Mate, what's up?' Neveah asked.

The group paused and focused on the Tribal with his weapon securely locked in his fists. Maledream continued to hear the voice in his mind. Paranoid to what it was, and highly confused, he raised one goggle and looked all around the canyon.

'Who are you?' he shouted.

His voice bounced off the walls and returned no yields. No matter where he looked, he couldn't see the intruder.

'Maledream,' the voice raged, repeatedly chanting his name to drive him insane.

'What's wrong?' Angelite asked with a worrying frown.

Silver could sense it, but he couldn't locate where the communication was coming from. His ears were keened the best he could get them.

'Where are you?' he shouted once more, ignoring Angelite's caring plea.

'What the hell's going on? Come on, settle down before you scare the shit out of us,' Neveah ordered, his voice stern.

He put his hand on Maledream's shoulder to prevent him from doing anything stupid. The Tribal ignored his old friend, and continued to glean every rock and shadowy crevice. Gradually, his eyes crawled up the canyon wall, almost in a trance-like state.

Voices from the others faded.

The intruding rasp repeated his name in a louder chorus, cutting through his mind like razors. As his eyes reached the top of the canyon, he saw, through his onyx goggle, a dark, billowing, phantasmal figure peering at him. Heat waves brushed over the being, as if it was a mist, blowing and distorting like a flame.

Feeling paralyzed, he couldn't open his mouth, nor look away, as he stared into the large, frightening, black eyes of the Anunaki Blood Adept. Maledream's sight grew darker. His onyx goggles afforded him little protection against its sheer intent. It felt like his skull was going to explode from the pressure.

Neveah tackled the young man to the ground, which seemed to break the spell once he landed a strong punch on the Tribal's jaw. Whipping him out of the daze, the Tribal's sword landed in the stony ground with a smack, corrupting the dead earth for a scant second with its crimson hue.

Maledream ripped the goggles off and shivered with a grim, ashen expression. He roared and let out the dread that swelled within. His voice loosened debris from the canyon walls. Dust and stones peppered the ground, which, in turn, alarmed the group.

'What the hell's wrong, for fuck's sake?' Neveah barked, shaking him.

In answer, the Tribal pointed up to where he saw the being. Neveah let go of him, turning to stare upwards in an instant with his own onyx eye-patch but, before he could see whatever it was properly, it moved out of sight. It was almost like a darting wisp of shadow. Maledream, in the meantime, vomited bile on the dry rocks.

'Shadow beasts again?' Neveah growled.

'I doubt it, not in this light,' Angelite replied, rushing over to Maledream.

Resting her hands on his shoulders, she pulled him away from the spot where he retched. Grabbing a spare cloth, she rested him on her lap and wiped his lips whilst wetting his clammy head with some flask water.

'I have a major concern,' Silver said, a tone of foreboding accompanying his concern. *'I believe it was an Anunaki, and I believe it was targeting Maledream. They must be after the blade. It was almost as if I could feel them trying to possess him.'*

'I must've snapped him out of it, just by fluke and instinct. I felt something was wrong right before this happened,' the Pack leader replied.

Neveah's eye rolled back towards the Tribal as the priestess continued to treat him with sincere care. She stroked his hair and face, whilst keeping one hand on his chest and chanting her healing Resonance.

'Neveah, me and John will check it out, we'll cut the bastard down,' said Boris.

'I've been eager to spill some blood,' Crazy John added, enthusiastically whipping out his large, polished knives.

'No, it's too dangerous. Our best bet is to carry on. I don't want any one getting taken out or being used against us, especially with what Silver just said. We had to deal with that shit against the shadows, remember?' Neveah answered with worry, clutching his large pole-arm.

'That's right. They're probably planning something far worse. Be on your guard and, whatever you do, do not stare into their eyes. The Anunaki have great mental

strength. They are cunning as they are frail, and they're not something to be reckoned with. If N'Rutas were here, I'm sure she would've been able to figure out what to do, but this is our test,' replied Silver.

'Some bloody test, I ain't risking my skin for no test,' Neveah roared, his temper flaring as he struck the butt of his weapon on the rocky ground several times.

Angelite raised her voice, 'look, just help Maledream walk. He's going to need more than my healing, the attack left him physically exhausted.'

'I'm okay...' Maledream muttered and coughed, rising slowly from Angelite's lap. 'Let's just go. Let's get out of here.'

'Aye, good suggestion.'

The Pack leader helped Maledream collect his sword. His strength returned with surprising speed once he stretched his aching limbs. The group quickened their pace. It was growing darker as they traversed the shadowy darkness that lay ahead of them. Now the sun had set below the ridge to leave what little light was left to seep into the canyon, the group removed their goggles.

'Let's create a little light,' said the priestess.

With a few gestures and playful melodies, Angelite tossed a few crystals from her hands. The stones emanated a soft yet powerful light. Controlling them with her Resonance, the crystals lit the path as they levitated around the group like neon comets, serving to illuminate the shadowy, creviced walls.

Silhouettes of the group, created by the movements of the darting shards, made Crazy John jerk nervously. No one blamed him. They all had their eyes cast for any sign or presence of danger. All turned silent, except for their scuffling of boots.

Maledream thought back to what he saw. The thought of losing himself in those large, black eyes made him feel cold. He wondered what happened. It almost felt like something was different, like there was a gaping hole inside his chest. Reaching into his pocket, he withdrew the cloth that Angelite used to dampen his head. Gripping it tightly, he peered at the priestess who led the way with Silver.

The Tribal was now aware of the ache in his jaw from where Neveah punched him, although he was grateful. He knew that the Pack leader probably saved his life. He began to wish that, as he stared towards the cloudy, moonlit sky, he was back at the Tribal camp with Larkham. The life he left behind was dangerous, but was comparatively safer than this.

'I've come so far, so, why the hell do I feel so depressed?'

The group travelled through the canyon for half the night, not daring to stop and eat with the looming threats that could exist in the darkness. They could relax somewhat with Angelite's glowing crystals. However, it was their only comfort.

'I think there are some gates up ahead,' Boris quietly uttered.

'Shine a little more light in front of us if you can,' Neveah said, his eye gleaming with hope.

'Already on it,' Angelite nodded, her crystal lights darting ahead of what was left of the straight section of canyon.

'I guess this means we made it?' said Maledream.

'It certainly does, the Watchman are professional soldiers from Meridia. We've made it!' she replied excitedly.

'Damn, just when we had the prospect of killing something...' Crazy John muttered.

'We did it lads and lasses! To Meridia we go!' Neveah cheered, raising his pole-arm skywards.

'Thank the spirits,' Maledream thought, letting out a relieving sigh.

The crystals illuminated the wooden and iron frames ahead of them. They instantly bolted in unison towards the salvation they offered, and crashed against the great barrier. To cover their rear, Angelite shone her crystal lights back into the darkness from where they travelled.

'I'm fucking tired,' Boris panted, unlatching her studded-leather slightly to let the hot air escape.

'Yep,' Maledream groaned, falling to his knees and staring at the tall doors.

They were around thirty feet in height and width. The canyon acted as a natural defence with these strong doors blocking the entrance to the port. No attacker could easily penetrate this careful, well thought-out perimeter.

'Right, now, how do we get in?' asked Neveah.

There was a long pause.

'They should have opened them by now, by there's no one up in the security tower,' Angelite uttered, beaming her glare up at the sentry points.

The large wolf sniffed at the thick gate for a moment.

'Well...' Silver said thoughtfully, before Neveah butted in, 'shit, I've said it for you. No one's alive behind there?'

'I can't sense any thought forms, no.'

'Fuck sake!' Neveah roared, smashing his large fists against the thick wood.

'There's no noise coming from the other side, either. Aside from that, the only light present is Angelite's.'

Those left standing collapsed in exhaustion and despair, only realising, then, that when they did, they were sitting in muddy puddles that seeped from under the doors.

'Water?' Maledream quizzed, wiping his wet ass and getting back up.

'The mechanism's broken,' Crazy John spoke as he examined the steel lock in-between the iron frames.

'Right, everyone get by me and help push this bastard open,' Neveah ordered.

Gradually, the gate began to shift and move across the wet surface of the mud. The large door heaved and groaned as all bodies pressed against it. Angelite's crystalline lights shone through the darkness beyond the door once it was finally flung aside. Pointing her staff towards the clearing, the lights shot quickly into the outpost.

They illuminated a gruesome sight in the docking area. Bodies were left strewn across the harbour and loading bays of the port. Neveah led the way forward, followed swiftly by Silver and Angelite, whilst the rest followed cautiously, all weapons drawn.

'This isn't what we unexpected,' Maledream sighed in a low tone, examining a well-armed guard whom wore solid steel and chainmail armour. 'Looks like scorch marks on this body, or what's left of him.'

'Must've been an ambush, probably from the sea,' Angelite theorized with a worried tone.

'Whatever it was, they certainly knew the humans weak points,' Crazy John rasped, glaring at the vicious, disembowelled jugulars.

'Cleanly cut, like how we did it back in the city,' Boris remarked.

'Aye,' Neveah grunted.

'By the spirits... look... the beach,' Angelite cried.

The scene was poorly lit by the moonlight, but it was enough to make out a glimpse of more corpses floating on the calm waves. Crashing against rocks and sand, the deceased Watchman floated back and forth with the tide.

Angelite could barely contain her stomach at the carnage. When the moon showed itself fully, both the sand and waves glowed with a crimson sheen. Blood smeared the beach, which in itself looked disturbed and lumpy all over. She stood closer to the Tribal, almost hoping his presence could comfort her in some way.

'If only we knew they were attacked,' Maledream cursed, stooping over another corpse and examining it.

'Aye, was also our only exit,' Neveah huffed, staring at the chilling scene.

Angelite looked away from the dead and towards some of the wooden and metallic vessels still sitting in the docks. Some ships in the distance lay on their sides, splintered in many pieces. If they were used as a likely escape, they failed in the attempt.

'Some boats are still here, which means whatever hit them, hit them quickly,' said Crazy John.

A tear slid down Angelite's cheek. The female assassin made her way to the priestess to give her a tight hug. 'Don't worry, Sweetie.'

'I reckon we should start fixing one of those ships in the docks, aye Crazy John?' Neveah prompted.

'I'll give it a go,' John smirked, whipping out his personal fixing tools from his backpack.

'Right, which ship do we think is seaworthy enough to fix up?' Maledream wondered.

'The ship in the centre of the piers looks like a good start,' Angelite said, pointing in its direction.

With haste, the group made their way towards the ship. Their footsteps sounded heavily on the old, wooden pier as it creaked with each stride. The ship only had one broken mast out of the three it sported. Its hull was also the least damaged from the rest of the fleet, which was either docked at port or split apart just out to sea.

'By the looks of things, this attack was just a one-off,' said Crazy John.

'I wouldn't put it past the Anunaki that we encountered earlier to have something else planned. Be on your guard,' replied Silver.

'Those things are rather tenacious, aren't they,' Boris muttered, staring at the carnage on the beach from the wooden pier.

Maledream shut his eyes and listened to the sweet sound of the waves gently thrashing the rocky shore, as if it could soothe his racked nerves. The smell of the ocean and cool air added to the sensation.

Once the group boarded the vessel, Crazy John disappeared into the bowels of the small, sleek ship to have a look at what he could fix, whilst Boris examined the upper deck for anything that might prove useful.

'Since it'll take a while to get this thing moving, I'll head back and take a look around on the beach. Might be something useful to salvage to speed things up,' said Maledream.

'I'll go with you. Angelite, stay here with the mutt. You need a rest, so find somewhere to sit down and eat something,' Neveah ordered, patting her on the shoulder and giving them each the thumbs-up.

'Ape...'

Weakly smiling, she nodded and rested her hand on Silver's fine, furry coat. She lit some nearby lamps with a click of her fingers, spilling light across the entire deck of the ship. 'Much better,' she sighed.

* * *

The pair trod slowly off the pier and back on the beach, leaving the others to get on with what they had to do on the vessel.

'Poor bastards,' Neveah cussed, finding the gawping expressions and dead eyes of the Watchman an unsettling experience.

'Not much we can do,' the Tribal sighed.

'Aye, they've got some fine-looking armour and weapons strewn about the place. If I find any short-blades,

I'll hand them over to Boris and John. We should salvage what we can.'

As the pair searched, the Tribal came across a man who was ripped in twain with his intestines dangling out of his ghost-white torso. Trying not to vomit, Maledream felt oddly compelled to take a closer look. The man wore some silvery-looking gauntlets, adorned with many symbols on them.

'Mate, have a look at this. What do you suppose this is for?' Maledream wondered, staring at the gloved armour that had a metallic chain attached to it.

'Aye, it's a failsafe. You attach it to your gauntlet, which this poor bastard has done here, so that if you lose your weapon in combat, it'll keep it in quick reach. It's life insurance. I'd grab it off him, if I were you. It's handy.'

Maledream smirked and ignored the bad pun.

'Well, I've lost my weapons in the past, so I might as well,' he nodded.

Once he removed one of them from the corpse, the Tribal strapped it on his own wrist and attached the chain to his weapon's hilt. Maledream was quite pleased with the find. However, once the metal-link locked into place, the runes on the gauntlet briefly illuminated with a hazy crimson.

'Did you see that?'

'Aye, ask Angelite about that,' Neveah grimaced, both men confused by the passing glow.

'Probably nothing to worry about. If they came from Meridia, then I expect they've got stuff similar to what Angelite uses,' said Maledream.

'Yeah, you're probably right, mate. It just doesn't help us when we're on edge,' Neveah chuckled in irony, both smiling.

'This chain's great. A bit long, but at least it won't be ridiculously out of reach if I drop it.'

'Aye, that's the idea... wait! Look in this hut. I've hit the jackpot.'

'Why, what is it?'

'Armour plating, shoulder pads, cloaks, and hoods! Oh man, and the mother-load of them all... tobacco!' he cheered.

The list was endless, both men jumped around like children at the treasure they had found in the dank storage cabin.

'I can finally have a good smoke, ran out of it in the forest,' Neveah uttered.

'I wondered what happened to you and your pipe,' Maledream smirked.

Whipping out his gloriously stained pipe, and filling it to the brim, Neveah realised he hadn't any means to light it.

Instead, he began sorting through the Meridian cloaks and various metal armours that were stashed in the crates.

'Right, I'm going to change into some of this,' said Maledream.

Removing his grotty, knee-length coat and discarding his old, sodden tops, he replaced them with new Meridian ones. They were woven from fine silks and warm wool. Interesting patterns were also inscribed into their fabrics, which added to their welcoming, comforting charm.

Both men changed their appearance drastically. Smashing many locked crates with their weapons, the pair delved deeper into more storage containers. They found robes that would no doubt suit Angelite, and looked far better than the roughly stitched garb she currently wore. They never looked the same after Reckless and his gang ripped them apart. Maledream's hands folded and clenched the robes as he put the events of that night behind him.

'Looks like the Anunaki are good at killing, but that's about it,' he said, adjusting his new, shining chest-plate and chain mail links.

His newly acquired dark cloak and hood draped over the runic, metallic shoulder pads to complete the set.

'Aye, damn hard strapping this shit on in the dark, I know that much. There's little here for Crazy John and Boris, but they usually rely more on their agility in combat anyway,' Neveah muttered.

'Yeah, let's bring some of this stuff back for Angelite and get going. You sure Crazy John can find something to fix that ship?'

'He's the greatest mechanic that I've ever known. There's not much he can do with wood, but that boat's made of thick metal as well, so he would've found and fixed something.'

With that, the two of them exited the cabin and quickly trekked back to the pier. Both clinked in their new armour as they strode across the creaking planks. They were proud of their new look, thinking of it as a much-needed improvement.

As both men approached the vessel, they noticed the third mast, that was once snapped, now stood tall again. They saw Catalyst humming with power as the priestess concentrated on melding the wood back together, whilst holding the large wooden-beam in place with telekinetic prowess. Swirling around her legs were bright, spiritual orbs, which gradually spread outwards as her Resonance grew on the wooden decking.

'She's at it again,' said Neveah.

'It's good to see,' Maledream smirked, strolling up the gangplank.

Angelite aimed Catalyst at the broken area of the wooden beam and unleashed the swelling energy, which flowed out of the swan statuette. Resonating green and golden energies reached out for the break in the wood, to amalgamate it solidly in place. Finishing her spell, she relaxed with a passing sigh, and the Resonance dissipated with static.

'Thank you,' she said, turning to smile at Silver.

'Don't thank me. I just encouraged you to believe it was possible. Catalyst has tuned to you nicely.'

Angelite weakly smiled, and then turned her sight to the gangplank to see a heavily armoured Maledream and Neveah with big grins on their faces.

'That's armour from Meridia, where on earth did you find it?' she probed.

Maledream, with both hands, lifted his blade and sank it into the wooden decking. He leaned on it confidently with one hand. 'A wooden hut,' he smirked.

'What else was in there?'

'Aye, these robes, and other bits,' Neveah grunted, lighting his pipe from one of the lamps.

'You'll have to show me. Did you see any papers lying around at all? It should have information for the equipment, and rosters for the Watchman who lost their lives,' Angelite pursued, inspecting the runes and embedded crystals in the finely forged armour.

'It's on the beach, but I don't think...' before Maledream could finish, Angelite brushed past him.

Neveah shrugged with a confused expression, and then nodded to Maledream to follow her back to the beach.

* * *

Meanwhile, high on the cliff tops that overlooked the Watchman port, the Blood Adepts surveyed the Cattle in unison.

'Is it time? All this waiting and planning is laborious,' one uttered in mind.

'Agreed, the conditions are most favourable,' another stated.

'Yes. Release them now. They have nowhere to run.'

* * *

Silver raised his keen ears, his eyes raced to the height of the cliffs looming above the harbour. Releasing a frightening howl, his cry echoed everywhere across the port's vast, natural walls, serving to warn the three who had just set foot on the beach.

* * *

'Silver?' uttered the priestess, pausing in her stride.
Before she knew it, the lumpy sand shifted beneath her.
'Angelite, watch out,' Maledream bellowed.
Neveah roared in retaliation and, throwing his pole-arm like a javelin, sent it flying past Maledream and

Angelite's scalps. With a crunch, the weapon's blade embedded itself in the horned cranium of an Anunaki warrior, killing it outright as it just emerged from the grains.

Angelite shrieked, having the presence of mind to reach for Catalyst. Its runes glowed with a fierce, golden light, barring another Anunaki warrior's attempt to take her life. It brought its monstrous claws upon her, screeching its talons against the rippling, golden shield like steel on steel, and forcing her to her knees.

Maledream's eyes widened at the sight. His runic weapon charged with energy in an instant, its symbols reacting to his nervous response. The scene was surreal. He watched the circling runes protect Angelite as the Anunaki continued its assault on her frail barrier amidst her cry.

His Relic Blade illuminated with a crimson glow, matched in colour by his newly attached gauntlets. Before he knew it, a torrent of power rushed through him and, with a blinding light and surge of speed, his sword sliced through the Anunaki with an echoing, sonic boom.

Angelite stared at him as he landed on his feet in shock and awe. Neveah watched with his one good eye, easily gleaning that something wasn't right, even as more warriors appeared from the shifting, lumpy sands. Wrenching the pole-arm out of the Anunaki's skull with a crunch, he saw the amassing horde lumbering towards them. It brought back the horrendous memories.

'Let's get the hell out of here,' he roared to them.

Maledream couldn't hear Neveah. All he could hear was his own heartbeat as he focused on the massing, scaly-horned horde that stumbled towards him. Bloody-wet sand covered every crack in their scales, and their claws were primed and ready to disembowel. Without warning, the Tribal lifted his blade behind his shoulders and charged.

'Maledream, what are you doing?' Angelite screamed.

'Run!' Neveah repeated, turning to grab Angelite by her arm to drag her back to the pier.

Chapter Fourteen

Deceitful Plan

'*He is a fool,*' uttered one Blood Adept, watching the scene below.

'*I agree, but don't you dare underestimate that weapon's potential, or that of the bony human who wields it,*' uttered another, their psychic powers easily manipulating the defective soldiers.

'*We must begin corrupting this Cattle, this Maledream,*' one ordered, the rest nodding in unison.

* * *

Blood-red specks littered Maledream's tunnel vision. Dark voices whispered to his conscious thoughts, to protect those he loved and to destroy his enemies. He sliced his sword through all opposition with the unstable energy of the Relic Blade, toppling any foes that dared get within reach.

* * *

Footsteps pounded heavily on the wooden boards of the pier. Neveah and Angelite looked back for a moment, and saw the Tribal was swarmed by many Anunaki.

'I wouldn't advise looking back,' Silver's thoughts raced as they gazed upon the carnage.

'Crazy John, Boris!' Neveah bellowed.

'Yeah?' Crazy John groaned from beneath the decking.

'Are we ready to set sail at full speed?' Neveah barked.

'Just about,' Boris hollered.

'Then fire her up!'

In no time at all, the engine hummed from within the confines of the vessel.

'Got it!' Crazy John shouted.

The ship bolted forth in an instant. Shifting the ocean with roaring hums and thrashes, the propellers launched the ship forwards, and caught all but Neveah off his feet. He swung his pole-arm with all his strength to sever the thick ropes that bound the vessel to the pier.

* * *

Maledream cut another swathe of Anunaki down with several quick, powerful blows. To him, strength no longer mattered. He couldn't feel his muscles amidst the blood-red eyeballs of the beasts he continued to slay.

'You're saving your friends and loved ones,' the voice echoed in his mind.

It almost felt that the sword was speaking to him. It burned his palms, yet he felt no pain. Instead, he felt connected to an immense, raw power. He deflected a blow from another warrior, its large form covered in oozing, radiated boils. With a sharp upstroke after the parry, his Relic Blade cut through the Anunaki with a crunch.

Everything seemed synchronised. He barely had time to register each of his foes, yet swiped at them all the same. All he could focus on was the need to be victorious.

* * *

'Why, Maledream, why are you fighting?' Angelite thought, staring at the battle from the ship.

'Look to the cliff. I could sense those elusive Anunaki. It's why I howled the warning,' said Silver.

'Is there anything we can do?' Boris asked, peering at the shadowy figures that watched the scene from their perch.

'I'm not sure, although, it would explain where all those warriors had disappeared to when we were *travelling here. The Anunaki have mass-mind controlled those rotting beasts. I was meant to return to N'Rutas, but it looks like I'm fated to travel with you.'*

'Aye, Maledream's travelling spirit has that effect,' Neveah replied, his tone grim.

Angelite struggled to come to terms with what she saw. She felt the dark energies emanating from the extremely powerful, psychic Anunaki. She returned her focus on Maledream fighting the mass of dark scales.

'Are we setting sail without him?' Boris wondered, her tone one of surprise.

'We've got no choice. What can we do against those odds?' Neveah bitterly muttered through gritted teeth.

Angelite peered at the rolling, crimson waves crashing on the shoreline. Gripping her staff with renewed hope that grew in her heart, she had an epiphany. The priestess ran up steep, iron steps at the rear of the ship.

'I'm coming,' she bellowed, her green and purple robes whipping in the wind.

'No, don't,' Neveah shouted.

Angelite stopped when she reached the bridge. She glared at Maledream on the beach, and then towards the cliffs.

'Stop, what the hell are you doing?' Neveah urged, tripping on the last step of the iron stair.

His jaw slammed into the metal grating. All he could do was grunt and groan in his daze.

'I'll be fine, keep the ship at the end of the pier,' she barked.

Angelite climbed up and stood on the wooden beam. Rolling her vision earthward, she stared at the ocean below.

'Is it deep enough? Spirits, help me,' She thought, gazing back to the beach and then to the water.

She swept her long hair back from her eyes as the winds of Resonance picked up around her. The robes she wore pulled and threatened her balance, but she stood firm. Catalyst's runes reacted and illuminated once she smacked the butt of the rod on the beam, and then raised it with both hands.

'Water and air guide and protect. Water and air guide and protect. Feel the anger of the tides, feel the fury of the winds. Answer my call, answer me.'

Catalyst's crystals glowed brightly as she channelled the Resonance of her spell. Her eyes glimmered with a rich, cosmic violet. Something within her commanded the very essence she sought. White-cold ethereal orbs spiralled around her. The very light of them brushed warmth on her spirit, and the wind strengthened.

'What's she doing now?' Crazy John blurted.

'She's saving him,' replied Silver.

***

Cutting through another red-eyed beast, Maledream's strength was beginning to weaken, even though the sword seemed weightless. He just couldn't stop the bloodshed. Suddenly, a blow knocked him from behind, causing him to lose his balance and jolt forwards into a large, swinging arm from another warrior. The hit sent him flying through the air.

Landing on his back, Maledream's chest armour chimed against a rock. He had almost lost his blade, save for the chain-link that kept it close to him. Yanking on the chord, he grabbed the hilt again, and stabbed the two-handed blade into the roof of a warrior's snout. Blood and pus spattered his face.

He struggled to get his wind back. The Tribal's world darkened as many Anunaki leapt to land a killing blow. Suddenly, a voice reached inside his mind.

'Run to me, Maledream. Run as fast as you can.'

The Tribal's strength returned to him upon hearing Angelite's sweet voice cut through the chaos.

'Angelite,' he roared.

With only a split second to spare, he rolled and narrowly avoided the heavy punches and claws from the leaping Anunaki that pounded into the sand. It was then he noticed that his Relic Blade took on a softer hue, changing from the familiar crimson to a golden shade. It eased the pain of his burning wrists and hands. Humming with high energy, the Tribal raised the sword aloft his shoulders, just as he stood upright from his roll, and then stabbed it in the soft, crimson granules beneath his feet.

'Retrinumun.'

A shockwave rippled across the fine grains. With a thunderous, bass echo greeting the air, the released Resonance burst in a spiralling, energetic nova.

Tonnes of crimson-coloured sand, and Anunaki alike, were flung skyward from the deafening, blasting wave. In those scant seconds, the sand superheated into liquid glass and, hardening in an instant, served to pierce many of the radiated warriors in a field of ridged spikes. Bloody, gangrene ooze dripped down their solidified, transparent prisons. The warriors that had escaped the epicentre of the nova, but were carried into the sky from the blast, fell back to earth with splattering thuds. A shower of sand greeted the Tribal's ears like rain and, at the same time, revealed a clear path for him to the pier.

'Run to me, run as fast as you can,' Angelite uttered through mind, her voice strong.

'I'm coming,' he cried, sprinting over severed heads, spilled intestines, and other innards of the carnage.

A horde of warriors gave chase once they had leapt back onto their rotting, thick-scaled legs. The Anunaki could not allow him to leave.

'Now is the moment,' Angelite muttered, thanking the spirits that she had gotten through to him.

The Tribal watched the priestess fall from the bridge of the ship towards the water with worry-widened eyes.

'Go,' her sweet voice resonated to him. *'Run. Run as fast as you can.'*

Falling towards the ocean, and clutching Catalyst as she did so, the lights of the spiritual orbs fell in free fall with her. The priestess raised her staff high above her head and, at the right moment, released the power she had stored in Catalyst to smack the swan statuette on the ocean's surface.

The deep waters reacted instantaneously. A boom resounded like a clap of thunder, and the saltwater beneath her feet leapt up in front of her, which encompassed the length of the entire harbour. The power released from Catalyst was like a meteor slamming into the ocean as a million gallons raced towards the sandy beach, and, to the surprise of the Blood Adepts watching the scene below, turned the rushing tide into a monstrous tsunami under her power.

Maledream raced towards the end of the pier where Crazy John had a rope waiting for him. With fierce intensity, the once-calm tide roared into a growing deluge. He eyed the wooden pier's planks rise and fall like a winding serpent as the water grew higher. The right moment to jump meant everything as the ship was ten paces away. He took a breath and leapt towards the rope. Roaring in success, he gripped it with all his might.

Neveah finally got up and rushed over, glaring over the deck with a grim expression.

'After you're done pulling him up, pull me up,' he yelled, hastily grabbing a loose rope on the bridge and wrapping it tightly around his torso.

With that said, Neveah dived over the side.

Angelite focused on the deluge racing towards the beach, breaking the piers and swallowing any splintered ships between her and the bloody harvest to which she wrought. With no fear, the Anunaki mindlessly charged into, and disappeared, under the huge tidal force that crushed and carried them back to shore. Catalyst hummed in the priestess's hands. She had spent her energy, and lost her concentration.

'I didn't think this far ahead,' she thought, biting her lower lip.

Watching in horror, the torrent that had just as quickly crushed the harbour began rushing back into the ocean with a low, bass groan. Hearing a roar from above, she watched helplessly as Neveah's large form crashed into the shallow water. Resurfacing with a strand of seaweed overlapping his shaved scalp, he cursed and grinned at her.

'Come here, woman, and hold your breath,' he said, grabbing her by the waist with his tensed, bulging arm.

'That water's going to crush us, pull us up,' he ranted, tugging the rope.

No one replied.

'You bastards listening? Pull us up, for fuck sake!'

Feeling a tug, his curse was answered. As if ten strong men pulled at the other end, the twosome was yanked upwards to the decking of the ship with great speed and surprising force. Angelite was briskly chucked over the bridge's beam by the Pack leader's bulging arm. Once she picked herself up, she was surprised to see it was Silver holding the rope in his snout. He easily pulled Neveah over the edge with a harder yank. Landing for a second time on his already bruised jaw, Neveah let out a groan whilst glaring at the wolf.

'Cheers, mutt,' Neveah jested.

'I'm a wolf, not a mutt.'

Once Neveah was back on his feet, the combined force of the ocean, and a burst of wind that whipped the masts of the ship, sent the vessel roaring ahead at incredible speed.

'We made it,' Neveah muttered in relief.

Angelite raced down to the ship's main deck, soaked from head to toe and, before Maledream could say a word, she gave him a hard, echoing smack across his face.

'Idiot!' she cried, clutching at his armour and clothing. 'You do that again... and...' she stammered.

Maledream was shocked, yet also relieved. Relishing her strike with eyelids closed, he wrapped his arms around her and hugged tightly.

'Sorry... what I'm going to say next isn't an excuse. Something had some sort power over me...' he sighed.

'I know,' she sobbed, slamming a clenched fist repeatedly into his newly acquired chest-plate. 'I don't care anymore, Maledream. I just want to take you and everyone else home with me, where we'll all be safe from this crazy continent. I don't want to lose any one again! You know that, you above all else should understand that!' she blubbered.

Angelite cried with relief as Maledream continued to grip her tightly. Silver watched the humans for a moment, and then returned his glare towards the beach that was now disappearing from view. He couldn't shake his foreboding senses. Below the decking, a soft hum increased in strength. Crazy John increased the power of the Meridian engine, speeding the ship even further into the open ocean.

* * *

'Madness!' roared one Blood Adept.

They helplessly watched the horde of warrior corpses float on the ocean's surface after the crushing tsunami.

'We still have time. Only a little further out to sea and we'll unleash the next weapon,' another replied.

'I can't wait,' said the third.

'I'll utilise it now. I will possess that Cattle, Maledream. There is a gaping hole in his soul, and it has only strengthened since wearing him down,' uttered the leader of the few.

'Once we have control of that Cattle, we can take control of the weapon,' said another.

'Indeed, and it seems that the red-haired breeder has great control over him. We will need to step up our powers and wear him out further. Remember, we need to capture her once we find any trace of the Cattles' breeding grounds. Get ready. This time we will not fail. She will not interfere with us...'

* * *

The group sat in a circle on the main deck, and took turns smoking from Neveah's pipe while downing some of the Meridian alcohols stowed from inside the vessel. Angelite disappeared below deck to change into her new

Meridian robes as the party watched the flickering flames of three lamps.

'This has probably been one of the worst journey's I have ever had the pleasure of taking,' said Crazy John, breaking the long silence.

'Aye,' Neveah grunted, scratching his groin and returning to his pipe.

Maledream sighed and glared at the patchy clouds. He wanted to say something, but apprehensiveness got the better of him as he tried relaxing. His hands brushed against the cold, wooden planks of the deck. Silver stood at the bow of the ship, ever watchful and away from the others.

'We've lost many friends. Once we get to this Meridia, we'll honour their deaths,' uttered a solemn Neveah.

'If you're lucky,' replied Crazy John, his tongue toying with the tip of his knife.

'Then it's sorted. Wait, what's that...?' Neveah paused.

Silver howled, alerting everyone to the ocean rising in front of the ship.

'This isn't possible!' Neveah yelled, getting up and out stretching his arms in dismay.

A monstrous creature rose from the ocean, and at such speed, that it rocked the ship with a rolling wave. Everyone struggled to keep their balance as the vessel shifted sideways with a groan of wood and metal.

The hairs on Maledream's skin turned on end. He recalled his vision on the beach. The powerful moonlight shone through the gelatinous, transparent beast and revealed its gory, twisting innards.

'It's a Behemoth,' Maledream bellowed.

'It's fucking disgusting,' Crazy John shouted, his voice drowned out by the low, deep-bass roar of the sky-scraping creature.

The beast approached, eclipsing the pale light of the moon. The sound of its hundreds' of erratic heartbeats wailed on eardrums. It groaned with a low tone once more, easily overpowering any voices as it postured to attack.

'Brace yourselves!' Neveah roared.

Angelite emerged from the confines of the ship, only to be greeted by the towering monstrosity. The ship was knocked by the Behemoth's own weight as it rammed the starboard side, almost capsizing the vessel and sending all the passengers flying.

The group regained their balance and drew their weapons once the ship steadied, but stared hopelessly at the sheer size of it. The monstrosity took its place by the stern of their vessel, glaring at them with its beady eyes, and emitting a series of rasping click-clacks with its mandibles. It lashed at them with its many slithering tentacles.

'Cut them down,' Neveah yelled, his bulging arms tearing into one such appendage with his pole-arm.

The creature's stench was abhorrent. The powerful smell served to disorientate them. Some struggled to keep their bile in their stomachs. Boris and Crazy John tried to cut through the tentacles, to no avail, whilst dodging the clumsy appendages that were each the width of their height. Silver weaved and dodged, under and over, between the attacks, on the slippery deck. Neveah, although strong, found it hard to cut through one of the lumbering, gelatinous appendages.

The consistent heartbeats of the Behemoth grew faster as it exerted more energy. Angelite shrieked as one such tentacle grabbed her.

'Angelite,' Maledream bellowed, eyes widened.

The Tribal rushed forward with his special blade, easily cleaving the tentacle with a welcoming, thunderous smack. He reached out towards her and, distracted by his desire to help the priestess, was yanked from the decking of the ship with great speed, and was flung high into the air.

With a guttural slice, Maledream freed himself. However, another appendage gripped a hold of him. Repeating his erratic cuts, he was juggled from one tentacle to the next. His companions could do nothing to help as they battled for their own lives on the slippery decking. Knocked hard by the appendages, he lost his grip on the sword. It dangled freely from his chained gauntlet. The gelatinous tentacle tightly entwined around his chest-plate, and gradually dented the strong, Meridian metal.

Meanwhile, Angelite grabbed hold of a lamp, its flame thankfully alive. She aimed it towards the Behemoth. Singing to the tiny, fluttering flame, it fluctuated to her Resonance.

'Flamash, Flamash, Flamash, Gionistisa Triatus. Fire light the beacon, fire be my light, fire be my guardian. Fire be my Sun, Fire be my creation, Fire give breath to the Ether.'

Everyone cheered her on. They were ever more grateful for her powers as the inferno grew in the midair. A circular stream of fire encircled the priestess. In one hand, she held the lamp aloft. With her other, she held Catalyst.

'Like a droplet of water to the ocean, like a candle lit flame to the sun. Flamash, Flamash, Flamash.'

The flame grew into a roaring sphere, easily six feet in diameter. The gloom was no more. The transparent Behemoth was seen in all its glory as the ship rocked against the growing storm. They saw the many hearts of the monstrous creature beating down its tough, gelatinous body, its veins pumping gangrenous blood through its spongy organs. Its tiny white eyes glared at them with tints of red. The constant chattering continued as they blinked in sequence.

Angelite roared as the power surged through her and Catalyst. She spun on the spot, her robes catching in the wind. The runes and crystals stitched into her new robes shimmered brightly against the light. Swinging the staff into the flames, she hurled the smouldering inferno at the Behemoth's chattering snout. For a split second, the cacophonous explosion blinded them all.

'That should have totalled it, surely?' Neveah uttered, regaining his footing and lowering his hand once the light faded.

Before anyone could answer the muscled man, a loud bass-groan filled the air and, as the group's eyes adjusted in the gloom, they watched the beast thrash the hull of the ship. It knocked everyone in an instant to the decking from the multiple impacts. The party grabbed hold of anything to stop them from falling into the fearsome, unforgiving ocean.

Tilting almost vertically, then back down again, the ship only just steadied itself. Its sails caught the full breath of the stormy wind, serving to push the ship back down into the sea with a harsh crash.

Maledream, still in the clutches of a tentacle high in the sky, opened his eyes after the fiery explosion. He saw a gaping hole in the injured Behemoth's skull, where its putrid brain fluid spurted profusely from the gaping wound. The momentum of the thrashing appendages worked to his benefit. The blade waved up and the hilt brushed his palm. Securing it in his solid fist, he roared.

'Die.'

The dark sword's runes resonated a shade of crimson. Wriggling as much as he could through the tight pressure that bound him, he sliced through the monster's tentacle in a flurry, and fell towards the Behemoth's gaping skull.

Roaring in pain amidst the battering, stormy weather, the Behemoth crashed against the ship once again. Its tentacles slithered and tightened on the masts, trying vigorously to break them with a vengeance.

'I'm taking you with me.'

Maledream's cry echoed to the decks below. The others watched him land and stab the blade into the Behemoth's skull with a thunderous bout of Resonance. It to let go of the ship and gutturally roared. The remaining tentacles raced from its underbelly to try to swat the Tribal.

'Steer us away from the beast, or we won't make it, he's going to finish it,' Silver said and, turning his head, saw Neveah was already racing up the slippery iron steps.

'We're leaving, no questions,' Neveah yelled.

'What?' the priestess screeched in protest, her voice drowned out again by another deep groan from the monster.

'I said we're leaving, or we're not going to fucking make it,' Neveah barely bellowed above the fierce noise.

With a roll of the wheel, the ship turned a sharp fifty degrees to the starboard at a fast pace of knots. The vicious storm picked up in strength, and rain drizzled softly on the ship as Angelite looked beyond the beast, to the horizon, where strobes of lightning illuminated the dark clouds.

Maledream struggled against all odds. He repeatedly hacked into the large, squidgy cranium. His hands burned from the raw energies, like it had done on the beach. He let out a cry each time he lowered the weapon. At the same time, he clumsily dodged its flailing limbs.

'Not long now, old man, till I'm one of those spirits you always talk about,' he panted, striking again, the sword ringing.

'I wish I'd stayed at the camp. Why did I leave?' he said, lashing out with both anger and worry in his words.

His mind was tormented with fear. He felt like just giving it all up. His resistance dwindled rapidly when he became aware that the ship was leaving without him. Anger swelled from within.

'So, this is all it meant, Neveah?' he growled, gritting his teeth, his cloak swaying frantically in the wind and threatening his grip.

He no longer cared. Stabbing his blade into the Behemoth, he used it to balance himself as the monstrous creature swayed in the storm.

'So, this is all it meant, Angelite? Wait, what am I saying? I feel...'

Yanking the sword free from the groaning beast's skull, he swung the blade repeatedly at the same spot. Great chunks of bone and gangrenous blood flowed and glowed against the blade's crimson runes.

'I...' he muttered tearfully.

Maledream's eyes widened and, rolling his vision to the blackened sky, released a blood-curdling scream.

* * *

Screaming, Angelite was held back by Crazy John and Boris as she tried to jump into the massive waves. She could only watch as a flash of Resonance ripped from the sky and into the beast with a boom. It fell limply into the ocean with a heavy crash.

'Maledream!' she screeched hysterically.

All they could do was watch from afar. The Behemoth quickly disappeared below the surface of the huge, roaring waves. The wind whipped at the masts and all fell silent. Their only comfort was the soft drizzle that graced their grim expressions in the darkness of the storm.

Neveah shook his head. Exploding in sudden anger, he punched and splintered the thick, oaken decking with his club-like fists. Silver, Boris, and Crazy John just watched him with depressing sighs.

Chapter Fifteen

City-State

Many depressing nights passed as the crew continued their voyage to Meridia. Everyone tried to cheer Angelite up, but to no avail. She lay on her bed in her cabin, left alone to sleep or mope.

Neveah stood on the bridge, watching the sunrays beam into the glittering ocean. Ever since the Behemoth attacked, they wondered if any other beasts lurked out there in the blue abyss. All of them were highly tense. With their numbers down a further person, it didn't lighten Neveah's mood, especially as he lost his childhood friend no less than a few days after finding him after all these years.

No one dared approach him. He just shouted obscenities at them if they did. So instead, the group let him stew. He was glad. Peace and quiet was all he could tolerate as they sailed through this barren ocean. His one good eye watched the horizon hypnotically as the ship bounced lightly on the waves. Neveah couldn't put his finger on how or why things had gone so wrong.

First, the Anunaki ambush. Second, the Behemoth's surprise attack. He hated such surprises and, after thinking long and hard about it, thought that the strange, Anunaki cabal had probably been following them since the canyon incident. The Pack leader reflected on what had happened, each time shrugging, thinking, and shrugging some more.

'I sense very strong energies,' Silver said, his fur coat easily catching Neveah's good eye as it shimmered in the sun.

'Energy... what's it good for?' Neveah grunted.

'No need to be pessimistic, Neveah. You really should celebrate the lives you saved, not the life you lost.'

'Shut the hell up, mutt! Keep your damn optimism to yourself,' Neveah snarled.

Silence fell on the two for a moment. The big man sighed and, speaking with an apologetic tone, replied, 'sorry, Silver. I was close to Maledream. He was like a brother. He's dead because I had to save our asses, as dark as that sounds. It pisses me off, and I'm frustrated to hell that I couldn't do anything more to help the poor bastard.'

'That's understandable. I'm sorry for being blunt.'

'Nah, forget it. I'll be all right.'

He scratched his eye-patch, then, stretching out his arms, crossed them behind his scalp.

'First time in a while that I've opened my trap. I should thank you for it. But still, I'm just so pissed off, agitated, and fucking want bloody murder at the moment. Blood's boiling, and thinking just gives me a headache,' he added, letting out another heavy sigh.

'I've not had a headache, save for when N'Rutas hit me for biting her leg when I was a pup.'

Neveah glanced at the large wolf and grinned at him.

'Aye, she's a weird one. Just about eaten all the grub she made for us, too. Not to mention we lost most of our kit because we left them on the bastard decking when that thing attacked. I'm so hungry, and it's the fucking irony of it that makes it worse. No fishing rods and we're in an ocean full of bloody fish, and I say fish loosely. Knowing my luck, if I stuck a rod in the bastard water, I'd catch one of those Behemoths.'

'Please don't,' Silver jested.

'So anyway, Silver, you were saying something about energy?'

'Yes, we're almost at Meridia.'

'You're pretty damn useless in a fight, but I guess you've got other talents,' Neveah chuckled.

'Ape.'

'Mutt.'

* * *

Meanwhile, in the living quarters below, Angelite's sore eyes flicked open as she led in bed. Her hands clung to Maledream's long coat. She would smell him and upset herself further. Her freckled face furled slightly every time, although, it now seemed she had no energy left to cry. The priestess let out a long-drawn breath, before shutting her eyes slowly, then opening them again.

'Home...' she sniffed.

Feeling the ship gently rock, she eyed the all-wooden cabin. This small quarter served as her home for the majority of the voyage. She spent her time lighting one candle after another in a lamp by her bedside. She always stared directly into the hot-white brightness while reflecting on her thoughts and emotions.

No light from the outside world had been allowed inside. Depressingly sighing once more, she peered over towards the key in the lock of the cabin's only door. She recalled, back home, what her teachers had taught her at an early age.

Open the door, then the door after that to keep advancing, they would say to her. Never fear, look back or never hesitate, or you'll be lost in your pain and sorrow. This was a hard lesson to learn. Many feelings of her past childhood kept trying to resurface, but she wouldn't let it happen. She wouldn't return to the first door she had opened.

The candle caught her eye again as she sat upright. Her head tilted whilst eyeing the gloomy room, subconsciously trying to find some sort of sign or compensation for her feelings. Brushing her long red-hair behind her shoulders, she finally found the courage to stand.

She glanced at Catalyst that lay resting against the wooden hull in the corner. She hesitated letting go of Maledream's coat for a moment. She didn't want to let go.

'I wish you were here, you would have loved my home,' she thought, grimacing as she fought back the unsettling sadness.

The priestess approached Catalyst, squinting at the ornate staff. She cradled it in her smooth palms and, for a moment, it hummed and sang to her faintly before the sounds disappeared altogether. She didn't know if she should smile at the cold, silvery object she now held in her hands.

'Best go up and see everyone,' she muttered, striding to the door.

She hesitated to unlock it for a moment as her rich, silken sleeve comforted her skin.

'With each step through a door, another awaits,' she muttered, thinking back to her teacher's philosophy.

'Land Ho,' Boris roared from atop the ship.

Upon hearing this, Angelite was now anxious to join the others.

'*Don't cry again,*' she thought.

* * *

'Check it out!' yelled Boris.

'Aye, it's amazing,' Neveah concurred, raising his pole-arm with his arms above his head and shaking it like a trophy.

'*That's definitely Meridia, the energies are very strong,*' said Silver.

'I can smell food already!' Neveah laughed.

Striding to the upper deck, Angelite joined the group to see what was making them so happy. She smiled with them, even it was all for show.

'It looks better than I imagined. Thought it was going to be like the city we came from. Still, doesn't look like I'll be able to gut anyone,' Crazy John grinned, before Boris levelled him to the deck with a punch to the jaw.

'Was only a joke!' he cried, covering his face with his arms once she was finished with him.

'Don't make jokes like that when she's around, you fucking idiot,' she angrily whispered to him.

Crazy John stared across the decking to see Angelite lost in thought with her robes and hair billowing on the soft breeze. He smirked and nodded.

'Aye, stop it you two, before I dish out some of my muscle specials,' Neveah ordered.

'Nice of you to join us, Angelite,' Silver said, noticing she had crept up behind them.

'Sweetie, are you okay?' Boris asked, leaving Crazy John to squirm on the planks.

'Yeah, I'm fine, thank you...' she murmured, before finding the courage to speak louder. 'We should be at the Port Sector soon. I will probably be taken away to be debriefed by my peers. And don't worry, you'll all be looked after, so feel more than welcome to wander around the place,' she weakly smiled.

Silver peered into her eyes with concern. She seemed devoid of any emotion. For now, he put his concerns to the side and turned his head back to the horizon.

In the distance was Meridia and, from what they all saw, the city-state sported many tall spires and vast pyramids made from ancient stones that shimmered against the blue sky.

'It's certainly something, and to think, we only thought of this place as a myth,' Neveah jested.

'You can call it your home now. It's very different from the dangers you were all accustomed to in the Dark Age lands,' replied Angelite.

'Not too peaceful, I hope, not that I'd get bored,' Crazy John muttered with a snide grin, fully aware Boris eyed him like a hawk.

'Well, I'm sure there's plenty to do there?' Neveah replied, grimacing at Crazy John's words.

'You'll love this place as much as I do, I hope...' Angelite uttered, placing her spare hand on Silver's head for comfort.

Sleek ships sailed on the horizon, although not very quickly, or at all. They seemed to be just off the shoreline.

'We'll be there very soon,' said the priestess.

'Aye, gather your shit, everyone, we're getting ready to leave this floater.'

Soon enough, the group's vessel entered a harboured area. Its beaten hull easily attracted the attention from the Meridian inhabitants. They eyed up the new strangers whom stood on the bridge. It was common knowledge for people to arrive with just half a surviving ship, or even on a shoddy raft, yet this was first time that a Meridian-built vessel returned in such a beaten state.

A high, circular city wall, more than a hundred feet in height, hid the bottom halves of the tall pyramids and shining spires, which had, on closer inspection, causeways interlinking them. Many exotic plants draped from these pristine bridges. The smell of incense permeated the air, reminding the group of N'Rutas's hut back in her volcanic glade.

There seemed to be no doors that led in the city. Instead, there were small archways that signalled the entrances through the thick, high wall. As the vessel docked, the port-man chucked them ropes to anchor the ship. In the distance, two men wearing robes, similar to Angelite's, raced towards the harbour. The priestess turned and faced the excited group.

'Those two approaching us are my teachers. The one wearing the dark purple robes is Elric. He is the friendliest and most down to earth person you will ever meet. Don't let your eyes deceive you, though, he can fight with a pole-arm just as well as you, Neveah.'

'Aye, is that so? I bet my biceps could crush him,' Neveah laughed, tensing his muscles with a slight, jealous undertone in a comical fashion.

He managed to force a small smile on Angelite's lips.

'The other gentleman in the dark red is my other teacher, his name's Eldred, and no, Neveah, he can't use a pole-arm,' Angelite smirked.

'Well, I guess that's a damn shame,' he replied, cheerfully grinning as he wiped his sweaty forehead.

Finishing their talk, Angelite led the group down the wooden ramp to meet with the two Resonance teachers.

'Greetings Angelite, we thought you'd never return since your brash decision,' said Eldred.

He was clean-shaven, his hair short, dark, and sporting fashionable curtains that blew gently in the wind of the harbour. He was a man of average height, with cold-blue eyes and a middle-aged complexion.

'Hello,' she replied, steadily gripping Catalyst, slightly unsure of what to expect from her teacher.

'Welcome back, and welcome to your, uh, new friends?' Elric said, breaking the ice.

His hair was also short, but spiky. He had an unshaved, black, five-o'clock shadow. He was almost Neveah's height and, surely enough, had latched on his back a magnificently crafted pole-arm. Sporting a lengthy, thick blade, it was richly encrusted with runes and Crystalline-Pathways in the fine metal.

'Aye, glad to be here, we've travelled from a city far across the ocean. We're tired, lost a lot of friends, and starved to hell,' Neveah said, taking a moment to shake each man's hands.

'I see,' Elric heartily replied.

After the quick introductions, Elric turned and uttered, 'well then, Angelite needs to be debriefed, and that could take a while, so why don't I show you all around while Eldred looks after her?'

'That would be perfect. I need to borrow the Grand Circle immediately for an evacuation. It's for a tribe living in the Dark Age lands,' she said, staring intently at Eldred.

'Of course, priestess, come with me and we will get the debriefing done quickly,' Eldred nodded in agreement.

Waving their goodbyes, the pair made their swift exit deeper inside the city through an alleyway, which was situated in the thick walls that protected the city.

'Right, now that's all sorted... wait a sec, is that a wolf? How did you tame it?' Elric asked with a confused yet frightened tone.

'You could call me a spiritual accident. My name's Silver,' said the wolf, staring oddly at Elric's charming yet twitchy grin.

'And you can speak through mind, fascinating... I take it you haven't been here before?' he quizzed, unable to take his eyes off the animal.

'Of course not, N'Rutas was the only one that came here, and that was around a decade ago.'

'I see, one of the Nephilim by the sound of that name. I believe I met her a long time ago. However, there are stranger sights here since Angelite left us well over two months ago. We have all been worried sick. We expected her back last month. When we spotted your ship, we couldn't believe we saw her on the deck. We made our way down straight away. I'm sure she had her reasons as to why she took longer than expected. I don't see her original companions with her, which is troubling. Right, manners, let me show you around Meridia behind these great walls. Follow me,' Elric finished.

The group followed him with renewed energy whilst breathing in the strange, exotic smells of incense, food, and wine that wafted on the ocean breeze from the nearby markets. Eventually, they came to a small entrance on the docks and followed Elric through the gloomy passage, which led a path through the high, circular wall.

The Pack reached out with their hands to feel the walls that were cold and clammy. The passage was around thirty metres in length, showing just how thick the Meridian walls were. On closer inspection, the metric ton stones had many ancient sea creatures, small and large, fossilized on the old architecture.

Swiftly passing through the tunnel, they entered a large plaza. The tall pyramids and spires had stairways leading all the way to their pinnacles. They looked far more arcane and wondrous than the bleak, ruined cityscape that they once called home.

Birds of many varieties, perched on the high causeways, chirped away at the descending dusk. People were everywhere, drinking and eating outside on stools among areas of rich, cut grasses. Crystal-clear water sprayed from many fountains in these gardens, which created a plethora of dazzling colours from the various, large crystals embedded in them. They almost seemed like they were fountains made of rainbows.

The air seemed to tingle as though it contained some magical quality. Everywhere, and everyone, looked perfect. No ill or dying, no one eating pestilent food, or drinking water riddled with dirt, disease, or parasites. The group felt cheated the more they looked on with envious jealousy.

Their lives had not been so fortunate.

'I'm finding it hard believing what I'm seeing,' Boris said, so moved by what she saw that she linked arms with Crazy John, much to his surprise.

'Now, before I go on,' Elric said, turning around to face the wide-eyed Pack. 'There's a few rules, I'm afraid...'

'Aye, spit them out,' Neveah nodded.

'I must ask you to attend the colleges here in Meridia. This is a special place, and it was once a city that was spoiled in ancient wars. I will be more than happy to tell about its history later when we get a drink in my favourite tavern. I expect you've got more than a few questions.'

'Aye, a fair few.'

Elric smiled, uttering, 'then I'll begin. The rules are simple. Number one is free will. That stands for your free will and the free will of others. Please respect everyone here and they'll respect you back. Rule number two, absolutely no violence. Rule number three, live peacefully. Rule number four is to learn a little philosophy. We teach everything here. We don't try to enforce it, as remember the first rule is free will. Therefore, it's entirely up to you to take it on, but I ask you try. It can be difficult adjusting to such a culture shock, believe me.'

'So, you're saying we can do what we want, as long as we don't go around punching, mugging, or stabbing the crap out of someone?' said Crazy John.

'Pretty much, yeah, but bear in mind that the rules are only there to help you settle in. The transitions you will experience here will shock you. Some have gone insane in the past. Moving from a life in the Dark Age lands, to that of Meridia, can have unexpected consequences. Some have searched for this place all their lives, yet once here, they cannot cope. You are lucky to have stumbled upon Angelite. She can guide you all through your new lives here.'

'Understood, mate. We'll learn a little while we're here. Hell, we have to, really. If any of my Pack breaks these rules, I'll break their necks, personally!' Neveah jested.

'I claim free will! Snap our necks and it's against the rules!' Boris said cheekily, to which Neveah wittily replied, 'aye, but I've not gone through the transition yet. I'm still your leader, and I'll break your ass! That's what my free will is all about,' he chuckled, slapping her gently on the back.

'That's why you need to learn some philosophy now you're here. It's all well and good that everyone claims they have free will, but unless you have the know-how with Meridian philosophy, you will end up taking it all the wrong way and intrude on one another's wills. You'll learn a great deal in time,' Elric continued, scratching his unshaven chin for a moment.

'Now, I take it that these rules are understood? I was like all of you once. I, too, was a refugee. This was many, many years ago. I experienced hardship only the likes you guys will ever know. Angelite had no clue about the outside world, like many born behind Meridia's walls. She got restless and demanded the chance to explore. Anyway, enough of that for now...' he said, continuing to lead them through the various, bustling streets.

'I'll tell you how this city is structured before we settle for drinks. We are at the outskirts, and although much of the city looks the same, you can tell which part you're in by the style of the buildings. There's different vegetation scattered throughout and, most importantly, there are different, circular walls that separate each circular Sector. The Sector behind us is the Port Sector, and if you follow the road's going further into the city, you will find the first of many inner-walls that span for miles. The second area is called the Social Sector, which is the most beautiful Sector, in my opinion. Not to mention the music, night-life, and the alcohol!'

'Sounds like my kind of place!' Neveah grinned.

'I thought so. You'll no doubt have a few interesting encounters. Do be careful, though, it can be considered rather raunchy at times, but I'll leave you to find that out for yourself,' Elric laughed. 'Now, the third area is the Craft Sector, it has many skilled artisans and crafters, the likes of which you have never seen or known. They make many things, ranging from my pole-arm, to some experimental water-powered vehicles, although that's still in the early stages.'

'Water-powered?' Boris pursued.

'Yes, water, or rather hydrogen, a base element of water. We believe in a clean and friendly environment, never to disturb the world's balance. We believe in healing the planet, and the best way to do that is to use the most abundant, clean resource that the earth has to offer, and that is water,' Elric nodded.

'But that's impossible, surely?' Crazy John frowned.

'I take it you've been using the last of the world's gas to power your vehicles back in the Dark Age lands?' Elric asked, smirking.

'Aye, used to own one such truck. Damn thing kept breaking down most of the damn time,' answered Neveah.

'There was nothing wrong with the engine till we fucked it at the battlefield,' Crazy John moaned.

Elric laughed at the comment, continuing to utter as the group entered another cross-section, 'they've only recently created a few prototypes of these hydro-powered vehicles because of our expeditions into the Dark Age lands. We rediscovered the technology, you could say. However, there are secrets we have unearthed here, too. We rediscovered this city when it emerged from the ocean at the turn of the Dark Age, or at least that's how it's told. It's taken many years to rebuild this city to how it was, and, with the extra help Resonance has provided us, it has made morphing stone and steel a lot easier.'

'Very interesting. Still, I don't think I'm quite grasping it all just yet,' replied Neveah.

'Same… carry on, though,' said Boris.

'Right you are. The Craft Sector is a good place to go if you want any armour or weapons. However, Neveah, how did you acquire that chest-plate? I must ask, because you're only wearing a partial amount of the kit. The Watchman usually wear all the armour and other trappings,' Elric wondered.

'Long story, but you can blame those bastard-lizards. I found this in a cache at the harbour we left,' Neveah muttered.

Hearing this didn't seem to surprise Elric. He merely raised an eyebrow and sighed.

'We'll talk about it in detail later, then. If it's what I'm thinking, then they didn't last long out there. That's a terrible shame. Once we get a full account from your statements, we can contact the families. We were trying to tie our bonds more closely to the Dark Age lands.'

'So, I guess you know what happened?' Neveah sighed.

'Angelite briefly mentioned it earlier. Naturally, it's not something anyone wants to touch on, but we have a commitment to the Meridian people,' Elric replied, his smile disappearing altogether before continuing in his lecture. 'Anyway, I'll get the details from you later. I'll look up the rosters for now. So then, the fourth Sector is, if you haven't guessed it already, the Educational Sector. They not only teach Resonance, but also the ways of the body, the spirit, and medicines such as alchemy. It doesn't matter what you choose, if you do choose, of course. You can learn martial arts, which would probably interest you the most, from the look of your rugged fighting forms. No offence,' Elric grinned.

'None at all, mate. I wouldn't mind learning some of that martial arts stuff if it makes me a better fighter,' Neveah nodded.

'Same here,' Crazy John added, his fingers twitchily groping the edge of his dagger in his pocket.

'It's perhaps the most revered Sector, as it stands for the foundations of all knowledge. Knowledge is power, my friends, and all living in Meridia safely guard it. Now, the fifth and final Sector is the Core of Meridia. It's ironically called the Core Sector, and houses many ancient scriptures and artefacts from the old world. There is some closely guarded things in there, such as old, giant skeletons from ages past, and other exotic creatures or peoples.'

'You mean the reptile creatures? Those Anunaki?' asked Boris.

'Them, too. The history of this place will shock you to the core... excuse the bad pun. This city doesn't allow for secrets,' replied Elric.

'Aye, so, what are these giants? Are we talking a little taller than me?' Neveah grinned.

'Well, no, about six times taller, actually,' the teacher said with a serious, yet playful undertone.

'Bullshit,' Neveah laughed.

'I'm not joking, I can assure you. You can see for yourself after we get something to eat and drink. You can't touch them, though, they're in the museums for protection, but you can look at them all you want.'

Neveah looked concerned at the thought of such giant people that once walked in the city. It made him feel small and inferior as he stared at the giant structures once more, and thinking whether or not the tall spires and pyramids were so large because of this apparent fact.

'Other experimentations are also exhibited, creatures long forgotten when this city was buried beneath the waves. We have some large ocean specimens as well,' added Elric.

'You mean Behemoths?' Boris uttered with a surprised tone.

'Behemoths?' Elric pursued, his brow raised in confusion.

'Yeah, Behemoths, one attacked us on the way here. It was at least half as tall as the Port Sector's wall. It was huge, like the size of six or seven ships added together,' she exaggerated.

'Ah ha, I think I know of the creature you're on about, although it has another name in our archaeological papers. Right, sorry for keeping you this long without food or drink, but any refugees need to know the house rules. Let's head to the tavern,' Elric said, leading them down another road.

The Meridian citizens littered the streets and, every so often, they and the patrolling Watchman would stop and stare at the bizarre adventurers. Elric brushed past a large crystal stone, which almost resembled the ones that the group saw inside the volcanic ducts. There were several dotted around every couple of miles, each with a different glow.

Neveah returned his senses to the teacher walking besides them. 'So, Elric, what's this favourite watering-hole of yours called?'

'The Goblins Tap, a great tavern, very nice music, food and beers and it's only a short walk.'

'Goblins Tap? Odd name if you ask me,' said Crazy John.

'I agree with my man, what's a goblin?' Boris frowned.

'A dimensional being,' Elric replied, jest tipped on his tongue.

'Okay? I'll stop with the silly questions,' she said, smirking.

Elric simply smiled at her and the rest of the group as they entered a bustling high street, filled to the brim with crystalline lights, chairs, tables, and a thin veil of smoke as the Meridian citizens began their fun-filled evening.

* * *

Meanwhile, Angelite followed Eldred through the many Sectors for what seemed like hours. They made their way towards to the Grand Circle, which was situated within a pyramid. It was here, within the Core Sector, where the planet received the main influx of energy from the cosmos.

'So, about this young man, this Maledream, you said he was swallowed by the sea after fighting one of those gigantic beasts?' Eldred asked diplomatically.

'Yes, teacher, he protected me for most of the journey. I hoped to bring him here, but it just wasn't meant to be, I guess,' she replied with a heavy sigh.

'Not all things in life can be worked out the way you want them, dear priestess. Rest assured, life is full of mysteries. Who knows what the universe has in store for you? Perhaps it was meant to happen, perhaps it wasn't. I'm sure you'll feel better in given time.'

Eldred brushed his styled curtains backwards. He refocused his vision on Angelite's staff and eyed it up hungrily.

'And that staff, dear Angelite? Where did you acquire such an item? I take it some fallen one created it for you?'

'Yep, a Nephilim called N'Rutas,' she said, fully aware the teacher was groping Catalyst with his eyes.

However, after hearing the Nephilim's name, he stopped staring at it.

'And did she have anything interesting to say? She is free to visit, but has not done so in many years now, or so I believe. Did she give you any other artefacts that you could hand over to the Order?'

'After I've gone over them, then yes, teacher, I shall. She gave me maps of the old world before the Dark Age, but I'd like to make copies first,' she said with a stern undertone.

The priestess had deep reservations. She didn't want Eldred to take over the study of her information. It was practically all she had compared to the journals she had retrieved in Maledream's city. Already, she felt Eldred was trying to take control. Even the sound of his voice was beginning to irritate her.

'Nothing like home, sweet home,' she thought, nervously twitching her lips.

'Of course you can make copies, dear priestess. However, please let me have them next,' he asked, his tone pitiful.

'Of course, teacher...'

'... *Whatever you say,*' she thought.

Angelite paused outside a grand pyramid. Steps ascended halfway up to show a large entrance, which ultimately led to the Grand Circle inside. The two-thousand foot-high pyramid sported many symbols carved in the great, ancient stonework that had lasted for millennia. Sea fauna was also immortalised on the archaic surfaces. However, most of the runes and writings, etched long ago, showed unfortunate erosion.

'There it is,' said Eldred.

'Thank you, teacher,' Angelite sighed, staring at the flight of steps with tired eyes.

'Who is it you want to summon? A man called Larkham and his Tribals?' Eldred pursued.

'Yes, teacher, I made a promise. I left Larkham with my Quartz Crystal Core. Before I left with Maledream, I agreed with Larkham that all the tribe moving at once would be too dangerous. Two of us travelling together would be less noticeable. It was a gamble.'

'I see. Because of your connection with the Crystal Core's frequency, you intend to open a rift between the dimensions. Good. Very good. You are certainly going to pass many of the highest graduates in the Order. I am very proud of you, and yet, also so envious. Still, you have a long way to go before you can match my skill,' Eldred smugly grinned.

Angelite wanted to flame him on the spot for his pompous arrogance.

'Be careful for what you wish for,' she thought, replying slyly, 'Indeed, teacher. I have mastered many abilities. My staff, Catalyst, will help me open such a rift,' she cheerfully nodded.

'I shall watch then, star pupil,' he said, turning to smile at her.

His eyes reminded her of a greedy snake from an old children's book. Eldred was much older, and she knew he had feelings for her. If you could call them that. Yet all she could do was to ignore his cold, blue gaze. She didn't want to give him any encouragement as his hand briskly fell on her hip.

'Right, well, uh, you lead the way, teacher, I guess,' she stammered.

'Of course, follow me,' he nodded, casually removing his hand and taking his time to stroll up the steps in his revered robes.

'I hate it when he does that,' she thought, gritting her teeth.

The priestess was glad he was in front. She hated the idea of him following and watching her. They soon reached the entrance and entered the cool shadow of the tunnel network that led down into the large chambers. Small glass globes, burning rich incense oils, hung from the sides of the crumbled entrance and along the walls leading in, providing a sense of comfort.

Angelite felt woozy from the steep climb but, after breathing in the strong and exotic smells, it seemed to restore her. She was more eager than ever to speak to Larkham. She quickened her scuffling feet and raced ahead of her teacher. She sped past glowing runes leading the way through the spiralling labyrinth, until she entered a balcony that overlooked the Grand Circle.

Impressive illumination burned in the form of crystals, runes, and torches, showing in full the huge, foreboding chamber. Many Watchman guarding it stood around, idly chatting, and taking little notice of Order of Spirit's sudden appearance.

'I'll watch from up here, priestess. Take your place in the centre of the circle so you can carry out your task. I'll be here to assist you, if, of course, you should have need of my help,' Eldred uttered, his tone almost one of belittlement.

'I'll be fine by myself,' she said, quickly making her move before she snapped at him.

'I'll show him how it's done,' she muttered out of earshot, gracefully skipping down the balcony's steps to the main chamber below.

She took her place at the centre of the Grand Circle. Drawing in a deep breath and brushing back the sleeves of her robes, Angelite swept her hair behind her shoulders. She was ready. Catalyst sang to her with a gentle hymn as she made some final, mental preparations.

Her mind was focused on Maledream. Gently nodding her head, she suppressed her thoughts and emotions.

Angelite stared at the large, glimmering lights above. She saw the large circular opening at the top of the pyramid, where one could view the stars at night. The circle beneath her feet was covered in a thin layer of dust, suggesting it had not been used for many months, which was unusual. However, Angelite swiftly shoved this aside in her mind, she had more important things to worry about. Her keen eyes stared at the Crystalline-Pathways and symbols that lay etched in the circle's flooring.

Closing her eyes, she began to channel the energies through her body, thus activating Catalyst. A soft humming resonated inside the chamber, which was duly heard and felt as the Watchman crossed their arms and watched the young priestess. Gradually, a chorus of ghastly choir singers echoed around the chamber, almost like whispers.

Passing a sigh, Angelite focused greater Resonance into the staff. The swan statuette glowed with a rich, violet energy that snaked its way down the shaft, activating its runes and crystals with a powerful, low-bass hum. The metallic swan sprang into life unexpectedly and, silently, its wings arced upwards as if it were to take flight.

Onlookers gasped. None had ever seen such a staff work so quickly, nor release such sounds, or even move on its own accord. Eldred looked on with a jealous fervour. His ears and mouth twitched to each of Angelite's verses.

'I summon forth from my spirit a rift through the gateways of the mind and body, to set free will and energy. I call upon this ancient temple to do as my energy commands.'

As her voice picked up momentum, Angelite's adrenaline spiked. She felt the staff augmenting her spell. Its metallic surface shone and glowed with each verse, mimicking her voice with reverb. The swan statuette gradually outstretched its long neck and shrieked.

The Watchman looked on with fascination. Eldred narrowed his eyes with continued envy. He could feel Angelite's immense and completely unexpected power in the Grand Circle. It crawled all over his skin, likened to that of insects irritating every cell.

She continued her song, and Catalyst echoed her power in kind. Angelite's melody lightly shook the dust all across the chamber. Now was the time to use the vast, golden energies that encircled her in the form of neon glows. Bright orbs of many colours flickered into existence, racing around her voluptuous, elegant form. The spectral lights took up most of the Grand Circle with their dancing flight patterns.

She lowered the butt of the staff to the marble floor with a clunk. Ions of crackling electricity danced off the crystals and runes. She felt the Resonance reaching its highest threshold. Raising and slamming the staff into the centre of the circle once more, she released the final burst of energy. The Grand Circle's runic symbols illuminated from the released Resonance. It was only a matter of time before it would dissipate. She had to act quickly.

'I summon forth from my spirit a rift through the gateways of the mind and body, to set free will and energy. I call upon this ancient temple to do as my energy commands.'

The interlinking Crystalline-Pathways of the Grand Circle pulsated like a heart. Her hair and robes flowed and billowed, defying gravity's will.

'Now open.'

Angelite finished, and her Resonance echoed on the airwaves as the flooring radiated many shades of colour.

Those that watched shielded their eyes from the extreme brightness that took the chamber. The priestess, with her spare hand, flung the other half of the Crystal Core needed to finish the spell, and channelled a beam of rippling, multicoloured light from her palm as she did so. It stopped and hung in the air.

Crystals that provided lighting at the roof of the chamber shattered into many shards, and the fragments fell in slow motion, as if they wrestled with gravity.

A vortex of swirling Resonance exploded from the Crystal Core, where time and space were defied. The priestess tore into the fabric of reality with her voice. Sweat dripped from her nose, but she pressed on with sheer determination.

'Just a matter of tearing through the constant.'

Eldred watched the priestess, and that of the circle, as Catalyst hummed and glittered like silver dust. He peered into the swirling, shimmering portal after the darkness was given light and substance. He saw an ancient city appear in the desolate horizon of the Dark Age lands.

Leaving the Dark Continent behind, many Tribals entered the Grand Circle through the dimensional rift. It took moments before everyone was through. The last to arrive was the old man. Larkham.

Once he had set foot inside the chamber, Angelite halted the channelling, energetic flow from her hands.

Closing the vortex with a shuddering thud, the swan atop Catalyst shrank in size as the power waned, and the chorus of high-pitched sounds subsided.

When she opened her eyes, she was met by many refugees. They all cheered and applauded her for what she had done. Angelite fell to her knees as Larkham approached her. She was pleased to see his friendly face.

'Well done, Priestess Angelite Rose. On behalf of all of us, thank you,' he said, kneeling down beside her.

'Don't thank me. I would do it all over again,' she panted.

'Here, have some water, my dear,' Larkham said but, before he could pass it to her, Eldred tapped him on the shoulder.

'We'll look after her. However, I must ask you all to accompany these guards so they can get you all washed up, and find you something to eat and drink.'

The thought of Angelite surpassing him so soon raised his blood pressure. Eldred glared at her staff, Catalyst, with glazed eyes. *'Why did that cursed Nephilim gift that to her, how dare it?'*

'Thank you very much, young man,' Larkham replied, wondering who had spoken to him.

'Meet the others at the Goblins Tap, they will tell you everything. Find Elric, he should be there,' Angelite uttered, before collapsing unconscious from exhaustion.

'Best get her some water, because if anything happens to that petal, you will answer to me, understand?' the old man uttered coarsely, his vision piercing Eldred's glazed eyes.

'Ah, yes, so uh, who do you think you are, exactly?' Eldred rasped.

'I'm Larkham, and I'm an angry old man,' he growled.

'I see...' Eldred hissed, finding it impossible to look directly into the old man's eyes before continuing with an overly arrogant tone. 'Well then, you dirty Tribal-types must be tired and in need of some rest. You can find that old pub, old man, in the Social Sector. People in the street will direct you, if you ask nicely.'

'Now that I'm here, boy, I'll use my intuition, thank you very much. Now, take care of Angelite before I take her to this tavern myself,' Larkham ordered.

'Who the hell does he think he is?' Eldred thought, his eyes widening in anger, his hands clenching in kind.

Brushing his stewing fury aside, Eldred casually clicked his fingers with an added flick of his wrist. Healers from the Order of Spirit marched into the circle immediately with the Watchman in tow.

Gently picking her up, they carried the priestess away and, as they did so, Catalyst fell limply from her fingers with an echoing clang on the cold marble.

It briefly hummed as it did so.

The Tribal leader stared at it with inquisitive eyes. His ears twitched uncontrollably as if it was trying to attract his attention. He could clearly remember that the priestess owned a wooden staff.

'I'll look after this for her,' Larkham uttered, his weathered hands edging for the valuable rod of power.

'No, I'll look after that,' Eldred brashly stated, hand bolting for the staff.

'Why the rush?' Larkham replied, stooping his suspicious brow, his old hand firmly secure on its shaft.

There was something in the young Meridian man that he did not understand, nor trust. The two men glared at each other. The Tribals, Watchman, and members of the Order of Spirit turned to them with interest. The latter two knew that Master Eldred was used to having his own way.

'It needs to be studied. It's no good in your feeble, old hands!' the teacher snapped, his hand reaching out.

It was then that all present gasped in fright. Catalyst let out a shriek and, in a heartbeat, it burned Eldred's palm when he touched its silvery surface. He yelped and cursed aloud as the staff hissed in retaliation.

'You're not trusted by the spirits, or by this staff, for that matter,' Larkham coldly returned, eyeing Eldred's gawking expression with contempt.

The shocked Meridian teacher uttered no words and backed off. He motioned to the group to follow him from the circle.

'Bastard of an old man, who does he think he is? Some guts for just arriving in my city,' Eldred thought, anger coursing through his arrogant, pompous veins.

Larkham smiled at his fellow Tribals as they followed the Watchman Guard out of the pyramid. He inhaled the smell of incense and was happy to have finally escaped from the Dark Age lands. He and his people awaited many decades to find a place of safety. As the Tribals strode out and onto the balcony, they bore witness to Meridia, shining within the last embers of daylight. Many of them fell to their knees, weeping or cheering at the view. This was indeed heaven to them, a place of harmony, a promised land. Many Meridian citizens awaited them as they exited the mouth of the entrance, bearing clean clothes, food, and sparkling water.

Larkham bid his Tribe farewell, with a promise that he would soon return. For now, he had to make his way to this tavern somewhere in the city. He missed his foster son.

However, *'something doesn't feel right,'* he thought.

Chapter Sixteen

Reunion

Sitting on oaken stools at a table, the Pack, Silver, and Elric conversed in the corner of the Goblins Tap, smoking tobacco, and drinking various beverages. As the drinks continued to flow, so too did the tales of heroism.

'Those bastard Vasps were bloody huge,' Neveah laughed.

'Crap your pants in the process?' Crazy John smirked.

'Aye, would have been their grub if Maledream hadn't of turned up. I miss that little shit, you know?' Neveah mumbled.

'Come on, don't depress us already. You've been a miserable bastard for the past three weeks,' Boris moaned.

'Sorry, but that bloke was my best mate. Bastard-lizards, I bloody hate them. One way or another, I'll make them pay,' Neveah spat, smacking his fist on the oaken table.

'You mean the Anunaki. I think I mentioned something about them earlier as we were walking here,' said Elric.

'Don't care what they're called. I just call them bastard-lizards. Get too close to the water, and that's it, they feast on your ass. Never thought I'd encounter any on the way, and those shadows were something else, too,' Neveah said, swigging a healthy dose of alcohol down his gullet with a satisfying grunt at the end of it.

The human conversation bored Silver. He glumly stared into the nearby fireplace. The smell of wood barely caught his keen nostrils as he then examined the tavern. Old armour and weapons graced the wall behind the bar. Some looked as if they had been powerful millennia ago.

Many people from all societies and cultures were gathered in the building. The spacious rooms hummed with the noise of chatting, laughing, and generally the sound of a good time being had. Some of the crowd took a keen interest in Silver. They were unused to seeing a wolf in their company, and many had never ventured outside Meridia's high walls in their entire lives. Wildlife, aside from the avian nesting in Meridia, seemed more like myth or legend to the city's inhabitants.

Sounds of instruments coursed through the air from around the corner of the Goblins Tap. Musicians played different styles of music, which varied from culture to culture at different intervals. The song would end, and applause would ensue from the other end of the tavern, leaving an altogether good sense of unity.

'Anyway, now you've all had something to eat and drink, I'll tell you a bit more about this city and its foundations,' said Elric.

'Please do,' Boris said, rubbing Crazy John's hand affectionately.

'I'll try to keep it as simple as I can...' Elric said, continuing at length. 'Our evidence shows that around thirteen thousand years ago, we humans were born by a race, a race known as the Creators. They were apparently of a celestial origin, similar to that of spirits. The theory goes that they wanted to feel what it was like to be physical, to enjoy all the senses of the brain, such as pain, pleasure, being real or solid. Therefore, they decided to cross the dimensions, so that they could experience life. We don't know true their motivations, but we do have evidence that our race did change. We humans were once very primitive. All life is formed out of building blocks, called DNA. However, a defect in our ancient cousins DNA meant that our skulls, for example, were growing too large, which led to problems with females giving birth. The Creators changed all that and saved us from extinction.'

The group listened inquisitively, but raised or lowered their brows in confusion or jest.

'Aye, but so, uh, it's slightly confusing. Haven't us humans been the same as we always have?' Neveah frowned.

'We used to be primitive cavemen called Neanderthals. We had no speech, knowledge, or technology, such as how to use simple weapons to hunt wild game. Before the Creators turned us from that path, we had no spiritual beliefs, so no religion. We didn't practice Resonance because we didn't have the knowledge, capacity, or DNA to achieve this. The Creators changed all that, they spliced our DNA with theirs. It's why we can use crystals to work with Resonance, and therefore augment our power that has been awakened since the Dark Age's arrival.'

'So, these ancient cousins of ours didn't know how to make weapons? And, instead of speaking normally, do you mean they could talk like Silver?' Crazy John wondered, his voice almost tipping towards laughter.

'They could make simple stone clubs or wooden spears at the very least, but, with regards to being like Silver, who knows. We haven't unearthed any real evidence of this yet, aside from the remains and other scant history we have access to. There's so much we don't know. After all, it happened so long ago,' Elric uttered, taking in large glug of his wine.

'Maybe they would've known of such things? After all, you said that their brains were getting bigger, which meant their skulls got bigger,' said Boris.

'Which must have been painful,' added Crazy John.

'Exactly, but they must have learned something out of all that? Like an animal instinct, maybe?' she wondered.

'Aye, all this explains to me is how Angelite can use that Witchcraft stuff, and how to use those crystals. I'll never get any of it,' Neveah smirked, inhaling more of his tobacco and casually slouching in his seat.

Elric smiled at each of them, and then took another sip of his wine. He cleared his throat with a harsh grunt. 'We'll never truly know if evolution had intervened before the Creators interfered. And yes, it is why we can use crystals because of our Creator ancestors. That is what our core societies believe. You could say nature itself didn't create humans perfectly, like many other species.'

'Yes, Neveah, it means I'm better than you,' Silver jested.

'Aye, it does, mutt, but I fancy a wolf flank if you don't keep your clever moments to yourself. Always wanted a dog, a man's best friend, and all that,' Neveah slyly laughed.

Silver groaned, ignored him, and lowered his bored snout to the floor with a heaving sigh. Elric tapped the table with his knuckles to attract everyone's attention.

'Right, I'll continue. Spirituality, or the sense of a spirit, never occurred to primitive man. Therefore, the Creators redesigned the human blueprint so that they could inhabit the newborns of the new humans in which they altered, to experience life, for example. To keep their sense of connection to the spirit, or faith, religion was created. They gifted and taught us philosophy, technology, and Resonance.'

Neveah's good eye stared blindly at his pint as he thought long and hard about all this information. He wasn't sure he understood it all, but he was happy to listen and enjoy the relaxing atmosphere in the tavern. The songs of the Goblins Tap carried on peacefully in the background, adding further atmosphere to Elric's historical stories. Ash and embers were renewed with more firewood when the barkeep had a chance to keep the warmth going in the growing cold of the oncoming winter.

Neveah added to the conversation, glancing at Elric. 'Religions. Never heard of them. They sort of like the Tribals? Back from where we were from, these people have spiritual beliefs.'

'Well,' replied Elric, 'religions are a spiritual practice to support whatever beliefs their followers hold. There are some religions present in the city, but they have been in sharp decline since the Dark Age. Most people, today, don't know what to believe, but they know, deep down, that there is something spiritual in the universe. Their beliefs are none of my concern, of course, and certainly, you're free to do as you wish in accordance of free will.'

'Aye, think I'm getting it now,' Neveah mumbled.

'You'll find it easier as the days go by,' Elric replied with his charming grin.

'I'm surprised you can remember all of that, to be honest,' said Boris.

'I've reread the historical scripts too many times to count. I'll go into more details about the Creators, this'll interest you...' Elric chuckled whilst scratching his five o'clock shadow. 'The Creators built this city. In fact, this is where the start of the new species of humans began their lives over twelve millennia ago, or so it says in the texts. They taught the newborns great things. Mind over matter, philosophy, you get the picture. However, because of their ignorant flaw, and breaking of the universal right of free will, the Creators also began to forge weapons of untold power and devastation. There was once an alliance between the humans, Creators, and the Anunaki, which spanned millennia. Of course, under the rule of the Creators, the city was itself the centre of this grand alliance.'

Elric finished for moment and took a sip of his drink.

'Those monsters were allied with us?' Boris asked with an inquisitive, raised eyebrow.

'It appears so...' replied Elric. 'Of course, tensions grew between all the races. Each started breeding programs to increase genetic stock, which means mixing DNA together, or, more commonly, the blood of many races. As you can see, this city has two very distinct building types. The pyramids are of Anunaki design, and the tall, rounded spires are of Creator design, which we humans tended to also favour. To that end, it is why they all have bridges or causeways linking them together. It doesn't just signify easy passage between each building. These bridges stood for unity for the various races that lived here, our ancestors, and their ancestors.'

'Wait a minute, so, you're saying we're related to these bastard-lizards?' Neveah spluttered on his pint.

Elric laughed, but reassured him. 'No, not precisely, although there are beings of what you would call half-breeds. They were the result of Creator, Anunaki or human unions. They weren't trusted in the slightest. These beings are called the Nephilim. N'Rutas is one such being, my friends.'

The Pack recoiled in unison. Neveah almost spilt his beer at hearing this.

'That old hag? Half bastard-lizard?' Neveah coughed.

'News to us, I thought she was a Witch,' said Boris.

Neveah and Crazy John nodded in agreement. They squinted at Elric.

'*I could've told you from the very start, of course,*' said Silver.

'Well, if there are such things as half-human and half-bastard lizard, then what are you, mutt?' Neveah uttered, eyeing him with suspicion.

Silver just shook his head. '*If you think my mother or father is human then you're ridiculous,*' the wolf scoffed.

Elric bellowed with laughter and came to Silver's defence. 'No, no, no. Silver isn't anything like that, nor would it be possible. The Creators are the original link between both the Anunaki and our own ancestors. It's why they can congregate. Evolution has made Silver the way he is. That's my guess, at least.'

'Aye, maybe,' Neveah muttered, lighting his pipe.

'That reminds me. The old hag gave Angelite that staff,' said Boris.

Elric looked surprised. 'I noticed her with it when you disembarked. I thought it was different from the original staff she owned before she left. She was in a rush, so I didn't have the time to ask. It doesn't surprise me, though, the few Nephilim that are still alive are the only ones with the vast knowledge inside their insane minds to fashion such objects. It can take many centuries of hard labour to get halfway to what the Nephilim can create in just a decade or so. In legend, the Creators made similar powerful weapons. They don't break or age, even if they appear to.'

'Like what sort of weapons?' Neveah wondered, his form shifting to the edge of his seat.

'When this city was formed during the alliance, they were said to have been created for close quarters combat or, at the very least, used in close vicinity of an enemy. Do you remember me telling you about the newborn humans, which were twice the size of a human today? They were the ones that utilised them in the Great War of Meridia and, of course, weapons like that are rumoured to be like daggers to them because of their size. They would be, let's say for example, a double-handed sword to a normal human of today?'

'Maledream...' Neveah muttered.

'Maledream?' Elric pursued.

'Yeah, Maledream. He found a blade that could shoot that Resonance shit from its surface. It could cut through anything that stood in its way. Turned him into a killing machine,' Neveah nodded.

'Surely, you're having me on, Neveah. Nephilim can make weapons that resemble the Creators' Relic Weapons, but none are known to exist,' Elric said, half-expecting the large Pack leader to turn around and make a joke.

'No, it's true. Maledream found such a weapon. N'Rutas advised him not to over-use its potential power. She feared that the weapon was awakening,' Silver replied, his tone serious.

'No, it can't be true. We would have found one by now, surely?' Elric politely protested.

'Elric, listen to us,' Boris said, leaning over the table. 'We can all tell you the same thing. You believe in things that might not have happened so long ago, but you have to believe us about this. If anyone has any knowledge on this, it's you.'

'I'll take your word for it. I can feel you're not lying, besides the serious looks on all your faces. How big was this sword?'

'Let's just say that Maledream had difficulty swinging that heavy bastard. It would glow strange colours, weird symbols would ignite on its surface, and a host of other things to boot,' answered Neveah.

'I see, this is serious,' Elric said, his hands finding their way to support his hairy chin as he thought over the matter carefully.

After several moments of silence, the group continued to smoke and drink. Elric found the courage to speak again. 'Now, after careful thinking, there are legends of such weapons back at the Core that hint of such objects. It's why I mentioned them after all, but there was no mention of them after that. It's as though they were wiped off all the records. This can only mean that someone, or maybe some secret society, kept these weapons for safekeeping. It's entirely possible, but it's a long shot,' replied Elric.

'Its mind boggling,' Crazy John groaned, casually leaning backwards in his chair.

'Indeed it is. May I ask why Maledream isn't here now, dare I ask? You mentioned him earlier, but no other details?'

'Aye, he would've been, but something seemed to possess him. He went down with that Sea Behemoth. He had the courage of a brave but stupid bastard when he had that sword in his hands. I don't get scared easily, but when over a hundred bastard-lizards jump out of the sand, and Maledream races towards them, any sane man knows the odds are stacked against him. Angelite managed to save the poor bastard. I've no idea how she snapped him out of his blood frenzy, but he was like a machine. Whoever it was that wanted him dead got their damned wish. Miss the bastard,' Neveah growled, shaking his head, and slamming his fist on the table in frustration.

'You sound like you fancy him, Neveah, just marry the guy,' Crazy John carelessly sniped with a snide-look etched on his grin.

Neveah didn't take his Packer's comment very well. Punching his knuckles together, he glared across the table with the look of killing him.

'Sounds like you all lost someone close to you. After all, surviving dangers with the company you keep develops special, instinctive bonds,' Elric said, peering across to Neveah.

'Aye,' Neveah grunted, swigging down more alcohol.

'Well, legend has it that there were around thirteen such weapons, although there could be more,' continued Elric. 'Obviously, we've none in possession, of course, and, if we did, who knows. We would probably heed the legends and keep them locked away. Only destruction would once again rain on this civilisation, which we desperately want to hold onto. The thing is, if that sword was really one of the Relic Weapons of legend, then it makes you wonder what happened to the others.'

'I know, I'd be king of the old city if I had one...' Crazy John chuckled.

'Aye, and if I had one, I'd shove it up right up your tight little asshole. So keep that clever fucking mouth of yours shut,' Neveah growled.

'Scary when you think about it. I wonder if we'll ever find out what happened to the other weapons,' said Boris.

Silence swiftly fell across the table for a moment as all contemplated this information, despite their intoxicated minds.

'I think that's enough for one day. Dinner is just about to be served, along with another round of alcohol!' Elric finished.

'Sounds good,' Neveah uttered, watching the waitress bring their food over in turns.

Most of it was steamed vegetables, although fish was also a staple part of the menu. Neveah hastily put down his pipe of tobacco, and Boris stood with her glass.

'Well, everyone, let's have a toast. We made it here under the leadership of Angelite and Neveah!' she cheered, causing the men to raise their glasses and join in.

* * *

Larkham's old knees occasionally cracked as he hobbled down the Meridian streets. Resting on both Angelite's staff and his rickety cane, he approached the Goblins Tap. The spirits barely whispered to the spiritual leader's ears. Smells of ale and food caught his dangly haired nostrils.

'Smells like the place,' he muttered.

The old man continued in his slow stride, and he drew the attention of many smartly dressed Meridians. He was aware that they were watching him as he walked up to the oaken doors of the tavern. After all, he looked a state from the poor living conditions to which he was accustomed. The sound of music inside caught his ears.

'Not heard that in a long while,' he said, pushing the door open, and almost coughing from the smoky atmosphere.

His eyes caught those of the tavern keeper. He edged closer to the bar and looked around, trying to find a clue to show him who exactly he was looking for. He heard roars of laughter from the rear corner of the tavern that was illuminated by a fire. A wolf was also sat with them. It caught Larkham's wandering eyes, and locked a sense of friendliness with his own.

'Odd,' Larkham remarked with a cheerful smile.

'Excuse me, sir, you want a drink, or you just planning on standing there?' asked the burly barman.

'Do you have water, kind one?' Larkham smiled.

'We certainly do. Are you another refugee, old geezer?' said the tavern keep as he reached for a glass.

The barman's hair was long and knotted with thick stubble covering his chin that gave him a rough-looking edge. Larkham noticed that his clothes were almost as dirty as his own were, yet he cleaned a mug carefully with a clean cloth before pouring the drink. With a smile, the barman sent the glass sliding into the old man's open hand.

'Thank you, Son. I'm looking for other such refugees. Have you seen any here by any chance?' Larkham wondered.

'Certainly, over there in the corner, they're with Elric,' nodded the barmen, pointing his finger at the group.

'Thank you kindly,' Larkham said, nodding a goodbye as he strode away with the pint of water in one hand, and two staffs in the other.

As he approached the group sat in the corner, they easily spotted him. Their body language turned threatening.

'Hey, old man, where the fuck did you get that staff?' Neveah barked, standing tall and planting his hands firmly on the table with a slam.

Larkham stared at him, and merely smiled through his mangy, dark beard.

'Hello, I'm guessing you know miss Angelite?' Larkham uttered to the group, before resting his pint of water on the table.

All eyes followed his every move.

'Aye, we may well do, but who the hell are you?' Neveah grunted.

'I'm also a friend of hers. She told me to meet you here,' he answered confidently.

Neveah's nerves settled whilst Elric decided to lighten the subject a little.

'It seems you have travelled long and hard, by the looks of you. Come, take a seat,' he cheerfully stated.

'Don't mind if I do, thank you,' Larkham happily returned.

He was pleased by the young man's manners, unlike the other Meridian, Eldred.

'So, I guess we should all get properly acquainted, before someone gets hurt?' Crazy John said, twiddling a dagger between his bony fingers before stabbing it into the oaken table with a thud.

After much discussion throughout the evening, Larkham and the Pack found a truce with one another. Much banter was afloat as they all became better acquainted. It was then, through their discussion, that they discovered this old man was Maledream's foster-father.

'I feel something is wrong, where is Maledream? Is he taking it easy somewhere?' Larkham wondered, his voice husky.

'We've talked about him too many times today,' Boris moaned, gently shaking her head and pouring a fresh glass of wine.

'Why? What's happened to him?' Larkham worried, squinting at Neveah.

'Aye, listen to me closely, old man. This may take you by surprise, and I ain't going to beat around the bush with what I've got to say next. Maledream went down in the ocean defending us from a giant beast of the deep. A Behemoth he called it.'

'I see,' Larkham muttered, taking a swig of his water.

'But, to my knowledge of what the spirits say, he isn't in the spirit world. This seems troubling...' Larkham mumbled.

'His soul hasn't joined with the Great Spirit?' Elric asked with a raised eyebrow.

'No,' Larkham bluntly nodded.

The Packers seemed confused by this statement.

'I believed him to be well and safely in Angelite's company, but the spirits can't tell me everything, only that he isn't a part of the energy. That boy is trouble, isn't he? There was no teaching him. I wonder where he is,' Larkham uttered, his voice growing a tad darker from the troubling thought of what could have happened to him.

'So, you're saying Maledream's alive?' Crazy John pursued.

'Aye, shut up, that's what the old man said. I don't believe that little bastard's alive, Larkham. If you were there, you'd have no doubts,' Neveah argued, although his one eye shined at the thought of the possibility.

'Neveah's right, Maledream had no chance. It can't be possible,' Boris sighed.

'And I get told to shut up at the thought of this?' Crazy John snorted.

'Aye... shut up...'

'Don't lose faith, trust in the spirit,' said Larkham.

'Then what can we do? Look for him?' asked Elric, his thoughts wanting to meet the young man and his Relic Blade.

'Aye, that sounds like a damn good idea to me,' said Neveah.

'Yes, but, how are we going to search the depths of the ocean for him, if he's even in the ocean?' Boris laughed.

'It sounds mighty confusing to me, young ones, but I'd say just give the rescue mission a rest for now. There is one thing you youngsters are good at and that's rushing into trouble,' Larkham smirked.

His weary eyes stared briefly at the happy patrons in the pub, laughing, drinking, and smoking, without an idle clue about what lay beyond Meridia's walls.

'Perhaps Larkham's correct, my friends. It would be foolish to assume we could hold our breath and swim to the depths to find him,' Elric said light-heartedly.

'Aye, but if he is alive, then that means I can take the piss out of him again,' Neveah said, his voice reaching a happier pitch.

'Sounds good to me, I've missed that too,' Larkham smiled, the two leaders' sharing a chuckle.

'Larkham's an older version of Neveah,' Silver thought, his feral eyes watching the humans ever more closely in the tavern.

Then, as his vision arced across the pub, he noticed that Catalyst, which lay against the table, close to Larkham, began to glow with a hue of violet and crimson. He keened his feral ears, picking up what he thought were sounds of a chanting choir. Rising on all four paws, Silver wandered closer to get a better glimpse of the glows.

'What's the matter, mutt?' Neveah wondered.

The staff, it's activating and Angelite's not here.'

'Huh?'

All got up and stared at it. Its runes, symbols, and crystals pulsated in rhythm.

'Can you hear that?' Silver pursued.

'It's singing. I'm not sure why, but it talks to you as if it is singing,' said Larkham.

'That's just plain weird,' Boris frowned, settling back in her chair.

'I agree with my woman,' Crazy John nodded, easily believing it was a great deal more evil than it appeared.

'I can assure you its fine. Violet is a sign of knowledge and psychic ability. Crimson for anger or raw power. I don't know what this means, though,' said the Tribal leader, picking up the special rod with his hands to examine it more closely.

Elric also leaned forward to inspect it. 'The Runes and crystals are a natural part of Resonance to aid casters. Many of these symbols were once lost knowledge. However, we have a whole archive on what they mean, but this staff has so many, and I believe it was created by a...'

'Nephilim?' Larkham said, cutting Elric's conversation short.

All he could do was nod and smile in agreement.

'I know of old legends of these creatures of the past, and of stories of such Creators that made weapons such as these. You said Maledream went down with a giant monster in the sea?' said Larkham.

No answer could be heard, yet all nodded in agreement as Larkham's weathered hands rubbed Catalyst's cold, metallic surface.

'May I ask how he achieved such a feat? I noticed he kept a sword hidden from me, but I could almost feel the weapon's presence. I take it he used this weapon to kill this Behemoth of legend?'

Again, Larkham only received nods in agreement. The Pack continued drinking and smoking with the occasional belch from the good food they had eaten.

'Your wisdom and intuition is something to behold, sir,' Elric said, sounding suitably impressed.

'Years of practice and of knowing thyself, my friend,' Larkham smiled. 'So, he found one of these weapons of my legends. That boy got himself into this, but I admit, I knew he had something up his sleeve when he left with Angelite over a month ago. I didn't worry too much, but I've had a few visions about him. A times of shadow and regret...'

'Aye, you're babbling, old man, get on with it,' Neveah interrupted, cheekily grinning.

'You share Maledream's sense of humour. You remind me a lot of him,' Larkham chuckled.

Neveah merely grinned as he leaned and relaxed in his seat. Silver sat by the staff and continued to feel the strong, spiritual presence of the energy that flowed softly off its shining surface. It seemed to soothe everything around its mystifying aura. The group relaxed once more, and spoke about other, more darker topics that came to mind.

* * *

The moon rose higher in the cosmic night-sky as Angelite briskly walked through the Meridian streets. She was on her way to meet the group at the tavern and, at the same time, could finally have a glass of red wine, which she had not had the pleasure of drinking for many, many months. She was glad to get away from the Core where the healers had helped her back to health.

'What a relief to get away from Eldred,' she thought, a sigh escaping her lips.

The wind gently brushed her as she passed through the various sectors that shone and reflected the pale moonlight. The Social Sector's nightlife was picking up in a city that knew no bounds of where fun had no end, especially for the younger generations. Smells of incense and oils were gone as the traders stopped bartering their goods. Instead, the aroma was replaced by the natural smells of the many varieties of plants, trees, and salt-ocean air.

All she could focus on was the lengthy journey she traversed. She thought of her friends that had lost their lives, both her Meridian companions, and then Maledream. Angelite briefly glared at the lunar sphere beyond the tall, shining spires and large pyramids. She wished that some of the events had never happened.

Entering the Social Sector, she made her way towards the tavern where she could feel the strong presence of Catalyst. Stopping in her tread on the cobbled path, the priestess's intuition kicked in for the briefest of moments. The wind blew her robes with a burst, her long hair following suit, then disappearing altogether as she focused her eyes in the direction of the Port Sector.

'What are you telling me?' she asked blindly to the wind. 'What is it? No, I'm being silly,' she muttered, eyeing the direction with a sense of importance.

Laughter caught her ears. The Goblins Tap lay around the corner from where she stood. Legs carrying her once more, she strode around the corner and stared at the many people going about their business. The nightlife was in full flow. Pushing the door open, she made her way through the bustling tavern.

'Over here!' Neveah yelled.

His voice was so loud that it could have rocked the foundations. She smiled and quickly navigated her way to the table to hug all her friends affectionately, then found a place to sit next to Larkham and Elric. Boris poured her a large glass of red wine and forced it down her neck with a mad laugh. Dark thoughts and events were soon put to the back of each individual's mind. It had been a long journey, but, at last, they could relax within the safety of Meridia's walls. Their new home.

Chapter Seventeen

Release from Darkness

'I've had far too many wines! I better leave before it gets too late,' Angelite blushed.

'Aye, that's fine by me, Sweet,' Neveah said, stumbling as he got up to give the priestess a bear hug, and almost crushing the young woman in the process.

'Now, if anyone bullies you, Angelite, just come find me, and I'll sort those bastards out,' Neveah slurred and laughed, before letting go of her so she could catch her breath.

'I will, don't worry. I've had such a nice time. Shall we meet tomorrow, say, around noon? We can have another drink and something to eat?' she said, grinning.

'Most certainly, priestess, I'll be here again tomorrow. We all need to have a serious talk at some point, though, after all, this is such cosy place,' answered Larkham.

'Don't know if I'm up for more of the serious shit, but I'll drink to that!' said Boris, raising another glass with a drunken, screeching laugh.

'Okay then, it's settled. I'm going before I drop. Elric, I take it you'll look after my friends while I'm away?' she said, grabbing Catalyst.

'Of course, my wonderful student, it's an honour for these fine people.'

Once she had thanked Larkham for looking after her staff, she waved goodbye. The priestess left the Goblins Tap, and the rest of the nightlife carried on. It wasn't unusual for it to keep going until the sun rose.

'Something's causing her to be on edge,' Larkham quietly uttered to Elric.

'I share the same thought, but, I'm sure that once she gets some rest, she'll be fine,' Elric returned.

Silver easily caught their words.

'Larkham, Elric, I will follow her in a few moments and keep a close eye on her until she is safely home. If anything is the matter, you'll hear me. Besides, I have been sat by the fire for the whole evening, and I should stretch my paws.'

The two smiled at the large wolf.

'You do that, my friend,' Elric replied with a sly wink.

Silver soon left the tavern to begin his surveillance. Using his keen sense of smell, he followed her trail through the illuminated, Meridian streets, but kept his distance.

* * *

The night was loud until Angelite strode away and towards the Port Sector, ever wondering why her senses were drawing her closer to the sea. A part of it was curiosity as she stared at the moon. Her true motive was to follow her aching heart. The wine had played its part. Catalyst's runes and crystals were faint in the glow of the light as she carefully made her way out the Social Sector in her elegant, windswept robes. The staff hummed with energy, more so than it did when it wasn't within the boundaries of the city, as if it was more alive than usual.

The sea breeze wafted in her nostrils once she had entered and passed the large tunnel leading into the port. Once out, she gazed at the sprawling ocean. She glanced at their beaten ship that was anchored in dock. Her eyes traced the vessel hypnotically rocking on the steady waves, with other vessels like it, in the harbour. Angelite sighed. She was relieved that she couldn't see anything out of the ordinary, although her thoughts swiftly returned to the Tribal and that of the decimated port in the Dark Age lands.

'Better get his coat and head back.'

She focused on the pier, recounting Maledream's act of bravery and, ultimately, the last time she was in his comforting arms. She was never sure if he felt the same way about her, although, it now seemed silly to speculate. Instead, she stared at the reflecting moon on the rippling ocean. The wind picked up again, blowing her robes and red-hair with a freezing sensation.

She hated these moments of nostalgia. However, just as she dwelled on her feelings, her premonition switched into action. Slowly, she turned her head from the pier to the dim, golden beach. In the gloom of the moon, she thought she saw someone crawling on the drenched sands. Dread seeped into her heart, but, at the same time, she couldn't turn away. The priestess slowly approached the strange, shadowy figure.

'Hello, are you hurt?' she called out.

There was no reply, as such, just a groan in the distance. Catalyst chimed, the sound flinching her ears, reinforcing the omen that dawned on her fear as she drew closer.

'Hello?'

No reply, yet she saw the shadowy figure rise fully to its feet, its motion like that of a puppet on strings. It held something long, dark, and thick in its outstretched arms. Holding her staff in a defensive pose, she muttered a few words of Resonance to prepare for whatever it was.

The feeling of being alone crept over her skin, her hairs rose on end. Catalyst responded in kind with its crystals, illuminating the area around her like a torch. Pausing in her tracks once more, she let the stranger stumble into the light.

Her eyes widened.

She stared at the ghastly appearance of Maledream. Angelite's heart fluttered. Thoughts raced through her mind as to how he could be here in Meridia but, before she had a chance to say or think anything else, the young man dashed towards her with unnatural speed. Now, with only ten paces between them, she stared at him in horror. His eyes were abyssal, and his aura dark strangled the very air.

'You, and all your kind, are ours now, breeder,' a raging, rasping voice bellowed in her mind.

The cracked chest plate he wore was unnaturally rusty, whilst shadowy-crimson energies seeped from the cracks of the old crystals attached to the armour. He raised the sword and was ready to decapitate her with one blow.

'Maledream, please,' she screamed, raising her staff clumsily, and ducking her head from the swing.

Catalyst sang and responded on its own accord to protect its wielder. The energy roared like a fierce inferno, creating a rippling, golden barrier of Resonance that surrounded her. Maledream smashed the Relic Blade against both Catalyst and shield. She successfully blocked the blow with an echoing clang resonating through the air. Adrenaline now pumping, the priestess leapt to one side to escape other harsh swipes from the dark entity that possessed the Tribal.

'You're all going to die,' the voice raged.

'We'll see about that,' she screamed in defiance, her eyes lighting with a bright, violet hue as she readied herself for another hit.

Multicoloured sparks flew from both the blade and the staff, accompanied by more harsh screeches, like steel on steel.

'You cannot defy your masters, Breeder. We are your birthright.'

Although shaken from fear, the priestess was filling with courage and conviction. Battering away another blow from Maledream's swings, she gathered raw energies in her spare hand and, channelling the Resonance through her quickly tiring body, blasted him away with a ball of bright, multicoloured light. Flying a short distance through the air, he landed heavily on the sand with a thud.

Rising off the ground, and laughing insanely, his abyssal eyes glared at her. 'You cannot stop this vessel. This blade will grow in strength the more I slaughter with it.'

Angelite empowered more energy in the staff as the possessed man renewed his charge.

'Maledream, I know you're listening. You've got to break free, snap out of it!'

She parried the accurate blow, but landed ass first on the damp beach from the force of the strike. She saw Maledream swing again and, managing to escape with a roll, the sword was sent plunging into the granules. Dark energies polluted the sand with red cracks as it struck, seemingly melting the grainy crevices into cracked glass.

'You cannot stop my new-found power,' it roared, dragging the sword out of the sand with an uppercut.

Angelite was barely able to block it below her knees. A flash of light signalled an energetic explosion and, as it faded, Angelite flew limp to the air as she was hurtled tens of feet in an arc. Landing on the solid cobbled-stoned pathway away from the beach, sharp, shooting pains racked her spine.

Thankfully, her weapon was still with her. Catalyst kept its chorus high, and slowly healed Angelite's wounds. It was then she saw her staff had large scrapes in it. However, the special alloy began to remould into its original shape, almost as if it was never damaged to begin with.

Struggling back to her feet, the possessed Tribal rushed at her once more, his sword primed for another swing across her exposed throat. Blocking the oncoming strike in a rain of multicoloured sparks, she enacted the exorcism rights of such supernatural beings.

'Illumani' Penetrana Sheol Dagadan.'

Gold energies surrounded her spare hand, and just as he was about to swing, he was enveloped by a rippling wall of golden energies. She caught Maledream in the Resonance frequency of her spell just in time.

'Be gone.'

Spinning on the spot, Angelite smashed the charged energies of Catalyst into Maledream's torso. Releasing another thunderous explosion that shook the ground, the creature's cold, abyssal eyes stared at her for a mere moment, before it was blasted backwards and towards the beach. However, it didn't end there. The puppet of Maledream steadied in midair, and landed safely on the sand with his feet, sending countless grains into the air as if a meteor had struck the beach.

'Is that all you have? You're truly pitiful, we shouldn't have overestimated your empty powers,' it mockingly bellowed.

Maledream primed the Relic Blade behind his shoulders and, by sweeping it in a downward arc, released a terrifying blast of crimson Resonance. After the sweep, the familiar sound of a sonic boom followed it. Angelite's pupils dilated as she watched a spear of crimson energy crash into her protective barrier, before inevitably overwhelming her.

Screaming in agony from the powerful Resonance, she crumpled to her knees on the ground. Catalyst struggled to keep her alive, even after absorbing most of the blast. For a moment, its silvery surface glowed white-hot in her hands, acting as an earth to dispel the surge.

'*Now, to end you...*'

Raising the blade towards the sky, the sword's energy created another batch of ions across its ancient, metallic surface. Its Crystalline-Pathways glowed red-hot.

'*I used so much of my power opening the portal, I can't keep going,*' she grimaced.

Catalyst fell silent. Its surface was cooling from the large energy it had to dissipate.

'*Spirits help me,*' she prayed, closing her eyes, tears beginning to stream down her cheeks.

She watched the Relic Blade gather more energy. The runes illuminated along its surface as it charged for a killing blow. Pausing with the sword aloft his shoulders, the shadowy being snapped its head to its flank to see a large, silvery object racing towards it. Crashing into him, the rushing mountain of muscle sent him reeling across the beach. It roared a terrifyingly powerful howl, and then positioned itself between Angelite and the possessed Maledream.

'*I'm sorry I couldn't have been here sooner, Angelite. Hurry, replenish your strength, I can't hold him back for long.*'

The shadow entity manipulated its puppet back onto his feet. Its abyssal aura grew ever larger. Tendrils of shadow erupted outwards from the Tribal's spine. With a roar, it charged at the feral wolf, trying to slice and stab his agile form. Each time he failed to do so, serving to frustrate the Anunaki.

Staring at the night sky as she recuperated, the priestess thanked the stars. With Silver fighting by her side, she felt she had to try even harder. Struggling to stand, she began to focus her healing energies as Silver bought her time.

'Feral beast, out of my way.'

Silver hopped to one side, ignoring the intrusive thoughts. He bounded out the way of its clumsy sword strokes, and dodged the tendrils of dark, snaking energy that tried to grab him.

'Maledream, wake up you stupid fool, wake up.'

Angelite watched them fight with violet-glowing eyes. Catalyst's symbols fiercely ignited as she focused more energy into the special staff. Crystals illuminated their way up the shaft as the resonating manifolds slowly charged their power to the sound of a low-pitched hum, which steadily whined louder as more time passed.

'I have no time for this.'

Raising the Relic Blade in the air, Maledream, with both hands, stabbed the weapon into the sand. The

Resonance exploded and arced out from the blade in the ground, much like a quake. A crack of power trembled across the beach, sending particles of sand in a circular radius pluming high into the air.

Silver was caught by an erupting strike of crimson lightning exploding from the sands, which threw his feral form skywards. Once the large wolf helplessly fell, Maledream raised the blade above his shoulders and, with a sickly, bone-crunching squelch, impaled the feral beast down to the hilt. Silver roared in defiance, howling with a bloody rage to suit, yet was powerless to do anything. His spine was fractured.

'Angelite, save him...'

With demonic fury, he smashed the dying wolf into the ground with a deathblow. Angelite watched in horror, she could barely contain her rage as she tightly squeezed Catalyst.

'No!' her voice echoed.

'No?' it laughed.

The priestess returned no words. Her feet edged forwards, her violet vision locked with Maledream's abyssal eyes.

'Well then, let's see your feeble power, breeding-scum!'

Leaping to the air, the Tribal defied gravity with the sword held aloft. Falling in an arc, and sweeping the blade down, struck with both the weapon and crimson energy simultaneously. She held Catalyst high, and blocked its passage in a shower of sparks. Another shield rippled around the priestess, serving to hold Maledream in place as his blade struck the staff.

Catalyst absorbed the blast of potent Resonance, the shock absorbed once more by the special metal. The energies of conflict wagered on as Maledream's dark tendrils from between his shoulders slithered against the golden barrier.

Without warning, the entity finally wrestled free of her trap, and then leapt and landed once more, landing another blow against her shield. This time, he rested his feet on Catalyst's shaft. However, her legs could only take so much strain from the weight and, without warning, Angelite's knees buckled with a crack. Both kneecaps popped out of socket. Falling backwards, she screamed as the entity's powerful, shadowy energies pushing her further into the earth.

Holding Catalyst up with her hands and arms, a round crater formed beneath her the more they held their powerful weapons in lock, such was the weight of the Relic Blade's released power. Angelite's spine ached against the pressure. She gritted her teeth.

'Maledream, listen to me. It's Angelite, please wake up. Please, Maledream, listen to me,' she cried in desperation.

His abyssal glare showed no emotion to her yields.

'It's no use, breeder, this feeble man never cared for you. I've shown him real memories of what he is, of the great deed's he shall bring us,' it laughingly rasped.

'Liar, he is kind and gentle,' she screamed, her arms, wrists, and muscles locked and almost at breaking point.

'You have no idea, do you? He loves nothing, especially you. He considers you just another breeder,' it cruelly laughed.

'Liar.'

She had her doubts, but she couldn't let this thing get the better of her. Another strong wave of emotion further opened up Catalyst's potential. As the shadowy tendrils closed in around her, she wept. She could hear a choir in all the madness of the crimson lights and multicoloured sparks. Something sang to her in the back of her mind.

'I can't hold on, I can't,' she thought, tears streaming down her cheeks, unable to turn away from the creature's dark stare.

'Die, Breeder.'

Angelite squeezed her eyes shut.

'Trust me, and trust in yourself, Spirit,' Catalyst hummed, every word echoing in her mind.

Without needing to reply, and acting on a gut feeling, Angelite gave in for but a moment. Catalyst suddenly took control of the energy flow. Flashes of bright orbs raced around Angelite and Catalyst in an instant. Swelling into a ball of energy, the bright light smashed itself into Maledream with a thunderous crack of power.

Throwing his body back to the beach in a violent push, he crashed violently back into the sand with a resounding thud. The swan statuette screeched with its neck outstretched. Angelite was lifted off the ground, to the sound of a high-pitched whine released by her staff, and her hair rose in unison against gravity.

Her robes viciously rippled as a sudden strong wind swirled around her, accompanied by a blinding white light. The reeling Tribal got up and, turning its shadowy, tendril-like wings around, faced and gazed upon the new and unexpected form of the transformed priestess.

'What manner of foolishness is this now, breeder? Where did this power come from? Impossible, you were finished!'

Raising its wings with another shriek, the swan atop Catalyst sprang fully to life, seemingly becoming a living entity as it fluttered its fluidic, metallic wings, which grew in size atop the staff. Its tail feathers grew in length and entwined down the shaft. As it did so, feathery, ethereal wings of multiple colours sprang from Angelite's spine. Her wings grew six times the length of her body on either side, which bathed her in an aura of multiple hues. Her skin shone with purity and, with a crack, her joints snapped back into place without pain.

Her piercing eyes shone violet as she floated a metre above earth. Her ethereal, feathered wings flowed and shimmered with the gentle current of the wind. However, Angelite recalled what N'Rutas had said. Catalyst could only keep this power going for three minutes at a push. She was short on time, and every second counted.

'Can I do this?' she thought, eyes glancing at the metallic swan.

'Breeding-scum,' Maledream roared, sprinting towards her with blade poised.

'Illumani' Penetrana Sheol Dagadan.'

Angelite sang with a chorus of a thousand voices behind her own as she bounded towards him, her gentle wings in pursuit. Light and dark, staff and blade, crashed into each other with a thunderous clap. She now possessed supernatural qualities, free from limited physical bonds. Pressing the shadowy possessor hard under her newfound strength, the light of her Resonance burned the Tribal's crippled form. Ethereal smoke wafted into the air.

Holding the staff in a parry, she deflected the blows that Maledream's clumsy limbs flung at her. Elemental sparks danced in spiralled arcs through the air to each clash of the special alloys and, each time, she counter-attacked after the parry, hitting the shadow of Maledream with great bouts of pure, multicoloured energy square in the chest. Her red-hair and robes glowed brightly and flowed in kind in the great, supernatural winds. Every movement and strike was perfectly synchronised.

However, the Anunaki's dark tendrils caught her off-guard suddenly. It grabbed hold of her staff, but with great pain. The Tribal raged as he tried reaching for her soul with the slithering tendrils. Angelite, with a spin of her wrist, and a quick lock of weapons, came eye to eye with him. Her wings tangled with the shadows, and metallic screeching echoed aloud.

'It doesn't matter if you destroy me, breeder. More will come, and you'll never triumph over the strength and resolve of our glorious Empire,' it raged, still trying to free itself from her bonds.

'Come and try,' she screamed, singing the rights of exorcism for a third and final time. 'Illumani' Penetrana Sheol Dagadan.'

Pulling her free hand backwards to build up the Resonance in her open palm, the Blood Adept saw her fate lines shine with powerful light, and helplessly watched her slam the energies into his vessel's chest with an echoing thud. A beam of silvery light shot straight through the Tribal's chest, which cut a swath of destruction through the sand and ocean with a deafening roar. A rush of air signalled the fall of the Anunaki. Her spell blasted it back into the void, littering the air with silvery ether.

The abyssal tendrils that once fought against Angelite's wings had dissipated in kind. The corrupted red-hot armours that Maledream wore shattered into fine, rusty dust. His body stood motionless from the spiritual blast that had shot through his heart, and his blue eyes seemed void of any consciousness.

The priestess sighed. Catalyst's power coursed through her being, humming and singing in her palms. Then, as the unconscious Tribal fell slump, she caught him in one of her gentle, billowing wings. In her higher state of being, Angelite glanced at Silver's bloodied and mangled body. Resting Maledream gently on the beach, she landed and strode to the feral wolf.

'You saved my life, Silver. Thank you. Now, to return yours,' she said, softly resting her main hand on his feral form.

She healed the wolf's broken vessel in a display of Resonance that emanated from Catalyst's power. Silver's wounds knitted together instantly, his fizzled hair returning to its original state.

'Awaken,' she whispered.

Catalyst's swan statuette fluttered and sang, rejoining Silver's spirit with his physical body in energetic hues of greens and gold.

From afar, the Pack, Elric, and Larkham, watched in awe with a few Watchman. No one could believe what they had just witnessed.

'She's either surpassed her teachers, or that staff is also something to be reckoned with,' Elric said, quickly rushing towards them with the others in tow.

'We'll have the chance to ask them our questions later. For now, let's get them back home,' Larkham panted.

'Mate, you're back!' Neveah grinned.

Chapter Eighteen

Grave Matters

Several days in Meridia had passed since Angelite's encounter. News of a battle in the Port Sector spread through the city. The port was closed until further notice by the order of the Watchman guild, who also worked closely with the Order of Spirit on the matter.

It became clear that Maledream's possessed form took a ride to Meridia on the back of a Behemoth, which had washed ashore the morning after the fight. However, rumours circulated around the city-state that the old, vengeful powers of the Anunaki would soon attack, which ensured a state of panic on the Meridian populace.

In response to these rumours, the Meridians began to mass-produce weapons and armour of various kinds. The Order of Spirit informed the city that there was nothing to fear. Wards were already present to protect against such a scourge, quelling some, but not all.

Deep in the Core Sector, Larkham and the Pack sat within a small council room fashioned from marble, discussing the issue. The only way in or out of the small, claustrophobic room was by a single metallic door, also inscribed in fine detail with runes and symbols. Elric and Eldred were also present, and they led the council in the decision-making. Eldred told them of the grave news, and encouraged them to think of ways to solve their spiralling problem.

Eldred spoke up during the meeting. 'We've told the citizens that there's no need to worry, but obviously, this is the first time in the history of this city that such an act against free will of a person's passage from the port to the inner-districts has taken place, and, of course, this has sparked outrage from everyone. Don't even get me started on the fishing fleets,' he finished, twiddling his hands in quiet anger.

'Indeed, your friend has brought with him a fabled Relic Blade of the Creators. We have left it on the beach for now. Everyone is afraid to go near the weapon and, of course, it's the main reason we've cordoned off the area,' added Elric.

'Aye, but if what you say is true about the bastard-lizards knowing the whereabouts of this city, isn't it wise to keep it as a defence? You speak ill of it, as if it's a dark omen, but it rips those bastards to shreds,' Neveah smirked, his lips uttering a good question as he proceeded to stuff more tobacco in his pipe.

Elric frowned with worry. It was something he didn't want to think about and, at first, he hesitated to reply. 'We're unsure of its potential, and that of the user's ability to resist such possessions to indirectly use its power. We have learned that it was the armour Maledream wore that allowed the Anunaki to control him. We're unsure which part of the armour, do you have any clue?'

Neveah groaned, recollecting events the best he could. 'Aye, there was something Maledream picked up that I didn't mind him having at the time. It glowed crimson, and had strange letterings on it, not like the ones you all have around this place or on your weapons. We didn't think much of it, though. We don't understand any of it,' he said, scratching his eye-patch in frustration.

'Of course not,' answered Eldred, painfully sarcastic and obnoxious in tone. 'It's the language of the Anunaki. True, our alphabets look similar, but only because of the alliance the Creators and the Anunaki shared in this ancient city's time. Only the Nephilim dabble in such languages now, for they share Anunaki bloodlines,' he finished with a bored sigh.

Elric merely glanced at Eldred and shook his head. It appeared that even he could not put up with him.

'It's not Maledream's fault...' Larkham interrupted, continuing to utter as he stared at each council member in turn. 'He is a curious young man. It has almost killed him in the past, and there is no doubt in my mind that there is something special about that young, cheeky fool. After all, to survive a possession isn't a feat anyone can do without great spirit. A strong spirit.'

'Aye, second that,' Neveah grunted, slapping the marble table with his palms in quick sessions like a drum before listening to Larkham again.

'Who knows what Maledream's spirit had to endure while his body was abused for sinister purposes? Angelite, I believe, is the key to his success. She has attended to his bedside since she fought for his soul and body. She's attracted to his spirit, and I firmly believe they are soul mates.'

Neveah bellowed in laughter. 'That little shit? It wasn't long ago that I was mocking him for not sticking it in her. Now that's connection.'

Larkham winked at Neveah, smiling back and joking in turn. Elric smiled with Boris and Crazy John at the silly jest.

However, Eldred stewed at the old man's comment, and barked, 'I can't believe we're wasting time talking about soul mates, or the size of his manhood. We have more depressing and important matters to discuss. My people are in grave danger because of your peo...'

'Choose your words carefully, Eldred. There's a few in here that won't take kindly to your next words,' Larkham firmly interrupted.

Eldred fell silent with a harsh shrug, before slinking back into his chair and avoiding eye contact with the old man.

'Aye, fine, have it your way, we'll talk about important things,' replied Neveah.

'Do you reckon Eldred's got the hots for Angelite?' Boris whispered to the Pack leader.

'Could well do, he keeps changing attitudes when she's brought up,' he murmured.

'Who cares,' Crazy John muttered.

'Eldred's right...' replied Elric, sticking to a neutral stance. 'The Anunaki now know we're here, and this is why we must think of a way to protect our city. I'm all for a joke. However, we must get down to some ideas and trade knowledge on what we know, and what we can do about our situation.'

The group chatted for hours over coffee, tea, and tobacco that were in abundance as the Pack, Elric, and Eldred piled on theories. The old Tribal leader focused on his thoughts in silence. All he saw in his mind was crystals in the shapes of human-sized skulls. He pondered over it for many hours, thinking it was nothing terribly important over the arguments that bounded back and forth across the marble table. He remained patient throughout, knowing in some way they were a clue.

'There are legends of crystal skulls, which are said to have had the power to save our world before the Dark Age arrived. An old prophecy was not fulfilled, so say the legend surrounding them. Again, we think it is another myth. The skull in our possession, at the Core, just seems to be an ordinary, but pure, crystal. However, our researchers do note that it wasn't made by human hands, its craftsmanship is elite to say the least, so it could possibly be Creator in origin.'

'This prophecy was fulfilled, but not as imagined,' Larkham's voice lowered as he went on in a trance, hunching over the table. 'They want to be reunited, these Skulls of Meridia. I have a feeling that, if we can find all of these skulls, then maybe, just maybe, we can fulfil an old prophecy. I have a feeling the spirits wish this.'

'The prophecy you're speaking of is about the skulls triggering humanity's golden age. Obviously, this hasn't happened, save for Meridia's existence,' Eldred stated.

'There is no greater idea going on the table,' Larkham frowned.

Everyone sadly nodded in agreement. All the Meridians could do was to prepare their defence.

'So then, everyone, what's our best choice of action? Does anyone know of any skulls that exist outside of Meridia?' Elric asked, although his tone was one of deflation.

'Now that you mention it...' Boris muttered. 'We did a little information trading as usual, back in our old city. At the time, we thought it was totally useless info, and, if you ask me, a load of shit. We heard that the most powerful Pack leader in the city, the Pack Baron, owned such a skull. The rumour is that it gave him abilities above any Witch or mortal. Sorry I didn't bring this up sooner. I swear there's something else we've heard about them, but I can't think of it.'

'Aye, it's okay. You ain't proposing on sending us back to the city?' Neveah pursued.

'What? We've only just got here,' Crazy John protested.

Eldred replied to the idea joyously. 'It's a great proposal! The best I have heard all day. Something supports your claims about a skull, Boris. Angelite found journals, which I have deciphered easily from the old languages. The author of one of the paperbacks mentions a friend owning such an object, just before the arrival of the Dark Age. It's possible that some brute has such an object of old,' he finished, clasping his hands and resting them under his chin with a patronisingly smug grin.

'Well then, would you mind going to get it, if that's the case? What do you think, Neveah?' Elric wondered.

Silence gripped the table. All eyes turned to Neveah for a final decision. He casually smoked on his pipe before giving an answer. He leaned back in his chair, and placed his feet on the table, crossed them in a relaxed fashion. The Council leaned further in their seats, expecting him to say anything at any second. He moved his arms, the table almost gasped. Then, casually placing his hands behind his scalp, he further relaxed himself, and stared blindly at the ceiling.

'So... are you going, or what?' Eldred piped up.

'Like fuck we're going.'

'What! You made us wait for that long, with a found tongue also?' Eldred barked.

'Aye,' Neveah grunted, eyeing the cocky teacher. 'I practically lost my whole gang getting here. The two sorry asses you see here, John and Boris, are all that's left of it. It's a month's travel time, maybe more depending if some of us live or not. So, what I'm saying, is, what's in it for us you pompous prick?'

Eldred stewed at the comment, turning his head away from the table.

'Well...' Elric intervened, 'you'll be thought of and treated as heroes. There isn't much we can offer you, personally, except it would be a good deed to yourself, and everyone else you know. If this wondrous city falls, over a million people will perish. Women and children are our main concern. Everything we have strived to rebuild over the past century would have been for nought. Please help us, for humanity's sake.'

'I guess...' Neveah mumbled.

'We'll do whatever you want,' Elric offered.

'Anything?' Neveah grinned.

'Anything,' Elric smirked.

'I'm not sure. I guess it means we'll get to kill those bastard-lizards?'

'I guess if any cross your path, sure. You could even think of it as payback for what they did to your friend.'

'What about better weapons and armour for my Pack, and this martial arts combat shit. Can teach us all there is to know?' Neveah pursued.

'You can have it, all of it, and more,' replied Elric.

'I'm going wherever Neveah goes, so will John,' Boris grinned.

'Fine, whatever,' Crazy John groaned.

'I'm sure we can forge some new weapons for you. We can also teach you Resonance if needed, it would be formidable,' Elric offered.

The pack fell silent after hearing this.

'Sorry to say this, but no, everything else except that stuff. We Packers are kind of, well, superstitious. We don't like all this Resonance stuff. We don't mind Angelite blasting the shit out of things, but that's as far as we'd venture with it. Just forge us some hard-ass weapons, armour, and any other training we need, and we'll do the dirty work for you,' Neveah smirked.

'Fair enough,' Elric nodded.

'Then it's settled, give them training for a month as well as time to relax and study. Meditate the ways a little more. If Angelite and Maledream are up for it, then perhaps they'll also join you,' Larkham uttered, leaning over the table and stroking his dark beard.

'Aye, old man, sounds good to me. Besides, we've fallen for this place, but it ain't the same as our old home. So, going back there and taking down the biggest brute in all the city would be a damn pleasure. I've got an old score to settle with that prick,' Neveah remarked lowly.

'I was unaware you had an old score with him,' Crazy John frowned, the only one daring to speak up.

'Aye, for a woman I lost to his hands many years ago,' Neveah winced.

All present were astonished, especially Eldred. *'Why any woman would choose you for a mate, I have no idea,'* he wisely thought without letting his venomous tongue slip.

'I wondered why you never wanted a woman,' Boris replied, sweetly toned.

'Aye, love eh?' Neveah grunted, his one eye filling with glistening anger.

It wasn't known for him to shed a tear, but he was close. He gave his blind eye a good scratch under his patch, adding, 'now, we ain't promising anything. If we find these skulls, we'll be as quick as we can to bring them back. How many are there? How many skulls should we be looking for?'

'Good question. Legends say thirteen such skulls existed, but apart from that, and what I mentioned earlier about them, that's all I can say,' said Elric.

'It's a start. Can we take the one you mentioned for reference? Angelite could probably look after it,' said Boris.

'Agreed,' Elric said, nodding his head frantically.

'It's been a long afternoon,' Eldred uttered drably. 'I have things to get on with, such as addressing the rest of the guilds on the matter. It's a long shot from all out war that will more than likely consume us all.'

With that, Eldred left the room in a rush, pushing the seemingly heavy doors open with ease. His richly decorated robes arrogantly flowed in his stride.

'What a damn shame, he had to leave us. Why hasn't any one tossed his ass into the ocean yet? You want me to save Meridia from the likes of him as well, Elric?' Neveah laughed.

'Naturally, we've been waiting for a hero such as yourself,' Elric returned with a chuckle.

'Right, let's get some rest and get ready for our training tomorrow to make us into better killers,' Neveah announced, raising his fist.

Elric smiled and thanked the spirits for a minor chance of salvation against the Anunaki. With a loose plan set in motion, Larkham joined Elric to chat more as they left the room, whilst Neveah bid Boris and Crazy John a swift goodbye. Making his exit, Neveah strode to Angelite's home located in the Social Sector.

* * *

Angelite gently stroked Maledream's face, smiling at him weakly, as he lay unconscious in bed. His chest rose and fell slowly as he continued to heal. She wasn't dressed in her usual robes, and instead wore a long, black skirt down to her feet, laced with many Meridian symbols. Her top was a lacy, frilly-pink blouse, woven from fine velvets that caressed her skin.

It was late in the evening. A gentle chilly wind crept through the window of their apartment in the Social Sector. Catalyst was never far from her reach as she slept next to Maledream on an adjacent bed, hoping in any way that he would wake up. The priestess had lost count of the tireless hours she had spent trying to heal him with her Resonance. Nothing seemed to work.

Larkham suggested that it could take a few days for him to recover, although it never did stop her worrying. She recounted the battle that had almost killed her and Silver. If it was not for Catalyst, then a single Anunaki may well have killed everyone in the city-state in a matter of days. The repercussions of such a thing happening was something she hated thinking about.

Sweet-scented flower petals were scattered everywhere from Angelite's homemaking skills, ranging from the dresser to the window seal, held in glass or crystalline bowls, and her room was painted in bright shades of pink and red, thanks to her personal touch.

'At least he's back,' she thought, stroking his stubbly face affectionately.

With a passing sigh, the priestess hopped from the bed. She strode calmly across the room to the open window to feel the breeze entering the room. The smells of incense were carried on the wind, adding further to the pleasant aroma of her apartment. Sparse, silver clouds traversed the open heavens in the reflections of her deep, green eyes. Peering to the streets below, she saw Neveah approaching her apartment at a steady stroll. It took scant minutes until he knocked on the oaken door.

'Come in,' she answered.

It creaked open. Neveah smiled at her and, as he stepped in, shut the door with an almighty slam. Both of them winced.

'You couldn't be any louder, could you?' Angelite smirked.

'Aye, don't know my own strength half the time,' he grinned and nodded. 'No use yet then, Sweet?'

'Nope, afraid not. Sorry I couldn't make it to the meeting, but I'd rather look after Maledream.'

'You've nothing to apologise for. Not much happened, except that in a month's time, we, or rather my Pack, will be heading out to our old city,' he said, easily watching Angelite's mouth gradually open to protest.

He raised his hand up with his palm facing her, uttering, 'let me finish. I was hoping you might join us.'

Angelite's eyebrow rose curiously. She sat on the window ledge and thought about Neveah's offer.

'Why? Why would you want to go back? I don't ever want to go back. It's a horrible place,' she stammered.

'Aye, but the Anunaki now know this city exists, or some shit like that, so the council came to a decision to send us back. We've agreed to look for these Skulls of Meridia.'

'I see, but what about Maledream?'

'Well, if the lazy shit wakes up, then he's more than welcome to come along for the ride. I don't think he knows you've brought Larkham and his fellow Tribals here either, so that'll be a shock for him when he wakes up,' he smiled.

Hope seemed endless in his one eye. This lightened the priestess's heart a little, as he continued.

'We'll be training in this martial arts stuff that they have on offer, to make us better fighters. We only have a full month to do this, and by then, we'll stand a better chance when we head back. Would be grand to have you come along, Sweet.'

The priestess thought about it for a minute as she stared out the window. She released a heavy sigh with sorry eyes staring at the clouds. Many had lost their lives in that desolate land, such as her Meridian friends that had died defending her in the library. Neveah also lost most of his men on the battlefield, and Maledream was considered another casualty until a few nights ago.

However, the Anunaki now knew of the city's existence. She recollected the Anunaki's threat before she banished him. This weighed heavily on her mind. She wanted to say no, although, she could not bring herself to say it. She averted her eyes from the glowing clouds and back to Neveah.

'Not to mention it'll be freezing, we'd be travelling around the time of the Winter Solstice... so, count me in,' she nervously smiled.

'I was hoping you would, but I'd like you to learn how to fight as well, Sweet. We had some narrow escapes, especially you. I fear that if that ever happens, and we're not with you, then it'll be easier for you to defend yourself,' he stated.

'Yeah, I know,' she said, eyes widened.

Her fears rose with the hairs on her spine as she remembered the night that Neveah was referring. The terror she experienced that evening was not easily forgotten. Her hand sub-consciously rose up and gripped her blouse.

'I will, don't worry. How will we travel back to the old city, though? Why are these skulls of Meridia so important?'

'Aye, well, we didn't talk about how we'd get back there in detail, but I'm sure Elric has a plan. There's something else I have to ask you, though. Have you seen the mutt?'

'Silver? I did this morning. He hasn't been the same since Maledream struck him down. I think he's still healing in his own way. He might be in the Social Sector resting in a park, bless him.'

'Good, I think he misses the woods or some crap, to be perfectly honest. He might even be missing N'Rutas.

Anyway, as I was saying about the skulls, Eldred found your journals and said it supported what Boris knew about a crystal skull, back in the city. We have to fulfil an old prophecy, from what old man Larkham was saying. These skulls are the key to surviving.'

'I see. He was very quick to read my notes. This time, I guess it is a good thing that he did, I suppose. I struggled to read the old language. I guess we don't have much choice then. The Anunaki know that we're here now, right? After all, I banished the Anunaki that possessed Maledream, and I think it would be wise to assume it returned to its origins,' she said.

'Aye, we only saw the last bit of the fight you had with it, and, by the spirits, you turned into something more unnatural than the spells we normally see you cast,' Neveah grinned, his tone one of being impressed.

'It was the first time I've experienced near-limitless power like that, but I really should thank N'Rutas when I meet her next time, if there is a next time. It was Catalyst that helped me,' Angelite smiled, lightly blushing from Neveah's praise.

'Aye,' he grunted, reaching for his tobacco and pipe out of his chest pocket as he strode closer to Maledream.

'Poor bugger,' he sighed, adding with a heavy heart, 'the armour he wore from the beach was tampered with, from what we understand, and that's how the bastard-lizards managed to possess him.'

'I thought as much,' she nodded.

She strolled slowly and casually to the bedside and sat on a chair next to the Tribal.

'His armour was crimson, much like the blade, but Maledream only had that once when he was angry. That happened back in the city when he stopped the Pack from, well, you know, and it glowed with his anger. However, at the Watchman port, it wasn't a natural anger. I felt something was manipulating him, and it seemed to work very well,' she said, her fingers twiddling her chin in thought.

'What do you mean?' Neveah wondered, puffing away on his pipe whilst sitting down on a chair opposite her.

'I'm guessing they wanted to use Maledream as a weapon. The blade he found is a Creator weapon. I presume they wanted to destroy Meridia with him. Luckily that wasn't the case...' Angelite paused, a brain wave struck, and her eyes widened.

'Wait!'

'Bloody hell, woman, don't screech like that,' Neveah blurted, coughing on his smoke.

'N'Rutas told us about those skulls, remember?' she said, bolting to him and shaking the Pack leader by the arms.

'Shit, you're right, that old bird went on for so long I think we forgot.'

'Go and tell them what she told us. It'll be of great significance to the council,' she said, speaking quickly in her excitement.

'Aye, will do. By the way, meet us at the tavern later,' Neveah grinned, his large form sprinting out the room once she nodded.

'Thank you, N'Rutas,' Angelite thought.

Maledream writhed in his slumber whilst Catalyst hummed away in the corner of her room. Angelite watched closely, clasping her hands on his.

* * *

'It's good to dream isn't it,' sounded a voice within Maledream's mind.

'You're in a world where no one can hurt you.'

The strange voice continued as he opened his eyes, yet all he saw was darkness. *'You're in a world filled with your greatest fears, which is why we'll take care of your dreams for you, Maledream. The world is full of pain. We will guide your hand of vengeance and sorrow. We'll take care of those that abandoned you so easily...'* the rasps faded.

Though all seemed black, the Tribal thought he saw a robed, black-eyed figure towering over him. Just standing there, watching in silence. Silhouettes of shadowy creatures darted in circles around him, whispering sinister dialects. Pain racked his heart, and he cried in silent anguish. Suddenly, faint lights darted before the Tribal's vision in the darkness. A strange song echoed in the distance, barely above the rasping whispers. No voice could escape from his vocal chords.

Strange ethereal writings, like neon lights, would rise and fade in similar hue. Nausea was Maledream's only comfort in this strange realm. All he could feel was fear, anger, and watch images of his friends leaving him when he went down in to the depths of the dark ocean. He struggled against the void, trying to awaken from a nightmare from which he had no control.

Then, from out of the gloom, he saw something glimmering. A skull of human origin stared at him in silence. Its surface was faintly outlined against each crevice, like a flame to warped glass. It came to him from the abyss, seemingly levitating in silence. Its hollow eye sockets pierced his vision. Slowly, it approached him, its jaw dropping and rising occasionally with a cold chatter. Guilt resurfaced, as if it ripped from his soul. He could do nothing but watch the human teeth morph into fangs. A laugh tore his mind. It grew in size and, opening its jaw, enveloped him.

It was over in moments. Maledream now found himself in a lush, green meadow. A confused expression was clear on his face. He wanted to cough and splutter, yet could not. With blurry vision, and a dizzy mind, his eyes rolled about his surroundings.

It was a strange world. It seemed to be daytime, save for a lilac aura surrounding everything from the fauna to the sky. Trees seemed to disappear and reappear like spectres, whilst some seemed to be buried upside down, with roots floating on-ends in the open air like dangling string. The faded grass he stood on grew in and out the ground in fast-forward and reverse.

He didn't know where to stand. It was then that he realised his feet were ethereal. Dizziness took him after he peered up at the ozone, where the birds flew forward, but upside down. Some also flew backwards, their songs reverse-like in tone to what they should sound like. Then, he watched the moon circulating the earth every three seconds, going through the monthly cycle of crescent moon to full moon, in that width of time. He tried to retch, but couldn't.

'*A dream, it's all a dream. It has to be. Where the hell am I?*'

The moon hypnotized his dreary vision. He watched it pass over his glazed eyes repeatedly.

'*I'm afraid it's not a dream,*' said an old, soft voice that seemed vaguely familiar to him from behind.

He sat upright on his knees.

'This place is wonderful, isn't it? You're an unfortunate soul to have been dragged here. Luckily, for you, I have friends here who keep me informed. You are here in spirit, Maledream. If you can guess who I am, then you may have found your way home.'

Maledream only wondered for a moment, answering, 'N'Rutas?'

'Correct.'

Turning his head, he saw something he did not expect. N'Rutas was a spirit, but in her Anunaki form, free from the weathered effects of physical time. Her scales glistened with silvery shades. The spectral robe she wore was difficult to see, but all the same, looked fantastically rich in detail. Runes danced off the seams in synchronous rhythm. Her eyes and pupils were slant like a snake's, yet were not large and dark like a true Anunaki.

'Don't be alarmed, Child. You know my intentions are good. It was hard work dragging your soul out of the void. The Anunaki imprisoned you there. I couldn't watch you suffer at the hands of those unborn, what we call the shadowy daemons that dwell in that hell. I could not restore you to your body without first freeing your soul from the void. It would have had dire consequences on your health, my poor Child. You're experiencing dark emotions because you still have a vessel to go back to in *the physical realm, as you, my young Maledream, have a Soul-Link.'*

Maledream looked on. He couldn't grasp entirely what she was talking about. The images of his memories flickered for a moment. She strode towards him.

'This sacred place is known in our world as the fifth dimension. You could say this is where the powers of the Resonance manifest and pour into our world. It is free from space, the material, the constant, save for the spirit. This is not paradise, but rather, the earth's reflection, the mirror of itself. Its echo, if you would like. This plane is the bridge to the higher-planes. I will now reconnect your soul, my Child. You have someone who cares greatly about you, still waiting on the other side of existence,' she said, kneeling down in front of him.

'N'Rutas, does that mean you, and even Angelite, have limitless power connecting here? Is this infinite energy?'

'Yes, although Angelite tires her physical form when using Resonance. She will get stronger in time. I was like her once, in my younger days. This dimension feeds your spirit and physical forms with the sounds of the universe. This dimension is also responsible for your dreams, Maledream. It is here where creation takes place within one's mind. You could say that this was once the plane where the Creators first resided, before they ventured further to our denser reality.'

Before he could ask another question, N'Rutas changed her tone and mood.

'It's been nice talking to you, Maledream, but something is coming. I shall deal with this personally. For now, I will reconnect your spirit to your shell. Don't worry, this will not hurt one bit, Child,' she said, her tone one of haste.

Her form shifted for a moment, a look of concern grew on her face.

'They have found my anchor, we must be quick.'

The dimensional realm around Maledream began to shift. N'Rutas raised her ethereal hand towards the sky, chanting, *'Larszarish Zandrishth Zuthell'el Carntanooria Zandalaar Naria'lith.'*

During her song, Maledream saw the spirit world rippling under her loud, powerful voice. Maledream felt the weight of denseness grapple him. He stared at N'Rutas, and found the strength to rise on his spiritual feet.

She smiled at him as he did so. Then, peering below, he saw a swirling vortex open between him and N'Rutas. He glared at his frail, physical form. He felt like not going back. Only when he peered at Angelite's caring face did that feeling wash away. His physical body began convulsing in the bed. All the priestess could do was clean the bile from his lips with a cloth. Nothing he saw in that hole shifted, yet everything else around him kept rippling and distorting with a low, bass groan. The comparison between the dimensions was frightening.

'*You must go now, Maledream,*' she uttered, her voice anxious.

He nodded at her, and then took one last glance at the spirit world. '*Thanks for everything, N'Rutas.*'

Chapter Nineteen

Back from Dreams to Reality

Maledream gasped when his soul slammed into his being, and jolting upright in the bed. For several moments, he could once again feel his heartbeat, feel his exhaling lungs, and feel every pulse flutter.

'You're awake!' Angelite shouted, hugging him tightly as he spluttered.

He panted and stretched his aching muscles. It felt good to be back. 'Glad to see you, too,' he coughed.

'Thank the spirits. I was afraid you'd never wake up. We were all worried, please don't do it again,' she said, breaking into a cry.

Maledream hushed her, and she hugged his aching ribs even tighter, almost squeezing the air out of his lungs. She stared into his pupils, her green eyes filled with tears.

'I promise,' he struggled to rasp, his voice croaky.

'Here, have some water,' she insisted, handing him a glass.

She was deliriously happy. He drank the pint in seconds. She instantly got him another one, and then another, before he insisted he was okay. She tried forcing a third down his throat.

'I'm all right, woman!' he protested through a cheeky grin, arms raised in defiance.

'I'm just looking after you! Drink!' she persisted.

The priestess wouldn't take no for an answer. Once Maledream finished the third and final glass, he took a moment to glance around the room. Angelite told him to lie still while she got him something to dress in.

'I feel something different in you, like something's opened,' Angelite said, looking carefully through the wardrobes that stored various assortments of Meridian clothing.

'If only I could tell you the half of it,' he groaned, rubbing his sore eyes. 'It was a strange dream. N'Rutas was in it, and from what I learned, it wasn't a dream, but something else. N'Rutas saved me in the spirit world.'

Angelite's jaw dropped, she slowly turned around with the clothes in her arms to face him.

'Are you sure?' she pursued, a serious look etched on her face.

'Certain, but I'll tell you and everyone else later about it. Are we going to meet up with them?'

Her face lit up with excitement.

'Of course, let's get you dressed. I can't wait until you tell me more! N'Rutas in your dreams, or rather spirit, I guess. I'm dying to hear more about this,' she squealed.

Angelite hastily chucked the Tribal his cleaned clothing. His leather armour was polished to the highest quality, and there were new mail-links covering the vital areas. It all looked upgraded, even his old coat was practically replaced with thick, durable materials.

'By the spirits,' he said, almost unable to believe how well his belongings had been treated.

'We're in Meridia, if you haven't guessed,' she grinned.

He squinted his eyes and raised his brow at the news.

'Never mind, you'll learn more in the next month before we set off again. A lot has happened, there's so much to tell since you were unconscious,' she said.

'I'm sure it has... wait, set off again?' he muttered, thinking back to how he saw the boat leaving before he blacked out.

Angelite caught his deepening sadness. She wandered back to by his bedside and sat next to him on the mattress. Placing her fingers on his lips, she forced a weak smile out of him.

'Maledream, you were brave and courageous. You're so strong, so don't feel stupid or inferior. I think you're amazing,' she gently murmured in his ear.

The Tribal looked away, but her hand forced him to look back at her again. Catching him off-guard, she kissed him softly on the lips, locking them together as they both closed their eyes. It felt like an age as she kept her supple lips moving against his, both enjoying the heart-racing feeling. Flirtatious adrenaline flowed easily through their veins.

'You need to get dressed,' she whispered, breaking the long kiss.

Angelite blushed, and her eyes glimmered with a deep forest-green. A faint, cheeky smile appeared on her cheeks, her light freckles adding to the cuteness.

'You're, uh, right,' he stuttered, embarrassment quickly taking him.

For a moment, Angelite stopped him thinking of his troubles, and for that, he was happy she did.

'I'll wait outside. Get dressed, and then we will go and meet up with the others. They can't wait to see you!' she said, excitedly clasping her hands whilst jumping from the bed.

Without saying a word, she left, closing the door softly to wait outside. Maledream relaxed for a moment to collect his thoughts. He felt exhausted, yet he was fully awake and hopeful of events yet to come.

He crawled out of bed. His leg muscles strained, and his back and neck creaked. Shaking it off with a satisfying grunt, he donned his cleaned clothes and armour. He slung his coat behind his right shoulder. Noticing a mirror across the room, he stared at his reflection. He recalled what N'Rutas had said to him.

His skin was slightly pale as he stared at his scrawny form with a smirk. His hair was un-knotted and brushed, slightly cut around the front, while a band kept his long, black, coarse hair in a ponytail. He noticed the addition of Tribal-like braids, which he guessed was Angelite's doing.

'Better get going,' he grinned, eyeing up the door through which the priestess had exited.

He opened it to see her expectedly waiting for him on her tip toes, her hands clasped behind her back. He took a moment to appreciate her frilly Meridian skirt and lacy top. Her blouse was looser around her cleavage than it was ten minutes ago.

'Feel any better in all that?' she asked, beaming him a flirtatious grin.

'I do, thanks,' he returned with a devilish smile, eyes briefly wandering.

'Follow me,' she said, pulling him by his hand.

Nodding, he followed her curvaceous, petite form down the oaken stairs towards the exit of the apartment.

***

Meanwhile, Neveah met up with his Pack and, at the same time, caught Larkham and Elric on the way. Like all good conversations, they decided that a drink was necessary. The Goblins Tap was quieter than it had been during the Pack's first visit. Rumours were on every patron's lips.

People discussed the arrival of outlandish refugees and that of the Port Sector, leading to a battle between a member in the Order of Spirit and that of a possessed man. Low lighting illuminated the dank tavern. Smouldering pipes filled the air with a blanket of smoke. Tensions were high, yet the musicians played on, as if to take people's minds off the bad omens.

'Well,' Elric said, pondering over the information given to him by Neveah. 'It seems that we should pay heed to her wisdom. Maybe she told you this by accident, maybe not, but if what she says is true, then you will have a long journey ahead of you. We estimate the Anunaki will not attack during the Winter Equinox and Solstice periods. That is, of course, if they dislike the cold or not, there is no evidence to support either theory. We think they will attack next summer. Nevertheless, we will stay vigilant around the city walls and build our defences. It was naive of us to think that we would be totally safe living here.'

'It was foolish. Through my stories, I have taught my Tribals about the creatures that live under the earth, or for that matter the deep oceans,' Larkham said, rubbing his hands together.

'Indeed, Larkham, I guess we've had a lot of arrogance running through the city since its rebirth,' Elric concurred.

'Sorry to sound patronising, Elric, but remember, nature crushed us once before, and it could do so again, in whatever way it chooses, whether it be by cataclysms, creatures, or beasts. You mustn't place your faith in these Creator weapons as our ancestors once did. Only wars and destruction can follow. It almost killed Maledream,' Larkham sighed, his hand raising a glass of water to his bearded mouth.

'Technology can save us this time round, now that we've got you here to help guide us, Larkham,' Elric smiled.

Larkham choked, almost spitting out his drink. 'Boy, I'm a spiritualist, not a true leader. I just look after those that wish to follow by my example. There are many fine people here in Meridia that can have my place. I'm getting old. Too old. Tired is the word for it. You need someone young, someone who has the potential, and someone who knows how to fight for the spirit of the people. That, I don't have...'

Larkham shiftily eyed up Neveah whom smoked his pipe and drank his beer, chatting nonsense and profanity to Crazy John and Boris. The Pack paid little attention to their serious conversation on their end of the table. Elric turned his eyes towards the Pack leader, pondering over Larkham's words for a moment, trying to scale his true meaning.

'You don't mean Neveah, do you?' Elric muttered.

Larkham laughed, staring into Elric's eyes, a wrinkly grin rising in his beard. 'Yes, he has the spirit of a true leader. He would be a good choice, but he has a long path to walk before he takes up such ideas or choices. Maybe, just maybe he is the one, my young Elric.'

'Perhaps you're right. I joked to him about it a couple of days ago, but not anything serious. Right, I think we need to make a summary.'

Elric got to his feet and asked for the attention of the others to speak of the mission, but then...

'You little shit!' Neveah bellowed, jumping on and over the table as swiftly as a gorilla to meet some newcomers in the tavern.

Moving his large, bulging bicep around Maledream's aching neck, he proceeded to force him into a headlock and rough up his hair and scalp with his knuckles.

'All right already, get off me, you big ass!'

'Aye, have it your way,' Neveah laughed, diverting his attention to the priestess to eye-up her casual wear.

'Looking damn good, Sweet,' he added, giving her ass a firm slap.

Angelite squealed and jumped.

'Someone started drinking early,' she smiled, her hand briefly rubbing her backside.

'Take a seat, you two,' Neveah grinned, kindly pulling up two chairs for them.

Angelite stared at the smiling group. Whispers from other patrons arose and heads turned, staring at them with fearful eyes. A feeling of being unwelcome set in, but it was something Maledream easily ignored. After all, he lived like it with the Tribals for much of his life. It was then that his gaze rested on Larkham.

'Old man, Angelite said to expect a surprise, but this I didn't expect!'

'You had better believe it, Boy,' Larkham winked, staring at Maledream's clean armour and clothing that meshed nicely together.

In return, Maledream eyed Larkham's new attire with a shaking head.

'But you still need a good ear clipping, you little bastard,' Larkham added, chuckling over times long ago.

'It's been too long,' Maledream cheerfully grinned, striding over to his foster-father, and, for the first time in his life, shook his hand, much to Larkham's surprise.

'How do you like it here?' asked Elric.

'I've had a strange month, and it only gets more surprising,' Maledream returned.

'Well met, Maledream. I'm Elric,' he grinned.

'You too,' Maledream nodded.

'Sit down, I'll go and fetch you a beverage,' said Elric.

'Thanks, it'll taste good knowing it doesn't contain piss, like in the old city,' Maledream chuckled, taking a chair next to Neveah and Angelite to face everyone else as they began to catch up.

As the group happily conversed, Maledream thought of the nighttime streets of Meridia. He felt compelled to love every inch of the city that they struggled and fought to reach. Now, he relaxed with his drink, and enjoyed the laughter floating across the table. The young Tribal's awakening had finally removed everyone's dampened spirits. Angelite was in the best of moods, there wasn't a moment she wasn't flirtatious with him. However, Elric had to drag the evening back to business.

'Now, before Neveah leapt over my head,' Elric jested, 'I was about to break some news. First, I must welcome Maledream. I'm glad to see he's made it to our wondrous city,' said the teacher, cheers erupting from the Pack. 'However, we, the people of Meridia, need all of your help, including you, Maledream, against the Anunaki threat that we fear will soon arrive on our shores.'

The Tribal didn't know what to make of this, but eyed Elric carefully and nodded with curved eyebrows.

'Your friends told me how you saved them from a Behemoth, and also, from my detective work, I believe that some of the armour you wore was designed on purpose, perhaps through the chained-braces to give the Anunaki a way to take control over you, and ultimately, to take control of your blade. Do you remember what happened?'

'No... I woke up after some disturbing nightmares,' Maledream answered.

'You ended up on the shore. It was a few nights ago that you and Angelite bumped into each other. To cut a long story short, my friend, Angelite banished the Anunaki possessing you. But she didn't kill it, so we're hazarding a guess that it crawled back to its origins.'

'I see. It all fits, I guess,' Maledream muttered.

'Indeed, my friend. However, not to worry, you're here now. Your sword's still on the beach, which means we had to close off the Port Sector as a result. It's still lodged in the sand, awaiting the return of its warrior.'

'I know, Angelite said on the way here,' Maledream sighed, not wholeheartedly believing the warrior nonsense.

'However, we believe that the Anunaki may attack Meridia. We have asked Neveah and his Pack, and I would like to extend the invitation to you and Angelite. It is a mission to find some artefacts, with hopes to fulfil an old prophecy to protect and save Meridia, and indeed, humanity as a whole,' Elric said, leaning closer towards the Tribal.

Maledream's ears winced as he thought it over. He had only just awakened from his coma, and now, it seemed, he was having this peaceful existence ripped away from under him. However, he couldn't let his friends go back alone. In some way, he felt deeply responsible for this entire mess.

'I'm in,' he said, reassuringly.

'Me too,' Angelite concurred.

'What do you want us to do?' Maledream pursued.

'You'll need to head back to the Dark Age lands, and find twelve artefacts that we've branded the Skulls of Meridia. It won't be an easy task, and we can only direct you back into the city where your journey started.'

'Are the skulls we seek like the one in the museum?' Angelite wondered.

'Yes,' Elric nodded.

'I can see where this is going, you mean of the Maya and such?' she added.

'Aye,' Neveah grunted, finishing off his mug of booze.

'I have with me the skull from the museum, which I mentioned before,' said Elric.

The teacher placed an object on the table, before carefully undoing the taut leather and twine that bound the skull and jaw together. All eyes graced the quartz, human-looking skull as they gazed in wonder at it.

'Quite a spectacle,' said Boris.

'Must be worth a pretty penny, especially to the Pack Baron back in the city,' Crazy John madly grinned.

Everyone was amazed at the attention to detail. Not a mark seemed to show it was chiselled with any tools. It seemed that no the artisan in Meridia could match such an exquisite object without spending many generations refining and defining it. The skull's sockets beamed a small amount of light from the tavern's soft illumination.

Elric stated at length, 'the Order of Spirit has tried tapping into this object, but it seems dormant, which is why we just left it collecting dust in the museum. We believed it was once an important object, although we doubted the legends and myths surrounding it. Of course, we have learned more about them recently through the documents collected by Angelite, which Eldred deciphered, and that of the information given to us by N'Rutas. These were gifts from the Creators. We may be in a position to, once and for all, fulfil what our ancestors failed to do. The prophecy of a golden age has passed, so it's a long shot to try and re-unite all of them.'

'What if the Anunaki own some of these skulls?' Crazy John interrupted.

The question rocked the table with silence.

'We can only hope they don't,' Elric replied, a sigh escaping his lungs at his valid and intelligent question.

'You're an asshole. Why do you always have to dampen the mood?' Boris groaned, the palms of her hands pressed on her face.

'We've got to try,' replied Maledream.

It was the least he could say to stop the guilt gnawing at him. The group calmed down and carried on discussing the skulls throughout the evening, considering what N'Rutas had said about them. They knew that the more information Elric had, the better he could assess the situation, to see what else he could muster before the end of the month.

'Now, I'll show you the maps,' said the teacher.

Elric reached below the table, wrapping his hands gently around some old parchment, intact from years of care. Larkham made a space on the oaken table for Elric to roll them out, using everyone's hands to hold the corners carefully on his instruction.

'It has been decided by the guilds to open an ancient tunnel network, known as a Labyrinth. Labyrinths are ancient structures that extend for many leagues in all directions across the planet. Since the shift of the continents, they have either collapsed, or worse. It is thought that, by using Resonance, we can quickly repair a way back to the city where you all came from, somehow.'

'Aye, so, I'm guessing it will take you a while to clear the way? Would a boat be too dangerous?'

'Indeed, my friend, we don't know how many beasts the Anunaki may have under their control, such as another Behemoth.'

'Then, what happens after this tunnel is clear?' Neveah wondered.

All eyes were cast at Elric's index finger as he traced a line from Meridia to the Dark Age continents, the trajectory of where the group was to traverse. The group seemed worried, confused, or both, wondering if it was correct.

'We must travel back in a straight line, if we can, it'll be the fastest route. We may reach the city in under a week, in that case, maybe even sooner with transport. These Labyrinths were used by the Creators, according to ancient accounts back in the Core,' uttered the priestess.

'I see, so, doesn't that mean that these bastard-lizards have knowledge of these tunnels, too? Wouldn't it make sense for them to attack from underground if that was the case? You said they lived in this city once. Even if it was a long time ago, they surely would've kept records of it, just like you have,' Neveah muttered.

'It's a possibility,' Elric conceded, before adding with a hopeful tone, 'however, it's more likely that they will attack by sea. We intend to keep it closely guarded, so don't worry.'

'You had better,' Larkham muttered, his eyes shifting to the teacher to continue his omen, 'because if you don't protect all your flanks with the long weapon of wisdom, then Meridia will not be standing if Neveah and the others don't get back in time, or in one piece.'

'Thanks for that, old man. I'm sure we can get them all back here before anything bad happens,' Maledream uttered, shaking his head.

'Don't get too cocky, Boy. Remember, these are dangerous foes, not to mention the other dangers that exist elsewhere in the Dark Age lands. Remember all my tales, Maledream. I'll quite happily repeat them for you,' Larkham smirked.

'Spare me, old man,' Maledream cheekily quipped.

'Larkham's right,' Elric said, breaking the light-hearted squabble, 'we'll have every possible front guarded. However, until then, focus on your mission for the skulls. You will have a month to train. Leave the defences to me. We will work with everyone in the city to ensure its safety. And Angelite, look after this skull, and make sure you pay close attention to it. In addition, copies of our maps will be ready for you, along with the other supplies needed before you begin next month. Everything will be prepared and waiting.'

All nodded in agreement to his words. Elric wrapped up the map and tightened the leather straps around its coiled body.

'Maledream, I recommend you pick up that sword of yours. We need to reopen that Port Sector. The sea is one way for us to harvest large quantities of food before the winter, and every day is costly as we need to prepare for a siege,' Elric stated.

'I will,' Maledream nodded, still staring blindly at the skull.

Larkham watched him, wondering what his adopted son was thinking.

'I think that's everything. You all know about the skulls. I have made you aware of the Labyrinth, which is being excavated as we speak. I think I've covered everything, so, any questions?' Elric grinned.

No one spoke, but all glanced at one another with positive smirks.

'Training begins tomorrow. I suggest you take this up, especially you, priestess,' Elric added, beaming his caring stare towards her with a worried brow.

'I will, don't worry. I'm not so naïve anymore,' Angelite smiled.

'Good. Right, I'm tired, so I bid you all good night. Remember to pick up your sword, Maledream, sooner the better. Farewell, and look after that skull,' Elric finished.

He got up, shook everyone's hands, and then left the group to finish their drinks before closing time. Neveah started one more conversation for good measure.

'So, Larkham, I take it you're not joining us?'

'I will stay here as an advisor, I think. I want to make sure that the fools running this city don't get carried away with their weapons of war,' Larkham drably replied.

'Aye, sounds like a plan. Besides, you might slow us down, you wrinkly old git!' Neveah jested.

'You be surprised, Boy! You're just as cocky as Maledream, but, I guess in time, you'll learn the error of your ways, much like him,' Larkham cheekily winked.

Neveah and Larkham traded bouts of laughter. Meanwhile, Maledream watched Angelite strap the skull back up, then realised...

'Where's Silver?'

Everyone shrugged.

'I'm going to the beach, then. I'll see you all later. Angelite, uh, is it alright if I go head back to yours after?' he nervously smirked.

The Pack heckled him with blown kisses.

'Of course, go for a walk, and clear your head. Find Silver if you can,' she giggled, turning around to snap at the Pack with a grin.

'Alright, I'll see you later.'

'Aye, don't forget, tomorrow we start training,' Neveah said, pumping his large biceps.

'Can't wait, catch you then,' Maledream lightly laughed.

***

Leaving the tavern, he put on his long coat and raised his hood. A chilly wind brushed his face with drizzle from the clouds. Maledream steadily made his way towards the Port Sector in the rain. Unable to read any languages made it difficult, but luckily, he was good at memorizing city streets. The Social Sector had fallen quiet. He travelled along the various cobbled paths, each one illuminated by large, glowing crystals in a myriad of colours.

Eventually, in his slow pacing, he found the Port Sector entrance guarded by several Watchman. They let him pass unhindered. He was expected. Without saying a word to the Tribal, they merely moved to the side and nodded. He crossed underneath the tall, circular wall that protected Meridia, and his boots eerily echoed down the dark passage.

Before him lay the docks once he exited the tunnel. He stood in the cold rain and breeze once more, and caught a glimpse of the moon behind the pale clouds. Shimmering, crystalline lights illuminated the seafront, which easily extended for miles around the circumference of the harbours and beaches.

Unsure of where to look first, Maledream took a stroll and followed the circular, cobbled path of the port. His thoughts soon wandered, his pupils glazed, as he stared at the glimmering ocean.

It was then Maledream saw Silver in the distance, sitting on the beach, staring in the direction of the rough sea. It seemed the wolf had been sat there for a while. His silvery, damp fur barely wavered in the wind. Maledream left the warmth of the illuminated stony path and strode towards him. He noticed that the sand in this area looked disturbed, unlike the rest of the calm beach. Glancing over at the piers leading out to sea, he noticed the number of ships docked in the outer harbour.

'I'm glad you're finally awake. Come and join me, Maledream. It's a pleasant night, isn't it?'

'It is,' Maledream replied, sitting down next to him with legs crossed.

He saw the Relic Blade sticking out of the beach, several metres in front of them both, buried at a slant angle, and covered in wet, sticking sand. The waves gently rolled around its dark, metallic surface as it glittered, distorted, and reflected the lights of the port.

'It's been there for days. I have watched over it for you. Do you remember what happened?'

'I'm afraid not, it's all a blur,' sighed the Tribal.

'Then, perhaps it's best left forgotten,' Silver replied in monotone. 'It was the fight you had with Angelite, or should I say, the battle with the Anunaki that possessed and controlled you.'

'So I'm told. Thanks for everything, Silver, and sorry for the hurt I caused.'

'No need to thank me or apologise. It has been a trip worth making, although, I do long to be home with N'Rutas. You're the only one I have spoken to in a while. Sometimes, I just need space away from you humans, no offence.'

Maledream smiled, before saying with a heavy heart, 'it's been some journey, but one that's going to get longer. We're to head off again in a month. Because of me, the Anunaki now know of this city.'

'Be silent,' Silver groaned.

The Tribal turned his head and raised an eyebrow.

'You humans either blame yourselves when you get upset, or you blame others for your mistakes. You never see it from a third person perspective. Selfishness doesn't become you, so just go with the flow, Maledream. You know it's your style, and besides, that's how it should be, it's called natural, and it's very simple.'

'I guess it was my mistake for being human,' he chuckled.

'Don't start. I had a rant with that ape, Neveah, just a few days ago,' Silver moaned.

Without saying a word, Maledream got up and strode to the Relic Blade. The cold ocean breeze and drizzle blew against him, coat flowing, hood rippling.

'That will all change,' Maledream muttered to the wind.

Gripping the hilt, and with a groan and a tug, pulled the blade out of the wet, sticking sand. Once Maledream had lifted it free, he rested on it lightly by its hilt.

The pair stood and sat motionless, studying the dark ocean waves over the horizon, deep in thought.

* * *

Meanwhile, deep within the Anunaki Empire, Lemuria City, Quetolox had learned of the troubling human settlement. He immediately ordered an army to be assembled to purge the last free pocket of human resistance. The lord of the Black Sect stood before the Queen in her royal chamber. Her delicate, albino hide glistened amidst the candles illuminating the large, brooding chamber.

She leaned forward from her crimson throne as her closest advisor spoke. 'Once everything is ready, my Queen, the assault will begin,' Quetolox rasped, his forked tongue tasting the warm air.

'Then it is so. However, Quetolox, make sure that you do not displease me, or you will have more than Cattle to worry about,' she hissed.

'As you wish, you're Majesty. The Red Sect has already initiated their Warrior Breeding Program...' Quetolox returned, barely able to keep his tone civil as the Royal guards eyed him, his anger silent. 'And then you will have your feast of true victory, my Queen.'

Turning on the spot, Quetolox exited the throne room hastily. *'I will deal with those Cattle, personally.'*

Quetolox's highly decorative regalia clinked and flowed with vicious sways, his one eye glimmering with fearsome power as he strode down the vast, grand halls of the Crimson Palace.

'You will all perish...'

Dream-State Drive Titles

Katie Marie's debut novel, Grey Wings

Jason is stranded in a dark city, and is in desperate need of help when he has no idea how he will get home.

So, when he collides with Aurelius, an Angel only in the mildest sense of the word - who has committed a crime worthy of great punishment, but has been handed a rare chance at redemption - Jason can see a way home.

However, their journey will be hampered by Fallen Angels, Earth Spirits, and Griffons - and none can say if everyone will make it home.

Suitable for children.

ISBN: 978-1-291-64632-0

Available in-store and at online retailers.

Dream-State Drive Titles

M.C.Chivers, Orchestra, Vol. II

Approaching the Dark Age Series

A moon has passed since Maledream and his companions arrived in Meridia. Training has been long and hard. Now, the group must endure a long journey to try to restore a long dead prophecy to satisfy a vain hope.

The plan: together, they will locate each of the twelve Skulls of Meridia, unite them, and trigger humanity's supposed golden age.

However, the Anunaki now know of Meridia's existence. Quetolox, leader of the Black Sect, has sanctioned a new army to be born in order to exterminate this new problem. Tunzuulizh, leader of the Red Sect, promised the council leaders that this new army would be unlike any other, and far more potent than the first that was responsible for the human's downfall almost two centuries ago.

Meanwhile, Ganzath, leader of the Purple Sect, discovers shocking revelations that has shaken his very faith and soul. He has two choices. Both filled with blood.

ISBN: 978-1-291-65928-3

Available in-store and at online retailer.

Dream-State Drive Titles

M.C.Chivers, Echo, Vol. III

Approaching the Dark Age Series

Maledream's heroic sacrifice has cost him his way home, and now he is stuck within the swirling, chaotic mists of Etherscape's twisted storm. Alone, he is confronted by the sky-scraping Phantom Titans as their dark, bellowing laughs tremble the rocky, forsaken landscape. Trapped, he swings and roars defiantly with his awakened Relic Blades', Aisling and Retrinumun.

Meanwhile, Ganzath leads his exiled Anunaki-kin across earth's vast ocean, in the hopes of reaching Meridia to strike an alliance with the humans. However, they are hunted by the chasing Anunaki fleet, under the command of Admiral Jun'Zwu.

Quetolox, Lord of the Black Sect, has a promotion in store for Tunzuulizh of the Red Sect for his loyal service. However, although Tunzuulizh is gracious for the promotion, he is emotionally compromised when Quetolox brands the Queen a traitor of the state. Both a patriot and a royalist, he must cope with his conflicted inner-struggle and cold-blooded empathy, all in the name of loyalty.

ISBN: 978-1-291-65930-6

Available in-store and at online retailers.

Dream-State Drive Titles

M.C.Chivers, Crystal Core Craft, Vol. I
The Meridian Archive Series

Angelite Rose, Priestess of the Order of Spirit, goes into great depth on how Resonance, the science of sound made magic, works in the first volume of this Compendium.

Not only that, but she has also supplied great knowledge on how Crystal Cores work alongside Resonance, and how they can be applied in a practical way when working with anything ranging from armour, weapons, or magic.

Note from the Author: The Meridian Archives are extras from my main series of novels, entitled: Approaching the Dark Age Series. These short novels contained within The Meridian Archives Series are intended to be extras in their own manner.

Freely available via Smashwords, Lulu, or Amazon in electronic format only.

Dream-State Drive Titles

M.C.Chivers, Dream-State Drive, Vol. II

The Meridian Archive Series

The Dream-State Drive. Ancient technology left over from when the Creators once graced the earth some 10,000 years ago.

Master Elric Lordante of the Order of Spirit has spent some time deciphering and testing this ancient travelling craft, said to be capable of faster than light travel...

As brilliant as it may sound, there is an unforgiving darker side to this wondrous machine.

Note from the Author: The Meridian Archives are extras from my main series of novels, entitled: Approaching the Dark Age Series. These short novels contained within The Meridian Archives Series are intended to be extras in their own manner.

Freely available via Smashwords, Lulu, or Amazon in electronic format only.

Dream-State Drive Titles

M.C.Chivers, The Tribals, Vol. III

The Meridian Archive Series

The Tribals are a descended remnant from when the Dark Age arrived. These are a nomadic, spiritual people that avoids all conflict, if possible.

They hunt and scavenge for any materials and food possible throughout the stricken lands, and are led by Tribal Elders that can commune with the spirits, either when they are asleep or awake. Elric Lordante delves into his past experience with them.

Note from the Author: The Meridian Archives are extras from my main series of novels, entitled: Approaching the Dark Age Series. These short novels contained within The Meridian Archives Series are intended to be extras in their own manner.

Freely available via Smashwords, Lulu, or Amazon in electronic format only.

Dream-State Drive Titles

M.C.Chivers, The Packs, Vol. IV

The Meridian Archive Series

Packs are vicious, ruthless war-bands that plague the Dark Age lands from one end of the continent to the other.

Like the Tribals, Packs are the end result of surviving humans since the arrival of the Dark Age, but instead of living in peaceful existence, they rape, steal and butcher their way forwards in order to live. Master Elric Lordante has had unfortunate business with them in the past.

Note from the Author: The Meridian Archives are extras from my main series of novels, entitled: Approaching the Dark Age Series. These short novels contained within The Meridian Archives Series are intended to be extras in their own manner.

Freely available via Smashwords, Lulu, or Amazon in electronic format only.

Dream-State Drive Titles

M.C.Chivers, The Order of Spirit, Vol. V

The Meridian Archive Series

The Order of Spirit is a guild dedicated to teaching, healing and spreading the word of the soul. Like many other guilds, they are based in the oceanic city-state known as Meridia.

It is an extensive Order, and one which many of the cities inhabitants have been members of at least once in their lives, for every Meridian can boast casting the easiest of spells. Written by Master Elric Lordante.

Note from the Author: The Meridian Archives are extras from my main series of novels, entitled: Approaching the Dark Age Series. These short novels contained within The Meridian Archives Series are intended to be extras in their own manner.

Freely available via Smashwords, Lulu, or Amazon in electronic format only.

Dream-State Drive Titles

M.C.Chivers, The Watchman, Vol. VI
The Meridian Archive Series

Those who guard Meridia's high walls are members of a guild, known simply as The Watchman.

They follow a strict set of rules, and follow the Free Will Constitution to the final letter. They work well with their sister guild, the Order of Spirit, and work to defend the city-state with both Resonance and sword. However, though it may not seem it at first glance, the guild can be highly political.

Note from the Author: The Meridian Archives are extras from my main series of novels, entitled: Approaching the Dark Age Series. These short novels contained within The Meridian Archives Series are intended to be extras in their own manner.

Freely available via Smashwords, Lulu, or Amazon in electronic format only.

About Dream-State Drive Publications

So, you have written a story and now you want to make that big leap into publishing.

Trouble is, many of the big publishing houses will only take on stories that are, quite often, only written by competent writers who are not disabled in the field of language. There are some, but they are rare.

What Dream-State Drive Publications seeks to do is to break this rule. DSD seeks to help writers, who are disabled in field of writing by their (your) Dyslexia, Autism or other language disabilities, to publish their (your) novels. By using the existing self-publishing model, DSD seeks to publish our authors' works - no matter the story content - as DSD is firm in the belief that anyone can write a story.

Those with Dyslexia, along with other language disabilities, can unfairly languish without a voice.

Dream-State Drive Publications seeks to change that.

If yourself, or someone else you may know, is writing or has written a story, and has dreams of publishing their novel, then Dream-State Publications could be their way forward.

To find out more, please visit the official Facebook page.

https://www.facebook.com/DreamStateDrive